Mothers

Cath Weeks

piatkus

PIATKUS

First published in Great Britain in 2017 by Piatkus
This paperback edition published in 2018 by Piatkus

3 5 7 9 10 8 6 4 2

Copyright © 2017 by Cath Weeks

The moral right of the author has been asserted.

*All characters and events in this publication, other than those
clearly in the public domain, are fictitious and any resemblance
to real persons, living or dead, is purely coincidental.*

A CIP catalogue record for this book
is available from the British Library.

ISBN 978-0-349-41066-1

Typeset in Bembo by M Rules
Printed and bound in Great Britain by
Clays Ltd, Elcograf S.p.A.

Papers used by Piatkus are from well-managed forests
and other responsible sources.

Piatkus
An imprint of
Little, Brown Book Group
Carmelite House
50 Victoria Embankment
London EC4Y 0DZ

An Hachette UK Company
www.hachette.co.uk

www.littlebrown.co.uk

We need in love to practise only this:
letting each other go.

Rainer Maria Rilke

For Nick J. Smith

PROLOGUE

For a long time afterwards, Steffie feared dust.

It was everywhere – on the furniture, in their oxygen, in their eyes. She was scared to sleep at night for fear that it was entering her lungs, clinging to her skin. They moved home, yet to her dismay the dust followed them.

She had tried everything: hoovering every hour, using microfibre cloths, air purifiers and even a wand that used a static charge to collect dust. Nothing helped.

Summer was the worst when the dust swirled thick in sunbeams. She couldn't retreat to bed since the bedding would be full of dust mites, no matter what she did. She couldn't fight it, couldn't get rid of it. On such occasions, she barely made it through the day.

It was called amathophobia, her fear: a feeling of dread when near earth or other fine particles. Most likely the root of the phobia lay in childhood, but not necessarily. Everyone, even the sane, feared dry particles on some level – the hardwired instinct to flee from something that could choke or bury you.

But to the amathophobe, dust triggered panic and a flood of hormones through the body causing difficulty breathing, nausea, sweating and increased blood flow.

All of which she had read covertly online.

There was no point telling anyone about it. What could they do? Besides, it sounded ridiculous when you said it out loud.

Still ... all that was many years ago. Things were different now. She only hoovered once a week, owned just two microfibre cloths, and the purifiers and the wand were gone.

Yet the dust was still there, silent in the air around her.

It came from concealing the truth. For just like secrets, dust always came to light – always returned, no matter how hard you tried.

And it was this that she was most afraid of.

THE ARTISTIC DIRECTOR

Of course it's competitive. You can't get to this level without being single-minded, ruthless even. Gather enough pupils in one place all wanting the same thing and you're bound to have a lot of tension and rivalry. It's what makes them great artists in the making.

But to suggest that someone might have done this deliberately . . . No. That is going too far. I cannot believe it.

Do you have news from the family? Will the child live?

Mikhail Alexandrov
Phoenix Academy of Performing Arts
Surrey Police interview transcript
20 February 2016

ONE

Being a good mother was all about learning how to let go – knowing when to hold on, when to release. Everyone knew that. It was the sort of thing that parenting experts discussed on daytime TV or in magazines. And to most mothers it was as realistic a goal as the full lotus position or world peace.

A child was one's mirror and it was no easier to say goodbye to them than to oneself. It was what made the idea that one day we would all part this earth so unthinkable. The human brain wouldn't even allow us to die in our dreams.

Steffie often thought this sort of thing whilst watching Jemima perform on stage. Steffie was no dancer herself, couldn't imagine having the concentration or poise to do what her ten-year-old daughter did so effortlessly. Yet she felt every move that Jemima made as if it were her own, found herself swaying as Jemima swayed, bowing slightly as the audience applauded.

At the Christmas show last month, a rush of emotion had hit Steffie as Jemima appeared on stage, like the blast of heat on opening the oven door that melted the mascara on her eyelashes. It happened every time – the sensation that she wasn't fully in control of her emotions. As Jemima leapt into the air, Steffie had reached quickly for her tissues and kept one scrunched in her hand throughout the performance, just in case.

Greg had smiled and rolled his eyes at her. But she could tell that he was feeling it too, that his sudden runny nose wasn't out-of-season hay fever. They had been separated for a year and Jemima's performances were the only times when they sat together in mutual rapture, or sat together at all. Their daughter was the sole surviving evidence of a marriage that had once been remarkable, if only because it had created her.

Sometimes, when Jemima disappeared into the wings, Steffie took the opportunity to discreetly observe the other parents. She liked to guess who they were, to match them to the children on stage. If a child was being spotlighted, their mother would be smiling awkwardly, battling the urge to cry. It didn't matter who the child was – whether they were one of the chubby ones in a bee costume or the principal dancer in sequined leotard, like Jemima. The mirror didn't judge, merely reflected the child back to their mother all the same.

That lethal mirror. It hadn't done anyone in *Snow White* any good, and it wasn't helping anyone in real life either.

'Mummy!'

Steffie opened her eyes. Jemima was standing over her, holding the cordless phone, which was ringing.

One of the benefits of raising a gifted child was that they rarely needed nagging to practise said gift; one of the negatives was that they often woke before daylight to do so.

Steffie took the phone. 'Hello?'

'Good morning, Steffie.' It was Jemima's dance teacher.

Steffie glanced at the bedside clock: seven thirty.

'Would it be possible to speak with you before class this morning?' Noella said.

'Of course,' Steffie said. 'Anything wrong?'

'Not at all,' Noella said. 'Just something urgent that I'd like to discuss with you. Shall we say eight thirty?'

'That's fine,' said Steffie, standing up stiffly. She put her hand to her neck, circled her head, but felt dizzy so stopped.

'May I ask your husband to join us?' Noella said.

'Please do.'

'Good. See you shortly,' Noella said, and hung up.

Steffie stood still, pursing her lips.

'Was that Noella?' Jemima asked. She was just beyond the partition that separated their rooms, pulling on her dance tights.

'Yes,' said Steffie.

'What did she want?'

'To have a little chat with us.'

Steffie gazed out of the window. If there was the slightest breeze out there this January morning, she couldn't see it. The tree in the courtyard was expectantly still, as though awaiting further instructions.

'So we'd better get a move on,' she said, turning away from the window. She scooped a leotard off the floor, handed it to Jemima. 'She wants to see us urgently.'

She tried to say this casually, but Jemima was no fool and as Steffie left the room she could feel her daughter's eyes widening, like burning holes in paper.

Greg always worked on Saturdays. He had turned fifty last year and vowed to give up weekend work, but it was hard to find something to replace the sense of purpose. It was just him living at The Fishing Lodge now, so called because of its vicinity to a ten-acre lake that was fished for carp. He had never fished, but the view from the decking was outstanding and of an evening, when the only company was the splashing of floats and the whirling of reels, he was glad of the sport.

That Saturday morning, he was off to work. His latest contract was at a manor house south of Chelton, the hamlet that

7

he lived in. He tended to work within a small radius of home to avoid hefty fuel consumption, since his business was eco-friendly. Lately, his hand-crafted kitchens were so sought after that he had started running a waiting list. So it was difficult to squeeze his work into a Monday-to-Friday mould. It was his passion, his life, more so now than ever.

Sometimes, when he thought about it, it seemed sad that he couldn't leave the lodge – where he and Steffie and Jemima had once lived so happily – because his workshops and all his gear were here. It was easier to be the one who left, rather than the one left behind. No one wanted to be that person. And so he didn't think about it often, didn't dwell on whether the situation was sad. He was lucky. Each day he told himself that. And some days he even believed it.

He was five miles out of Chelton, when his mobile rang.

'Mr Lee?'

He recognised the accent immediately. Noella was the only French person he knew.

He pictured her at the end of the phone: her petite form in black – always black – with her hair swept up and, rather unexpectedly, a tattoo of a swallow on the back of her neck.

'Sorry to trouble you so early,' she said, 'but I've something urgent to discuss with you.'

'Go ahead,' he said, braking the truck, pulling over. He needed to be still, ready, if this was what he thought it was.

'I need to do so in person,' Noella said.

'Oh.'

'Would you be able to meet us in the studio at eight thirty? Steffie and Jemima will be there also.'

He looked at the clock on the dashboard. 'No problem.'

'Excellent,' Noella said.

He hung up and reached for the leather attaché case that was once a proudly procured anniversary present from Steffie and seemed now like a wrinkled apology for all that had occurred between them. He sighed, pulled his clients details from the case and phoned them to set their meeting back. And then he took off again, sniffing firmly, gathering himself together.

There was no need to feel bad about this. It was good news, inevitable.

He put on the radio, tuning in to Radio Dorset. A happy song by The Mamas & the Papas was playing. He tapped his fingers, squinted at the sunshine on the frosted tarmac, told himself that everything was going to be all right.

He was just parking the truck near Noella's school when his phone rang again. He was late and thought it would be Steffie ringing to ask where he was. So he answered the phone without looking at the screen. 'Steff,' he said, reversing.

'Greg?'

'Olivia,' he said, stalling the truck in surprise.

'Where were you last night? I waited for you,' she said.

He paused whilst he thought of what to say. Firstly, he needed to park. He was in the middle of the road. He started the engine, parked up, turned the engine off. 'Greg?'

'I'm here,' he said.

He watched as a little girl walked along the road towards him wearing a furry deer hunter hat, presumably on her way to Noella's. She was spinning a pair of ballet shoes in the air by their straps. Her mother looked infuriated, tugging the child's hand.

Poor kid. Not all ballerinas were created equal. Jemima would never have spun her shoes. And they never had to tug her to class, even in the early years. She had always woken them by pulling off their duvet, urging them to get up immediately or she would be late.

He smiled to himself at the memory of his bossy little girl in owl pyjamas, always so alert, even at dawn.

He couldn't think of anything to say to Olivia.

'I'm really sorry,' he said. 'I've got to go into a meeting. I'll call you later, OK?'

Then he locked the car, turned his collar to the cold and hurried to the studio.

Steffie couldn't find a parking space on Peach Street, had already circled the block three times and was now running late. Noella's School of Dance was the only business on Peach Street, and all the residents parked on the road. It was too early in the morning for anyone to have moved yet.

'I wonder what she wants to see us about,' Jemima said, leaning forward to speak. At ten, she was old enough to ride up front, but Steffie still kept her in the back seat where she deemed it safer.

'I don't know,' Steffie said. 'And at this rate, we're never going to find out.'

As they turned on to Peach Street again, Steffie spotted Greg in the distance, approaching on foot. She would have recognised the black donkey jacket anywhere. Jemima hadn't noticed him yet, but she would do so at any moment and would start calling for him, the sound of which always saddened Steffie immeasurably.

He had worn that jacket for such a long time, she thought. It was the sort of coat that dustmen had worn back in her childhood, whistling loudly, carrying metal bins on their backs.

She had told him this the first time she saw him wearing the coat, on one of their first dates: that there was nothing wrong with being a dustman, if that were his profession. He had laughed, his eyes creasing in the corners. He had dry, rough skin that was prone to being crêpey, even back then. It had reminded her of filo pastry – of something delicate, delicious. Now it reminded her that he was old.

She eradicated the mean thought the moment she had it. She

was trying to work on being mindful, on having only kind thoughts.

Well, good luck with that, as her mother always said.

Jemima had spotted him now, was banging on the windows with her palms. 'Daddy! *Daddeee! Daddeee!*'

Steffie breathed deeply, trying to slow her heart down but it was beginning to make a racket within her, like clacking castanets.

Greg was waving at them, pointing. He had found them a parking space.

She smiled.

That was nice.

She got out of the car, pushed her hair from her eyes, hoped she looked attractive, suspected that it was too early in the morning to be true.

'Hi,' she said.

'Hello,' he said. He was freshly shaven, raw-cheeked, had shaving foam on his ear.

'You've got . . . ' She went to reach up, but thought better of it.

He tugged his ear. 'Ah. Thanks.' Then he turned to Jemima and held out his hand. 'Shall we?'

Jemima skipped forward to him happily, and they set off.

The height difference between them was cute. Jemima was petite for her age; Greg was six foot three. Steffie trailed behind them, feeling the flutter of sorrow that often accompanied seeing Greg. She listened to their conversation – to the easy flow of words between father and daughter, Jemima's voice lower pitched than normal, snug, nuzzled, safe in Daddy's company.

Noella was waiting for them inside the studio; she looked agitated. 'Thank you for coming,' she said. 'Please.' She gestured to the row of chairs at the back of the room. 'Sit.'

Steffie and Greg sat down immediately. There was something about Noella that made you do as you were told.

'Would you like to get changed, Jemima?' Noella said, bending down, her hands between her knees, as was her habit when addressing her pupils.

'I *am* changed,' said Jemima, folding her arms. She wasn't going to be got rid of that easily.

Steffie tried not to smile.

Jemima, neither sullen nor petulant, was steadfast and resolute. She was a match for her mistress, and her mistress knew it. With her pale skin, dark hair and eyebrows that formed arrows of concentration or indignation, Jemima could be French, so Noella often said.

Noella gave a little sniff. 'Well, go hang your coat up and begin stretching,' she said, clapping her hands. 'Chop chop!'

Jemima slowly walked away, dragging her coat behind her along the vinyl floor.

Noella waited a moment before speaking. 'So the reason I asked you here is because the Phoenix Academy have offered Jemima the chance to audition with them.'

She paused, her eyes flitting between them both, scanning their reaction.

Steffie didn't know quite how to react. If she had been wearing a hearing aid, now would have been the time to fiddle with it, stalling.

'The Phoenix Academy?' Greg said. 'Should we—'

'Yes,' Noella said. 'You should have heard of it.'

Once again, Steffie tried not to smile.

'The Phoenix is an outstanding dance academy,' Noella continued. 'It's been in the news of late because it has appointed a new artistic director . . .' Noella glanced over her shoulder at Jemima who was now at the barre, warming up. 'None other than Mikhail Alexandrov.'

'Gosh,' said Steffie.

Who was Mikhail Alexandrov?

Noella's voice was rising. 'I was fortunate enough to study with Mikhail in Paris many years ago,' she said. 'He was considered the Nureyev of his time, but then sadly was injured. This will be his first teaching post, and as such it will catch the attention of the world.' She clasped her hands together and rose on to tiptoes. 'And he wants Jemima!'

'Well . . .' Steffie said, shifting in her seat. 'That's fantastic . . . But how does he know about her?'

Noella blushed. 'You mustn't be cross,' she said, sitting down on the piano stool, her black dress flapping behind her. 'But I sent him a video.'

There was a dull silence.

Jemima stopped stretching and watched them intently in the mirror.

'Noella . . .' Steffie began carefully. 'Greg and I looked into specialist education last year. We did a lot of research, as I'm sure you remember. And in the end we decided that early specialisation would be too restrictive – that Jemima would be better off at Wimborne Comprehensive.'

Greg was nodding slowly, emphatically.

Noella bowed her head. 'I know,' she said. 'And I'm sorry if this feels intrusive or like overstepping the mark . . . But in the last six months Jemima has really blossomed. Her talent is extraordinary – too much so for a conventional school. I understand why you might think otherwise, but trust me – I know what I'm talking about. And so does Mr Alexandrov.'

Jemima had left the barre and was creeping forward, trying not to be noticed.

'This way, Jemima would have the best of both worlds: a top-notch artistic environment combined with academic excellence,' Noella said. 'If she's to fulfil her potential, then she needs professional training as soon as possible. Don't you see?'

Yes. Steffie did see. Yet it wasn't a clear vision but a pickled one with all sorts of feelings attached. She was struggling to decipher which feeling was the strongest. Surely pride, excitement? But fear and apprehension kept bobbing up too, like plastic ducks in a water barrel.

She gazed at Noella. 'Why didn't you say this last year when we were looking at senior schools?'

Noella frowned, hesitated. 'Because Jemima has really accelerated of late. And also I happened to bump into Mr Alexandrov in London a couple of weeks ago. I didn't think applications would be accepted this late in the day, but to my surprise he said he would assess Jemima's tape ... And he loved it!'

'Well, maybe you can give us some details,' said Greg, folding his arms. 'So we can look into it.'

'Of course,' Noella said. 'Anything you need.'

'Does that mean ... ?' Jemima asked, arriving within reach of them.

Steffie turned to look at Jemima, having temporarily forgotten that she was in the room, that this was about her.

This was what happened sometimes when discussing children's lives, when discussing what was best for them. No matter how much you tried to stay focused on them, they somehow still got lost in all the dialogue.

'Is this what you'd like to do, Mims?' Steffie asked gently, ignoring the raw feeling in her throat.

It wasn't because she didn't want Jemima to go to the academy. She wanted only what was best for her daughter. But there was a little something else wrapped in there too, something that she would unwrap later when no one else was looking.

'I think so, Mum,' said Jemima, twisting her fingers awkwardly as she spoke, her cheeks turning Barbie-pink.

'So she's in?' Greg said. 'Just like that?'

Noella shook her head. 'No. I should have explained ... Mr

Alexandrov is happy for her to join in at final audition stage. I mean, it's very late, for entry in September. He was very kind to—'

'So when does he want to see her?' Greg asked.

Steffie glanced at him. He didn't sound cross, but he was evidently uncomfortable with something – possibly the same thing as her: that this was a decision that appeared to have been made for them. Even if it were the right decision, no parent surrendered their role of chief executive without some resistance.

'In a fortnight,' said Noella.

'Wow,' Greg said, sitting back in his chair heavily. He gazed at Jemima in wonder. 'Must have made a good impression, eh?'

This small encouragement set Jemima off – sent her spinning around the studio, a blur of hair and tights and tulle. 'Epic!' she was saying. 'Epic!'

Noella watched her, laughing. 'It's very exciting for all of us,' she said, placing her hands on her hips. 'Yes?'

Steffie was watching her daughter.

She could feel the excitement, could feel herself spinning as Jemima span, could feel the immensity of the opportunity, the privilege of being singled out.

'It's not local, is it,' she said, more to herself, more a statement than a question.

Greg looked at her in mild surprise. This didn't appear to have occurred to him yet.

'No,' Noella said. 'I'm afraid not. It's in Usherwood, Surrey.'

'So she'll be leaving home,' Steffie said. 'She'll be boarding.' Again, these were not questions.

'Yes,' Noella said.

'OK,' Steffie said.

'OK?' said Greg. 'Are you saying—'

'I'm saying . . . ' Steffie said.

15

Somewhere within her, the last two emotions were slogging it out, punch-drunk, before the victor held up its hand. Pride had fought off worry. Everyone was cheering.

'I think we need to focus on Jemima,' she said finally. 'On what she's capable of . . . I mean . . . look.'

They all turned to watch Jemima.

Alone, in the middle of the studio, she was dancing her favourite piece unaccompanied by music. It was Prokofiev's *Cinderella*.

'This is probably the piece that she'll do at the audition,' Noella said, her voice wavering with emotion. 'Isn't she magnificent?'

She was.

Jemima had accelerated. She was moving up and on. She was a beautiful helium balloon longing to rise. They were the chunky rope holding her down, and back.

'Just tell us where to be and when,' Steffie said.

She often thought of that helium balloon in the weeks to come, of how much Jemima in that moment – the moment of decision, at the crossroads that changed their lives – had seemed like a thing of beauty, straining to be released from captivity.

That in itself should have told her everything.

Balloons were not robust. Their overstretched skin was filled with nothing but air. And air was filled with nothing but dust.

She should have seen it coming, should have seen the misfortune that was heading their way.

Yet she did not.

And they continued forward, unable to avert disaster before it hit.

I wasn't surprised, really. I mean, you can't come to these things and not have a bit of fire in your belly. I'm always saying to Freddie that if he doesn't big himself up, no one else will.

I'm not being funny, but you could tell that she wasn't used to being at auditions at this level, among students of this calibre. And that's just sad.

Truly, I felt sorry for her. Totally out of her depth.

This isn't being recorded, is it?

I'd hate the parents to think I was being a bitch.

Mrs L. Rawlings
Phoenix Academy of Performing Arts
Surrey Police interview transcript
20 February 2016

TWO

The danger in indulging your child's dreams was that eventually those dreams would lead them far from home. After all, few aspirations were met by pulling up the sofa cushions or gazing down the plughole. Home might be where the heart rested, but ambition lay down the road, beyond reach. That was the whole point of it.

Steffie accepted all this – had known for some time that Jemima wouldn't be long for Wimborne, would outgrow her parochial home town. She just hadn't expected to surrender her only child quite so soon.

It was the moment that many mothers dreaded, letting go; so much so that perhaps there were those who would flatly refuse even to consider it an option. Some might reject the offer on the table; some might coax, manipulate, fudge facts. And others, like Steffie, would fantasise about doing all those things, but would in fact let their child go, and turn to Netflix for distraction.

Steffie had been practising for this event for many years. Back in the days of preschool, she had dropped Jemima off and then hurried away to her car, telling herself not to look back, to drive away quickly.

Then on the first day of school, she hadn't gone to the event that they were holding at the toy shop in town – the sparkling wine and cake for 'grieving mums' – but had got on with her day like any other, telling herself that it wasn't a big deal, that life moved on.

It was the same during every dreaded wardrobe sort-out, when she held too-small dresses in her hands, stretching them a little, wondering whether they would do for one more summer ... before realising that they couldn't possibly fit and that she was to drop them into the bin bag and walk away.

Sometimes, even then, she would lie in bed at night panicking about whether she should have given away the sweet little hat – the one that Jemima had worn that entire summer – whether she could buy it back if she went down to the charity shop first thing in the morning ... What if it had already gone? Oh my goodness. What had she done?

Then she would check herself, tell herself off.

Let it go.

She wasn't the only one – far from it. There were businesses born of this condition: from the seamstresses who created patchwork teddy bears from outgrown beloved outfits, to the boom in dog groomers hired by all the mothers who, realising they were to have no more children, acquired a puppy instead.

Back away, step away. Mothers told themselves this on a loop – during little routine moments, like the daily school run, and the bigger defining moments, like letting one's child leave home aged eleven to attend a dance academy.

Steffie had already familiarised herself with the Phoenix Academy website, perusing the images of dancers sashaying in branded leotards. She had noted the name of the shop in Usherwood that sold the uniform, had driven the one-hundred-mile car journey on Google maps, had calculated the total school fees; she had read the very healthy cafeteria menu and hoped that Jemima would like tofu.

Steffie zipped up her coat. It was unusually cold in the school tonight. Noella kept the studio at a carefully maintained temperature, checking the air-conditioning dial often – was doing so now, since some of the pupils were shivering. The pianist, a young student wearing spectacles that were bandaged with tape, began to play a trilly bit of jazz. Noella shot him a look and the music stopped.

'Where were we?' Noella turned to the class.

The girls, and one wiry boy, took their positions at the barre, right arms extended and curled into a position that Steffie thought looked uncomfortable, unnatural.

'And one, two, three ... supporting leg, don't bend it ... And seven, eight ... Heels! ... One, two ... In first position ...'

Jemima was at the front of the group, set apart from the others at Noella's request. Her hair was in the traditional bun and her expression was blank. Nothing broke her concentration whilst practising, unlike her classmates who twitched and yawned.

They had known for several years that Jemima was talented. Greg's mother, Vivienne, had been the first to spot it. An ex-professional dancer, Vivi had performed with Sadler's Wells Ballet during the fifties and sixties. One Christmas, they were staying at Greg's parents when *The Nutcracker* came on television and three-year-old Jemima, spellbound, tried to copy what she saw. 'She's got the gift!' Vivi had declared with unmasked delight.

Shortly afterwards, a tiny tutu had arrived in the post, together with a CD of a *Swan Lake* production that Dancing Grandmammy had performed in and a ballerina snowglobe.

Vivi had worked her charm; as had genetics.

And so it began.

Jemima grew, as did her requests. She begged for lessons and leotards and dance DVDs and tap shoes. Greg constructed a studio for her in the garage at the lodge, complete with barre, mirrors and heater. He would have done anything she commanded – always dissolved around Jemima quicker than a pink wafer in tea.

Steffie shifted her position on the plastic chair and watched as Jemima demonstrated a perfect pirouette.

'Now that,' said Noella, 'is how you do it!'

Jemima allowed herself a flicker of a smile, before falling back into line.

Steffie was the only parent at the class tonight. More often than not, that was the case. Most parents dropped and left. Steffie, however, always stayed, not for any reason other than the fact that she liked listening to Noella's instructions and the rippling piano music, and watching the children's reflections in the tall windows. It was hypnotic, soothing, and sometimes the only time during the week that she stopped.

'And down ... down ... keep your back straight ... up ... up ... And down ... down ... and up ... up ... And down ... And with the opposite arm ... stretch ...'

She gazed up at the windows now, watching the children's shadows dance in the glass. The windows were tightly sealed, keeping winter at bay.

Yet it wouldn't be long until spring, when Noella would unwind the cords on the walls and pull the windows open, little splinters of white paint falling down, like dry snow.

The studio had its rhythms and cycles, which they had been familiar with for many years. Leaving here would be difficult, Steffie thought.

The class had ended. Jemima was waving at her.

Like many mothers, Steffie, on sight of her child, could conjure a smile out of nowhere, like pulling rabbits from a magician's hat.

She smiled warmly at Jemima and waved back.

*

'So what are her chances of getting in, Steffie?'

Steffie paused, Stanley knife mid-air, cardboard box at her knees. She was unpacking a delivery of inflatable love hearts on sticks for a Valentine's window display. 'I'm not sure,' she said.

'They must be pretty high for this man to be fast-tracking her to the final stage?' Her mother paused to sit up straight and stretch her neck. She was making a fabric heart garland to hook along the counter. It was a dark day. The trees were moaning outside and the rain was tapping on the windows. The string of fairy lights outside the shop were shaking up and down, like fireflies trapped in jars.

Steffie stood to turn the main light on. Then she cut the cardboard with a decisive flash of the knife and out popped the love hearts.

She realised that her mother was waiting for her reply, her mouth a line of enquiry.

'You'd have thought so, yes,' Steffie said.

Her mother nodded. 'So what does Greg say about it?'

'Well, he's pleased . . . but cautious,' Steffie said. 'I'm meeting him later to go through it all properly.'

'Good. Because it's a huge decision.'

'Yes,' Steffie said.

Her mother shrugged, continued to work on the garland. 'These places can be very competitive. Vicious even.'

'Yes, Mum,' said Steffie, trying not to sound vexed.

She pushed the box of hearts into the narrow hallway at the side of the shop, the idea of working on the window display suddenly less appealing.

With a sigh, she leant against the counter, watching the traffic passing by. An old man, barefoot in sandals, appeared at the window, looking at the cake tins, necklaces and scarves. Nothing here for him, she would imagine; although they did sell men's socks.

'She really wants to go to this school,' Steffie said. 'She hasn't stopped talking about it.'

'Of course she hasn't. It's her dream.'

'So we have to give her this chance.'

'Yes,' her mother said, laying her work on the counter. 'But you need to do it with a happy heart ... And that's the difficult bit.'

Hearts again. Hearts everywhere.

'I am happy about it,' Steffie said.

'That may be so,' her mother said, 'but I'm still concerned about you.'

'Concerned?' said Steffie. 'Why?'

'Because you're forty-four.'

Steffie laughed. 'And what's that supposed to mean?'

'Nothing,' her mother said. 'Only that it's a tough age. Your body's gearing up to a big change. And Jemima's your precious little girl.'

'Which is why I have to let her go,' Steffie said, picking up a bejewelled pen from the counter display and shaking it so its charm jingled.

'Yes.'

Steffie put down the pen and gazed at her mother, at the soft lines around her eyes, at her ash-blonde hair that was starting to look thin, no matter how much she bouffed it up with spray.

'Mum,' she said, placing her hand on her mother's hand, 'is there something else you'd like to say? If so, speak now or for-ever hold thy peace.'

Her mother was thinking about it, her head tilted to one side. 'No,' she said.

'Good,' Steffie said.

'Good.' There was a pause. 'But promise me you'll tread carefully? And you'll look after yourself?'

Steffie looked into her mother's eyes. This close they were watery, faded. 'Promise,' she said.

Greg knocked on the door, cringing at how flimsy it sounded. With a good kick, the door would probably come right off its hinges. He hated that Steffie and Jemima were living here. It felt so inadequate.

He cleared his throat nervously. This was the first time he had come to the apartment to see Steffie on her own, without Jemima present. It felt date-ish, although circumstances said otherwise and Steffie would be annoyed to hear him say so. Even so, he ran his hands through his hair and tucked his shirt in as he heard her footsteps approaching.

'Come on in,' she said, opening the door and smiling.

She looked as though she hadn't slept well last night. He could always tell. She walked with her shoulders higher than usual. It was so subtle it would take sixteen years of intimacy to recognise, which thankfully he had.

He hovered over the couch for a place to sit down.

'Sorry about the mess,' she said, scooping up toys and stationery. 'Jemima's Second World War project: she's making a Lego spitfire.'

'Should have said,' he said. 'I could have helped.'

'Sorry.' She looked crestfallen. 'I didn't think.'

'Don't worry,' he said. 'Looks like she's getting along fine without my input . . . Here. Let me help.'

They carried the Lego to a table that was crammed with ballet books and Steffie's shop paperwork. He felt a little pang of pleasure as their fingers touched briefly and he glanced at her, but she was intent on clearing a space on the table – on proving that the apartment was perfect. And she had almost managed it until she turned too quickly, sending the paperwork spilling to the floor in a swishing waterfall.

'Oh, flax seed,' she said.

He bent to pick up a handful of paper. 'Let me—'

'Leave it,' she said, with forced cheer. 'Why don't you put the kettle on?'

He sighed and went to the kitchen, which was three paces away.

As the kettle wheezed to life, he thought of the day she had moved in here – this time last year. It had been a grim day all round – wet, cold – and nothing seemed to fit where it should. But Steffie wouldn't acknowledge that, trying instead to squeeze things into tight spaces. *Perfect!* she had said. *Look, Jemima! A room of your own!*

A room? That was a stretch. Jemima's room was separated from Steffie's by a thin partition. To a constructor like him, it was excruciating. To a man, a husband, a human with feelings, it was hell.

She hadn't been able to keep her red kettle. It was too big for the narrow counter space. So he had to take that back to the lodge. She pretended not to mind – went and bought a small plastic kettle from Argos that took several lifetimes to boil. Back went the Venetian mirror too, the art nouveau lamp and the oil painting of Big Ben. None of them fitted. And none could be replaced at Argos. Yet she kept saying things like, *Look, Jemima! You can see Noella's studio from here!*

But the next morning, when he had come to collect more books and china that didn't fit – *Just whilst we get settled*, she had stressed – he had noted that her eyes were puffy, as though she had cried herself to sleep.

The kettle clicked off, finally, bringing him back to the present, and he made the tea.

By the time he returned to the lounge, Steffie was drawing a vertical line on a notepad. She was going to write one of her pros and cons lists. 'I don't think that's going to help,' he said, setting the mugs on the floor.

'Why not?'

'Because we just need to decide if we're doing this,' he said. 'Don't complicate it with lists.'

She was about to object, but changed her mind and put down the pad. 'OK,' she said.

This instant compliance caused his forehead to tighten with worry. She was never easily led, was strong-willed. What did this change signify?

He was always looking about her apartment, her possessions, her self, for change. For despite the assurances that the situation was temporary, that she needed space to think (space! Here!), the fact remained that she was single whilst separated from him and could more or less do as she wished.

Steffie wouldn't remain single forever, and the thought filled him with dread. She was attractive, with dark spiralled hair – the sort that made men think of kinkiness and negligées, at least him anyway. She smiled readily, revealing dimples either side of her mouth. Her eyes weren't blue, grey or green but somewhere between all three, depending on the weather and the colour of her sweater. Her body was slender, sometimes angular during hectic times. And her favourite colour was violet, which when worn made her eyes look blue.

'So I'm thinking that we should just do this,' she said.

'And I think we need more time,' he said.

'But we don't have more time.' She pulled her sleeves over her hands. 'Noella needs a decision by tomorrow.'

He reached for her mug of tea, handed it to her. 'Noella can wait,' he said.

'Maybe,' she said. 'But the academy can't.'

He frowned. 'Doesn't it annoy you how this has come about? That she sent Jemima's video off without our permission?'

'Yes,' Steffie said, 'a bit. But then you know what Noella's like. She's so driven. She just gets carried away.'

26

'Hmm,' he said, drinking his tea.

She stood up, went to the window, her hands in her pockets. 'This is a great opportunity for Jemima, no matter how it came about.'

He sat forward so that he could pull a piece of paper from the back pocket of his jeans. 'So ... I've had a look at our finances – how much it'll all cost. And we can definitely afford it ... Business is going really well.' He smiled at her, his toes warming slightly.

'Good,' she said. 'That eliminates a lot of worry for a start.'

A sudden downpour of rain hit the windows. They both turned to look. The sky looked turbulent, chargrilled clouds speeding by.

'Let's just go for it,' he said.

'OK,' she said, smiling with a sudden blush. She wasn't normally coy. It was because she was treading an unfamiliar course. She would be so fixed on doing the right thing by Jemima, she would forget to look at her own feet.

He thought of her being here alone in September. It made him feel unbearably sad.

'Come home, Steffie,' he said.

He hadn't meant to say it, not out loud at least. He had surprised himself.

And her too. She was gazing at him with an expression that he couldn't read – was probably better off being in ignorance of, like doomsday tea leaves at the bottom of a cup.

'I can't do that,' she said.

He stood up, but made no move towards her. She wouldn't want him to draw closer. That was the one thing he knew.

'Let me make this up to you,' he said. 'Let me make all of this better. I'll do whatever you want. I'll—'

'Just be there for Jemima,' she said. 'At the audition.' And she went to the kitchen where she began to run the tap and wash up.

'Of course,' he said. He gazed around him. She had taken his mug of tea. Evidently, the meeting was over. 'Well,' he said, 'I'll be off then.'

She turned the tap off, didn't look at him, though. 'OK,' she said.

'I'll leave the costings with you,' he said, looking about for a safe place to put the piece of paper. 'Where shall I ...?'

'On the table, please,' she said.

At the door, he paused. 'I'm going to make this up to you. No matter what it—'

'See you soon,' she said, trying to smile.

He gazed at her. Leaving her anywhere was always wretched. Leaving her here was worse. The place reminded him of the little flat she'd been living in when he first met her, except that it was smaller.

The idea of having pushed her back in time to a state that she had outgrown put him in mind of schooling systems whereby children were kept back year after year, outgrowing their classmates, their knees too big for their desks, their humiliation apparent.

'I'm sorry,' he said.

And he left, closing the flimsy door softly, reverently, behind him, securing his wife as best as he could with the poor materials that he had to work with.

PARENT OF CANDIDATE
DAISY KIRKPATRICK

Daisy's been dancing since she was two years old. Maybe eighteen months. Yes, eighteen months, actually. We knew then that she was exceptionally gifted. Many of the board of trustees at the Phoenix are personal friends of ours. You see, my eldest son, Hector, attended here. He's now on sabbatical in the States and—

No, I didn't see what happened. I heard all the commotion and went running like everyone else, but I was too late. It was awful. Terribly traumatic. I don't think I'll ever forget it.

You should know that I've informed my lawyers. My husband is currently out in the Middle East on—

Toxic? The Phoenix? Absolutely not! Why on earth would you think that?

Mrs U. Kirkpatrick
Phoenix Academy of Performing Arts
Surrey Police interview transcript
20 February 2016

THREE

'An affair is a very difficult thing for a marriage to overcome, Steffie. But for the record, I think you're doing ever so well. I really do.'

Steffie nodded, sniffed. During these sessions, she always kept a tissue in her hand – it would start as a flat sheet and end up as a ball. She never cried here, though. For Steffie, tears were private – secret tears that were warmer, fatter for being harboured indoors and not aired.

Her counsellor, Yvonne, was very pleasant: a fifty-something who wore glasses on a chain around her neck and kept a fan on her desk that lifted her hair and ruffled the paperwork.

Steffie had been coming here once a week for three months, to the upstairs office that was only four doors along from her own shop, the Silver Tree. Yvonne's services had been recommended to Steffie by a mum in the school playground, whom Yvonne had just helped through divorce.

I don't want you to help me get divorced, was the first thing Steffie had said to Yvonne.

Yvonne had laughed. *But of course not!*

Steffie had liked her right away – the way she tucked her stretchy top down over her tummy, the way she kicked her shoes off to rub one foot with the other, the way she got so hot during sessions that she had to turn up the fan and flap her blouse. *It's my age*, she would say with a regretful smile.

This, Steffie thought, was a real human.

Not like the chair beside her.

The chair – a wooden chair with a burgundy padded cushion – was sometimes Greg. She often had to turn to the sorry little chair and converse with it, to tell it how she felt or to listen to its point of view.

Today, she had just told the chair that she wanted to forgive it so badly, but she was finding it hard.

And the chair had just told her that it was OK; she could take all the time she needed.

What a chair.

Sometimes, she had told Yvonne recently, seeing Greg was like being presented with a Krispy Kreme selection box just before you went bikini shopping.

'You often use humour as a shield, Steffie,' Yvonne was saying, hands arched and resting on the arms of her chair.

'I do?' said Steffie.

'Yes. And humour's good. It's healthy ... But not if it's masking the way you really feel.'

There was a pause. Steffie listened to the fan whirring, watched it lifting Yvonne's fringe.

'You don't need to put on an act, or a brave face,' Yvonne said.

'I disagree,' Steffie said. 'I'm a single parent. I can't have a meltdown in front of—'

'I meant here, Steffie,' Yvonne said gently. 'You can drop the mask here.' She smiled. 'It's safe.'

Steffie squeezed the tissue ball. She noticed Yvonne's gaze dropping slightly, observing the tension in Steffie's hand.

It was safe here, perhaps. But Yvonne didn't miss anything. She would notice every time Steffie tensed her shoulders, every time she held her breath or squeezed the tissue ball.

But Yvonne didn't know about the dust – about the dust-balls lying on the black rim of her open laptop, minuscule yet boulder-like; about the layer of dust on the glass surface of her desk that was threatening domination; the dust swirling in the sunshine by the window, like a swarm of dirty flies.

'Let's talk about the guilt that you feel concerning your marriage,' Yvonne said.

'Well, that's easy to explain,' Steffie said. 'It's because of Jemima.'

'Because you moved out and took her away from Dad?'

Steffie nodded.

'Because he cheated,' Yvonne added.

Again, Steffie nodded.

'Yet it is you who bears the guilt,' Yvonne said.

Steffie shrugged this time.

'You had a right to feel hurt and angry, Steffie – a right to buy yourself some time and space.'

'Yes,' said Steffie. 'But Jemima misses him. And it makes me feel terrible.'

'Why?'

Steffie paused, clenched the tissue ball. 'Because I know I should be able to forgive him, but I just can't.'

'You can't?'

'No,' said Steffie. 'Every time I get close to it, something inside me tells me to get back, not to let him off the hook. It's awful … Some days I wish so much that things were back as they were – that we were all living at The Fishing Lodge, that we were happy, that he never met that woman—' She broke off.

'Say her name,' Yvonne said.

'I can't,' Steffie said. 'She makes me too angry.'

'What do you want to say to her, Steffie? What would you tell her if she were here now? What would you tell Olivia?'

32

Steffie laughed. 'Well, that's easy. I'd tell her to go to hell.'

'So tell her. Here she is,' said Yvonne, holding her hand out and turning her head as though ushering in an invisible guest. 'Tell her what you'd like to say.'

Steffie turned to the ghost. 'Go to hell,' she said.

'Say it louder,' Yvonne said.

'Go to hell.'

'Again.'

'Go to hell!'

'And again. Louder, Steffie.'

Steffie stood so forcibly, her chair toppled back. 'Go to hell, Olivia! Go to hell!'

She stopped. Her heart was racing, her breath haphazard. She straightened her top, picked up the chair.

'Good work, Steffie,' Yvonne said. 'But we need to press pause as our time is coming to an end and I'd like to reflect on the session.'

Steffie glanced at her watch. 'Sorry, but I need to make a dash for it. I've got to pick up Jemima early today.'

Yvonne smiled. 'As you wish . . . I'll see you next time.'

Steffie left, hurrying downstairs to the high street, passing the Silver Tree on her way, glancing in at her mother who was serving a customer whilst Steffie was at 'Pilates'. She wasn't comfortable telling anyone about the counselling, least of all her mum, who would make more of it than was necessary.

She looked at her watch again and began to run. She was taking Jemima to Noella's straight from school. Greg had agreed to meet them at the studio. They were going to give Noella their decision and then take another look at Prokofiev's *Cinderella* before confirming it as Jemima's audition piece.

To Steffie's surprise, however, when she arrived at the school, Greg was leaning against the wall, arms folded, waiting for the gates to open.

Her heart gave a lurch on seeing him unexpectedly, combined with the shame of having just repeatedly wished his mistress would go to hell.

Sometimes she wanted to ask him whether he had seen Olivia, whether there was still any contact between them, but she found it hard to form the woman's name on her tongue, let alone discuss details. It put a barrier between them that she found impossible to peek over, despite the fact that Greg was desperate to pretend it wasn't there.

'Afternoon,' he said.

'I thought you were meeting us at Noella's?' she said, walking straight past him and through the school gates, which had just opened.

'I thought I'd surprise Jemima.' He drew level with her. 'Is that OK?' he asked, his voice lowered.

The usual parents were gathering in the playground, around the eaves, around the picnic benches; the same parents each day, talking to the same people, often in the same spots.

Steffie had always noticed the glances that were shot at Greg on the rare occasions that he ventured into school. He was better-looking than she was, she thought. At least, that was what some of the mums would be thinking. And now that they were separated? Greg was like a beast set off the leash.

Except that it wasn't really like that. Many of the mums were reading their phones or talking about SATS, IBS or other initialised subject matters. No one was outwardly unpleasant, but Steffie knew how to navigate the path in order to avoid whiplash. Amongst the practically perfect, there was a stigma attached to separation that she sometimes found difficult to deal with, which was why she didn't like Greg joining her with his ripped jeans, his oily caramel-coloured hair and his truck parked out front as though he were about to go and lop down a tree or wrestle a bear.

The other dads who did the school run did so in suits or work-at-home daywear.

Jemima had appeared in the stream of red jumpers that was spilling from year six like over-zealous ketchup, and was now sprinting towards them, her rucksack jumping on her back.

'Daddy!' she shouted. And then stopped, recalling that it wasn't cool at her age to look so pleased to see a parent.

Still, she took his hand and off they went to Noella's studio, Steffie trailing behind as usual.

Steffie wasn't submissive, mousy. It was just that when you were the one living with the child, when you all met up, the other parent took centre stage. It was just fair. In everything that had happened – was happening – she wanted to be fair.

They found Noella waiting for them in the studio, standing by the piano, hands clasped high on her chest.

'Well?' she asked, before they had even entered the room. 'What have you decided?'

Noella hadn't been completely truthful with the Lees. Not that she had lied. She detested liars. Growing up with four brothers in southern France, the ease with which her brothers had distorted the truth had always amazed her. They lied as easily as throwing rocks over the neighbour's wall, as easily as poaching apples from trees. They lied all the time about everything, just to save themselves.

She wasn't a liar, but there were certain things that she had omitted to say.

For one, she hadn't told the Lees about her history with Mikhail Alexandrov, about the fact that she had slept with him whilst studying in Paris – twice, four times, a dozen; had lost count.

It was irrelevant and would cloud the issue. Jemima's future was the most important thing here.

She had also failed to point out that if Alexandrov were prepared to fast-track Jemima, then other academies would too. In other words, the child was good enough to go wherever she liked, whenever.

But this wasn't for her to highlight. It would be patronising. The Lees could work this out for themselves.

They were good people, she thought. Unusually, touchingly, they didn't appear to be interested in pushing their daughter for their own gain. She admired them for that, but still she was scared that they were going to say no, that Jemima would be going to Wimborne Comprehensive in September.

So she held her breath that afternoon, waiting for Steffie to reply.

She wasn't sure what was going on between husband and wife – why Steffie would want to be estranged from such a handsome, gentle man, who could pick up his daughter with one hand to kiss her.

Steffie looked pale today in a sky-blue ski jacket and faded jeans – a puffy cloud of motheryness. Noella hadn't ever wanted children, didn't see the appeal. Mothers were well-worn, softened by the endless chafing of little feet and limbs and cotton on skin.

Noella, by contrast, knew that she appeared bleak, sharp. Yet she was also uncompromised, undistracted.

She looked up at the windows with a shiver. It was wet and cold out – a nasty January, this one.

Unconsciously, she touched the little swallow on the back of her neck. She often forgot it was there and yet when she did remember it, it was always with the same sweet pain. She could feel the slight rising of the ink on her skin, the etching of the wings.

It had been so good to see Mikhail at their chance meeting last month – so fateful, fortunate.

The world of dance, like any specialist industry, was a small one and you often bumped into the same faces repeatedly. Yet still she hadn't expected to see him after all these years, especially not in Soho, for he was not what one might describe as a social animal.

She tried not to look shocked or grateful when he said he would consider an application from her.

Standing outside The French House in Soho with people jostling for space in thick coats, she blew on her mulled cider and hoped that her lipstick had stayed on – that her cheeks looked prettily pinched and not sallow, that the silvery trails of grey in her hair were not illuminated underneath the Christmas lights. She would be forty next year and was aware that her looks were time-sensitive, could change by the hour now.

Mikhail, the same age as her, had not changed. She could barely hear him above the chatter around her, above her beating heart. But she heard him say that yes, she could send him her pupil's video.

'You won't regret it,' she had told him, as though he were committing already. Which he most definitely was not.

What he said next had startled her. He had leant in closer to whisper, his mouth brushing her ear. It was an accident, but it sent a shiver down her spine. She could smell his familiar scent; not cologne, he was too subtle for that, but something intriguing, undetectable: the trace of blue in the cigarette smoke, the drop of moisture in mist.

'Look out for the *étoiles*,' he had said.

She had gazed at him in incomprehension. Whatever could he mean?

She wondered momentarily if he were drunk. He rarely used to drink, didn't appear to be drinking now. She took a step back from him to assess him more clearly, treading on someone behind her who yelped. 'I'm so sorry,' she told them.

'What *étoiles*?' she said, turning back to Mikhail.

But he was gone.

She looked for him – around the outside of the bar, in the crowded room upstairs. Perhaps he had gone to the bathroom.

She lingered, made excuses to her friends as they left – told them she would catch up with them shortly.

Yet she didn't see him again that night.

'We want to go ahead with the audition,' Steffie said.

'Yes!' said Jemima, punching the air.

Noella clasped her hand to her mouth. 'Really?'

Steffie nodded. 'Yes.'

'Woo hoo!' Jemima said, jumping up and down. She was still wearing her school uniform and began to pirouette, her checked skirt rising, her *Frozen* pants on display.

'That's fantastic!' Noella said. 'Thank you! So, wait … Today's the twenty-seventh. So that gives us …' She counted the days on her fingers. 'Eleven days … Can Jemima rehearse after school every day this week?' Suddenly, she paused, staring at Steffie with her dark eyes. 'Could I come to the audition?'

Steffie laughed. 'Of course, Noella. I assumed you would.'

'Perfect,' Noella said.

Greg was smiling affably, but outside as they parted on the corner of Peach Street, he hesitated, frowning. 'I think it was the right choice,' he said. 'But we need to keep Jemima's feet on the ground.'

'I know,' Steffie said.

'And ours.'

'Yes.'

She watched a sparrow pecking around the base of a tree a couple of yards away. The poor bird was shivering.

'Well, I'd better be off,' Greg said.

Today, she didn't want him to go. It was upsetting, the thought of him walking away.

She set off decisively in the opposite direction, her footsteps making hollow sounds on the cold pavement. She wouldn't think of Greg walking away, would concentrate on the day ahead, like she always did.

She was going to do an hour's work at the shop whilst Jemima rehearsed – would relieve her mum of some of her duties. Her mother didn't work at the shop full time, just when Steffie needed help. It gave her mum – a widow – a means of meeting people, of being connected and useful. And wasn't that the whole point of parenting, or at least a major part of it: being useful?

And that, Steffie realised, was the grating bit in all of this, the little fishbone in the tooth – the secret discomfort that she had felt at Noella's the other day and had wanted to take home and unwrap alone.

Someone else would be Jemima's cook and cleaner and wardrobe adviser and confidante and best friend and guardian soon; because Steffie wouldn't be there to be any of those things.

She gave a little sniff. No use being selfish, self-indulgent. This was what Jemima wanted to do. It was her course in life.

Despite her intentions not to do so, Steffie found herself glancing back over her shoulder at Greg.

He was in the distance, about to turn the corner, elbow raised, talking on his phone.

Her stomach dipped. Who would he be talking to? A client? Olivia?

It didn't help matters, this separation pickle. It didn't help her deal with the possibility of Jemima leaving home. It didn't help make her feel loved, settled or safe – all of which a mother had to feel in order to let go.

But she was going to do it anyway, loved or not, because Jemima was the most important person in her life and her happiness was everything.

She upped her pace and when she arrived at the Silver Tree she tossed her coat to one side and began to talk enthusiastically to her mother about audition dates and Prokofiev's *Cinderella*, and the well-documented benefits of Pilates.

PARENT OF CANDIDATE
ZACHARY WILLIAMS

Everyone always says Z's a bit of a live wire. And I can see that. I really can. Someone even had the nerve to say they thought he was 'on the spectrum'. What's that supposed to mean, anyway?

Zach's a good lad. Got a bit of spirit in him, that's all. If the modern kids weren't so robotic – I blame all this testing – then they'd be more like him. He just stands out because he's got a bit of personality. Good for him, I say.

My wife says he's out of control because I'm too soft. But I'm away a lot on business and when I see my kids I don't want to spend all my time telling them off. My dad used to take the belt to me. He was a right twat, 'scuse my French, and I swore that when I had kids I'd do it differently.

No, I didn't see it happen. I was in the auditorium. Zach had just performed. The first I knew of it was when I heard all the screaming.

My initial thought was that it was someone screaming because they hadn't been selected. No word of a lie.

Mr T. Williams
Phoenix Academy of Performing Arts
Surrey Police interview transcript
20 February 2016

FOUR

Jemima was a typical ten-wannabe-fifteen-year-old girl. She wore her hair long and back from her eyes in a cherry-red hairband – she was a big fan of cherry. And she wore Doc Martens boots everywhere, which Steffie thought made her legs look too thin – made her overall look off-balanced, like Minnie Mouse. But her best friend Pippi wore the same boots and she had even thinner legs, and whatever Pippi said went.

Jemima, despite her dancing prowess, wasn't especially academic, wasn't at the top of the class. Wimborne Primary was an Outstanding school within an affluent catchment area. Many of the parents were doctors, solicitors; one was a TV newsreader; another a former Olympic athlete. At drop-off time, the narrow road outside the school was a marinade of resplendent four-by-fours, grinding forward with passive ferocity, parked skew-whiff on double yellows and 'do not park' zigzags.

The mothers were mostly either unmade-up, dressed in faded cardigans and carrying eco shoppers, or clad in Lycra, traction trainers and neon armbands. Then there were the working mums, like Steffie, who moved too quickly for anyone to note their attire.

Steffie and Jemima, living only minutes away now, walked to

school, slipping between parked cars, waving a thankful hand to drivers for not mowing them down.

The atmosphere was jovial as the children entered the gates, dragging gym bags, hockey sticks, trumpet and violin cases, their hobbies bearing heavily on them. Everyone was very pleasant, exchanging greetings. And yet Steffie always sensed that there was something lurking underneath – that the kitten had spiky claws.

It was impossible for it not to be competitive here. The pool was too full of big fish, slapping against each other, with few prepared to lurk gloomily on the bottom.

It wasn't just because most of the pupils were wealthy, intelligent or both. It was apparently like this everywhere now, so Steffie's friends assured her.

After university, she and her friends had dispersed around the country, settling wherever their careers led them. But no matter where, the story was the same: competition, pushiness, pressure.

Where teatime conversations with a ten-year-old might once have been about tadpoles, boy bands or how to make cake without eggs, Jemima often wanted to talk about algebra – about how on earth to do it – or subordinating conjunctions.

Subwhatties? Steffie would say.

Jemima now kept her laminated SATs Companion sheet propped on the table before her as she ate of an evening. Steffie had given it a quick perusal. It was an overwhelming spelling and grammar maze, set out like the London Tube map. Conjunctions. Subjunctive forms. Determiners. Adverbial phrases.

Jemima seemed to think that she had to know all of these terms and what they meant and how to *demonstrate* them *appropriately* and *concisely* and *consistently* in her written material.

It was these sorts of topics of conversation – more frequent of late, in the run-up to the year-six SATs – that made Steffie realise that Jemima would be under pressure whether she went to Wimborne Comprehensive or the Phoenix Academy.

As far as education went, there was no easy run now.

Up and down the country, parents were downloading test papers, hiring tutors, stealing a march.

Some of the parents in the playground were beginning to complain, albeit in hushed tones, that their children were tearful about coming to school, were suffering from tummy ache or insomnia. No one voiced it loudly and Steffie noted that most mums edged into the conversation hesitantly, unsure how the recipient might react. One never knew. Even the hippiest parents could shock – could be spied leaving the head's office with extracurricular homework.

There was, at the school, a quiet underbelly of discontent and sadness. Some people found it easier to voice things online than confront stressed teaching staff. Facebook campaigns and online petitions were currently circulating, urging parents to strike in protest of the forthcoming SATs. *Give our kids their childhoods back!*

Striking was one extreme, racing at the front of the pack was the other. And somewhere in the middle was Steffie, along with many other parents.

The middle stood with their legs rooted, yet their eyes on the horizon, watching those advanced children wistfully.

Soon they would be specks in the distance, too far ahead to catch.

Perhaps it wouldn't harm for their own child to do a little extra maths or reading this weekend. They were spending far too much time watching telly and come to think of it had been getting pretty lazy lately . . .

It was very difficult, standing still during a race, as those who often did it knew.

The options were either to leave the race or to win it. Standing still, as others nudged past, trampled you, was soul-destroying for both parent and child.

So what if you did leave the race, went on strike, gave up? What if you were told on parents' evening that the school was sorry, they had done all they could, but your child wasn't going to pass any exams – they were a huge failure, all before puberty?

Steffie had spent a lot of time mulling over these things, choosing her stance. And the thing she had discovered was that she didn't have to stick to her position. She could change at will, striking some days, racing on others, or standing quietly at the back. It all depended on what was going on, how high the stakes were. But the choice was always there, greeting parents in various guises, from deciding whether to attend the parents' social evening to weighing up whether to download a SATs paper.

Sometimes, it wasn't difficult standing still; it was bliss.

The Phoenix Academy would be no worse than anywhere else. But Steffie's closest friends were urging her to apply caution, nonetheless.

'Especially at a ballet school,' one of her friends told her. 'A lot of ballerinas are anorexic.'

That was surely true. Any career whereby weight was a significant factor was going to motivate eating disorders. But then Steffie knew of several teenagers at Wimborne Comprehensive who were anorexic. An eating disorder could happen anywhere.

'And then there's the worry that you could be defining Jemima's future too early in life,' said another friend, an educational psychologist.

That one was hard to get around. Yet it was Jemima who had defined herself; Jemima and her inspiring Dancing Grandmammy.

Steffie's own mother, Helena, had always been slightly reserved about it all, faintly disapproving of the training that Jemima endured – that her only grandchild had muscle definition and what could only be described as a six-pack.

But there were several other children in Jemima's class who were in the same situation: a child heading for the British gymnastic team, one who was swimming for Dorset, another who had been scouted for Southampton football academy.

That was four amazing talents just in one class in a small corner of the country.

It seemed to Steffie that everyone had a talent now; and rightly so. Whereas in the past, many an undiscovered skill had wilted in the grave, now it appeared to be at the other extreme with the faintest sign of aptitude being exploited, like trying to extract milk from a dandelion stalk to fill a pint glass.

It was all well and good. Steffie had been into lots of things herself as a child: flower-pressing, stamp collecting, netball, swimming. But she couldn't remember it being anything other than fun. Pastimes were literally a way of passing time.

But now it seemed as though one's child had to be doing something, not only constantly, but to an exceptional level.

Playing 'Chopsticks' on the piano was no longer impressive. Swimming without armbands wasn't a milestone. Learning to ride a bike didn't warrant a special certificate from Dad.

What do you do? was no longer the parental icebreaker. Far more likely was: *Which team does your son play for? How long has she been playing chess? When's she doing grade-four cello?*

The bar had been raised so high, everyone was having to leap higher and higher to reach it.

All of which made Jemima's recent success not only rather unremarkable, it also transformed Steffie's playground status from One Not to Watch to Dark Horse with Hidden Agenda.

Lots of parents spoke to Steffie at school that week – people who had rarely spoken to her before now. They had heard the news about Jemima, since Pippi was very much a chatter, as was her mother.

Everyone was very pleased for Jemima, they kept saying; so pleased.

'Well, this is what Jemima wants to do, after all,' Steffie said, edging away. 'We're just supporting her.'

'Of *course*.'

From now on, no one would ever believe Steffie when she claimed that she wasn't a pushy parent.

It was nice that they were all wishing Jemima good luck. Yet Steffie couldn't help but wonder what this obsession with constant comparison and with hobby-pushing was really about, and how it was going to play out.

You could strike, opt out, home school even. Yet the high bar would remain, a new version of a glass ceiling for modern times.

Some would deny its existence. Some would try to pull it down. Some would ignore it, wouldn't even try to reach for it. Some would strive for it their whole lives and never get there.

And some, like Jemima, would reach it effortlessly, and then have to work out quickly, urgently, how to stay there.

The only other person who could influence Jemima, aside from Pippi, and Louis from One Direction, was Noella.

Everything that Noella said was The Truth.

Jemima drank four large glasses of whole milk a day, *in order to maintain bone density, vital for dancers.* Whilst it was Jemima who often said this, they were Noella's words.

And now, with the audition less than a week away, Jemima was so imbued with Noella-isms, it was hard not to think of her as just a little bit French.

First thing in the morning, then after rehearsals and then

before bed, she would lie on the lounge floor of their apartment with her headphones on, visualising the moves of her audition piece.

It is vital, she kept saying, *to visualise before a performance. If one can see the moves, one can achieve them.*

'Hmm?' Steffie said, reaching into the back of the fridge for a tub of coleslaw. She was sure there was one there somewhere; unless she had left it at the supermarket checkout. Sometimes, she did that.

'Visualising!' said Jemima, folding her arms, raising an eyebrow. 'Were you listening?'

'Of course,' said Steffie. 'Now go and wash your hands for supper.'

Jemima didn't move. 'Noella says she thinks the place at the academy is already mine.'

'She does?' Aha. There was the coleslaw. 'Well, Noella should keep her thoughts to herself.'

Jemima looked stung. Her mouth flopped open. Down went the hands to the hips. 'Why? What's Noella—'

'Calm down, Mims.' Steffie smiled. 'No one's criticising Noella. I just mean that we should take things one step at a time. No one's guaranteed anything at this level and I don't want you to be disappointed.'

'Well,' said Jemima over her shoulder as she paced from the room, her back straight. Such excellent posture often made her look arrogant, which she wasn't. 'Noella says that cultivating a positive attitude is tantric to success.'

When Jemima had left the room, Steffie laughed to herself.

Tantric? Wasn't that what Sting was famous for?

Jemima meant tantamount.

Such moments reminded her that for all Jemima's talent, maturity and determination, she was still little, impressionable, vulnerable.

As Steffie hooked the jacket potatoes from the oven and sliced open the skin, the steam tickling her nose and eyes, she made another vow to watch Jemima closely throughout this process; to keep her safe, grounded, secure.

Later that night as Jemima slept, Steffie crept around in her usual fashion, like a courteous burglar, stuffing her pockets with strewn objects. When the apartment was tidy, she sat down at her computer and began her routine of scrolling through the Phoenix website.

She had seen everything there was to see, including the photograph of Mikhail Alexandrov, MA, ARAD, Dip PDTC.

He was exactly how she had expected him to look: intense, handsome, slightly scary.

What else could she look at?

She flicked back to the home page and saw that a news item had just been posted.

We are delighted to announce our new Six Étoiles programme.

During final auditions for entry September 2016, Mikhail Alexandrov will be selecting six étoiles ('stars') from current year-six candidates.

The étoiles will enjoy extra tuition and will be showcased internationally throughout their careers at the academy.

'The étoiles will set a standard for the other pupils and for onlookers around the world,' Mr Alexandrov said.

Good luck to all the candidates who are auditioning next Saturday!

Further details of the Étoile programme to come.

Steffie stared at the screen and then went to phone Greg, before deciding not to.

Then she picked up the phone and dialled anyway.

When he answered, she could hear the television murmuring in the background. 'Greg,' she whispered, 'sorry to ring so late.'

'What's up?' he said.

She pictured him in his pyjamas and sweater, sat in bed. He had always liked watching television in bed at night, whereas she had preferred reading. For a long time, when she had first moved in here, she had found it funny reading in bed without the flicker of a blue light on the page.

'It's going to be even more competitive than we thought,' she said.

'Hey?' Greg said.

She could tell from the tone of his voice that he was deep in some Miami-based crime scene. It had always surprised her that such a placid man could watch violent programmes without flinching. *But it's not real*, he used to tell her.

'Only eighteen children will be offered places at the Phoenix for Jemima's year,' she said.

'But we knew that,' he said. He had turned the volume down.

'And then six will be chosen to be *étoiles*,' she said.

'Whats?'

'*Étoiles*,' she said. 'It's French for star. Six of them will be showcased internationally.'

'Oh,' Greg said. 'And are we bothered about that?'

'We're not,' Steffie said. 'But Jemima will be. The auditions will be even worse now – even more intense.'

There was a pause.

'Well, she can only do what she can do,' Greg said.

'Yes,' Steffie said.

'Night then,' he said.

'Night,' she said.

And they hung up.

AUDITION CANDIDATE NO.1

I didn't even know they'd gone up there. I wouldn't have gone, even if they'd asked me to. I always stick to the rules. That way you don't get hurt, unless there's an earthquake or another natural disaster . . . My mum says that you have to be ready for anything. We have a panic room at our house. And I have to text my mum as soon—

Oh. I was in studio four practising my piece and then I went straight to the auditorium. I was with my mum the whole time. She was trying to keep me calm, but sometimes she makes me worse.

Please don't tell her I—

You've probably already seen her. Or heard her. She can be a bit loud . . . Yes. That's her. That's my mum.

She kept trying to put a flower in my hair, even though I told her it would fall out.

I did the audition with the flower and it did fall out, right at the end.

Beatrice Jones
Phoenix Academy of Performing Arts
Surrey Police interview transcript
20 February 2016

FIVE

'What do you mean: showcased?' Helena asked. She was leaning against the shop counter with her back to the main entrance, looking at the view through the large windows. The Silver Tree was shoe-box shaped, with windows at the back and front, creating the illusion of being lighter and bigger than it actually was. From the back window, you could see almost all of Wimborne and the hills beyond.

The beautiful view was the reason Steffie had chosen the site for her business, that and the fact that it was placed lucratively in the middle of the high street, with office blocks at either end. A gift shop specialising in expensive-looking yet affordable items, it was a convenient stop-off for locals.

The shop did very well, and it served Steffie well also. She was happy here, so far as Helena could see. Retail wasn't what she had set out to do in life, but running the shop was enough of a challenge to keep her occupied, but not gruelling to the point of collapse.

'Well, I suppose it means that she would be one of the principal dancers,' Steffie said, 'and would get to perform abroad.'

'Abroad?' Helena turned to look at her daughter who was opening a box of new stock. 'And you're OK with that?'

'I think I have to be,' Steffie said, pausing to pick a piece of fluff from her jumper and letting it drift to the floor.

'But it's a lot of pressure for a young girl,' said Helena, lowering her voice, since two women had entered the shop. 'International travel, on top of her education?'

'But it might not happen,' Steffie said. 'She might not even pass the first audition.'

'The first *final* audition.' Helena stood up, straightened her jumper and smiled at one of the customers who was examining a glass teardrop. 'Hand-blown in Pembrokeshire,' she said to the customer, coaxingly.

Steffie began unwrapping a box of toys on strings: a puppy, dragon, tiger and zebra, which were to be hung in the window. The rest were going in the toy section; not that there were really sections in the shop. It was too small for that.

Helena gazed at the back of her daughter's head, at the mass of curls. 'I just hope it's not too much for her,' she said. 'Young people have so much pressure these days.'

'Come on, Mum,' Steffie said. 'You could at least sound a little bit positive about it.'

'I am positive. I'm just asking questions . . .' Helena said, then turned to the customer. 'That'll be nine pounds fifty, please. Would you like it gift-wrapped?'

The glass items always sold well – recycled glass hand-blown into friendship hearts and teardrops, on satin ribbon. They could be hung in windows to catch the sunshine, or in trees outdoors. Helena had one in her kitchen window – a pink heart that reminded her of the mint shrimp sweets Steffie had gorged on as a child.

Steffie had spent a lot of time reading books, eating mint shrimps, as a little girl. She used to read whilst sitting in the tree in the back garden and in the tall grass by the wall, sucking mints, chewing grass. She had long legs, which had looked grasshopper-like. She had plenty of friends, loved swimming in the river across the field, and bouncing up and down the driveway on her spacehopper, the dust clouding around her.

Those were wonderful days – hot, sticky days of Wimbledon finals, fishing with jam jars, big hairstyles and home-knitted sweaters.

And look at it now. Look at Jemima's life compared to Steffie's – at how scheduled and pressurised and accountable it was.

Steffie had tried to eat a dead bumblebee once; Jemima was allergic to honey.

It wasn't Steffie's fault. She was painstaking, conscientious, doing her utmost to protect her daughter and raise her well, in accordance with the rules now in place.

Helena turned to watch Steffie who was climbing into the shop front to hang up the animals. It was just beginning to rain. Soon the windows would be awash with water, the car lights splodges of red beyond. Helena liked being here on wet days most of all, sitting behind the counter with a mug and a biscuit, watching the humdrum life beyond.

Wimborne was a nice place to live – a quiet town whose movements were largely predictable. She had raised Steffie here, mostly alone, since her husband, Steffie's father, had died during Steffie's teens. Steffie had attended Wimborne Primary, where Jemima now went. Yet the comparisons ended there. For the town, the school and the parenting styles had all changed beyond recognition.

'Well, that's that job done,' said Steffie, wiping her hands on her jeans. 'Cup of tea?'

'Please,' Helena said. 'But I'll make it.'

Steffie smiled, but was looking tired, creased at the temples. It was Thursday today. Monday was audition day, pressing ever nearer.

Still, Helena thought, as the kettle boiled, Steffie had turned out all right, despite all the idleness and time-wasting and bumblebee eating and wild-river swimming. She was kind, responsible, a good mother.

Helena poured the water, stirred the tea pensively.

All you could do as a parent was go with the flow, move with the times. And hope like crazy that everyone around you was sane and knew what they were doing.

Greg was in his workshop on Friday morning working on the order for the manor house when Olivia rang again.

He didn't hear the phone above the sound of his electric saw. He wasn't working alone on the job as it was too big; he had two workmates with him. They were building the cabinets by hand in exposed oak, which they had darkened with ammonia to reveal the tannins in the wood.

This afternoon, the furniture painter was coming to hand-paint the wood in slate blue. The clients were sparing no expense, with original stone flooring being shipped from France.

As soon as the floor arrived, they would start installing the kitchen. They were all working hard and fast, to exacting standards.

It was one of his workmates who shouted to him that his phone was ringing.

He put down his saw and took the call outside in the dim morning light. It had rained overnight, and moisture was dripping from the gutter and tree branches. He shivered, thinking how easy it was to forget that it was winter when you were knee deep in sawdust and sweating.

The couple at the manor house were reasonable, but they wanted the work completed quickly. He thought it would be them calling to say they had made up their mind about whether to go for granite or slate worktops.

But it was Olivia. 'Hi,' she said. 'How are you?'

'Good,' he said.

She sounded slightly out of breath. He could hear her high heels clipping as she walked briskly. 'I thought I'd give you a call, as it's been nearly two weeks.'

'Two weeks?'

'You said you'd call me back.'

'Oh,' he said. 'Yes.'

'After all, it's Friday and it would be nice to make plans for the weekend ... I mean, do you want this, Greg? Where do you actually see things going between us?'

Too many words, he thought. And too much going on with Steffie at the moment, with the audition looming.

Thinking of Steffie did not help, it merely stalled him.

Slate, he remembered. His clients had left a message last night to say they had decided to go with slate.

'Greg ... ?'

Olivia had stopped walking. He pictured her at the end of the line, waiting, frowning.

She wasn't someone who tolerated being messed around, he knew from experience. His first impression of her, aside from the fact that she was very attractive, was that animals and small children would recoil from her, narrowing their eyes, as though she were cigarette smoke.

Her appearance was highly groomed, perfectionist. To other women, her look would say that she was to be respected, envied, and could rock a backless dress; men translated it slightly differently.

He had met her the summer before last, whilst installing an eco kitchen in her impressive home. An environmental consultant, she had inspected his credentials thoroughly. Only when satisfied that he didn't use tropical hardwoods, that the paints were water-based, that he used LED lighting in his workshop and an eco energy provider, had she allowed him to install the whopping stainless-steel kitchen that shone so brightly he grew tired of seeing his reflection whilst he worked on it.

And then one Friday night that summer, when he was lost in his work and had stayed later than intended and the sun was beginning to dip, she had opened a beer and perched on the swinging chair in the garden, wearing a low-slung vest and jeans, bottle pressed to her lips, and had asked him to join her.

She was pretty, he had considered, sitting there with the pink foxgloves in flower behind her.

Her daughters were staying the night with their dad, she told him delicately.

He had shuffled about with indecision as he packed his tools away. The temptation was great.

But he couldn't – couldn't even talk to her, or linger.

He got into his truck with heavy limbs and drove home, laden with loneliness. The lodge had felt quieter than usual, stiller; even though Steffie was lying right there in bed beside him.

He had tried to put his arm around her that night, but things were too far gone between them, and she hadn't even bothered to recoil but merely pretended to be asleep.

The following Friday night, when the same thing happened again – the vest, the foxgloves, the absent children – he had agreed to a bottle of beer with Olivia on the swinging chair.

She had made the first move, waiting for him to finish his beer, for him to loosen up before making contact. She had kissed him tentatively, her eyes watchful.

She had smelt of vanilla, a scent that reminded him somehow of Christmas. The moment owed everything to that perfume.

All this he thought as he held his phone and gazed beyond the lodge to the lake that was still and silver, like a giant plate covered with foil.

'Greg?' Olivia said. 'Are you still—'

'Yes,' he said. 'I'm here.'

His nose and eyes felt itchy. He pinched the top of his nose to stave off a sneeze.

He was always covered in sawdust. Come the end, when things had deteriorated to the point of intolerance, Steffie had disliked that about him the most, he had sensed – had withdrawn from the smell of wood on his clothes, the shavings in his hair. It got so that she wouldn't go near him when he was working or just after working, which was most of the time.

'And what do you think?' Olivia said.

He didn't want to be mean to her, wanted to do the right thing by her, but was unsure what that was.

He had always been squashy, malleable when it came to women. As a boy, his little sisters had run rings around him – wild, crazy rings that burnt holes in the grass – like witches playing with fireballs; setting light to dustbins, hanging from trees by ropes, pulling the tail on the neighbour's cat.

His mum, Vivienne, was performing with Sadler's Wells at that point, so they had a nanny, who didn't appear to mind whether the twins danced with the traffic or threw darts at each other. His stockbroker father was rarely home. So Greg took the role of father-figure willingly, not wishing to see the twins buried.

But on meeting Olivia, all this had changed. He had wanted to do something reckless for once; to put his own needs first, no matter how selfish or harmful that might be. He hadn't thought about it, it had just happened. He had been overwhelmed by loneliness and rejection, by a craving to be loved, needed.

The affair had only lasted a few months – for the duration of his work on the house, in effect. It had been fervent at first, dizzying, but those sensations soon descended into gut-wrenching guilt that rendered him unable to eat or sleep.

Miserable, ashamed, he had ended things between them in the autumn. Olivia had accepted the news with unpredicted dignity.

Things settled down. He forgot Olivia, tried to revive things with Steffie.

But then on Christmas Eve, Olivia's drunken ex-husband had phoned the lodge to speak to Steffie.

He wasn't in the house at the time – was out in the workshop putting the finishing touches to a ballerina figurine he had hand-carved for Jemima – but he knew as soon as he entered the kitchen that something was wrong.

He could still see the look on Steffie's face when she turned to look at him, holding the phone in her hand.

Steffie had moved out in the New Year, taking Jemima with her.

A year had passed and now Olivia was contacting him again, treading lightly, seeing where things stood.

'It's a bit hectic at the moment,' he said. 'There's this audition ...'

'Audition?'

'My daughter's auditioning for a dance academy.'

'Oh.'

'So maybe I'll call you afterwards?'

'Maybe?' she said.

'Definitely,' he said. And then he considered that this sounded too much like a promise. 'I'll call you ... And we can talk then.'

She exhaled heavily. 'OK, Greg,' she said.

This evasive behaviour would have got him nowhere twenty years ago. Yet at their age, the circle was far smaller. Olivia probably didn't have that many men on her radar, which was why she had taken a shot at a married man in the first place presumably, and was now back for more.

It was all rather sad: her desperation, his loneliness, his having hurt Steffie – and Jemima by default.

He had tried his best to get Steffie to forgive him, to mend their marriage, for Jemima's sake if no one else's, but she was struggling to accept the betrayal.

He didn't blame her. He hadn't forgiven him either.

He put his phone away and walked slowly back to the workshop, noting that he didn't feel half as happy now as when he had walked out only minutes before.

It was why he loved his work so much, why he was in no rush to reduce his hours or to ever retire. His work didn't confuse him, didn't play with his feelings. He moulded it, shaped it, built it into something beautiful and lasting.

He thought he had done the same with Steffie, that their marriage was as robust and carefully crafted as the kitchens that he created.

But it wasn't so.

Yet before he let go of whatever it was that still remained between them, he needed to hear it from her. She had to stand before him and tell him unequivocally to give up – that she was never going to forgive him.

PARENT OF CANDIDATE
BEATRICE JONES

Oh my God, I love watching Bea dance. I get all, you know, hormonal as soon as she dances. She's my little princess and my best friend and I just don't know what I'd do . . .

Sorry. I'll be all right in a sec. Just give us a sec.

Oh my God. It was horrendous. There was such a commotion. I was petrified. Everyone was. We were all petrified. I mean, you don't expect this sort of thing to happen at this level, do you? I can't imagine what I would do if anything ever . . . I love Bea sooooo—

No. I didn't talk to the family, wouldn't be able to recognise the child.

Were they even there this morning? Or did they just appear? I didn't even notice them.

Mrs P. Jones
Phoenix Academy of Performing Arts
Surrey Police interview transcript
20 February 2016

SIX

Noella changed her mind five times, packing and unpacking the outfit that she would wear to arrive at the academy. First she chose something that she wore when teaching – a black top and full skirt. But that seemed too draconian. So then she opted for jeans and a frilly top. So it went, swinging back and forth between smart and casual until she felt giddy.

Then she couldn't close the holdall.

'Damn it!' she shouted, drumming her fists in exasperation on the bag, before realising the time. She was meeting the Lees in ten minutes on the corner of Peach Street. They were driving her to Usherwood and then after the audition she was spending the night in London with friends and returning by train tomorrow.

She pulled up the window and tipped her head out to look up the street. No one there yet.

She slammed the window shut and sat down on the bed, gnawing her fingernails, eyeing the swollen bag.

In the end, she went for the black top and skirt.

She sat in the back of the Lees' car, aware that every time she scowled she was forging a deeper crease between her eyes. She hadn't known about the line until the other week in London when a friend of hers – an ex-ballerina who was now a Chinese medicine practitioner – told her that the deep line between her eyes denoted frustration and anger.

What deep line? Noella had said, jumping up to consult a mirror. *Oh,* mon Dieu! *I never knew that was there!*

See? her friend had said, smiling over her cup of chia tea.

The problem with ballet dancers was that a lot of them were rich and well-connected. Naturally, there were the wild cards, like herself. But the majority of her friends had left ballet to become beauticians or crystal healers, so they could tell others that their faces were cracked and old.

And the problem with being around people like that – the self-assured, the over-privileged – was that eventually you grew tired of constantly being found fault with.

At least, that was Noella's experience. Coming from the rural outskirts of Bordeaux, her family had eaten bread straight from the wooden table, with their backyard chickens running in and out, pecking their toes. It had been a leap for her to adjust to life at ballet school in Paris.

Sometimes she wondered why she had tried to fit in for so long. Yet here she was, about to turn forty and still travelling to London to see her old friends from the Parisian ballet school – many of whom had settled in London – to court their good opinion.

And here she was once more, hoping to get the biggest approval of all.

She glanced sideways at Jemima, who sat with admirably good posture in the passenger seat, her hands clasped between her knees, her eyes staring straight ahead. There was no knowing what she was thinking.

She hoped that Jemima's nerves wouldn't show today. If her limbs were twitchy or stiff, Alexandrov might overlook it – would be insightful enough to see her potential. But having a strong mind was a vital part of being a professional dancer and his board would be looking for evidence that each candidate could survive the course.

Noella had been strong enough. She had been a good dancer. But twelve years ago, she had suffered an Achilles tendon rupture that felt as though she had been shot in the foot. She had thought at first – after several operations – that she might dance again, but it was not to be.

Bitter, broken, she had fled the profession and Paris in order to open a dance school in rural Dorset, where she could brood unheeded.

Her school wasn't the Bolshoi – a fact that she tried to overlook each day, without much success.

'Nervous?' she asked Jemima, placing her hand lightly on the child's knee.

Jemima didn't reply. Noella then noticed the wire in her hair, realised that Jemima was listening to headphones – no doubt Prokofiev's *Cinderella*.

The Lees were quiet up front, although it was very early in the morning – still dark out. Steffie's arms were folded; Greg was driving. Noella had not heard them exchange a word. It was going to be an odd trip. And perhaps a fruitful one, not only for Jemima but for herself.

Over the years, if she had doubted her staying power in Wimborne, had doubted her decision to wither into her fourth decade unnoticed, Jemima Lee had persuaded her otherwise.

Jemima's talent, her virtuosity, had given Noella a sense of purpose and pride.

The idea of facing each day without her, of unlocking the studio each morning and watching the luckless, unremarkable and ungifted go through their moves hour after hour, day after day, was crushing.

Without Jemima, there would be no substance to her life, no brilliance.

Jemima could not fail at her audition. She had to excel – to rise to the top and take Noella with her. Everyone would want to know who Jemima Lee's tutor was – this last-minute non-private-academy-trained entrant from rural England. The attention would attract a different calibre of pupil to Noella's studio – could even warrant her opening a bigger, more prestigious school nearer London, somewhere where she would be less of a joke.

She glanced again at Jemima, who was oblivious to the weight of her tutor's expectations, and then closed her eyes, tried to let her forehead relax, tried to smooth the pesky line between her eyes.

Steffie got out of the car and stood looking up at the building, her breath visible in the cold air. The academy was set within Danube House, a handsome art deco property on the outskirts of Usherwood, within forty acres of land framed by spruce trees.

It was mid-morning and the sunshine was brilliant, earnest. A bird of prey was circling the lawn, gliding in the Mediterranean-blue sky. The trees were shimmering with icy droplets, as though adorned with glass pendants from Steffie's shop.

It felt safe, remote.

The boarding pupils – one hundred and fifty of them – danced, studied and slept within Danube House. The west wing had been heavily renovated in recent years to house state-of-the-art studios and an auditorium. Otherwise the property looked authentic, timeless, graceful. Steffie could almost hear the pattering of ballet shoes, the whisper of excited voices backstage.

She reached for Jemima's hand and squeezed it. 'Here we are then, sweet pea,' she said.

'Gulp,' said Jemima, raising her shoulders and holding them high in a mock grimace. She was still at the joking stage. That might change, Steffie thought.

Steffie opened the passenger seat of the car and unhooked Jemima's costume which was hanging in a plastic sleeve: a classic black leotard with short white tutu.

'Impressive place, hey?' said Greg, once he'd parked the car on the gravel to the side of the building.

'It's epic, isn't it, Daddy?' said Jemima, skipping to him.

Steffie watched Jemima with excitement. To think that Jemima could be living here, on her way to greatness . . . Steffie allowed herself to picture for a moment what that might look like.

And then a Mercedes pulled up on the driveway behind them.

Car doors slammed and two people approached: a woman and a girl with plaited hair sticking out from a sequined beanie hat.

'Morning,' said Steffie brightly.

The mother, a short, officious-looking woman in a felt *Downton Abbey*-style hat, shot Steffie a smile before heading for the academy entrance. 'Come on, Daisy,' she called over her shoulder.

Daisy was tiny with large bug-eyes. She was carrying a rucksack on her back that looked to be twice her body weight. As she passed, she gazed gormlessly at Jemima.

'Hi,' Jemima said.

They stood watching the woman and child enter the academy, and then Noella clapped her hands. 'Well, what are we all standing here for?' she said.

Steffie wasn't sure why they had been spellbound, but they had. It wasn't just the odd mother and daughter with their fast-paced little legs, but the aura of the building. It was the sort of place that one had to pause and admire before consuming, like a beautiful Italian pastry.

'Shall we?' said Greg, motioning to the ornate door.

Inside, there was no sign of the mother and daughter.

The four of them gathered at the foot of a marble staircase that was panelled either side in mahogany. Pearl lamps adorned the walls and at the top was a shrine-like alcove containing a vase of lilies and decorative panels etched in gold.

Greg gave a soft whistle of admiration.

At the top of the stairs, a door was ajar. They headed there, their feet clipping on the marble flooring.

Beyond the door was the reception desk: a circular space-age construction housing large screens. Behind the reception, lay a high-ceilinged shop with shelves of clothes, fastidiously organised as though not to be touched.

The place was teeming with people, despite the lack of cars outside.

'Probably arrived by helicopter,' Greg muttered into Steffie's ear.

She smiled, but felt suddenly anxious. 'Do you know how many people are auditioning?' she asked Noella.

'I suspect forty or so,' said Noella. 'And from them, they'll select their eighteen.'

Steffie's stomach churned. She gripped Jemima's warm hand and led her forward to the desk.

'Welcome to the Phoenix Academy,' said the red-lipsticked receptionist. 'And whom do we have here?'

Jemima cleared her throat, but no words came.

'Jemima Lee,' said Steffie.

'One moment.' The receptionist tapped her screen, began to type.

Greg was gazing at the silver panel above them. 'Do you think that thing comes down at night and seals the desk off, like a pod?' he asked Steffie.

'I've no idea,' she said. It was the last thing on her mind.

Noella was examining the site map on the wall, tapping her hand on her leg.

They were all on edge.

'Your audition's at four o'clock,' the receptionist said, giving Jemima a plastic card. 'Warm-up's from three o'clock in studio three. Through the lift to the first floor, third door on your left. This card will get you into anywhere requiring a security pass. Just swipe it against the wall panel and hey presto!' She smiled broadly. 'Here's some paperwork for Mum ... Mr Alexandrov will be giving a presentation in the auditorium at noon.' She opened a pamphlet to reveal a map and circled the auditorium with a pen. 'Good luck!' And she turned to the next family in line.

A man beside them was on his mobile, talking intermittently in English and possibly Japanese. 'We need substantial international trade data,' he was saying. 'Not wishy-washy horse crap ...'

Next to him, a toddler was jigging his legs, clutching his pants. It wasn't clear to whom the child belonged. 'Pee pee,' the boy was saying on repeat.

'Don't bite your nails!' a woman behind them said to a young girl, who was already in her tutu, legs blue with the cold. 'No one wants to see that.'

The woman to Steffie's left sounded furious. 'I told you there would be a queue,' she was hissing to the man beside her. 'Why the hell don't you ever listen to me? I told you there would be a queue!'

Steffie glanced down at Jemima who seemed to be having difficulty swallowing. 'Let's find a quiet place to fill out these forms,' she said. 'There's a café somewhere.'

Jemima perked up at this. 'Can I have a KitKat?' she said.

'Good morning and thank you for joining me. It's a privilege to have you here.'

Mikhail Alexandrov was tall; his muscular arms, resting on the rostrum, were tanned. He was wearing a logo-emblazoned black T-shirt and black jeans; the staff seated around him on stage were wearing the same.

'As the new director, come September, it is my intention to take the Phoenix to even greater heights. By the end of today, some of you will be joining me. We can't take all of you. We'd love to take all of you. But we can't.' He paused, allowing his words to register.

'If we reject you, don't be too disheartened. We are human. We make mistakes. We may choose people who will prove to be mistakes, and many worthy pupils will slip through the net. We can't always get it right. But we try our best.'

Jemima twitched her legs nervously. Steffie reached for her hand. Jemima had refused to take her coat off yet, was peering out from her fur-trimmed hood like a hedgehog at dusk.

'Many of you will have heard by now,' Mr Alexandrov continued, 'that this year we are running a special Six *Étoiles* programme.'

There was an immediate buzz of conversation around the room, as heads bent to confer. The panel of staff on stage were nodding encouragingly, smiling.

'Once you have secured a place in year seven,' he said, raising his voice to hush the chatter, 'we will call ten of you back for one final audition. From these ten pupils, we will select six *étoiles*. Once you are an *étoile*, it will remain your privilege throughout your time with us.' He flashed a smile. 'So yet another reason to impress me today.'

Once more there was an outbreak of noise around the room. Steffie noticed that the stubby-legged woman and girl were sitting two rows in front of them, still wearing the *Downton Abbey* hat and sparkly beanie. The woman was nudging the girl exuberantly as though she had already been selected.

Steffie took in the other people around her, noting the expensive coats and jewellery. It was mostly mothers and daughters, although there were a few fathers and sons dotted about.

Behind her, the man was still talking in English and Japanese about international trade data, albeit in a hushed voice. He was with a boy with white-blond hair that was gelled up at the front, and a woman with thick drawn-on eyebrows. Steffie took all this in with what she thought was a discreet backwards glance, until the boy noticed and winked at her.

Steffie turned front-ways again, her cheeks burning.

Mr Alexandrov was talking about the prestige of being an *étoile*, about what it would mean professionally.

The family in front of Steffie were German by the sounds of things – she could hear them whispering to each other. And then her attention was drawn to a mother who had just arrived with a clatter and a grimace of apology. The woman came to a halt near Steffie, leaning against the wall, her arms draped over her po-faced daughter, her thighs locking the child in place. Steffie watched them, fascinated. The mother kept fiddling with a flower in the girl's hair, which the girl kept trying to shed, like a horse flicking a fly away with its tail.

'There are only eighteen places on offer. And for the six *étoiles* . . . ?' Mr Alexandrov held out his hands. 'Well, this could be the springboard to a glorious international career.'

Steffie shifted uncomfortably in her seat. Greg was eyeing her above Jemima's head, his mouth a pondering circle. He appeared to be thinking the same thing as her: it was going to be tough – very tough.

Once Jemima changed into her tutu and held the barre and listened to the piece on her headphones and beheld herself in the mirror, she was *in the flow*, as Noella called it.

Noella came into her own now, murmuring instructions, straightening Jemima's limbs; and Steffie felt the familiar sensation of slipping away. There was always a moment at these things – the moment before the performance, even at the humble town hall – when she had to let go.

She did so now, and sat down on the bench with her back against the wall, Jemima's coat and clothes on her lap. Greg stood nearby, arms folded, gazing around the room, looking mildly daunted.

It was hard not to compare, for your eyes not to flit between Jemima and the girl next to her and the girl along from her. They were a line of faultless performers, so far as Steffie could tell – all with similar posture, weight and skill sets. She had no idea how the panel would be able to judge them apart. But there would be some red-eyed candidates going home tonight, dejected, inconsolable, for sure.

It was a lot for young children to compute. Most adults found rejection in any form unbearable and went to great lengths to avoid it, yet these children were facing it head on – baring themselves to be assessed, judged, cast off. There was no telling whether such pressure would steel their souls or crinkle them.

It would have been so much easier, Steffie thought, were there a scanner available so that you could ascertain soul damage, like the ultraviolet scanners showing the harmful effects of sun on skin. Yet there was no such scanner and most of life's gently pulsating waves of inspiration and injury were immeasurable.

'Sienna Black and Isobel Quinn, please.' A lady in black uniform wearing a headset stepped forward from the door, waving her clipboard, summoning the candidates. The girls who had been along the barre from Jemima ran dutifully forward, leaving their families gathering bags behind them, calling out hurried 'Good luck's.

There was a little swishing sound and then the door closed and it was just Jemima at the barre.

Steffie rose to speak to the lady in black. 'How long will Jemima be in the audition?' she asked.

The lady consulted her clipboard. 'About forty-five minutes. She's the last candidate because she needs extra time. The panel haven't met her before so they'll also want to interview her.'

'Oh,' said Steffie, crestfallen.

She hadn't thought of that – hadn't gone through any questions with Jemima. She gazed at Jemima now, who was stretching her leg as high as her ear. Was it too late to run through a couple of responses? She looked at the clock on the wall. The audition was in ten minutes.

She sat back on the bench, smoothed her hand over Jemima's coat.

It would be fine. Jemima would be fine.

She was just feeling better when she saw that Jemima was hurrying towards her, her face crumpled, upset. Noella was dashing after Jemima, trying to call out discreetly but her voice was echoing across the room nonetheless.

'Jemima! Come back!'

Faces were turning to look at them. Greg unfolded his arms, stared at Jemima in surprise.

She stood before them, chin lifted slightly. 'I want to go home,' she said.

'You what?' said Steffie. 'Why?'

Jemima threw her headphones on to the bench. 'I can't do this. I'm rubbish. Did you see that girl next to me? Did you see her? I can't do this. I'm not as good as them. I want to leave.'

Steffie stood up, touched the tight bun on Jemima's head. It felt smooth and prickly at once. 'It's OK, Mims,' she said.

'You're just nervous. As soon as you get in there, you'll be fine. And afterwards you'll wonder what all the fuss was about.'

Greg echoed the same, squeezing Jemima's shoulder consolingly.

But Noella had joined them and was cross. 'This is time wasting, Jemima,' she said. 'You need to be focused, in the flow, not crying into your mother's lap.'

'Now hang on . . .' said Steffie. She raised her eyebrows to Noella, as if to say, *Come on, let's be sympathetic, shall we?* But Noella was having none of that.

'*In. The. Flow,*' she said, tapping her watch.

At that moment the lady with the headset stepped forward and shouted, 'Jemima Lee?' And then, 'Oh. Of course,' when she realised that Jemima was the child standing nearby – the only remaining candidate.

The woman frowned. 'Is there a problem?' she asked.

'Yes,' said Greg.

'No,' said Noella, speaking over him.

'Could we have a moment, please?' said Steffie.

'Of course.' The woman nodded, stepped away.

Steffie straightened Jemima's leotard, brushed the dust from her tights, smoothed her bun, placed her hands on Jemima's shoulders.

'Look,' she said, taking a deep breath, 'if you don't want to go in there, you don't have to. We can go home. If that's what you want.'

The moment she uttered the words, gave her daughter the option of escape, she sensed a change in her.

'It's OK, Mummy,' Jemima said, with a little quiver.

'Good girl,' said Noella.

And then Jemima joined the woman with the headset, who promptly led her from the room.

'Good luck!' Steffie called out.

And then she sat down on the bench, as the door closed with a whoosh of air that could have been a draught but felt like the air being sucked out of her in a rush. She felt so deflated.

All the build-up, all the busyness and worry and dashing around and planning; only for Jemima to be led off by someone else, away from her, out of her control, beyond reach.

It was the hardest part of parenting: the sudden realisation that there was nothing more you could do.

PARENT OF CANDIDATE
ISOBEL QUINN

Isobel came to dance relatively late. She's very academic and we were loath to restrict her so early on. But Mikhail's a close friend and encouraged us to audition at the Phoenix.

We always come to these things as a whole family. It's important for Issie's siblings to support her. My husband's a top Consultant Respiratory Physician at Guy's Hospital, but he always clears his schedule for auditions.

I find it shocking how other people don't come as a family, how there's only ever a few people making an effort. I mean, if you can't support your children—

No. Issie didn't even talk to her, that I know of. Issie's profoundly shy. In fact, one of the reasons we have encouraged dance is in order to help her to—

Oh, it's just horrendous, tragic. I really feel for the family. I suppose it means she's out of the running for the *étoile* programme now.

Mrs E. Quinn
Phoenix Academy of Performing Arts
Surrey Police interview transcript
20 February 2016

SEVEN

'Blimey,' said Greg, rubbing his face, feeling drained all of a sudden. 'For a moment, I thought she wasn't going through with it.'

'Me too.' Steffie was sitting down, clutching Jemima's clothes on her lap, her head tilted in the direction of the door, listening, even though everything was soundproofed and there would be no clues as to the progress of the audition.

Greg gazed at the spot where Jemima's rival had stood – her silver jacket draped over the barre as a lasting reminder of victory, like an expedition flag on a conquered mountain. He didn't need to take a closer look at the jacket to know that it would be embossed with the logo of an elite dance academy in the Home Counties. The entire family was gathered near the barre: a weary-looking mother in flared jeans and sensible shoes, a greying father who kept consulting his phone, three sombre siblings sitting in a line reading Kindles.

The father had just walked to the middle of the room to speak on his phone. 'No, I'm at my daughter's audition ... You'll have to refer the patient to ... Yes ... Fine.' And he returned to his family, his shoes squeaking on the vinyl floor.

So the father was a doctor – someone fairly important by the sound of things, Greg thought, eyeing the man.

'I don't think that girl was any better than Jemima,' he whispered to Steffie. 'Do you?'

Steffie shrugged. 'Probably not. Jemima just got intimidated.' She glanced about the room. 'And who can blame her?'

Earlier, when they first arrived in the studio, they had been surrounded by slender children with groomed hair and sinewy limbs that as good as gleamed as they stretched. And all around the children were groomed parents and siblings whose interest in the proceedings had ranged from mild to obsessive.

Some of the parents and tutors had murmured encouragement and instructions; some had hissed through clenched teeth; one woman in the corner had actually shouted at her child: *For God's sake. Not like that!*

'We knew it would be intense,' said Noella, who had been gathering her belongings from the barre.

'Yes,' said Greg, nodding.

Noella frowned at him regretfully. 'I didn't mean to push her,' she said. 'I just didn't want her to blow this. We've worked so hard to get here and I believe she has a great chance.'

'Sure,' said Greg. And left it at that. After all, they were all feeling the pressure, feeling fractious.

He turned to Steffie. 'If she's going to be in there for a while, do you fancy a quick stroll outside?'

'OK,' Steffie said. 'But what about all this?' She held up Jemima's clothes.

Noella stepped forward. 'Leave her things with me. I'll wait here. Go,' she said, smiling.

She was acting subservient, meek – un-Noella-like.

Apology accepted, Greg thought.

They left the studio and went back down the corridor to the lifts.

Outside, they walked in silence, heads bent against the cold.

'This way?' Greg said, gesturing towards the thin path that ran down the middle of the lawn, like a hair parting.

Steffie nodded, wrapping her scarf around her face.

He glanced back at Danube House. It was handsome – similar to the school his mother had trained at, only in Kent. It felt very enclosed, safe-guarded, with security passes in the building and cameras on the grounds. Jemima would be well cared for here, he thought. And yet there was something about it that unsettled him.

It was the pressure, he suspected. The atmosphere was glass-like, precarious. Not only were the stakes high at entry level, but the standards of everyday life would be high too. Being in a pressurised container like this would only suit a certain type of child. The problem was that it was only afterwards that you knew for sure which type your child was.

At the end of the lawn, the path descended down a stone staircase to another lawn. 'Shall we?' Greg said.

Steffie nodded, then stopped and looked back at the building. 'Where do you suppose she is? Which of those rooms?'

He turned to look, running his eye along the first-floor windows to the third room. 'That one?' he said, stooping and pressing his head close to hers and pointing.

Her scarf had dropped. His cheek was briefly touching hers.

'Steffie . . .' he said, reaching for her hand.

But she pulled her scarf up and turned away to admire the view that was presenting itself to them.

He stood still, inhaling the unpolluted air. Before them were hundreds of spruce trees. There was no life beyond, from this viewpoint.

The air was so refreshing, the view so enchanting, it reminded him of the Italian Alps, of where they had honeymooned; thirteen years ago now.

Memories like this – of happier times, before things had

deteriorated – were painful to recall. Sometimes he couldn't remember what that felt like: to be that free and light, before parenting had weighed in, slowly unpicking their marriage.

He took a sharp breath in, felt the cold air meet his lungs.

They had stayed in the Dolomite Mountains, north Italy, close to the Austrian border. Their mountain lodge had smelt of spruce and mountain larch, with dragons and eagles carved into the eaves.

He closed his eyes briefly in sweet memory, and then glanced at Steffie, wondering whether she looked at the landscape and saw the Dolomites too. It was unlikely, however. Her thoughts would be with Jemima.

So what she said next rather surprised him.

'Do you remember the pool in the mountains?' Her voice was muffled, wrapped in her scarf.

He looked at her, tried not to smile. 'Yes,' he said, 'I do.'

She wasn't looking at him, was staring ahead at the view.

The pool in the mountains had been a still mirror of warm brine water in the meadows. By day, it reflected the Dolomites. By night, it was alight with Alpenglow – the golden glow on the mountain tips as the sun sank. Swimming, just the two of them, they had felt weightless, timeless.

Suddenly, he had to say it. 'Please come home.'

She opened her mouth to reply, but didn't.

He pressed on. 'You have to forgive me, Steffie,' he said. 'It was a stupid mistake that I regret ... You've no idea. If I could go back and change everything, I would.'

He stopped, waited for her to speak. But again she said nothing.

'Do you think you can ever forgive me?' he said.

She gazed at him, her rapidly blinking eyes the only sign of motion from beyond the scarf. 'I don't know,' she said.

He felt his shoulders sink. 'Have you tried?'

She pulled the scarf down. 'Of course I have!' she said. 'But it's not that easy. As soon as I think we can give it a go, for Jemima's sake, I find myself thinking about that woman – about you and her together – and then I feel like punching you. And I don't want Jemima to have to live like that.' She was angry now. Her gloved hands were curled in frustration.

'I'm sorry,' he said miserably. 'I don't know how to fix this. I don't know what to do.' He felt the back of his throat swell. 'I just want you to come home . . . I love you.'

She gazed up at him, bit her lip. One tear escaped down her cheek, landed in her scarf. The movement seemed to waken her. She looked at the building as though remembering Jemima. 'We should get back,' she said.

He made no move to leave. 'Please try,' he said.

She nodded. 'I am trying,' she said. 'More than you realise.' She hesitated. 'I'm seeing a counsellor.'

He smiled, bent his knees to level with her. 'You are?' he said. 'Well, that's great. But I thought—'

'I don't,' she said, reading his mind. 'I don't like the idea at all. But I didn't know what else to do. And I like the woman I'm seeing.'

'Well, I'm pleased,' he said.

This was the first positive thing he had heard in a long while about his marriage.

She suddenly looked worried. 'Don't tell Mum,' she said. 'She'll make more of it than needs be. I've only been going a couple of months and it's just a casual thing, you know?'

'Course,' he said. 'But I'm still proud of you.'

She should have done this years ago, when things first went wrong. But she hadn't been ready to.

It was a big step. They both knew so.

'Thank you,' he said, trying not to sound gushy, overblown. 'This means a lot.'

Again, she shed a tear. She dabbed her cheek with her thick glove and the tear was gone.

'So do you want me to go with you?' he said. 'Aren't marriage counsellors supposed to be—'

She frowned. 'It's not a marriage counsellor,' she said. 'It's a general one. It's for me. Not for us. Not for our marriage.'

She said this very bluntly. He saw the regret in her eyes. But still it was done: the door had been opened a fraction and she had slammed it shut again.

The silence swelled between them, filling what they couldn't say: that they had so much work to do and no idea how to do it.

'Come on,' she said. 'Let's go.'

As they walked towards the building, Greg sensed that there was something else that she wanted to say. She kept glancing at him, her step faltering.

And then she said it. 'Have you had any contact?'

'Contact?' he said.

'With her?'

At that moment, the door of Danube House opened with a swell of noise from within, and closed heavily again. A family approached down the driveway. It was the man they had heard earlier during the auditorium meeting, speaking incessantly on his phone in Japanese. Greg had wanted to grab the phone off the man and tell him not to be so rude.

The man, presumably with his son and wife, was still on his phone. 'Now, listen here, buddy ...' he was saying. The mother was scowling, the boy was tossing a ball into the air and catching it behind his back with one hand.

'That's the boy who winked at me,' Steffie said quietly.

Greg tutted.

'Come on, Zach,' said the mother. 'This way ...' Then she glared at the father. 'For God's sake, will you get off that bloody phone?'

Greg realised that he and Steffie had stopped what they were doing, what they were talking about, in order to observe the scene before them. The people here had a habit of doing that, he thought; they made you drop everything and stare, albeit discreetly.

But Steffie had remembered their conversation and was looking up at him, arms folded, waiting. Her eyes were deep green today, reflecting the spruce trees.

He recalled the conversation too, kicked the gravel underfoot, wondered how to give an honest response.

'It's a simple enough question,' she said. 'I would have thought—'

'Yes,' he said.

'Yes, what?'

'Yes, I've had contact.'

She looked stung, confused. 'But ...'

'Look,' he said, plunging his hands into his pockets. 'You asked the question and I've been honest. I don't want any more lies.'

'But you ... ' She looked about her, as though lost.

'She started texting me a few weeks back and then calling,' he said. 'She's been trying to meet up. But I haven't. I haven't—'

'You haven't what, Greg?' she said.

'I haven't met her. I've tried to avoid her as much as possible.'

'Avoid her?' she said, raising her voice. 'That's not good enough! Try changing your phone number. Try not replying or speaking to her at all!'

He looked at his feet. She was right. He could be stronger.

But there was something else to this, something more that he couldn't tell her.

He was lonely. He wanted contact – with Steffie. But failing that, Olivia might have to do.

And that, he knew, was the truth.

'What is it, Greg?' she said, staring at him, scanning his eyes. 'Do you want to be with her? Is this what all this is about?'

'No,' he said. 'Course not. I want to be with you. I want you and Jemima to come home.'

'Then why can't you break contact? Why can't I just trust you to do that?'

She began to cry and he felt ghastly. He stood with his hand in mid-air reaching forward to her.

And then the front door of Danube House opened again and another family trailed out. This family, however – like themselves, Greg sensed – were unremarkable, didn't warrant a stop-everything stare.

Both parties passed each other without acknowledgement.

Steffie took off her gloves and pulled a tissue from her pocket, dabbed her eyes. 'This is ridiculous,' she said. 'This is Jemima's big day and here we are, doing this.'

'It's not ridiculous,' he said. 'It's our marriage. It's the most important thing there is.'

She gazed up at him. 'Yet look how you treated it,' she said.

There was no comeback to that.

'Let's go,' she said.

As they went back up the marble staircase, he spoke to her, his voice low but hurried. There were people everywhere now, coming in and out of the academy. 'I won't ever see her again,' he said. 'If that's what you want.'

'Of course it's what I want,' she replied.

'Then it's done,' he said.

At the top of the stairs, just as they were about to go through the room to the reception, she turned to him, stood on tiptoes and kissed him lightly on the cheek. 'Then we've got a chance,' she said, before disappearing through the door.

He was stunned.

Jemima had told him last week that the venom of an

Egyptian cobra could turn a human's insides to goo. How she knew such a thing, he didn't know. Children knew all sorts of facts like that. The other day, he had found an old note in his wallet that said: *Dear Daddy, I love you. Did you know that vykings ate pufins? From Jemima.*

He felt like that now – as though he had been bitten by that cobra.

It was all he could do to summon the strength to make his way to the studio. Steffie didn't seem to think this was a big deal, was acting as though nothing had happened. But he felt luminous, light.

That was all he had wanted – a hint of hope. And he had been given it.

They sat back down on the bench where they had sat before. He couldn't stop himself from looking at Steffie, couldn't remember having ever felt more love for her – not even in the Dolomites.

But she wasn't on honeymoon, far from it; was looking worried, tapping her feet, consulting her watch.

Noella was pacing up and down before them. The studio was very quiet now, most candidates having been and gone, aside from a few lingering parents, hovering as their child stretched post-performance.

Just along from them, on the bench, a young girl was crying noiselessly, knees drawn to chest, fists to eyes. Her parents were crouched before her, murmuring soothingly. Presumably she had messed up the audition.

Greg felt for her, wondered if that might be them shortly, consoling Jemima. It couldn't be the reason not to go to these things; and yet the thought of rejection – of witnessing your child's pain and not being able to do a thing about it – was sickening.

'She's been gone longer than I thought. It's a good sign,' Noella said, not looking happy, though. 'A very good sign.'

'I wonder how she's got on with the interview side of things?' Steffie said. 'I didn't realise they were going to do that. We didn't—'

She broke off. The studio door had opened and Jemima was approaching with a member of staff.

Greg tried to assess his daughter's expression, but she was giving nothing away. The only difference between how she looked now and when they had last seen her was that her hair had come unclipped from Steffie's carefully prepared bun and was hanging in frazzled strands around her eyes.

Jemima put her hand to her face to wipe the hair away, smiling shyly.

Steffie stood up. 'How did you get on?' she said.

Jemima frowned at them, curling her mouth, as though telling them to apply caution, discretion. They were surrounding her, the three adults, drawing closer with intrigue, unable to stay back.

'Jemima,' Greg said. 'Tell us . . . Is it good news?'

She nodded, smiled.

Greg glanced at Steffie, who was making a high-pitched squeal.

'Did you pass?' Steffie said.

Jemima nodded again. 'Yes,' she said, beginning to wobble with the effort of keeping it all in, since the other candidates were glancing her way, hungry for information, to find out whether their chances were greater or lower with this latest result.

'*Mon Dieu*,' said Noella in a whisper.

And then Jemima burst into tears, and he and Steffie moved forward instinctively to embrace her. And somehow they ended up pressed together, the three of them – a bundle of heartbeats and tears, trembles and joy.

*

Had he known that in less than a fortnight his world would be smashed beyond recognition, he might have held them both a little tighter.

But he hadn't known that, couldn't have known that the sense of fragility in the air at the Phoenix hadn't just been due to the pressure, but a sign of his own vulnerability – that his happiness was as weak as a crystal bauble on a demolition site.

And so at that time, with his wife and child secure in his arms, he knew nothing of glass and splinters and fractures; only knew pure, complete happiness.

AUDITION CANDIDATE NO.2

My father's a top Consultant Whispery Tree Physician at Guy's Hospital.

Whispery Tree? That's what I call it. It's to do with breathing?

He clears his schedule to come to these things to support me in my endeavours so it's very important for me to appreciate that and not jeopardise my chances. Other people would give an arm and a knee for this opportunity and here I am, not even knowing I was born.

Yes, I was warming up in studio four with the girl with the loud mum who kept putting a flower in her hair, and with the other girl in the sparkly hat. I thought she might audition wearing that hat.

My parents told me not to look at them and to concentrate on myself.

I'm not ever allowed to talk to anyone at auditions.

No, my mum told me not to talk to her too, even though she was friendly and said hello to me in the café. She had a bag of gobstoppers and offered me one. They made her tongue purple, which was funny.

That was the last time I saw her.

Afterwards I wished I'd taken a gobstopper.

EIGHT

Children used to do things without the need for discussion or safety measures, Helena thought. They went swimming in quarries, climbing into derelict buildings, racing on motorbikes along disused railway lines. All these things Steffie had done, and more. None of it had happened following discussion; most of it without Helena's prior knowledge.

It was the same when Steffie had gone to university. Steffie was interviewed by Manchester University, and then off she went.

Helena had driven her to Manchester at the start of term, had taken Steffie for lunch in a place that she would never be able to find again in a million years.

Fish pizza, they had eaten. She could remember that.

And that was it. Occasionally, Steffie came home on the train, mostly to use the washing machine and to get a good night's sleep. But otherwise, she had left home.

Not like now. Helena had noticed that the local university was advertising a spa hotel on campus so that you could spend as much time with your student offspring as you wished, even though they were supposed to be away from home, spreading their wings.

That sort of thing seemed to be encouraged from an early

age now: parental participation. Steffie was forever going in to school for information days and meetings. It was well meant, in theory. Everyone wanted to be involved in their children's lives, especially their education; and it was a proven fact that children fared better at school when their parents gave a hoot about their advancement. But still, from an onlooker's point of view, Helena worried about the pressure that modern life put on Steffie.

Gone were the days when you dropped your child off at the school gate and that was the only point of contact.

Steffie often looked tired, Helena thought. When she wasn't running the shop, she was organising play dates, going to PTA meetings, taking Jemima to dance class, helping with her homework.

Whenever Helena dared mention that Steffie's load seemed heavy, Steffie always replied the same way: *It's just what needs doing, Mum.*

Still, it was an awful lot to juggle. Helena helped out as much as she could – as much as she was allowed to. But Steffie often resisted help, prided herself on getting it all done, even though she looked weary and had little time for herself, aside from 'Pilates'.

Helena knew it wasn't Pilates – knew Yvonne's sister very well, who had blurted out clumsily in the Co-op last month that she had spotted Steffie in Yvonne's counselling offices. 'It's a small town,' the sister had said with an apologetic shrug.

Helena wasn't sure why Steffie couldn't tell her about the counselling. Yet if she were to guess, she would say that it was because the issue with Greg was too sensitive, too painful.

They were clearly still fond of each other – maybe even still in love – but fate had treated them poorly. It was heartbreaking to see. Yet Helena had not given up hope of a reunion.

Greg was a good man. But he had slipped.

'Slipped' was a silly way to put it, she felt. It implied that an accident was involved — that someone had oiled the soles of their feet, or in this case, their belt buckles. And yet sometimes it was easier to see it as a slip, rather than a plunge.

Helena should know. Her husband had slipped too, with his secretary. But she wasn't about to tell Steffie. Steffie had adored her father. There was no sense in ever changing that.

So she indulged Steffie by playing along with the Pilates cover, and often found herself wondering how much Steffie would tell Yvonne about the past.

Steffie wouldn't be able to say everything. There wouldn't be full disclosure. There would be little mental drawers left closed. Even if she tried to open them, they would grate, get stuck.

Poor Steffie.

And before long Jemima would be packing her bags for Usherwood. At the raw age of eleven, she would be leaving home, stepping into the unknown.

It had been hard enough for Helena when Steffie had left aged eighteen for Manchester.

Helena would have loved to cling. A widow by then, who else did she have in her life but her lovely little Steffie? Steffie in her blue wool coat with the acorn buttons; Steffie with her Snoopy apron on, helping make egg soldiers for supper; Steffie with her hair in ringlets bringing Helena a cup of tea in bed.

Sweet little Steffie. Helena had a lifetime of mental snapshots, of moments, of aromas, of songs, of tastes. To this day, she could smell gingerbread, Earl Grey, summer rain, old books, and recall a Steffie moment with the click of her fingers.

And just as fast, it was gone.

You could try to hang on, with photographs, videos; maybe even by literally hanging on and never letting them go. The system certainly seemed to be aiding and abetting that now.

It wasn't like that in the eighties, especially not where students were concerned. Parents hadn't been involved in student life, were embarrassing appendages. There were no university spa hotels encouraging them to linger then. The very thought of it would have been absurd, awkward – like the time Neil Kinnock was in a pop video, or Bill Clinton played saxophone.

The whole point had been for Steffie to leave home and face a series of initiation tests – coping with over-zealous drunken boys or exam pressure. Helena had tried not to picture details.

And that was part of learning to let go, Helena felt: teaching yourself to look away, not to see the details any more. For the more you saw, the more you drew closer; the more you knew, the more you understood; the more you clung.

There came a point where you couldn't be that involved any more, when you watched, even advised, but didn't control.

She hadn't ever visited Steffie in Manchester, aside from at the end of term to collect her. They had relied on weekly pay-phone calls to communicate, enduring the brutal sound of the pips going before they had a chance to say goodbye. And she had written to Steffie every fortnight without fail.

Letters, phone calls. They were the lifelines then – reliant on money not running out during the call, on postal vans not breaking down.

So Jemima would be leaving home, but communications were far more advanced. And Steffie and Greg would be able to visit her on weekends – would be actively encouraged to.

But still she felt for Steffie, that she was surrendering her daughter too soon; for it was a surrender of sorts, a relinquishing of duties.

It wouldn't be easy, especially not since they had been living so closely together in that apartment. Helena had offered to have them at her cottage, but Steffie hadn't wanted to do that – had wanted moving out of The Fishing Lodge to be impermanent, unworkable in the long run.

There was some logic in that, Helena supposed.

Yet the two of them had lived for a long year cooped up in the flat, knowing each other's every thought and move.

And if the trick to letting go was not seeing the details, then Steffie's living arrangements wouldn't have done her any favours come September.

Helena sighed, drew down the metal shutters at the front of Steffie's shop. Steffie was currently at a Roman exhibition at school. Tomorrow, there was an achievement assembly in the afternoon. There was always something.

And then in September . . . it would suddenly go quiet.

Helena put up her umbrella. It was raining lightly. She glanced back at the shop to check it was secure, and then drew her coat tighter around her and set off home.

As she walked, she thought of a niggling secret she was harbouring. It wasn't anything huge, illicit. It was just that she couldn't tell it to anyone for fear of seeming disloyal or critical.

She wasn't a pessimist, wasn't overly cautious or nervous. But she had a bad feeling about all this.

It wasn't just the stress of being in a competitive arena at such a young age, although she wasn't a fan of that. It wasn't just that Jemima was leaving home so early in life, although again it wouldn't have been her first choice for her granddaughter.

It was something else.

She couldn't quite put her finger on it. The only way to describe it was an uncomfortable feeling of doubt.

It was hard to ignore it, no matter how much she tried. There were few things as unsettling, as maggoty, as doubt. Questions kept wriggling inside her – questions that no mortal could hope to answer. Because that would mean that they could see the future, whereas Helena could not; could only feel doubt.

*

'So something that I'd like to talk about today, Steffie, is why things broke down between you and Greg in the first place.'

Steffie nodded, gripped the tissue ball in her hand.

'Can you pinpoint when things began to deteriorate?' Yvonne said. She was wearing a tropical-looking blouse and floaty trousers, despite the frost outside. She looked warmer than usual – the fan on her desk had broken, so she had cranked the window open. 'Tell me if you get cold, by the way.'

Steffie glanced at the window, at the shutters that were fluttering intermittently. It was an unremarkable day – rainless, light on traffic. Occasionally a car passed, parked in the high street below, wheels crunching, doors slamming, and Steffie remembered that there was life beyond. That was how quiet and still it was.

'Things broke down after the affair,' Steffie said.

'Yes,' said Yvonne. 'But before that.'

'I don't remember,' said Steffie.

She didn't want to be difficult, obstructive, but she didn't like where this conversation was headed.

Sometimes, it was a game of tennis in here.

Yvonne smiled. 'I think you can do better than that,' she said.

'I'm not sure that I can,' Steffie said.

There was a silence. Steffie missed the fan – its distracting whirring sound, the way it shifted the energy in the room, refreshed it.

Instead, everything was still. And she hated that. Because when it was still, she could see the dust.

'What are you doing with your hands, Steffie?' Yvonne said.

'Hey?' said Steffie.

'Your hands.'

Steffie looked down. She was still clenching the tissue ball – was holding it with both hands, pressing it.

'Are you angry?'

'No.' Steffie dropped the ball on to her lap.

'What might you be angry about?'

Steffie shook her head. 'Nothing that I can think of.'

'About Olivia?'

'Well, no one would feel good about that, would they?'

Yvonne didn't reply, was gazing at Steffie.

'Are you going to get your fan fixed?' Steffie asked.

'Does it matter?' Yvonne asked.

'Not really,' Steffie said.

This was weird.

The unspoken rule here was that Yvonne chatted things through with Steffie, who felt better afterwards. It wasn't supposed to be like this.

Yvonne hadn't cleaned her desk or her keyboard recently. There was a dark blue lamp on the desk with a shade that was layered with dust. It made Steffie shudder. She straightened her back, felt her pulse quicken defensively.

'Sometimes marriages unravel when children come along,' Yvonne said. 'Parenting can put untold pressures on previously perfect relationships . . .' Yvonne cocked her head. 'Shall we talk about that?'

'Yes,' Steffie said, fixing her eye on the wall clock. If she really stared at it, time might speed up.

And it did. She managed to get through the session without saying very much at all.

Yvonne glanced at her watch. 'Well, I'm afraid we're out of time. But perhaps before we meet again you might like to reflect on the things we've discussed and see if you can come up with some answers to share with me, hmm?'

Steffie didn't answer. She had no intention of reflecting or coming up with answers. She was too busy watching the dust cloud behind Yvonne's head that had suddenly appeared as the sun streamed in.

'See you next week,' Steffie said, grabbing her bag and heading out.

'There's no need to be afraid, Steffie,' Yvonne called after her.

Steffie halted, turned.

'I'm not the enemy,' Yvonne went on, smiling. 'I'm here to help.'

'Of course,' Steffie said, returning the smile. 'Thank you.'

It was a shame, Steffie thought, as she returned to the Silver Tree. She had liked Yvonne, would miss her. She was a wonderful listener and made great coffee.

But Steffie could never go there again.

PARENT OF CANDIDATE
FREDDIE RAWLINGS

I knew Freddie was going to get in, to be honest. When you come to enough of these things, you can pick the winners out from a mile off.

I'm not being funny, but Freddie's been dancing at a high level for years and takes it very seriously. At Christmas, he threw all his chocolate in the bin. He only eats healthy stuff like fruit and rice. He's ever so fussy. And he weighs himself all the time. It's great to see him taking care of himself. It's so important, especially nowadays with so many obese kids about. I'm always saying to his little sister, Savannah . . . she's six and such a sweetie . . . that she mustn't get fat and how Freddie won't eat chocolate any more and she's started doing the same thing. She even wants a pair of pink scales for her birthday!

Anyhow, I knew he was going to get in and that certain people would struggle.

Yes. I picked her out as someone who was going to . . . well . . . I shouldn't say it, especially not now. But I knew it wasn't going to end well.

Not obviously *that*, no. I didn't predict that. No one could have.

I'm just saying . . .

It's hot in here. Is it hot in here?

Mrs L. Rawlings
Phoenix Academy of Performing Arts
Surrey Police interview transcript
20 February 2016

NINE

On the Thursday after the audition, Greg rang Olivia and left a message, saying that he needed to talk to her as soon as possible.

Afterwards, he felt better – more like his old self.

He sensed that change was on its way. Steffie's kiss on the cheek at the Phoenix might have been casual, impulsive, caught up as she was in the emotion of the day. He wasn't to make a big deal of it – that seemed to be the main message to take away.

Yet he couldn't help but feel cheerful as he got back on with sawing a piece of oak that morning. The flooring had arrived from France for the manor house, so they were beginning to install the kitchen tomorrow.

It was a well-timed distraction – a good anchor to keep him grounded, restraining him from moving too quickly.

He had always been that way around Steffie, having to stop himself from revealing all his cards, surrendering all weapons and dignity. When he had first met her, it was all he could do not to declare his love rather than say hello, not to propose marriage on their first date rather than a bottle of wine with the main course.

He had known from the start that Steffie would make a great mum. He hadn't ever considered not having children, but nor had he planned how to acquire them. Having children had felt like a natural course in life for him, like getting a job or going grey – something that would happen along the way.

It was the same with his idea about what his ideal wife might look like. Were he to have examined it, he would have realised that the image he carried close to his heart was rather like that of his own mother. No man actively set out to marry someone like their mother, and yet if she was a good one – a loving mother – the imprint would be there, irrevocably.

Steffie and his mother, Vivi, didn't look alike. They didn't have similar mannerisms or opinions. Yet they shared one thing that mattered to Greg so greatly that he scarcely acknowledged it, for it would have been like constantly talking about the sun or oxygen.

Both women loved their children so fiercely that it was unquestionable, indubitable.

When he was a child, his mother had been away a lot, dancing, sometimes for entire summers. But she was always there, somehow. She had stayed up late to sew costumes for school plays, making cakes for sales, joining in the egg and spoon race on sports day – phoning them from abroad to say goodnight, writing to them, leaving them notes in lunch boxes. She proved that love didn't have to cling or even be present to be there.

And so it was with Steffie, who worked tirelessly to keep everything smooth, to earn respect and prove her worth. No one would ever question whether she loved her child – especially not Jemima.

He stopped work, wiped his brow with his shirtsleeve, took a swig of water. Then he heard a rustling noise and looked up to see a deer standing in the entrance of his workshop.

He froze, enchanted. Sometimes foxes poked around, birds got trapped inside and flapped around the rafters, and once a badger had run into the workshop before spotting Greg and running straight out again. But never a deer.

It seemed enormous, incongruously placed. It was female; a doe. She cocked her head at him.

'Hello,' he said.

And then she scrabbled her legs in panic, kicking up dust, turning and disappearing from sight.

He sighed, picked up his saw, got back to work.

As he sawed, eyes narrowed protectively, he thought of the day he had finally spoken to Steffie for the first time.

They were both working for a plastics supplier in Oxford – Greg as a sustainability manager, before retraining as a carpenter, and Steffie on a management programme. He often saw her in the lift and on coffee breaks in the lounge, but she seemed too cool for him to speak to. There was no dress code in the office. Steffie wore T-shirts that said things like *Morgan, Paris*, with bootlegged leggings and Sketcher trainers. Her hair was dyed blonde at the time – a mop of cryptic spirals – and she wore red lipstick that made her lips look larger than he now knew them to be.

He had tried to find a way to talk to her, something to lead the conversation with, but failed each time. Until one day in the lift he noticed that she was reading the back of a Radiohead CD and he saw his chance.

'You like Radiohead?' he had asked.

'Don't know yet,' she said, peeling off the price label. 'My boyfriend just bought it for me.'

His heart winced.

'If I don't like it, he's dumped,' she added. And then the lifts pinged and she stepped out.

He stood gazing after her. Then the lift lurched and he continued his journey upwards, unsure whether that contact had been successful or not.

After that, he didn't see her for a fortnight. He was beginning to wonder whether she had left the company, when he bumped into her at the coffee machine in the lounge, noted her hazelnut arms and guessed that she had just got back from holiday.

'How did you get on with the CD?' he asked.

She gazed at him expressionlessly.

'You said you'd dump your boyfriend if you didn't like the CD?' he said.

'Oh,' she said, selecting tea with extra sugar at the machine, 'just kidding.' And she began to walk away.

Without thinking he had run around in front of her, holding a steaming coffee that was burning his fingers. 'I'm Greg Lee,' he said.

'Hello, Greg Lee,' she said. 'I'm Steffie Pinkerton.'

And she walked away in her silver Sketchers, her curls bouncing on her back.

'Your phone's ringing, mate.'

Greg looked up, wiped his forehead with his sleeve. His workmate had arrived, was taking off his jacket, unloading his tool bag.

'Thanks,' Greg said, picking up his phone and taking it outside, his limbs aching from over-exertion.

He sometimes did that – got lost in Steffie, in the memory of her: a cocktail of spiral hair and sugary tea.

The sound of Olivia's voice brought him back to reality.

'I'm really sorry,' he said. 'I know this is difficult . . . and unfair . . . but we can't have any more contact.'

He heard her sharp intake of breath down the phone, and flinched.

He shuffled his feet, gathered his thoughts.

'I'm trying to . . . well . . . I need to try to put things right with my wife. I owe her that and I owe myself that and I'm sorry for everything that's happened but I think it's best that we don't contact each other any more . . .'

He was talking too quickly. He paused. She wasn't saying anything.

'Olivia . . . ?'

'I'm here,' she said quietly. And then she sniffed – a faint sound that betrayed the fact that she was crying.

He closed his eyes, guilt pressing heavily on his shoulders as though forcing him to his knees. Yet he remained standing, trying to be some kind of a man about it – a very small six-foot man.

'I'm so sorry,' he said. 'I really am.'

She sniffed again. 'OK, Greg,' she said. And then she hung up.

He stood for a moment, gazing at the lake behind the lodge. A kingfisher was flying above the water, its reflection following it as though a multicoloured fish were skimming the surface of the lake.

And then all was still.

His time with Olivia had been like that: pink foxgloves, vanilla; a flash of colour . . . and then stillness.

He pushed his phone into his pocket, turned away and went back to the workshop to get on with sawing oak.

There had been no chance to speak to Mikhail in person at the Phoenix. Noella had wanted to take him to one side, to mention old times, mutual friends, Jemima's excellence – translated: Noella's excellence. Yet she hadn't even glimpsed him, aside from during his presentation in the auditorium.

It felt as though she were being held on the peripheries, somewhere she hated being. All the other Home County-based tutors would be dining with Mikhail, moving in his circles, sweet-talking him over wine. And here she was, stuck in the provinces. These things were supposed to be unbiased, but Noella was experienced enough to know that no one was either impartial or immune to flattery.

She would have to do something about it. Few of the other competing tutors or parents could lay claim to having slept with him; at least, she hoped not.

Was Friday night too intimate a time to phone him?

No, it was perfect; just intimate enough.

She would drink a glass of wine first, whilst she ran through her words. She would mention Delphine, her old room-mate. That would get him going. And the all-night bar, Bartok, that they all used to meet in, just ten minutes from school in Paris. She wondered if Bartok were still standing. It had been tatty, dilapidated, even then.

At the thought of Bartok, of Paris, of Delphine, she suddenly felt overheated by guilt. She unwrapped the scarf from her neck and tossed it down in agitation, as though flapping away the past.

Focus, she told herself. *Focus on the future*.

When she had finished the glass of wine, she picked up the phone.

'Misha,' he answered.

She had forgotten that he used to call himself this, that it was how he was known to close friends. She felt a surge of pleasure at this display of intimacy, before realising that he couldn't possibly know it was her calling.

'It's Noella,' she said.

'Noella?'

She closed her eyes, felt her chest rise and fall in frustration. He didn't know who she was.

'Jemima Lee's tutor,' she said.

'Ah!' he said. 'Noella! Yes. I'm glad you called.'

'You are?' she said, leaning back against the wall of her kitchen. The fridge was purring, rattling a glass fruit bowl that was perched on top. She put out her hand to still the bowl.

'Yes,' he said. 'I have some news for the Lees.'

'You do?' she said.

Why was she answering everything he said with a question? She pinched the top of her nose to compose herself.

'Yes. But I'll call them myself to tell them in person.'

'Is Jemima—'

'I'll see you very soon,' he said, and hung up.

She listened to the silence emanating from the phone, looked at the shards of yellow light that were hitting the kitchen floor and walls from the streetlamps outside, and put her hand to her heart. It was racing, uncomfortably so.

She had been out-manoeuvred. What else did she expect from a masterful performer? He knew every trick, knew how to turn and side-step. He had rid himself of her, just like that.

He didn't want to talk to her, to engage her in chat about the past, to reminisce about personal bests on stage or in bed. She was forgettable, irrelevant – not only to him, but to the ballet world at large. If it were not so, he would have taken a moment to ask how she was at the very least.

Fine. At least she knew where she stood.

If Alexandrov and the world of ballet were going to ignore her, then she would up her game – would apply a no-holds-barred approach to proceedings.

She poured another glass of wine, which she drank too quickly, causing her thin body to shudder.

The phone rang while Steffie and Jemima were watching a cookery programme. They were in their pyjamas, eating bowls of cereal. Nights like this weren't exactly riveting, yet Steffie relished them – the almond smell of Jemima's freshly washed hair, their inane commentary about whether the TV chef used too much salt or wore coloured contact lenses.

It was the small rewards that counted, as every mother knew: the smiles when they spotted you standing there after school, the bedtime kisses, the grateful *I love yous* when you got something right. Steffie grabbed these moments greedily now, knowing that in only a few months they would be rare. If she could have bagged them up – the smiles, cuddles, kisses – and popped them in the freezer, with no expiry date, she would have.

She kept staring at Jemima too. She couldn't help it. She kept staring at her little hands and eyelashes, the curve of her upturned nose; and combing Jemima's hair with her fingers. She was doing that, when the phone rang.

'Gerroff, Mum!' Jemima said, pulling away.

Steffie paused the television with the remote control.

'If that's Pippi's mum,' Jemima said, 'tell her yes.'

'To what?'

'A sleepover,' Jemima said. '*Please.*'

'Here?' Steffie said.

'Duh!' said Jemima. 'It's way too small here for a sleepover. It's at hers.'

'When?'

'Tomorrow,' Jemima said, as though it were agonisingly obvious.

'Oh, but I thought—'

Steffie was going to say that she thought they were going to the cinema together, but Jemima was shouting at her now. 'Hurry up, Mum!' The answer machine had picked up. 'Too late.'

Steffie sighed.

It wasn't Pippi's mother anyway. It was someone with a foreign accent. It took her a moment to realise who it was.

Jemima worked it out before her, was ushering her towards the phone. 'Quick!'

'Mr Alexandrov,' Steffie said, plucking up the phone. She put her hand to her chest, stilled herself.

'Ah, good evening,' he said. 'Mrs Lee?'

'Yes,' she said.

Jemima was hopping from foot to foot as though she had wet herself.

'We haven't had the pleasure of meeting yet, but will do soon, I hope ... Is now a good time to talk?'

'Yes. Of course,' said Steffie, trying to think what the nature of the call would be. They had received the welcome pack, were filling out the paperwork, getting together the first lot of fees ...

'Excellent,' he said, 'because I have some good news for you.'

She pictured him at the end of the line in his fitted black top. His Russian accent was more pronounced over the phone, more charming, enthralling.

Jemima was now praying, eyes to the ceiling, feet marching.

'I'm delighted to tell you that Jemima has made it to the shortlist for my six *étoiles*.'

Steffie put her hand to her face in surprise. 'Oh my goodness,' she said. 'That's fantastic!'

Jemima had stopped marching and was gazing at Steffie with wide eyes.

'The final audition will be on the same basis as before, except that it'll be in the main auditorium in front of an audience. I'm hoping that will add a little *pizzazz* to proceedings.' He paused. 'Does that sound all right?'

'Yes,' she said. 'Absolutely.'

'Good,' he said. 'Then is it possible for Jemima to see us again here at the Phoenix a week on Saturday – the twentieth of February?'

Steffie thought quickly, unable to see her diary in her

mind – unable to see anything but blank dates and spaces. 'Yes,' she said. 'That's perfect.'

'Excellent. I look forward to meeting you then. In the meantime, we'll email you further details.'

'Lovely,' she said.

When she hung up, Jemima tugged Steffie's arm. 'What is it, Mummy?' she said. 'Am I going to audition to be one of his stars? Am I going to be one of his *étoiles*? Am I?'

Steffie gazed at her daughter in her ballerina-emblazoned pyjamas. Jemima's cheeks were flushed with excitement, her hair was bristling with static. She was standing upright, as Noella had taught her to do, her fingers crossed in the air before her as she waited for the news that would alter the course of her life.

Suddenly, the enormity of the proposal hit Steffie and she began to hop up and down as Jemima had been doing.

'Oh, my goodness,' she said. 'Oh, my goodness! Yes!' She scooped Jemima into her arms, kissing her forehead countless times.

And then they held hands and jumped up and down, like footballers did when they won the Premiership. 'He wants you to audition to be an *étoile*, Mims!' she shouted. 'You could be an *étoile*!'

EMAIL CORRESPONDENCE FROM
LAPTOP OF MIKHAIL ALEXANDROV

From: MikhailAlexandrov@Phoenix.Org
Sent: 12 February 2016 12.38
To: Tim Freedman
Subject: RE: RE: West Wing Renovations

Hi Tim,
    That does help. I'll get the paperwork from Sandra.
    Thank you,
    M.

From: TimFreedman@FreedmanLtd.co.uk
Sent: 12 February 2016 12.35
To: Mikhail Alexandrov
Subject: RE: West Wing Renovations

Mikhail,
    Suggest you write to those people coming to
the auditions and warn them in advance about the
construction work, so they know some areas will be
strictly off-limits. Also get parents to sign disclaimers,
claiming responsibility for their kids whilst on site. Sandra

in your school office will know about this as she just did it for all the other pupils.

Hope this helps,

Tim

From: MikhailAlexandrov@Phoenix.Org
Sent: 12 February 2016 09:14
To: Tim Freedman
Subject: West Wing Renovations

Morning Tim,

I understand that you're starting work on the west wing this Monday. As such, I wanted to inform you that I have an important audition taking place in the studios of the west wing on Saturday 20 February, just so you're aware that there will be pupils on site, including a fairly large audience.

Good luck with the work.

Kind regards,

Mikhail

TEN

Valentine's Day was a Sunday this year; Steffie was glad it was hidden at the end of the week, an afterthought.

She had been thinking of Greg rather a lot, since kissing him on Monday. It was only a kiss on the cheek – the sort of thing that friends did all the time without consequence; yet she and Greg hadn't been friends for a long while, not since she had found out about the affair.

Could there have been a meaner time to have found out about it than on Christmas Eve, whilst making star biscuits with Jemima?

She had been making the icing, whilst Jemima rolled out the dough. Jemima kept sneezing because she had poured too much flour on to the counter. Steffie, who found whizzing icing sugar in the electric mixer a challenge, given that it filled the air with menacing particles, was trying to ignore the flour clouds in the air, was drinking sherry in a large wine glass and singing along with 'O, Holy Night' on the radio ... when the phone rang.

It would be her mother. Her mum always rang on Christmas Eve with some last-minute catastrophe. It wasn't ever a real problem – *I can't get salt flakes anywhere!* – simply that her mum loved the drama of eleventh-hour festive preparations.

But it wasn't her mother. It was a man's voice.

She knew right away that it wasn't something pleasant because the man sounded drunk. She would have hung up, but he was saying something about Greg.

Her immediate thought was that Greg had been injured, before remembering that he was out in the workshop, working on a gift for Jemima. He was varnishing – hardly dangerous.

'Your husband's been screwing my wife,' he said. 'Thought you'd like to know.' And then the line went dead.

'Was that Grandma?' Jemima said, rubbing her nose and leaving flour there.

'No,' Steffie had said.

'Dancing Grandmammy then?' Jemima knew this was a babyish nickname – a name from infancy, but it had somehow stuck.

'No,' Steffie said again.

The anger and fear had risen so quickly, she hadn't even felt it coming.

'Look at all the mess!' she shouted, turning to look at Jemima accusingly. 'For goodness' sake, Jemima!'

Jemima jumped in shock, pushed her bottom lip out, held the rolling pin mid-air, uncertain whether to continue.

And it was then that Greg came in, wiping his boots on the mat, pulling his hat off and tossing it on to a chair. And then he stopped.

He knew that she knew, she could tell.

But they waited until Jemima was in bed before discussing it. Even then, they had to be quiet. Steffie couldn't shout at him and smash plates. Jemima was home, and it was Christmas Eve.

Having to keep it quiet, to suppress it all, to be dignified and measured, made it so much worse.

Somehow it had set a pattern for things to come. Steffie ultimately dealt with the news by pushing it away – far easier to just move out with Jemima than stay here simmering around

Greg. She couldn't say what she wanted to say – that he had broken her heart so succinctly it was doing well to beat.

No one declared love after uncovering infidelity. She should have done so a long time ago, but had neglected to do so. And she had paid the price for that.

And now she was living away from him, but was softening.

What was this softening?

Laziness? Amnesia? Nostalgia? Loneliness? Lust?

Possibly it was all five. Possibly these were the chief reasons why many women forgave their cheating husbands, and vice versa.

You began all hard, firm, indignant. And slowly the whole thing began to slide.

What the heck? She still loved Greg, was only human. If she slid, she slid.

She shivered, rubbed her arms. They had been airing the flat this afternoon, but it was getting cold. She pulled the windows shut and turned to Jemima, expecting her to be wearing her hat and scarf ready to go out. But she was sitting on the sofa, back straight, eyebrows raised.

Steffie knew that look, knew that something tricky was on its way. 'Ready for our walk?' she said hopefully.

Jemima was not going to be diverted. 'I want to make a cake for Dad.'

'A cake?' said Steffie. 'What for?'

Jemima shrugged. 'Just thought it'd be a nice thing to do. Dad doesn't get home-made cake now he's on his own.' She jumped up with her usual agility, crossing her legs one in front of the other and holding out her arms. Even when she wasn't dancing, she was prancing. 'Pleasey pleasey lemon squeezey.'

'Oh, Jemima . . .' said Steffie.

Jemima was yanking her arm, pulling her to the kitchen. 'Do we still have the heart-shaped baking tin?'

'Heart?' said Steffie suspiciously. 'Why—'

'Just tell me,' said Jemima.

'No,' Steffie said. 'We don't. It—'

'Didn't fit?' Jemima said, with a funny look on her face.

Steffie sighed in resignation, opened a kitchen cupboard and peered inside. 'How will you get it to him?' she asked the baking trays and a frail spider who looked starving.

'We'll drive over there,' Jemima replied.

Easy as.

They had to wait for the cake to cool and the icing to set. By which time, it was beginning to get dark – was Valentine's night.

Steffie was ordering stock online for the Silver Tree when Jemima appeared before her, holding the cake out on a plate. 'Can we go to Daddy's now?' she said. 'I'll carry it like this.'

'Don't be silly,' Steffie said. 'We'll put it in a tin.'

'It won't fit. The icing will squidge.'

'Fine,' said Steffie. 'Grab your coat.'

No doubt she was sounding gruff, but she didn't want to do this – go to Greg's on Valentine's night procuring a sprinkly cake. The whole thing could be misconstrued, which was no doubt Jemima's intention. It wasn't as if she had ever worried about her father's cake intake before.

There was little traffic in Wimborne at that time of evening. They were out of town and at Greg's front door within ten minutes.

The lodge was set to the right of the driveway and garages. There were two garages, the left one being Jemima's dance space. Over the years, Greg had personalised it, carving a *Jemima's Studio* sign to hang above the door, decorating the walls with photographs of her idols. When she stayed with him, he sometimes found her asleep out there on the beanbag, exhausted from practice.

114

Steffie pulled into the driveway and gazed in the direction of the front door.

From the door, you couldn't see arrivals to the house, could only hear tyres on gravel, see headlamps lighting the foliage and spiders' webs. This Steffie knew from the times she had waited for Greg's parents to arrive on Christmas Eve, Jemima by her side shivering in a dressing gown, gazing up at the sky for Father Christmas and Dancing Grandmammy, as though they would arrive together. It would be hard to say whom she considered more magical.

Steffie switched off the engine and turned her attention to the large black car she had pulled up alongside; not Greg's old truck, but a polished vehicle that suggested affluence.

It wasn't unusual for there to be other cars scattered around the driveway – workmates', clients'. But there was something about this one that was troubling her. Maybe the fact that it was here, as well as them, on Valentine's night.

'Whose is that's, Mummy?' said Jemima.

'I don't know,' Steffie said.

'Well, don't just sit there ...' said Jemima, unclicking her belt. 'Come on.'

Steffie remained seated. The black car was higher than theirs. On the dashboard, she could see a plastic tiara. There was a princess sunshield in the side window.

She had a bad feeling about this.

Jemima was waiting for her, having managed to slide out of the car whilst holding the cake still on the plate. Lithe and nimble, she would make a good cat burglar.

'Come on!' said Jemima.

Steffie followed hesitantly. Jemima was already there, lit by the security light that she had prompted. 'Will you knock, please, Mummy?'

Steffie obliged.

115

She could hear voices inside – a woman's voice, heels approaching on floorboards.

Oh, flax seed.

But it was too late.

The door had swung open and there in the doorway, in the threshold of Steffie's old home, was a woman in a long cardigan, skinny jeans and heeled boots – the pointy sort that Steffie shied away from wearing for fear of looking hard. This woman didn't look hard, though. Her cardigan was fluffy, her lip gloss glisteny, her blonde hair straight and smooth. She smelt of vanilla and candyfloss – one of those sweet perfumes that teenagers liked.

Steffie thought she was going to be sick. She stood staring, speechless.

Luckily, Jemima wasn't fazed at all. She rose on tiptoes, holding the cake steady, trying to look beyond the woman. 'Is my dad here?' she asked.

She sounded bossy, kick-ass. *Good*, Steffie thought. One of them ought to.

'Yes, he is,' the woman said, gazing at Jemima, and then at Steffie. 'Greg?' she called over her shoulder.

Steffie couldn't keep eye contact with the woman, gazed instead at the potted bay tree to the right of the door. Someone had added a ribbon to its base and a silver heart to its top, like a Christmas tree star. Who would have done so?

Steffie realised that she couldn't stand here – couldn't be stood looking like this when Greg appeared any second now.

She backed away, trying to sound cavalier, blasé. 'Come on, Mims,' she said. 'Just leave the cake for Daddy . . . It's getting late and you've got school tomorrow . . .'

She retreated to the car, grappled with the door handle and sat behind the wheel with her heart pounding.

Calm thoughts. Kind thoughts.

Calm and kind. She was calm and kind.

No, she wasn't.

She wanted to punch Olivia. She had pushed over a chair in Yvonne's office in rage just at the thought of Olivia's face.

And now she had seen her face and it was worse than she had thought – or better. And Greg had promised not to see her, to break all contact.

Oh, what an idiot she was, to have softened.

It was all coming back to her, her form. She was stiffening up, sitting there in the car. This was what they meant when they said that old spinsters dried up. It wasn't so much drying, as hardening, Steffie thought. If love melted the soul, hate solidified it.

She started the car and eased forward in order to see what was happening at the door. Olivia – for it was surely Olivia – was saying something to Jemima, had the nerve to be laughing. Steffie tried to lipread. All she could see was Olivia's shiny hair under the lights.

Jemima was handing in the cake. And the door was closing.

Olivia had gone, the security light had switched off. Jemima was standing momentarily in the dark, her head bowed, her back to Steffie. And then she walked towards the car.

She got into the back seat, clipped on her belt without a word.

As they turned the car around, the security light came on again as the front door swung open. 'Daddy!' Jemima said. 'It's Daddy!'

Steffie stopped the car and Jemima jumped out and ran to her father. They embraced in the middle of the driveway, Greg holding Jemima up high, her feet off the ground.

They talked for a few moments, Greg crouched with one knee up and one on the ground so that Jemima could perch on him.

Steffie surreptitiously drew the window down an inch and listened.

'Cake ... So kind ... Thoughtful ... Audition Saturday ... Thank you ...'

This was the essence of the conversation. Then Jemima broke away and skipped to the car.

Greg was walking towards them, frowning, looking upset.

How to do this without knocking him down?

He banged on the window, but Steffie was accelerating away.

When she glanced in her rear-view mirror, he was standing with his hands behind his head, in the position that police made people adopt before arresting them.

'Why didn't you speak to Daddy?' Jemima asked.

Steffie didn't answer that question, faked a happy voice instead. 'Pleased you did that?'

'Yes,' Jemima said. 'Daddy said he's going to have it for tea. He also said that he had a guest with him that he was trying really hard to get rid of.'

'That's nice,' said Steffie.

'No, it isn't, Mum,' said Jemima. 'Didn't you hear what I said? Daddy's got someone there who's—'

'I heard,' Steffie said abruptly. She softened her voice. 'I'm sure he'll love the cake.'

They travelled the ten minutes home in silence. When they pulled up outside their apartment, Jemima suddenly spoke. 'Was that Daddy's girlfriend?' she said.

Steffie felt her cheeks redden. 'No,' she said. 'Why would you think such a thing?'

'Because she's really pretty?' Jemima said.

Steffie felt a stab of sorrow in her chest. She turned to look at Jemima. 'Really?' she said. She turned forward again, pressed the car keys into her palm to stave off tears.

'Well, *I* thought so,' Jemima said. And then she got out of the car and began jumping up and down on the pavement, practising her *sautés*.

Steffie sat for a moment watching the sun setting at the end of the road – the grey clouds tinged with pink that were moving slowly between the gap in the buildings, reminding her with their heaviness, yet their opacity, of passing dinosaurs.

Kids could be so disloyal, so hurtful; and at their most cruel when they didn't intend to be. For they were merely relaying the truth as they saw it: the simple injurious truth.

MORNING SCHEDULE FOR
ÉTOILE AUDITIONS
PHOENIX ACADEMY, USHERWOOD
SATURDAY 20 FEBRUARY 2016

9 a.m. Beatrice Jones
9.45 a.m. Isobel Quinn
10.30 a.m. Daisy Kirkpatrick
11.15 a.m. Freddie Rawlings
12 p.m. Zachary Williams
12.45 p.m. Jemima Lee

ELEVEN

Luckily, Steffie hadn't liked Radiohead, but it still took her a long time to dump her boyfriend. In the meantime, Greg had continued to bump into her in the lift, to suggest musical alternatives, to work out when she might be in the coffee lounge and happen to be there by the machine when she got her sugary tea.

If she suspected that these frequent meetings were contrived, she didn't let on. She became very friendly towards him – telling him that the scratches on her hands were made by her flatmate's unstable cat, that she took sugar in her tea because her mother had given her lots of cake from an early age and if she didn't keep it up she would become hypergluconic.

'Is that a word?' Greg asked her.

She laughed. 'I don't think so.'

She laughed readily. And she made him laugh in turn.

He knew almost from the outset that he was in love with her. It was just a case of making her see that she loved him too, or could do.

Yet more often than not he watched the back of her head walking away – those curls, tightly wound, hiding her thoughts.

And then one weekend he was running through the gardens of Corpus Christi and there she was sat in the middle of the lawn, reading a book, wearing a sundress, straw hat and cowgirl boots.

Out of the office, endorphins high from exercise, he felt it was now or never.

He approached her. 'Hi,' he said, pulling his shirt up to wipe his forehead.

Slowly, she lowered her book, raised her eyes to his bare midriff. 'Hi.'

'I was wondering if you'd like to go out with me sometime,' he said, lowering his shirt, putting his hands on his hips, trying not to sound out of breath.

'OK,' she said.

He wanted to do a little jig, but didn't. He nodded solemnly. 'OK,' he said. 'I'll get back to you.' And he went to walk away, but then turned back and said, 'How about tonight?' And then, rather rashly, he knelt down and kissed her, despite being sweaty, despite the picnicking family beside them.

She was every bit as sweet-tasting as he had imagined her to be, after all that sugary tea, after those pink mints she was eating from a paper bag on her lap. And the smell of her perfume on her skin, mixed with sun lotion and summer saltiness, made him weak-kneed.

They went out for four years before he proposed. He would have done it sooner, on the day he kissed her at the park, but she was not a woman to be rushed. And he had all the time in the world for her.

First thing on Wednesday morning, Greg called into the Silver Tree. Steffie was behind the counter, flicking through a catalogue. As the shop door tinkled, she looked up, putting the catalogue aside. When she saw it was him, her smile faded.

He came to a halt before the counter, hands resting on it. 'Steffie . . .' he began.

On the way here, he had gone through the words several times. It had sounded OK, acceptable. But now he felt like a moron.

Evidently, she thought so too. 'Greg,' she said coldly.

'I'm sorry,' he said.

She gazed at him. 'That's all you ever seem to say,' she said.

'Well, what else can I say?'

She picked up the catalogue again, flicked through it in a manner that suggested that she wasn't really taking it in. 'Try coming up with something to tell your daughter, for a start.'

'What do you mean?' he asked.

She shrugged a shoulder. 'Only that she asked me whether that woman was your girlfriend and I didn't know what to say.'

He sighed. 'She's not my girlfriend. Tell her that.'

'No,' said Steffie, tossing the catalogue aside. 'You tell her.'

They stared at each other. He glanced around the shop. It was quiet here today – no customers. Yet it was still early.

He turned back to Steffie, who had begun tidying a revolving stand of earrings on the counter. 'Like I tried to tell you on the phone yesterday,' he said, 'I didn't want Olivia there – I wasn't expecting her. I was trying to get rid of her when you arrived. It was just bad timing.'

'I'll bet,' said Steffie. She gave the stand a push and it circled around – a blur of shining metal and coloured gems – before coming to a halt, earrings wobbling.

'I'm not seeing her any more,' he said. 'You have to believe me.'

She sat back down, folded her arms. 'No, I don't,' she said. 'Because I'm not interested, Greg. Not right on top of Jemima's audition. I just want us to be civil and friendly, for her sake.'

'That's what I want too,' he said.

'And then afterwards,' she said, 'we can kill each other.'

He wanted to think she was kidding, but you never could tell.

He studied her, trying to do so discreetly. She was wearing a toffee-coloured jumper that he hadn't seen before. Maybe it was new. Eventually he wouldn't recognise any of her wardrobe from old. He noticed also that she had painted her nails the same toffee colour. She didn't normally paint her nails. Maybe it meant something, or nothing.

'How's the counselling going?' he asked.

She looked away. 'Good,' she said.

'Have you—'

'What we talk about is confidential, Greg.'

'Oh,' he said. 'Yes.' He tapped the counter nervously. 'Course.'

A clock chimed out in the corridor. It reminded him of why he had come here, or the official reason at least.

'Just wondered what time I should pick you up Saturday?' he asked.

'Well ... About that ...' she said.

He felt the hair on his head suddenly recede in apprehension. For a moment, he thought she was going to tell him not to come to the audition.

'The Phoenix have invited all the parents to a coffee morning,' she said.

'Oh,' he said, relieved.

She reached for a clip from the counter display and pinned it into her hair – a sparkling cupcake clip. 'So we need to leave earlier than we thought.'

'OK,' he said. 'So what time?'

'Seven o'clock?' she said.

'That's fine,' he said, smiling.

He was included, not shut out.

She could have shut him out – made up some excuse about

how his presence would unsettle Jemima, just to punish him. Yet she hadn't.

'Thank you, Steffie,' he said.

She plucked the hairclip from her hair, stuck it back on the display. 'For what?' she said. 'It's you doing all the driving.'

But she knew what he meant, he sensed.

'Well, I'll be off,' he said.

'OK.' And she picked up the catalogue and resumed reading.

He left the shop, the doorbell tinkling behind him.

As he walked alongside the shop window, he glanced inside. To his surprise, Steffie was watching him leave.

On Friday, the night before the *étoile* audition, Noella went into her studio, unlocked a cupboard door behind the piano, and flicked on the light.

She stood on a footstool to reach the top shelf of the cupboard, squinting as she pulled down a shoebox, prompting a small avalanche of dust.

She sneezed, took the shoebox and went out to the piano stool.

For a moment, she sat with the box on her lap, drawing snaky paths on the lid with her finger in the dust.

She could remember doing this as a child – drawing patterns in the gravelly soil in their back yard. No one had ever been there with her, as far as she could recall. She had played alone, whilst her brothers – older, freer – had roamed the surrounding cornfields and tobacco fields.

She hadn't been happy as a child. For although the village of Galgon had been her homeland, it had been too hot, too arid for her. The dry land – colourless commons and fir-tree plantations – had nothing to offer her, had wobbled with the heat, searing her eyes.

From the earliest age, she had longed to escape.

It could have been anything – any number of professions that she might have chosen as an exit route. She was precocious at school, academically advanced. Yet something about the ballet drew her like nothing else.

It was the notion of being underneath a spotlight – of being free, incandescent, admired; none of which she had been, sat in the dirt clouds of Galgon.

She took a deep breath and eased the lid off the shoebox.

In a rush, as she touched the photographs, ballet shoes, key ring, lipstick, letters, postcards, she could hear her friends' laughter, could feel the cold of the floor in her old room in Paris, could smell the perfume and hair products; could feel the scratchiness of the blankets drawn to her chin in bed.

They had been inseparable – Noella and the five other girls with whom she had shared a corridor. The Six Swallows.

They had got drunk one night during their first term at the ballet school and had all had tiny black swallow tattoos inked on the back of their necks. It was daring, given that they wore their hair up most of the time, and would have resulted in immediate expulsion from the school had their superiors found out.

It was their secret. They had taken great pleasure in coming up with ways of disguising the tattoos in rehearsals: concealer pens, foundation, plasters, scarves, hooded sweaters.

They had all laughed so much about it.

It seemed stupid now. And yet it still meant something to Noella – the little tattoo; although its meaning had changed.

Once it had felt rebellious, anarchistic. Now it was a poignant reminder of how each and every one of the Swallows had fallen from the sky.

The tattoos, the laughter, the drunken nights had been a ruse, a cover-up for how fragile they each were; fragile because they were human, and what the ballet school asked of them was often not.

126

They were to train constantly, socialise rarely, eat little. This was the life of a top dancer. They all knew it was so – knew what they had entered into at the outset.

Noella's room-mate, Delphine, had been the most vivacious of them, and yet she wore arm-warmers permanently, covering the bloody patches on her arms where she scratched them in her sleep. The girls next door were both anorexic; everyone knew so. The other two Swallows were obsessive compulsive and alcoholic, respectively.

Not a wonderful line-up, yet not an entirely unusual one at the school.

From the shoebox, she picked up a silver necklace, pressing the Mackintosh pendant against her lips. It smelt ever so faintly of perfume, still. She closed her eyes, sighed with longing. And then waited for the guilt that always came, crushing her breath.

Mikhail Alexandrov was the first man she had ever loved. She had wanted him from the first time she had seen him. He was intensely attractive and had made his way through most of the female students at the school. But not yet amongst the Swallows.

It would be them next, they joked – probably Delphine, whose beauty had caught his eye. And it was this that was so cruel, Noella had felt. For she had fallen in love with a man who barely noticed her, who preferred her pretty friend.

Yet even with Delphine, Mikhail appeared tentative. Their corridor was famed for its neurosis and he perhaps was wary of its creakiness, its fragility, its female brittleness. Others in the school joked that it was the lunatics' wing, a joke that made Noella bristle with indignation because everyone here – especially the perfectionists – was flawed, some more obviously than others. It was easy to spot the too-thin, the repulsively arrogant. Others, like Noella, were more secretly afflicted.

To those who observed her, Noella would appear abrasive, uptight, yet ultimately well-meaning, compassionate.

And this was their error.

For a child raised in a warm climate, it was rather ironic; or perhaps biologically sensible, given that lizards were built for the heat too. Because whereas her friends were red-cheeked and giggly, Noella was cool-skinned and steely.

A sudden noise made her drop the necklace. 'Dammit!' she said, jumping up from the piano stool. It was the buzzer on the door downstairs. She glanced at the studio clock. Quarter to nine. Who would be here this late?

She gathered the shoebox together, pushed it inside the cupboard and slammed the door shut, before hurrying to the stairs.

The buzzer was going again. 'OK,' she said. 'OK. I'm going as fast as I can.'

Downstairs, she was surprised to see Jemima and Steffie standing on the pavement, squinting in the rain.

'Apologies for disturbing you so late,' Steffie said, hands on Jemima's shoulders, 'but Jemima couldn't sleep. She wondered if she could have just one more run-through before tomorrow?'

Noella smiled. 'Of course, *ma chérie*!' she said, reaching out to take Jemima's hand.

Steffie raised her eyebrows at Noella apologetically. 'Sorry,' she said. 'Hopefully it'll only take a few minutes. Really, she should be in bed.'

'It's no trouble,' Noella said, ushering her ward up the stairs to the studio. 'Honestly.'

Jemima moved beautifully that night, possibly the best that Steffie had ever seen her dance, even though she was in her pyjamas and dressing gown. Perhaps it was this that gave the sequence a dream-like feel – her dressing gown flapping behind her as though she were flying with Peter Pan.

Steffie had kept consulting her watch, disapproving of the lateness of the hour. Yet Jemima had insisted on dancing at Noella's one last time.

And looking at her now, asleep in bed, it seemed to have done her some good.

Steffie pulled the covers up over Jemima's shoulder and stood gazing down at her. There was just enough light from the lounge to see Jemima's face, to watch her chest rise and fall.

How many times had Steffie watched her daughter sleeping over the years, just as she was doing now?

She never tired of it. It was a secret delight; for sleeping children appeared uncannily similar to their mother's first glimpse of them. Somehow sleep robbed them of growth, of affectations and influences, and there they were again: babies.

Steffie wondered what the total might look like – the tally of hours spent watching Jemima sleep. It was only a little bit here and there, but it would add up.

These were not wasted hours, though. They were gorgeously rich and warm, like the inside of a baby's clenched hand, the hot folds in their chubby legs.

Steffie looked lovingly at Jemima's little hand, which was lying above the covers. Jemima always slept with one arm under the sheets, one arm out.

She was holding something. Steffie peered closer to look and then smiled. Jemima was holding a tiny pair of ballet shoes – a cheap bag charm that she deemed lucky.

Gently, Steffie prised the charm from Jemima's grip. No point her holding it and scratching her face by accident in the night.

She sat down on the chair next to Jemima's bed, shifting to get comfortable on the lumps and bumps of the pile of clothes beneath her.

She gazed at Jemima, listened to her rhythmic breathing, thought of her dancing in her dressing gown.

That image, that memory, would stay with her always.

Quietly, she began to cry.

'Oh, sweet Mims,' she whispered. 'What will I do without you?'

Suddenly, Jemima shifted position. Steffie froze.

She sat still, waiting, listening.

It was all right. She could hear Jemima breathing again, softly snoring.

She rose, wiped the tears from her eyes with her sleeve, placed the little ballet shoes on the table beside Jemima, and left the room.

THE EVENING NEWS

Tonight, in Surrey, a child is in a critical state after an
incident that took place earlier today at a dance academy. The Phoenix Academy is shortly to be under the
management of internationally acclaimed dancer Mikhail
Alexandrov. An official police inquiry has been launched
to uncover how the ten-year-old child, who is to remain
unnamed, fell twenty feet through unsafe flooring. In
a statement issued by the academy, Mr Alexandrov
expressed deep regret and stressed that the academy was not to be held responsible for the incident.
Wheresoever the blame lies, the fact remains that tonight
a ten-year-old who was auditioning to become one of Mr
Alexandrov's future stars now lies in intensive care in the
Royal Hospital, Guildford.

Jeanie Morris
BBC South East
20 February 2016

TWELVE

Every Friday night, Helena hosted a book club in her living room. Sometimes the books even got discussed. The women, all seventy-somethings, mothers and grandmothers, fond of a G&T, weren't difficult to distract. Even if they used books as the basis for discussion, there was a lot of off-piste chatter and gossip.

Tonight's book was about a smother mother, or snow-plough parent, so it said on the back.

'What the heck's a snow-plough parent?' one of the women said, tossing the book on to the coffee table.

'Go look in the mirror!' said another with a cackle. 'But try not to mow us all down as you pass!'

'Who? *Moi*?'

Helena smiled to herself as she handed out the drinks. No one was ever a smother mother or a snow-plough parent by their own admission – all claimed never to have heard of such a thing.

'Chin chin,' one of the women said. And the air peeled with the sound of clinking crystal glasses.

'Down the hatch!'

Normally, Helena joined in emphatically. But tonight she was too preoccupied for joviality. Tomorrow was pressing heavily on her.

For tomorrow, if Jemima passed the *étoile* audition, she would be elevated to a different universe; a star, with indescribable amounts of pressure and stress.

She sat down glumly on the sofa, wedged between two women who were chatting over her head. 'I blame the schools,' one was saying. 'They put far too much pressure on the children.'

'Yes, but that's because of the parents ... Parents have such high expectations nowadays ... My son was telling me that they've put rails up at his local football club, to hold back the parents. Seriously. Rails!'

Helena nodded absently. There had been a piece in the press last week about how it was predicted that someone was going to die soon at one of these children's football matches.

It was all so out of perspective, so out of control. But what to do about it? No one appeared to know where the problem lay, who had lit the fire and who was stoking it. But it was roaring all right. Everyone felt its blaze – even the grandparents.

One of the women pulled the book club paperback from her handbag and set it on her lap, smoothing the front cover pensively. 'To be perfectly honest, I think the smother–mother label is cruel and unfair.'

'To the kids?'

'No, to the poor mother.'

'But she's overbearing!'

'Oh and that's a sin?' said one of the women, bringing her glass down heavily on the table. 'Well, pardon us mothers for loving our kids!'

'Too right. I laboured a combined sixty-four hours to bring mine into the world – fed them, clothed them, kept them clean for twenty-four years when they were living with me. Only to be told, what? Back off, Mamma. You're too much?'

'I agree. No one thinks of it from the mum's point of view. Sometimes they're just ... you know ... '

'Lonely?' someone said.

Helena sipped her G&T thoughtfully, watching the fire flickering in the stone surround.

She could remember her loneliness the year Steffie had left for Manchester as though it sat with her here now, holding her hand.

That year, their home had felt as though it were actively mourning – creaking at night, the wind howling Steffie's name down the chimney. She had found it hard to sleep, had missed her daughter so.

She had consoled herself by buying lots of Wedgwood china, the housewife's choice of the eighties. Her favourite pattern had been Jasperware, with its white etchings that she longed to pick off, like snapping icy spikes from a Christmas cake.

But in truth nothing – neither china nor cake – could fill the gap.

She hadn't ever really let Steffie go. It had been about letting Steffie think she had gone, that she had been released, when really she hadn't – was being watched constantly, albeit from a distance, sometimes a long one.

All mothers did the same; some stood nearby, others remotely; all were watching.

There was something beautiful about it, a mother's watchful eyes. It was angelic, shepherd-like; deeply misunderstood.

The mother didn't look that way constantly because she had no life, had nowhere else to look, but because she had no choice. Her eyes, her thoughts, were automatically set that way. Changing that would be like trying to remove the salt from the sea.

'I'd love to smother my grandchildren,' one of the women was saying now, finishing her gin. 'But they've got more allergies than a bees' hive dipped in peanut butter. I'm scared to even bake a cake.'

'That's nothing. My son told me last week that I need to learn about boundaries ... I told him to take any fencing issues up with his father.'

Splutters of laughter ensued.

Helena smiled, rose to go to the kitchen for more gin.

As she chopped the lemon, she glanced at her reflection in the kitchen window. She could picture Steffie beside her, rolling dough, hair in bunches, Snoopy apron tied around her neck.

She sighed fondly, her heart coiling in nostalgia.

Children were such marvellous anchors. They made limp marriages feel robust, mealtimes uplifting, wholesome. They made Christmas magical, broke awkward silences, were truth sayers and realists, all whilst believing in fairies and dragons.

And they loved unconditionally.

For the lovelorn, the grieving, the weary, the disappointed, the misguided, the depressed, the unfulfilled, the stressed ... their child was a lantern in the dark.

She put the lemon slices, ice bucket, gin and tonic bottles on a tray and returned to the lounge.

Not long now until Jemima would be on that stage, she thought, with a ripple of worry in her tummy.

On Saturday morning, there was a very mixed atmosphere in the Phoenix café, Steffie thought: a fusion of sobriety, nervousness, competition, with little cohesion or warmth. She had expected it to be more intimate than this, and was disappointed.

They had arrived at quarter to nine and were handed a cluster of paperwork at reception about expected behaviour, data protection and equal opportunities, plus an urgent disclaimer about the west wing being off-limits due to construction work, which they dutifully signed. And then they had followed little blue arrows to get here – arrows that said: Étoiles' *coffee morning, this way!*

It had all felt nice, welcoming. On arrival in the café, they had set about the trestle tables, glad of refreshments after their journey, pouring tea, helping themselves to biscuits. Only to discover, on sitting down and absorbing the room's goings-on, that they were the only ones helping themselves to the complimentary coffee-morning wares – that everyone else was queuing for skinny lattes, organic smoothies and granola bars from the over-the-counter service, which was open for visitors and residents.

'Oh well,' said Steffie, feeling hot. She took off her coat and recalled that she was wearing a lambswool turtleneck that had seemed cosy at dawn but now felt as though she were bound in hessian.

'Were we supposed to help ourselves?' said Jemima, glancing around the room.

'Yes,' Steffie said, smiling. 'Don't worry.'

'Let them pay if they want to,' Greg said, swallowing a custard cream in one. Steffie frowned at him.

'What?' he said. 'I'm starving!'

She gazed around the room. The coffee morning had not been well organised, since the *étoiles* were scattered around the room, sandwiched between visitors in suits and Phoenix pupils in branded weekend wear. It was impossible, without purposefully going over to introduce oneself, to have a conversation with any of the other parents.

Most disappointing. And to think they had rushed here for this.

Still, Jemima was unfazed, as usual. She was drinking orange squash, kicking her legs backwards and forwards underneath the table, nibbling a jammy dodger, humming quietly to herself like any other normal child – albeit one that liked to hum Prokofiev.

Noella was unusually quiet, had been quiet the entire

journey. She was sipping her tea, reading a dance magazine that had been lying on the table.

Steffie wondered what the other parents would think, looking over here at them – at a man in a donkey jacket scoffing biscuits, at Jemima in her scruffy sweater, at the widow-like woman in black accompanying them; and at Steffie, glowing in lambswool.

Jemima had insisted on wearing her favourite grey sweater with an ice-skater appliqué that had been washed so many times it was beginning to peel and fade. Steffie would have chosen something smarter for her, but Jemima wanted to wear familiar clothes and in hindsight she was probably right. Not like Steffie in her new itchy sweater and expensive Toffee Soufflé nail polish – items intended to make her feel better about being here amongst the elite, and about Olivia.

She glanced at Greg. They wouldn't speak of Olivia again, she sensed.

Steffie was doing her best to forget her, but it was hard not to keep picturing her face, even though Jemima had told her over macaroni cheese during the week that she thought Steffie was just as pretty, if not more so, than Daddy's new *girlfriend*.

A familiar voice stopped her flow of thoughts and she turned to look at the man seated two tables away. She recognised him and his family – the white-blond boy with the gelled-up hair who had winked at her, the father speaking Japanese. The father was on his phone again now. The mother, arms folded, looked to be at saturation point, presumably with the incessant phone calls.

The boy was called Zach, Steffie recalled. She unfolded the paperwork in her hand and found the audition schedule.

'That must be Zachary Williams,' she said.

Jemima looked up. 'Who?'

Steffie nodded subtly in the Williamses' direction. 'Over there.'

Jemima gazed over at the family, slurping her squash through the straw. The boy was sitting with his legs splayed, his arms behind the chair. Everything about him screamed spoilt, but there was something likeable about him, Steffie thought. Perhaps it was the fact that he didn't appear to take himself too seriously. He was wearing a T-shirt that said: *Believe in your selfie*.

'Have the auditions started?' Jemima said.

'Yes,' Steffie said, feeling her stomach dip nervously. 'Beatrice Jones is in there at the moment.'

'And then who?' Jemima said, peering at the audition sheet.

'Isobel Quinn.' Steffie glanced her watch. 'She'll be warming up by now.'

'No, she's not,' Jemima said. 'She's over there, look ... She was the one warming up next to me last time. Remember?' She pointed at the family furthest from them, nearest the door. 'Can I go and say hello?'

'Well ...' said Steffie doubtfully. For despite the fact that Steffie had wanted this to be a friend-making opportunity, she didn't want Jemima breaking with protocol and barging in on people.

But Jemima was scraping back her chair, pulling a paper bag from her sweater pocket. She was going to offer the girl a gobstopper.

'Mims ...' Steffie said.

'Let her go,' said Greg.

Steffie watched as Jemima made her way between the chairs in her denim shorts and polka-dot leggings. She couldn't hear what the Quinns were saying to her. The mother, whose demeanour was tired, guarded, was smiling tightly, glancing over at Steffie. The mother kept biting her nails. The father, wearing a smart blazer, was playing with his phone.

'He's a doctor,' Greg said to Steffie. 'Someone high up, I reckon.'

'Oh,' said Steffie, watching the family. The other three children were sitting rather robotically at the table, reading Kindles. Isobel was smiling shyly at Jemima, shaking her head.

And then Jemima was returning. She sat back down, resumed slurping her squash.

'Didn't she want a sweet?' Steffie said.

'Nah,' said Jemima.

The Quinns were rising now in a sudden flurry of movement. It was evidently warm-up time for them. Isobel was smoothing her ponytail flat, her silver jacket shimmering under the lights. Her family looked grim with intention, all six of them.

Steffie's tummy lurched again. She didn't know how much more of this she could take – the agonising *and then there was one* factor. She regretted coming here so early.

And then someone spoke right by her ear, causing her to jump.

'Howdy doodle day!'

It was Zach. He stood with his hands in his pockets, grinning at Jemima.

The father had finished his phone conversation and was approaching them with an apologetic expression.

'How's it hanging?' Zach asked Jemima.

Jemima blushed, smiled. 'It's hanging well,' she said. And then her eyes clouded as though she weren't sure whether that was the right answer, what it was exactly that she had been asked.

The father drew level with them, rubbing his hands together. 'Now, Zach buddy,' he said, 'don't go troubling these good people.' He extended his hand in greeting to Greg and Steffie. 'Ted Williams,' he said. Then he glanced around the room and leant in closer towards them. 'Right old hornets' nest here, isn't it?'

'Yes,' Steffie said uncertainly.

'Course, these things are always uptight as hell,' he continued.

'Oh, right?' said Greg.

'Full of nutters and psychos who would kill to get a place.' He narrowed his eyes at them as he spoke, as though suddenly wondering which category they fell into. 'I always say to Z, do your best, buddy. And if you don't get in, I'll sue their ass!'

Steffie smiled, wondered privately whether the man was quite sane himself.

'Well, it was nice meeting you,' he said. 'Come on, buddy.' And then his phone rang and he turned away with a 'Yuhello'.

Greg was gazing at Steffie, trying not to smile. She laughed quietly down her nose and picked up her tea again.

'Come on,' Zach said to Jemima, motioning for her to stand up. 'Let's go to the rec room.'

'The where?' Jemima asked.

'Just down the corridor. It's got loads of cool stuff in it. It's a chillax place.'

Jemima stood up. 'Mum? Dad?' she said, looking at them in turn. 'Can I?'

Steffie chewed her lip, looked at Greg.

'OK. But you haven't got long. I want you back here for ten o'clock sharp,' Greg said, tapping his watch. 'Got that?'

'Yep,' said Jemima. 'Thanks, Dad.'

'Laters,' said Zach, holding up his hand in farewell.

And the two of them left.

Noella lowered her magazine and looked at Steffie. 'Is that wise?' she asked.

'Seems harmless enough,' Steffie said with a shrug. 'It might do her good. She's not on for another three hours, after all.'

Noella nodded, picked up her magazine again. 'As you wish,' she said.

Steffie sipped her tea, gazed at the empty space where Jemima had been sitting.

And it was then that the Kirkpatricks arrived.

Steffie recognised them at once – the mother in her *Downton Abbey* hat, looking as officious as ever, Daisy trailing behind with her large eyes and her stringy hair and her sparkly beanie.

'No, you can't have anything to eat,' Mrs Kirkpatrick was saying over her shoulder. 'You don't have enough time before the audition to digest.'

They stopped at the table nearest Steffie's, Mrs Kirkpatrick dropping her handbag on the table with a thud. 'Oh, for goodness' sake, Daisy,' she said, in a hiss, 'will you stop whining? Have you forgotten that we're here for you today? *You?*'

Daisy didn't look in a position to forget anything, looked as though she had never forgotten a thing – as though the chance would be a fine thing. Her brow appeared oppressed with information and instructions and dos and don'ts, to the point that her sparkly beanie was sagging like a too-hot pancake.

'Now go network,' said Mrs Kirkpatrick. 'Scram!' She flapped her hand at Daisy, who made her way towards Steffie's table, before realising that there was no child there.

'Oh,' said Daisy, halting.

Steffie took pity on her. 'They've gone to the rec room?' she offered.

Daisy made her way towards the door. Steffie glanced at the mother, hoping she hadn't incurred her wrath by interfering, but Mrs Kirkpatrick was rooting through her handbag for something.

Then she sat back in her chair, tilted her head back and squeezed something on her tongue. She caught Steffie watching her. 'Bach's Rescue Remedy,' she said.

'Ah,' said Steffie, smiling knowingly.

Mrs Kirkpatrick smiled back. 'It's not easy, is it?' she said.

'No. It isn't,' said Steffie, warming to her.

After all, Steffie thought, everyone here was just trying to do the right thing by their child, wanted what was best for them.

'Daisy doesn't appreciate how much I do for her,' Mrs Kirkpatrick went on. 'She has no idea.'

'I know what you mean,' said Steffie.

Mrs Kirkpatrick stared at Steffie then, her eye flitting up and down her as though assessing whether Steffie could possibly know what she meant.

'My husband is in the Middle East this week,' she said. 'And my eldest son, Hector, has just announced that he's spending the summer coaching soccer in the US. And to complicate matters, my daughter's doing her grade-eight viola on Monday.'

Steffie tried to look interested, but had switched off at 'Middle East'.

There was a crashing noise over by the door then, which made everyone turn to look. It was the first *étoile* back from her audition.

Steffie consulted her schedule: Beatrice Jones.

The mother, who had accidentally knocked a potted plant over with her large holdall, was bent picking up the plant, whilst the girl – a thin-faced child with pretty, ripply hair that was adorned with a mauve flower – looked mortified.

'Sorry, everyone,' the mother called out and then took Beatrice's hand and led her to the counter.

Steffie watched them with fascination. She recognised her as the same mother that had arrived late to the auditorium talk the other week. She had a hypnotic effect then, and now, on Steffie, who found herself unable to look away. She had black hair that was as straight as a door, and sturdy thighs that rubbed together as she walked. She was wearing Lycra leggings and a hoody with TEAM BEA JONES emblazoned on the back. The child was wearing a matching mini-version of the sweater.

'What would you like, sweetheart, hmm?' the mother was saying. Her voice was extraordinarily loud.

Beatrice replied inaudibly.

'How about one of those cupcakes, sweetheart, hmmm? One of the sprinkly ones with the flowers and hearts? Have you seen them? They look gorgeous. Are they freshly baked? They look freshly baked … Go on, treat yourself. You deserve it, hey?' The mother bent down now to hug the child and plant a kiss on her lips. 'Mwahh! So proud of you, hon. So proud!'

'What the heck?' said Greg, craning his neck to see.

Then another voice spoke behind Steffie and she turned to look.

'Is this seat taken?'

It was a woman whom Steffie hadn't seen before, but who was equally eye-grabbing. She was very tanned, wearing sparkly eye shadow that had escaped on to her cheeks. Her legs were slender in leggings and Uggs.

'I … uh …' Steffie was about to say no, that their daughter would be returning, but the mother was already pulling the chair away.

'Ta,' she said. Then she shouted, 'Over here, Freddie.' She waved at a sullen-looking boy with long hair who was dragging his hand along the café counter. 'What, Savannah?' She turned to the little girl by her side. 'Oh, for Christ's sake! You need the loo again? What's wrong with you? … Pete?' She looked about her. 'Pete? Can you take her?'

Pete, a jaded-looking man with a portly build and a newspaper tucked rather optimistically underneath his arm, reached for the child. 'Come on, Savannah,' he said.

The mother was coming back towards Steffie now, hitching up her leggings, brandishing a leopard-skin purse.

'Are you here for the *étoiles*?' she asked.

'That's right,' said Steffie. 'Are—'

143

The mother scowled. 'Not being funny, but it's not very clear what we're supposed to do, is it? I mean, are we supposed to—'

'Mum, I wanna Orangina,' said Freddie, joining them with a flick of his fringe.

'OK,' she said, turning away.

'And that was that,' said Greg.

Noella finished her tea and stood up noiselessly. Dancers could do that, Steffie noted – could move without sound, like insects.

'I'm just popping to the shop, Steffie,' Noella said. 'Would you like to join me? There's some lovely merchandise, so I've heard.'

'No, thanks,' Steffie said. 'Have a good look for me, though. I'll wait here for Jemima.'

She watched Noella walking away, back straight, heads turning to look at her as she moved. It wasn't that she was attractive, exactly, Steffie thought, although she wasn't unattractive either. It was just that she had that strange quality that many of the people here had: the ability to draw and hold the eye, like a plastic sucker pad on a shower door.

And yet ... no one seemed the slightest bit interested in them – in the Lees of Wimborne.

Why was that? she wondered.

She sighed, glanced at her watch. Jemima had four minutes to get back here on time.

PARENT OF CANDIDATE
DAISY KIRKPATRICK

Daisy rehearses for two hours every day, without exception. My husband says I push her too hard, but if this is what she wants to do then I have to push or she won't achieve it. You can be all touchy-feely about it if you like, but that won't get results. Did you know that recently an academic at Cambridge said that behind every gifted child stands a pushy parent? In my opinion, Daisy is privileged to have me here supporting her, devoting time—

No, Daisy wasn't involved. Absolutely not. She knew that area was off-limits and besides, nothing would have got between her and securing an *étoile* position.

There was no way that she was with them.

They said what? Then they're lying.

Mrs U. Kirkpatrick
Phoenix Academy of Performing Arts
Surrey Police telephone interview transcript
21 February 2016

THIRTEEN

Greg rose and poured himself a mug of coffee from the vat on the trestle table and got Steffie another tea. He held a custard cream in his mouth for want of somewhere else to put it.

When he got back to the table, he saw that Noella had disappeared and that Steffie was flicking through the paperwork they had been handed earlier.

He gazed at the family sitting nearest them – a tanned woman with two kids and a depressed-looking husband who was trying to read the paper.

'Who are they?' Greg said quietly.

She glanced up. 'The Rawlingses,' she said. 'Freddie Rawlings.' She pointed to the schedule. 'On at eleven fifteen.'

'Oh,' he said.

The boy was swigging a bottle of Orangina and kept flicking his long fringe away from his eyes. He seemed unhappy about being here, or indifferent at least. His knee was drawn to his chest and he was picking at a scab.

'Leg down!' said his mother, slapping his knee. The boy dropped his leg and folded his arms, rolled his eyes.

'Savannah,' the mother said, turning her attention to the little girl sitting beside her, who was nibbling a chocolate brownie, 'you can't eat all that.' The mother plucked the brownie up and began to tear it into chunks, crumbs raining over the table. 'Think of the calories.' She lowered her voice. 'Do you want to get fat?'

The little girl stuck out her bottom lip, shook her head. 'Uh uh.'

'Well, then. Just one piece,' said the mother. 'Here, Pete,' she said, pushing the plate to the pot-bellied father. 'You eat it.'

The father didn't reply, just reached underneath his newspaper for the brownie.

Greg looked away, picked up a sheet of paper that Steffie had discarded. 'Anything interesting?' he asked.

'Hmm?' she said.

He read the piece of paper, which was about expected behaviour of parents at auditions.

'Did you see what it says here?' he said, nudging Steffie. 'That parents are in no way to interfere with the panel's decision and that offensive or violent behaviour will not be tolerated . . . Is that really necessary?'

'Hopefully it's just a formality . . .' said Steffie. 'It says here that there'll be approximately two hundred people in the audience.' She frowned. 'I'm not sure that Jemima's aware of that.'

'Well, good,' he said. 'No need to make her more nervous than she is already.' He picked up his coffee and sifted through the paperwork. 'Have you seen that bit of paper about the west wing?' he asked.

'Yes,' she said. 'I think it's the green one.'

'OK. I'll have a read,' he said. 'See what they're up to, construction-wise.'

'Uh huh,' she said absently, reading again.

Greg read the gist of the green information sheet and then sat up abruptly, slopping his coffee over the table. 'Bloody hell,' he said.

'Here.' Steffie handed him a napkin. 'Use this.'

But he didn't move to mop up the spillage. He was waving the piece of paper, staring at Steffie. 'Jesus, Steffie,' he said, 'we should have read this properly.' He stood up, pushing back his chair, getting its leg caught in the chair next to it, shaking the chair agitatedly to set it free. 'We need to go,' he whispered to her. 'Now!'

She stood. 'OK,' she said uncertainly. 'Can I ask why?'

He tried to set his face to placid as they manoeuvred across the room, between tables, past bulky bags and wriggling children wielding drinks. At the lifts, he hit the button several times. 'We signed that disclaimer when we arrived.'

'And?'

'About parts of the west wing being off-limits,' he said.

'I don't understand . . .' Steffie said, frowning.

'The rec room's in the west wing,' Greg said. The lift arrived with a ping and whoosh as the doors opened. 'It's dangerous.'

Steffie followed him into the lift, her voice hushed. 'Isn't that where—'

'Yes,' Greg said. He consulted the site map on the wall and the row of floor buttons, realising that he didn't actually know where the rec room was.

Steffie pointed to the map. 'There, look . . . Near the auditorium, near the dance studios. Up one floor.'

'OK.' Greg stabbed the up button. 'Good.'

He folded his arms high on his chest as the lift rushed upwards, leaving his stomach behind.

'She should have been back by now,' he said, consulting his watch.

'It's OK,' Steffie said. 'They won't have gone in there if it's all taped off. They're probably somewhere else . . . They're sensible.'

'*They?*' said Greg, turning to look at her. 'We don't even know them.'

'Maybe not,' she said. 'But we know Jemima. And I don't think she would ...'

Whatever she was going to say, she didn't finish it; either because she doubted the conviction of her words or because the lift had arrived.

They hurried along the corridor. Everything felt more serious now. Gone was the bustle of the café. In its place, was a sterile white corridor with shiny flooring. The setting was so white, so silent; it had a disorientating effect, as though you were lost inside a giant syringe.

'Greg,' Steffie said, 'I sent Daisy Kirkpatrick in there too.' Her tone had changed. She no longer sounded confident. 'What if ...?'

'Hush,' he said. 'No use panicking until we know what's what.'

They passed studios one and two on their left, and then the auditorium on their right. The doors were closed, but as they paused there was a burst of applause and cheering from within, the sound of which squeezed Greg's chest.

It wasn't just the sudden recollection of the auditions, of the daunting task awaiting Jemima, but the impact of realising that they had lost their daughter – even temporarily – in this sanitary, uptight place.

And Greg knew then that there was a parenting circle: that at eleven o'clock there were ghettos and knives, drugs and jagged glass; and at one o'clock pristine corridors of high expectations, perfection and polish; and at midnight, the two met, shook hands. Equally dangerous, equally lethal.

He swallowed, tried to stop his mind from over-dramatising things. His back was damp with sweat. He reached for Steffie to steer her forward, as she was slowing down.

They were passing studio three and four. And then they came to a halt outside the door marked *Recreation Room*.

The warnings were clear enough at this end of the corridor: several cones and metal signs – red tape across the rec-room entrance and a large notice on the door: *Do Not Enter; Danger.*

Greg gazed at the closed door. 'Well, they didn't go in there, then,' he said. 'Thank God.'

Steffie's head was cocked to one side, thinking. 'Where else could they have gone, do you think?' She rifled through her bag. 'I've got a map here somewhere. Maybe we—'

She was interrupted by a noise – a rushing sound, like a sweeping broom.

And then the rec-room door swung open and Zach Williams was there, grinning, about to limbo underneath the tape.

He stopped when he saw them, smile vanishing. 'Oh,' he said, his mouth lingering in a tight circle.

'Oh?' Greg echoed, folding his arms, amazed that that was the child's only response. 'What are you doing in there?' He shifted position, trying to see past the boy. 'Is Jemima with you?'

There was another sound then, the shuffling of limbs, and Jemima slipped forward.

Greg stared at her in astonishment. 'What on earth . . . ?'

Jemima stood rigid, her eyes cast down, her hands fidgeting.

He felt Steffie's hand touching his arm lightly, calming him down, telling him that she had got this covered. 'Jemima,' she said softly, 'come here, please.'

He admired it – Steffie's ability to be calm; for he felt like going nuts.

Jemima bent down slowly, went underneath the tape and stood before them, head hung.

The door opened wider with a creak then and two more children appeared: the Kirkpatrick girl with the sparkly hat, and the boy with the long fringe and sulky mouth.

'What?' Greg laughed now, as there seemed little else to do. How had the second boy got here? he wondered; he hadn't even seen him leave the café.

The other three children lowered themselves under the tape in turn and then stood in the corridor next to Jemima, in a line, hands in pockets, meek. Or in the sulky boy's case, smirking.

If Greg had been able to control his anger up to that point, seeing that cocky child smiling lost him the battle. He took a step towards the line-up, flapping the green sheet of paper at them, which he was still holding.

'Have you any idea how dangerous it is in there?' he said. 'It's off-limits, dangerous! It's a construction site. Not a playground!' He pointed at the signs on the doors and the floor. 'What were you thinking?'

At the end of the corridor, the lift pinged, and then came the sound of fast little footsteps.

'Oh no,' said the Kirkpatrick girl.

'*Daisssyyyy!*' her mother was shouting. She looked livid as she accelerated towards them.

When she drew level with the group, the mother yanked Daisy away from the others and bent over to scold her, prodding the child's chest.

'What the *hell* do you think you're playing at? I've been looking *everywhere* for you for the past half-hour!'

That wasn't exactly true.

Greg watched the woman, her forehead creased with anger, her cheeks flushed, her mouth spraying furious saliva. She had no idea that she was being watched, that she looked so repulsive – or at least made no show of knowing. She didn't seem to care what anyone thought. Greg didn't know whether to admire that or be appalled.

'What is this to you? Some sort of bloody *game*, hey? Do

you have any idea of the *sacrifices* I've made to bring you here today – the *mountains* I've moved? Hey? You think it's easy being a *parent* to you? Hey?' She was still prodding Daisy's chest, the child giving a little wince each time it happened.

Daisy's bottom lip was beginning to jolt, her large eyes brimming with tears, the sight of which quelled Greg's anger to a vague sensation of disappointment in his own child.

'Perhaps we should take this back to the café,' he said. 'Break the kids up, calm them down. I expect they just got a bit carried away. It's a lot of pressure for—'

Daisy's mother turned to him. 'Café?' she said, scowling. 'Calm down?' She grabbed Daisy's arm and put it underneath her own arm, as though carrying a baguette. 'You're coming with me, young lady,' she said, turning away. 'You're on in fifteen minutes. *Fifteen minutes!*'

Greg stared after them as they hurried off, Daisy giving a backwards glance at the other children before being wrenched forward again.

He scratched his head, exhaled.

He looked at Jemima.

What was there left to say? Mrs Kirkpatrick's outburst had shaken her. She was white-cheeked, on the verge of tears. Even Freddie was no longer smirking. Zach was leaning against the wall, pulling a thread that was hanging from his T-shirt.

Steffie spoke then. She reached her hand out to Jemima. 'I'm not sure where you boys are going,' she said cordially, 'but we're going back to the café. You're welcome to come with us.'

The boys didn't reply, simply moved slowly behind them as they all proceeded down the corridor.

'I'm so sorry, Daddy,' Jemima said, beginning to whimper as the lift arrived.

He didn't have a reply for her yet; nodded instead.

Inside the lift, the two boys began to whisper to each other conspiratorially. Maybe they already knew each other before today, or had bonded quickly. One of them began to snigger. Evidently, any remorse had been short-lived.

But Greg was no longer angry, so he let it go. Everything felt to be sliding away. It was the come-down after a shock, his adrenalin-charged body now sagging, airless. He wanted to sit down, to put his head in his hands, to wish it all away.

When they returned to the café, Greg was surprised to see that neither of the boys' families appeared to have noticed that the children hadn't returned on time or, in Freddie's case, that he had even been gone at all.

'Hi, Freddie,' his mother said, without looking up. She was trying to persuade her daughter that skimmed milk was better for her than Orangina, less fattening.

Greg was about to tell them what the children had been up to, but the father seemed engrossed in his newspaper, so Greg clamped his teeth together and walked on past.

As Zach sat back down, Ted Williams raised his hand in greeting. 'Hey, buddy,' he said, high-fiving his son.

Back at the table, they took their seats, Jemima slumping, practically climbing into her sweater.

'Why did you go in there?' Greg asked calmly.

There was no point shouting, being cross. Mrs Kirkpatrick had facilitated that part for them, to devastating effect. Poor Daisy would have a sore spot where the mother had poked her. Her nails had looked sharp.

'Didn't you see the red tape?' said Steffie. 'It's dangerous in there. We had to sign a disclaimer saying that we're responsible for you today.' She turned to Greg. 'We should have realised that the rec room was part of that – or at least checked it out when they said they were going there.'

Greg nodded. 'Yes. But then again, you heard the woman tell us about the west wing when we arrived, Jemima. We didn't think for one moment that you'd ignore danger signs. You're nearly eleven.'

'Mims ...' Steffie said, reaching for Jemima's hand, her voice wavering. 'Why would you do that on such an important day?'

Jemima shrugged.

'Probably because most of the kids here are so privileged that they don't care,' Greg said. 'They're bigger than the rules.'

'But that's not Jemima,' said Steffie. 'Is it, love?'

Jemima shook her head, began to cry.

'Oh, don't cry,' said Steffie, reaching forward to wipe Jemima's face. 'Don't spoil your pretty face right before your audition. You want to go in there and shine. Don't let this spoil it. Not after all your hard work.'

Greg sighed, stood up. 'I'm going for a walk.'

'Wait,' Steffie said, rising. 'We'll go with you.'

Noella returned then, clutching a shiny carrier bag.

'What's going on?' she said, looking at each of them with an expression that couldn't make its mind up between curiosity and consternation.

'Don't ask,' Greg said.

'Nothing,' Steffie said.

Jemima stood up, sniffed loudly.

'Let's go,' Greg said.

'Where?' Noella said.

'Maybe a walk round the grounds.'

'A walk?' said Noella cheerfully. 'Excellent!'

As they left the building and stepped outside, Noella took Jemima's hand authoritatively. 'Whatever's taken place,' she said, 'you must forget it. For now it's time for you to begin to focus – to inhale fresh air, to move your body, to get into the right mindset. Because today, Jemima Lee, you are a dancer, nothing less, nothing more. A great dancer.'

Jemima was listening to all this, but kept glancing back at Greg.

They were lucky to have Noella with them, he thought. Left to their own devices – their clumsy, self-serving, parental devices – they would have ballsed this up and wouldn't have been able to turn it around in time.

'Thank you,' Steffie said, at his side. She was nestling into her coat, hands in pockets, as they traversed the gravel forecourt, heading for the lawn.

'What for?' he said.

'For not going ape.'

'Going ape,' he said, smiling. 'I haven't heard that expression in years.'

She smiled too, but it soon vanished.

'We should have checked out what the rec room was as soon as they said they were going there,' he said. 'The woman told us expressly about the west wing – even circled the map.'

'I know,' Steffie said.

'So why didn't we? What happened?'

Steffie appeared to be thinking about this. 'I don't know,' she said. 'But something happens here, around these people. I get . . . distracted.'

Steffie didn't say any more on the subject. She didn't have to. He knew exactly what she meant.

The people here – the children, and especially their parents – arrested the eye, the senses. They sucked you in and when you came to again, you realised you had forgotten yourself.

He wasn't entirely sure what that meant.

He thought about Mrs Kirkpatrick, salivating, prodding her daughter.

He had once read a parenting column that suggested that you should always act as though there were a secret camera recording you. That way, your responses would be modified, improved, putting you on your best behaviour.

Yet none of these people — neither the children nor their parents — seemed to care about onlookers, or even to notice anyone else.

They were either utterly selfish or single-minded, or excessively confident; maybe all three.

'We can't stay out here for long,' Steffie said, consulting her watch.

'Leave it to Noella to decide,' he said, watching the enigmatic character in black who was holding his daughter's hand, leading her away.

Enigmatic perhaps, but purposeful. For Noella knew how to get results, had got them here today.

She was the same as these people here, he realised. It was he and Steffie who were different, displaced.

Yet what about Jemima? Where did she fit in?

Well, that remained to be seen. But after this morning, after her blatant disregard for safety or rules, he wasn't as sure as he might once have been.

'I think Jemima should be warming up by half eleven,' Steffie was saying. 'I can't believe how fine some of these kids have been cutting it. It's as if they don't care.'

'Oh, they care all right,' Greg said.

Something in the way he said this — the edge in his voice — made her turn to look up at him. 'What do you mean?'

He shrugged, wondering how much to say. He didn't want to make Steffie anxious. It was just that he suspected that Mrs Kirkpatrick had inadvertently hit the target when she accused Daisy of playing games.

There were definitely games being played here. He just didn't know what the game was, hadn't been handed the Object of the Game along with the other paperwork.

Everyone else had a copy of the rules, though, and knew what they were doing.

Freddie could flick his hair and smirk all he liked, but from what Greg had observed there was no way his mother would let him get away with losing. Or putting on weight.

Time would tell, Greg thought. There were only six places, after all. Four of them were going to have to lose today.

He watched Jemima, who was skipping happily now, laughing with Noella as though nothing untoward had occurred. And he considered just how spell-bound his daughter was by her French idol – how powerful idols were.

Yep, I spoke to the parents, introduced myself, you know,
like you do. To be honest, I didn't think that much of them.
Wouldn't say boo to a goose. Seemed a bit out of their
depth. I know that sounds harsh, but the kid was flaky too.

They said something about how everyone's out to
get you at these things – that they're all nutters, pushy
parents.

Bit paranoid, if you ask me.

Mr T. Williams
Phoenix Academy of Performing Arts
Surrey Police interview transcript
20 February 2016

FOURTEEN

The auditorium was high-ceilinged, air-conditioned and overwhelmingly busy. There were at least two hundred people in the audience, if not more; pupils dressed in black Phoenix sweaters, guests in black winter coats. There was so much black, the heads seemed to be levitating above the bodies.

'Gosh,' Steffie said apprehensively. 'That's a lot of people.'

'Jemima can handle it,' Greg replied.

Steffie wasn't so sure. Jemima had been doing so well, but after the rec-room incident she had suddenly seemed terribly nervous.

'Well, here goes,' said Greg. They entered the room, going all the way down the aisle to find some empty seats. As they walked, Steffie was aware of heads swivelling to look at them. It was quite dark in the room, lit only by subtle wall lighting and green fire exit signs. She began to feel queasy, warm in her turtleneck sweater again.

'Did they really need so many people here?' she asked Greg, as they settled into their seats in a row right at the back.

'I expect it's to test the kids' nerves,' he said. 'If they're selected, they'll be performing in front of far bigger audiences than this.' He was taking off his jumper. There was a crackle of static and his hair rose at the back.

'And why is it that we want Jemima to be selected exactly?' Steffie said.

He threw his jumper on the seat next to him, tapped her leg lightly. 'It's all going to be fine,' he said, staring ahead of him, waiting.

Steffie gazed at him. Whilst she knew him intimately, at that moment she had never felt so separate from him.

It couldn't have been more apparent then that each human being was on their own, ultimately detached, singular. No matter how well she knew him, she couldn't climb into his thoughts, his being – had to endure this inside her own shell. As did Jemima. For no one could be with her on that stage, even if an entire dance troupe were with her. She alone had command of her body and mind.

Never had Steffie felt so alone, so mortal.

She folded her coat on her lap, and then Jemima's coat on top. It was a dusky-rose coat that Jemima had had for years, but was loath to part with, for the simple reason that there was a ballerina appliqué on the lapel. Steffie fondled the appliqué now, touched its velvet padding that felt cushiony like a puppy's paws. She emitted a little sigh, smoothed the coat tenderly.

It had been awful leaving Jemima earlier because it was obvious that she was suffering. She had felt small in Steffie's arms as they hugged goodbye – smaller than Steffie could recall her ever being, even as a toddler. She was trembling all over, pale-faced, and for an instant Steffie considered calling time on the whole thing.

But Noella was magnificent, emboldening Jemima with words that made Steffie ripple with pride and anticipation. They were the sort of words to inspire troops, the sick, or anyone else facing near-death.

As they left Jemima in the corridor outside studio four, Steffie had glanced over her shoulder, hoping that Jemima would be gone, but she was still standing there in her black leotard and white tights. She wasn't wearing her tutu today, in order to better display her movements. It made her look barer, less fortified. Steffie had stopped, hesitated, but Greg had pulled her forward, away.

There was a flicker of movement on the stage before them now, and Steffie caught sight of Zach Williams waiting in the wings, stretching.

Her stomach churned. Jemima was on after Zach.

She gazed up at the ceiling, at the ugly mesh of wires and lights.

The dust that would be up there, she thought, fretfully – on that equipment.

Mikhail Alexandrov was standing up at the front to talk to someone. She watched him. He was throwing his head back to laugh, clapping his hands. Then he sat back down at the table, joined his intimidatingly long panel of judges.

The lights were dimming. The audience hushed in response. And Zach entered the stage.

Gone was the cheeky caricature. In its place was a serious boy who moved astonishingly well.

'Told you so,' Greg said in her ear.

'Told me what?' Steffie replied. What had he told her?

But she didn't find out, forgot to ask him later, because the child on stage had seized her attention and kept it throughout the performance.

He had chosen a long, complicated free-form piece that she didn't fully understand, but the panel seemed to – several even stood to applaud at the end as he stood there, chest heaving, smiling widely.

As Zach left the stage and the lights slowly rose, Steffie's heart began to race.

The boy was brilliant – stunning.

It occurred to her that she hadn't actually seen any of these children dance before, knew nothing of what they were capable of.

Was Jemima up to this? Was she as good as that?

Her hands felt clammy. She rubbed them on her coat to dry them. 'Oh, flax seed,' she said.

Greg tapped her hand again. 'It's all right,' he said.

'Stop telling me that,' she said.

'Well, it is. Everything's fine. There's nothing to worry about.'

She gazed up at the lights once more, and at the rows of heads before them that were illuminated on top, their hair glowing universally white.

She tried to imagine what Jemima would be doing, tried not to picture a small child standing there, gazing after her mother, petrified; a dismembered insect that couldn't fly.

She shook her head. Not that image. Another one. Jemima dancing.

When Jemima began to dance, she would no longer be from Wimborne Primary, but something celestial, luminous, causing the audience to murmur, and Steffie to sway as she always did in the mirror of her child.

'That's it,' Noella was saying, her hand lightly on Jemima's back. 'And hold ... And release ... Good girl ... Excellent.'

Jemima, holding the barre, was fully stretched but very stiff. There were drops of perspiration above her top lip and on her nose. Her eyebrows were arched, her knees shaking.

In her eyes was a look that Noella had seen many times before – a silent pleading to be released, a soul who was desperate to find a panic button, an emergency cord to summon a team of heroes to come running forward and take the victim somewhere safe.

It was a look that said that Jemima was going to mess this up.

Noella had to do something for her – had come prepared. It was risky. Yet this entire profession was risky: the stress on the body, on its muscles and nervous system. You couldn't set foot on stage without risk.

She glanced at the clock. It was only ten minutes until Jemima would be called to the wings.

She looked all about her, checking there was no one in sight. No one else had cause to be here or in the vicinity, since Jemima was the last audition of the morning.

It was unyieldingly quiet.

'I have an idea,' she said. 'Carry on stretching.'

She hurried to the side of the room, where her bag was on a bench. The studio, so busy an hour before, was empty now, although the scent of its guests lingered: a subtle blend of nerves, perspiration, stress.

She returned with her bag, looking furtively about her. 'I brought this only as an emergency,' she said. 'I hoped we wouldn't need it. But I think we do.'

Jemima stopped stretching. 'What is it?'

Noella moved closer. 'If I do this, you must promise not to tell anyone,' she said.

Jemima looked even more frightened now. 'OK,' she said.

Noella unclipped her bag and pulled out a hip flask. 'Brandy,' she said. 'It's excellent for relaxing the nerves . . . Here.' She glanced over her shoulder, before unscrewing the lid. 'Take a swig.'

Jemima was frowning at the flask. 'Should I? . . . Isn't that breaking the law?'

'Nonsense. We used to do this sort of thing all the time in Paris. It's what top dancers have to do, Jemima. It's the sacrifice you have to make.'

'Oh,' said Jemima doubtfully.

'Take it!' Noella said. 'Quickly!'

Jemima grabbed the flask and took a sip, grimacing.

'That was barely anything,' Noella said, pushing Jemima's elbow up. 'Drink!' She watched Jemima take a longer drink. 'Good,' she said. Jemima was shuddering, shaking her head, wiping her mouth on the back of her hand.

Noella snatched the flask and hid it in her bag, then produced a breath spray. 'Open, *ma chérie*,' she said.

Jemima obliged, Noella squirted Jemima's mouth and the deed was done.

'Right,' Noella said. 'Now we have to summon our muse.'

'I can't,' Jemima said, hopping about. 'I need the loo.'

'What?' Noella said. 'At this late hour?' She put her hands on her hips, scowled. 'Why didn't you say earlier?' Then she thought of what had just occurred and of what the child had still to come, and softened her tone. 'Well, it can't be helped. Go quickly, then.' She shooed Jemima away. 'It's just down the corridor, on the left. Chop chop!'

And Jemima ran from the room.

Sitting on her own in the studio, Noella felt cold. She rubbed her arms, began to pace up and down, wondering whether she had done the right thing.

Of course it wasn't the right thing. Yet she had seen far worse in her time, involving dancers younger than Jemima. Vodka colas, whisky milks.

Steffie and Greg would be furious. Yet Noella had warned them that this would be a highly competitive environment – hostile, even.

Had she used that word? Had she actually said it might be hostile?

It had been implied. For surely hostility meant the same as highly competitive, was synonymous with perfection and success.

164

Noella thought so; knew so.

The higher you rose, the more lines you had to cross. Her contemporaries at dance school in Paris had all left home at an early age, were single-minded, intent only on winning, would have stopped at nothing to get where they wanted to be – even the sweet ones, like her pretty room-mate, poor doomed Delphine.

It was no different here.

If the Lees hadn't picked up on it yet, on the toxic atmosphere, then they were imperceptive, naïve. Or misled by their hopeful love for Jemima. They didn't want to see the hard little lines of the children's mouths, the sneaky glances, the fake smiles, the anxious breathing. They didn't want to see the Phoenix as a pressure cooker of small sweaty bodies sparring for centre stage. They didn't want to see the relentless regimes, the physio appointments, the eating disorders, the badly wired brains.

Yet they would all be here, as sure as the floor and walls.

Jemima had needed something to take the edge off and Noella had helped her; that was all.

Noella shivered, wondering why the studio was so cold. It didn't help the nerves. She glanced at her watch. What was keeping Jemima? She was supposed to be in the wings by now. The woman with the headset would be marching along in a minute, outraged by their tardiness.

She began to walk up and down again, her arms folded.

Jemima had been too long. There was a problem of some kind. Perhaps she had an upset tummy from nerves, or had been sick.

She would go and find her.

She plucked up her bag, Jemima's duffel bag of clothes, and ran from the room.

*

The shop was always busy on Saturdays, but today Helena could barely cope with it. It was as though there was an event on the shopping calendar that she wasn't aware of. The doorbell kept jangling and more customers entered, cramming into the compact space.

Ordinarily, she would have enjoyed the bustle, but today she was finding it hard to concentrate. Her heart kept tripping about as though tipsy. And when she went to wrap goods in tissue and pull Sellotape from the dispenser, she found that her hands were shaking, clumsy.

She bit her lip, smiled apologetically at the customers, hoped no one noticed.

During an opportune moment, she pulled her phone from her bag and sent Steffie a text.

Everything OK?

Steffie replied right away.

All OK Mum. Hope shop OK. Just about to go into auditorium so need to switch phone off now. Will text afterwards. Here goes! Xxx

Helena slipped the phone back into her bag. Half a dozen more people had just entered the shop, shuffling politely for space.

She checked her watch. Twelve thirty. Jemima was on in quarter of an hour.

Her heart felt now as though it were being fired out of a canon – completely out of control, doing dangerous leaps and plunges. She was too old for a dare-devil body, for maverick organs.

She didn't have time to consider what to do about it, since one of the customers was asking her about the hanging animals in the window, about what they were made of and stuffed with.

She didn't want to climb into the window to check the labels, didn't feel agile, steady enough today. She would knock everything here and there. 'I uh . . .' she said.

'Oh look,' the customer said. 'There's one here.' There was a giraffe dangling from the front of the counter. The customer bent to examine the toy, just as another customer approached.

'Do you have another flower-shaped slate clock, like the one over there?' the woman asked. 'I'd rather not have a display one.'

Helena nodded. 'I'll go and check. One moment, please.'

Normally she knew where all the stock was, but the slate clocks were new. She wasn't sure where Steffie had put them.

She was hurrying to the stock room at the side of the shop, when suddenly the walls seemed to be closing in on her. She stopped still, put her hands out to her sides, her hair line breaking out in perspiration. 'What in God's name . . . ?' she said.

She thought she was dying.

But it was nothing like that.

It was all the doubt that she had been feeling over the past few weeks coming to a head inside her – snagging her windpipe, like a fish hook.

She knew for certain then that she was right – that Jemima shouldn't be there, not in that academy, not trying to be one of those *étoiles*.

Because something awful was going to happen.

Steffie was sitting stiff-backed, waiting for Jemima to appear on stage, as were Greg and the rest of the audience. People were beginning to talk, a wave of voices rising louder and louder through the auditorium.

Her eyes were burning with nervousness. She stared at a large phoenix crest on the wall that appeared to be wobbling in a heat haze. She blinked and the phoenix settled.

'What time is it?' she said, even though she was wearing a watch, hadn't stopped checking it.

'She's three minutes late,' Greg replied.

'Should we go and look for her?'

'No,' Greg said. 'She'll be here any second.'

Steffie closed her eyes, summoned Jemima to her mind, pictured her coming on stage in her black leotard, white tights.

'Ladies and gentlemen, boys and girls . . . '

Steffie's eyes snapped open. One of the academy staff, wearing a microphone headset, was addressing the audience. 'Do we have a Jemima Lee here?' the woman said.

Steffie looked at Greg in alarm. 'We need to go and check on her,' she said.

'OK,' Greg said, standing up.

They made their way to the end of their row, brushing knees, knocking bags, and then hurried down the aisle.

'Jemima Lee?' the woman was saying, her voice booming.

There was something wrong. Noella was always punctual, precise; as was Jemima, her ardent disciple.

They went out to the corridor where the silence seemed foggy, grainy. Fear, Steffie knew, was like sand kicked into eyes.

'Maybe they don't realise they've been called,' Greg said. 'Try ringing Noella.'

Steffie pulled her phone out of her bag as they ran to where they had left Jemima: outside studio four, at the end of the corridor.

'It's gone straight to voicemail,' Steffie said, hanging up the phone.

Greg pulled the studio door open. It made a swooshing sound. They both stared at the empty space of studio four.

'What now?' Steffie said. She was trying to think of a logical explanation. Perhaps Jemima had taken a turn for the worse, was feeling sick. 'Toilets!' she said.

They ran to the ladies' toilets. Inside, with Greg propping the entrance open, Steffie crouched on the floor, looking underneath the cubicle doors. There was no one there, no noise other than the cistern making plaintive dripping sounds.

They went back to the corridor and looked at each other, confounded.

Then they walked back along the hallway, slowly now, looking through the port holes in the other studio doors.

'Let's check again in the auditorium,' Greg said. 'She might be there by now.'

'That's true,' said Steffie, doubting it as she said it.

They returned to the auditorium and saw that the stage was still empty, the audience talking all at once in a muddle of voices. The lady with the microphone was speaking to Mr Alexandrov. When he saw Steffie and Greg, he approached them, tucking his shirt into his trousers with a neat motion, running a hand through his dark hair.

'Mr and Mrs Lee?' he said. He took Steffie's hand as though shaking it, but then clasped his other hand around the handshake in a gesture that was more affectionate than she would have expected.

'Yes,' was all she managed to say.

'We appear to have lost Jemima,' he said. He turned to Greg now, shaking his hand. 'Was she nervous? Do you think she's run off somewhere?' He looked back at Steffie. 'She is hiding, perhaps?'

She thought about this. 'I don't think so,' she said. 'I mean, she was nervous, of course. But . . . ' She trailed off. She couldn't think of anything else to add.

'It's very strange,' Greg said. 'Her tutor is very punctual and—'

'One moment, please,' Mr Alexandrov said. He pulled his mobile from his pocket and took the call, his finger pressed against his other ear. 'Yes, please. Check everywhere,' he said. 'Well then, do it again . . . Thank you.'

He hung up. 'I am sure we'll find her shortly,' he said. 'We can all wait.' He bowed his head in parting and turned away, grabbing a member of staff to speak with them.

'Do you think she's hiding?' Steffie asked Greg.

He was opening his mouth to reply, when there was a commotion behind him and they both turned to look.

Halfway down the side of the auditorium, a fire-exit door had burst open. The audience seated nearest the door were standing up, shouting. Steffie couldn't see what was happening. There were too many people in the way.

But then she caught a glimpse of the person in the fire-exit doorway.

It was Noella, face taut with shock, flapping her arms, shrieking.

'Oh,' Steffie said, putting her hand to her mouth. 'Greg,' she said, turning to him. But he was running to the main exit, as were Mr Alexandrov and a team of staff.

Steffie stood still for a moment, the blood pounding so intensely in her ears that she couldn't hear anything; just a hiss. Around her she could feel the thud of cinema-style chairs jumping up as bodies stood – could feel the heavy vibrations of footsteps and voices en masse.

And then she hurried forward, following Greg out of the room. He was already lost in the throng of people moving down the corridor. She could see colours flashing, limbs moving on white floors, against white walls.

They were entering studio three. The hissing sound was so loud now, she couldn't hear above it.

She stopped abruptly in the room's threshold. There were fifty people or so gathered to the left, motionless. Somehow the energy of the room had pulled them that way, as though the floor were on a tilt and they were all liquid. But their eyes were being summoned elsewhere.

In the middle of the room, underneath a hole in the ceiling above, was a small body.

The face was turned the other way, the black leotard curved

slightly on the spine, the white legs curled as though sleeping, the arms splayed, one wrist dangling limp, smashed.

People were beginning to move, to pull out phones, to cry, talk, whisper.

Steffie took in the details at once, her gaze resting on the sparkly beanie on the head of the body. There was no mistaking it. That hat belonged to Daisy Kirkpatrick.

She could hear a little better now, the hissing was abating.

That wasn't Jemima lying there. That wasn't her daughter.

She was looking about for Greg, when she felt someone small pushing against her to enter the room. A crowd had quietly amassed in the doorway, filling the space around Steffie with hot anxious breath, warm bodies.

Steffie rocked to the side as the small person squeezed forward and stood just beyond her, hands clasped to mouth, wearing a black leotard that made her look as thin as liquorice laces.

Then the child began to scream.

Steffie stared at her in horror.

'Come away,' the mother said, pushing forward, holding out her hand to her daughter. 'Don't look. Come away, Daisy. *Now*!'

No. I absolutely one hundred per cent did not go into the rec room.

Daisy Kirkpatrick
Phoenix Academy of Performing Arts
Surrey Police interview transcript
20 February 2016

FIFTEEN

'Oh, God. No!' Steffie said, panic hitting her bloodstream. She could feel someone behind her, close to her, holding her shoulders. It was Greg.

She went to move forward, but he was gripping her too tightly. 'Let me go,' she said. She didn't say it loudly. She couldn't shout, move, think. She had entered a hazy field that was hot, freezing, deafening, silent, slow, speeding.

'Steffie,' Greg was saying. 'We need to wait here. We can't go to her.'

His voice cracked, broke.

It reminded her of once before, a time that she could not touch, but that smelt of blood, of terror, of dust.

She stared at the dark hole in the ceiling, at the black void on white plaster, her eye then falling to the black leotard and white tights below, to the debris scattered on the floor.

She was struggling to breathe, gasping for air, as the dust swarmed around her.

'Greg . . . ' she said. She wanted to tell him that it was back: the dust, the amathophobia. But it was too late. She didn't have enough oxygen. She was fighting consciousness, was soaked in sweat.

'It's OK, Steffie,' Greg said, clasping her head between his hands to get her to look at him. 'It's OK. *Breathe.*' He inhaled markedly, so that she might do the same. 'That's it. Deep breaths. That's it.'

She fought it, breathed with him, felt the attack waning.

Someone was shouting behind them. Mr Alexandrov was pushing through the doorway crowd. 'Get back! Please! Let them through! Step aside!'

The people who were gathered to the left of the room remained there, slowly getting larger as others joined them, a puddle becoming a pool.

Greg pulled Steffie to one side, supporting her by the shoulders. 'It's OK, Steffie,' he kept saying quietly. 'It's OK.'

A man in a checked shirt with grey hair was hurrying into the room, followed by Phoenix staff.

The grey man was kneeling down on the floor in the middle of the room. He was saying something about airways.

'Can we move her?' a member of staff asked, kneeling down beside the doctor. The other staff around him were opening first-aid bags, all talking at once.

'We have to,' the doctor said. 'But do not move her neck.'

Another member of staff was talking on his phone. 'Possible spinal injury and skull fracture,' he was saying.

Steffie held herself rigid, watched as the men — sweating, clenching their teeth — manoeuvred the body on to its side. 'What are they doing?' she said.

'I don't think she's breathing,' Greg said.

Steffie held her own breath. She still hadn't glimpsed a face, an expression. And then there it was suddenly as they turned the body; acid white, blank.

Jemima.

She felt herself recoil, devastated. Greg was still holding her, locking her in place. 'It's all right, Steffie,' he said.

The doctor was lifting Jemima's jaw upwards, a look of

174

concentration on his face. Then he crouched, watching her chest, listening to her mouth and nose.

'Hush up!' he shouted to no one in particular. He listened again, his cheek close to Jemima's mouth.

'Is she OK?' Greg called out, the sudden sound of his nearby voice making Steffie's scalp prickle.

The doctor didn't reply. He was pinching Jemima's nose, his mouth pressed against her mouth. He watched her chest. Then he began to push it, compressing it rapidly.

Greg dropped his hands from Steffie's shoulders. The doctor stopped. Everyone stopped, waited. The doctor was listening to Jemima's mouth again, watching her chest.

Then he sat back on his heels, wiped his forehead. 'OK,' he said.

There was the sound of communal breath being released.

The doctor was looking around him, wiping his face on his sleeve. 'When will the paramedics be here?'

'Any second now,' one of the staff said.

Steffie realised that Noella had drawn near, was speaking to her, saying something, crying. 'I'm so sorry.' But Steffie did not heed her, was moving towards Jemima.

She wouldn't be allowed to touch her. The staff were watching, waiting for the opportunity to tell anyone so, to shout if necessary. Yet still she approached.

Up close, crouched down, hovering, she could smell the fabric conditioner on Jemima's leotard. The conditioner was cherry fragranced, on Jemima's insistence.

It was her sense of smell that she would remember most about this moment in weeks to come, perhaps because touch had been extinguished. She could smell the coldness of the floor that Jemima was lying on, the putrid smell of fear in the air, the dry smell of smashed concrete, plaster and dust.

Sneaking from Jemima's nose down to her ear was a trail of

blood. The sight of it filled Steffie with a powerful urge to hold her child.

'Jemima . . .' she said.

And then there was a clamour behind them and Steffie turned to see a team of paramedic staff running in with boards and stretchers.

She jumped up and stepped back. Greg joined her, gripped her hand.

They watched as the paramedics spoke to the doctor, who was saying that he wouldn't advise a cervical collar. It would increase the pressure on the neck veins. The paramedics would use a padded spinal board and would manually support the head.

'What's the smoothest way out of here?' one of the paramedics asked.

'Straight down the corridor to the lifts,' Mr Alexandrov said.

The paramedics were easing Jemima on to the spinal board, assisted by the doctor. There was a lot of grunting. The doctor's shirt had a fat line of sweat in the middle.

'Steady!' the doctor was shouting. 'Easy now! Steady!' He was leading the paramedics forward – men in green uniforms with tattoos and shadowy chins bearing Jemima away, accompanied by swarming Phoenix staff.

'Where are you taking her?' Greg called after them.

'The Royal Hospital,' one of the paramedics shouted over his shoulder, as they hastened down the corridor. 'Guildford.'

'Can we travel with you?' Greg said.

'If you like. Though it might be better to follow in the car so you've got your vehicle. It's all signposted. Can't miss it.'

They were easing the spinal board – Jemima – into the lift. There was no room for Steffie and Greg.

Steffie looked at the closing doors in panic and then noticed a fire exit to her left. She ran to the door, pushed it and descended the stairs.

'Steffie!' Greg shouted after her.

She ran down the steps, her legs and back juddering. She missed a step, foot skidding down, then regained her balance and carried on. At the bottom, she pushed the bar down on the exit door and went outside.

She was on the forecourt. The ambulance was there, back doors wide open. Two police cars were arriving, kicking up the gravel on the driveway.

The doors of Danube House opened and the paramedics came out bearing the board, followed by the staff who were hovering anxiously.

The paramedics were easing Jemima into the ambulance, strapping an oxygen mask to her face.

Greg had followed Steffie down the stairs. He appeared now, out of breath, grey-skinned with fear. He began to talk to the doctor.

They were closing the ambulance doors, raising the ramp.

Steffie stepped up on to the metal ramp of the vehicle. 'Shall I follow in the car?' Greg shouted after her.

'Come with us,' she said.

He jumped on to the ramp, into the ambulance just in time. The paramedics slammed the doors behind them and put the siren on.

As they drove along, speeding smoothly, Greg stared at Jemima, at the child lying unconscious underneath the mask. They wouldn't know the extent of her injuries until she was scanned in hospital, the doctor had told him. She was stable for now; her airways were clear.

Good luck, was the last thing he had said.

Greg wondered who the doctor was. How fortunate it was that he had been there. He had a feeling that the man had saved Jemima's life, or at least had improved her chances of survival.

Chances of survival. Was that term applicable? Was Jemima fighting for her life?

He stared about him in confusion, knowing nothing, understanding nothing.

He thought of the sparkly hat. The doctor had taken the hat carefully off Jemima and then had flung it on to the floor in his haste, where it had skittled away with a rustling sound like a glittery rat.

He thought of Daisy Kirkpatrick coming out of the rec room earlier – of the two boys, of the one with the long fringe smirking.

He thought of Mrs Kirkpatrick and her sharp nails; of the other parents at the coffee morning; of Noella leading Jemima away across the grounds that morning.

He thought of the big hole in the ceiling above Jemima in studio three.

Why was it there?

Jemima had fallen through the ceiling somehow. But from where? And why?

Why would she have been there, when she was supposed to be in studio four getting into the flow or whatever Noella called it? And why hadn't Noella been with her, getting her ready to go on stage?

None of it made sense.

He gazed about him, around the insides of the vehicle. What were they doing here? How was this even happening?

It seemed impossible, incomprehensible.

He realised that he had left his coat in the auditorium. He looked at Steffie. She had nothing with her either. They were both sitting on pull-down seats at the side of the ambulance, backs bumping on metal.

She caught him looking at her jumper, evidently following his train of thought. 'My coat's in the auditorium, I think,' she said. 'I don't know where my bag is. And there's a duffel bag somewhere with Jemima's clothes in.'

He thought that she might cry then, but she didn't. One of the paramedics, who had Jemima's head locked between his hands, was speaking to the other about heart rate, blood pressure and medical stats that Greg didn't understand.

'Is she going to be OK?' he asked them.

The ambulance had stopped momentarily. All was quiet, still.

The man holding Jemima's head didn't reply, hardened his lips to a thin line. But the woman, who was the other side of Jemima, holding a compress to her head and helping secure her in place, said, 'We hope so.'

The ambulance was moving forward again. Greg's back jolted against the vehicle wall. 'Is she breathing?' he said. 'Do you think—'

'She's stable for now,' the woman replied, with a sympathetic crease of her eyes that wasn't quite a smile. 'They'll be able to tell you more shortly.'

'What do you think they'll do first?' he asked.

Again, the almost-smile appeared. 'A CT scan to determine the level of brain or spinal injury ... if any,' she said. 'And to check for broken bones.'

Greg's stomach shifted.

Brain injury. Spinal injury. Broken bones.

What if Jemima died? What if their baby girl died?

He stared at Steffie in horror. She stared back at him. Her eyes were red-rimmed, her lips blue.

That's not going to happen, he told himself.

'It's not going to happen,' he said out loud.

Steffie reached for his hand. She felt frozen.

And then the ambulance stopped again.

There were voices outside, muffled conversations, tyres screeching, sirens, doors slamming, footsteps.

The back doors swung open and daylight and winter poured in. They had arrived at the Royal Hospital.

The ramp was lowered, the padded board lifted skilfully down. The doors of the intensive care unit rushed open with a blast of hot air and the paramedics began to hurry forward, carrying their precious cargo into the warm mouth of the hospital.

Noella was the last one to leave studio three. She was aware of the crowd dispersing – of people seeping steadily away. She was aware of the blood inside them – aware that beyond those fine clothes and cosmetics, beyond the hair follicles and skin cells, were organs that relied on blood and oxygen, that were intrinsically ugly and remarkable at once.

Never before had she been so aware that humans were blood, water, liquid.

And then it was just her standing there on her own. Held tightly against her body was her bag, hidden in the lining of which was the pewter hip flask.

At her feet, was Jemima's duffel bag. Poking out of the top, she could see the familiar faded appliqué of the once-sparkly ice-skater. She quivered with guilt, pushed the sweater down out of sight.

The police would be here any minute. She had heard them arriving as everyone left, their caterwauling sirens approaching.

She stared up at the terrible hole in the ceiling.

Scattered on the floor below, where Jemima had landed, were splinters of wood and plaster and concrete.

'You can't be in here,' said a voice behind her.

She turned to see two plain-clothed men walking towards her, circling the area where Jemima had lain. Beyond them were half a dozen policemen in uniform, radios crackling.

'I was just going,' she said.

'Can we take your name before you do?'

'Noella Chamoulaud,' she said.

'And you're . . . ?'

'Jemima Lee's tutor,' she said.

'In that case, don't go very far. We'll need to ask you a few questions.'

'Fine,' she said, picking up the duffel bag. 'I'll be in the café.'

Jemima was being taken at speed to the children's intensive care unit. Two men in burgundy uniforms wearing bandanas were pushing her on a special wheeled carrier, her head secured by padding. Steffie and Greg hastened after her, scarcely noticing where they were going, with little hope of ever finding their way back.

On the children's ward, they went past murals of clowns and princesses and fairies and dragons, before coming to a side room where the doors were closed behind them. The men in burgundy disappeared and in their place arrived two nurses and a doctor. The doctor introduced himself briefly, but Steffie didn't get the name, didn't process it. She was too busy watching what was happening beyond.

Jemima's leotard was being cut down the middle and her tights were being removed by the nurses. A man in a rugby shirt and jeans was splinting her wrist, elbow and heel. There was a confusion of conversation, of equipment, as staff barked instructions, grappled with plugs and charts. Jemima was being hooked up to a new oxygen mask; her bare chest was a graph of wires and tubes. On her index finger there was a sensor pad, like a one-fingered glove, and the nurse was fitting an intravenous line into her right arm, suspending a bag of clear liquid on a pole above the bed.

The doctor, who was consulting a chart and tapping his pen on his teeth, turned to speak to Steffie and Greg. 'We've paged a head-trauma specialist,' he said. 'Dr Bernie Mills. He'll be here any minute.'

Steffie only heard *head trauma*. It was as though they were learning a new language where trivia wasn't relevant, and only horrifying words reached the brain – that and the beeps of the medical paraphernalia.

She glanced around the room, registering where they were based. They were in a small private room. There were two green chairs with wooden arms, yellow curtains with a gingerbread man design, a large window, a wooden bedside cabinet.

She rested against the wall. She couldn't get warm despite her woollen sweater, couldn't feel her toes. Her fingers were numb, yellow-tipped.

There were voices. Steffie looked up to see that the doctor had been joined by two others in white jackets who were crowding Jemima's bed, discussing intracranial pressure, linear fracture, venous sinus groove, other things that Steffie couldn't understand.

She opened her mouth, found that it was speechless. Greg stood beside her, hands hanging limply by his side.

They wanted to take Jemima for the CT scan, but were waiting for the specialist to assess her first.

'Ah, here he is,' said one of the doctors, turning to greet a tall man in a petrol-blue shirt and corduroy trousers. The other medics stepped aside reverently for him.

Steffie watched. The tall man was shining a torch into Jemima's eyes, observing her chest, listening to her heart, reading the monitors. He began to mutter in a low voice to one of the doctors, whilst writing on a clipboard.

Then he approached Steffie and Greg. 'Hello,' he said. 'Bernie Mills.' He had a kind voice, but he looked grave. Steffie pressed her back into the wall for support. 'We need to scan

Jemima to ascertain the level of injury sustained ... How far would you say she fell?'

Steffie couldn't even guess, hadn't allowed herself to think of the hole in the ceiling, of how it had got there. She looked at Greg for help.

'Twenty feet, or thereabouts,' Greg said.

'Was the fall broken?'

Greg appeared to be considering this. His reactions seemed slower than usual, his mouth taking a while to form words. 'I ... I'm not sure. She somehow fell through a ceiling on to the floor below.'

'And what was the flooring made of, do you suppose? It was a dance studio, I understand.'

'Yes,' Greg said, sounding slightly more animated. 'It was vinyl. It would have been thick, sprung, to reduce impact injuries.' He glanced at Steffie.

They were both seeing it: this hint of hope.

Steffie felt herself rousing a little.

'We know that she's fractured several lower limbs,' the consultant was saying. 'The fact that Jemima's still unconscious could indicate skull fracture, and possibly swelling and tissue damage. But it's impossible to say without seeing the scan results.'

'Will she ... ?' Greg began.

'We need to be prepared for anything,' the consultant went on, dropping the torch into the breast pocket of his shirt. 'But let's be positive. Children have been known to escape accidents virtually unharmed. They're resilient. Their hearts and lungs are stronger than ours, and they're soft and their skeletons bounce. All of which will go in Jemima's favour.'

'Good,' Greg said, nodding slowly. 'So when will we know?'

The consultant glanced at his watch. 'Hopefully we'll have a full set of results by teatime.'

Teatime, Steffie thought. It sounded so homely, so far away.

She realised that her mother didn't know yet. How to tell her this?

The consultant was looking at her. 'You're in shock,' he said. 'There's a family room down the corridor. Go and make yourselves a strong tea.'

Steffie nodded, but didn't move. She was looking at the consultant, willing him to say more – to promise them that Jemima was definitely soft and bouncy and strong, that the floor had been special, expensive; that this was still going to end well.

The consultant sensed her disinclination to leave. 'Jemima's going now too,' he said gently.

Steffie wished he hadn't said it quite like that, for it made her cry. She pictured Jemima walking across the café that morning in her shorts and polka-dot leggings, clutching the paper bag of gobstoppers.

She was glad now that Jemima had worn her favourite grey sweater. And she was glad that her daughter was the one with the sweets and the kind heart. She wondered where the gobstoppers were now, and Jemima's sweater – where their coats and bags were. Somewhere in the Phoenix. She thought of the sandwich wrappers that she had left on the dashboard of their car, of the banana skin that Jemima had tossed from the moving car into the hedgerows earlier with a delighted shriek.

Little bits of them were scattered about the area, like debris after a tempest.

'It's all right,' Greg said, taking her arm, as the nurses kicked the brakes off Jemima's bed.

Steffie stopped crying almost the moment she started. She couldn't cry – not with her child lying there like that. She stared at Jemima's pale face as she passed by. The paramedics' oxygen mask had left strap marks on her tender cheeks. The blood spilling from her nose had dried, darkened. Her beautiful hair bun was straggled, hanging loose.

Jemima was being wheeled down the corridor, equipment in tow. Steffie followed a short way behind, stopping when she reached the nurses' desk, when the group went through a set of double doors.

Every drop of blood in Steffie's body seemed to be bubbling, every bone snapping.

Even with Greg's arm around her, she felt she would fall.

She kept her eye on the doors that Jemima had disappeared through. What had the consultant said?

Escape unharmed. Resilient. Strong. Soft. All these things would be in Jemima's favour.

'Resilient, strong, soft,' she said.

She hadn't realised she was speaking out loud – had not meant to.

Greg began to cry.

Like most men, he didn't wear it well. It was a sound, a sight, that she abhorred. For when Greg cried, it meant that things were hopeless. She had only ever seen him cry once before – on the previously unchallenged worst day of their lives.

He clapped his hand to his mouth, stamped his feet.

And then the assault had abated. 'Come on,' he said, leading her away.

PARENT OF CANDIDATE
BEATRICE JONES

Oh my God. There's no way I'm letting my daughter attend this academy now. Not Bea. She's scared stiff. Isn't that right, sweetie?

I mean, children crashing through ceilings at auditions? Falling to their death? It's a nightmare. Talk about *trauma*.

Sorry. I shouldn't have said that so bluntly. But we're all a bit freaked out, you know?

Bea hasn't said a word since it happened.

Not one single word.

Isn't that right, hon?

Mrs P. Jones
Phoenix Academy of Performing Arts
Surrey Police interview transcript
20 February 2016

SIXTEEN

If it were true that buildings and rooms eventually acquired the nature of the task being undertaken within – that funeral parlours and their contents were imbued with morbid pessimism, temples with sacred permeating light – then nowhere said it more effectively than the family room at the Royal Hospital.

Every fibre in the cushions, every thread in the sofa fabric, every hardened spilt coffee granule, every dried used tea bag was infused with a sense of quiet agony. Were you to remove the objects from the room, they would still be carrying pain within them – a dull morose energy that dogs would whimper at.

Steffie took a step into the room, then stopped. There was a hole in the middle of the sofa. White stuffing was shooting up out of the upholstery, like a hot spring.

'This is awful,' she said, turning to Greg.

He gazed about him. 'It's not great,' he said. 'Tea?' He approached the kitchen counter hesitantly. There was a kettle, a jar of coffee with no lid, a plate of tea bags, a bowl of sugar cubes that were suspiciously off-white.

'I s'pose,' she said, perching on the edge of the sofa. The room was grey – grey walls, grey sofas, grey carpet – and it was very large, perhaps unnecessarily so. It reminded her of the stock that arrived at the shop in huge boxes, only to reveal something minuscule within. The room's size made it feel loose somehow, unstable.

She looked over her shoulder at the chairs beyond – plastic chairs in a circle as though an AA meeting for ghosts were in progress. In the far corner, a television was talking to itself. Above it on the wall was a photograph of men walking through the rain carrying red umbrellas. The red was the only splash of colour on the painting, in the room. It reminded Steffie of the blood on Jemima's face, and she turned away.

'Drink this,' Greg said, handing her a mug. 'I gave the cup a good wash.'

'Thank you,' she said.

They went to a table and chairs by the wall, underneath a book shelf, and pulled back the chairs, flicking crumbs from the seats. There was no one else about, but someone had been here not so long ago. There was a steaming cup of coffee on the table. Someone had been caught unawares, deprived of their break.

Steffie picked up a flyer from the table as they sat down. When she saw that it was about bereavement counselling, she dropped it.

'Oh, God,' she said, putting her head in her hands. 'I don't know what's going on ...What are we doing here? How did this happen? I just can't take it in. Can you?' She gazed at Greg.

'No,' he said, shaking his head. 'I've been trying to piece it together. But none of it makes sense.' He glanced around the room. 'It feels surreal – just being here. Sat here, like this.' He jerked his head in the direction of the door. 'And Jemima ... like that ...'

She ran her finger around the lip of the mug. 'What's going to happen?'

'I don't know,' he said. 'But you heard the doctor. We've got to stay positive.'

'Yes,' she said.

Resilient, strong, soft.

'She'll get through this,' she said.

She could feel his eyes on her. He was battling saying something.

'Yes,' she said intuitively. 'I had a panic attack.'

He continued to gaze at her, then nodded slowly. They would discuss it at some point. But not now.

They drank their tea in silence. It tasted stale, but she couldn't have cared less. She was picturing Jemima being scanned – picturing X-rays that didn't have any cracks or grey areas.

This room was the only grey area.

She looked at Greg again. 'Where did she fall from, do you think?' she asked.

'I don't know,' he said. 'Or what she was even doing there in the first place. Wherever it was, it wasn't where she was supposed to be.' He sipped his tea, his lips pursed white.

'And why did she go into the rec room?' she said. 'It wasn't like her at all – especially not before the audition. What was she thinking?'

She thought of Jemima standing there in her grey sweater outside the rec room earlier, head hung, contrite.

What had that signified – the shame? Had she been led astray, acting out of character to impress her new friends?

Steffie wished now that they had dug deeper at the time, hadn't let it go so easily. And yet she had been more focused on the audition than anything else – on Jemima not stuffing it up. The last thing they had needed was an emotional inquest.

'And what about the others?' she said. 'Why would they have wanted to go in there?'

'God knows,' Greg said. 'Something to do? Boredom? Or . . .' And then his eyes narrowed and he stared at her.

'What?'

'Nothing,' he said.

'Please,' she said, touching his arm briefly. Their touches were light, even in the circumstances: tissue-thin exchanges that couldn't hold water or hope.

'Well, it's just that I had the feeling that the kids were playing a game of some sort.'

'What do you mean?' Steffie asked.

'I dunno,' Greg said. 'It sounds stupid saying it out loud. But I just thought they were play-acting, setting a trap almost.'

'What sort of trap?'

'Oh, I don't know,' he said, putting his cup down. 'As I said, it sounds daft.'

Steffie was thinking about this – about whether the children were capable of scheming to such a degree.

It was impossible to say. They were just kids, weren't they?

Yet what about the parents?

She thought of the odd assortment of people in the café that morning who had held her attention so effectively, ghoulishly even.

And then she laughed drily. 'You're right,' she said. 'It does sound daft. This is a dance school, for God's sake.'

She sipped her tea, gazed at the photograph of the men with umbrellas.

Sometimes, though, she thought, children committed murder.

What if Greg were right? What if Jemima had been led into a trap?

She thought of the two boys smirking in the lift on their way back to the café after the rec-room incident. And Zach's father with his pseudo-Japanese, telling them that these places were full of psychos. Why would he have said that?

Was it true?

'Have you heard from Noella?' Greg asked.

'Noella . . .' Steffie said, as though recollecting a name that she hadn't thought of in years. 'No.' She turned in her seat to look at Greg. 'I'd forgotten about her. Why wasn't she with Jemima?'

He had that funny look again – narrow eyes, staring at her. 'Exactly.' He folded his arms. 'She was in charge of Jemima. She had responsibility. So something went wrong, didn't it? And she's not told us otherwise, so that puts the blame on her, so far as I'm concerned.'

Steffie put her head in her hands again. 'No,' she said. 'This isn't happening.'

'It is,' Greg said. 'And the police will get the truth out of her.'

'The police?' she said.

Somehow, in all the chaos, the trauma, she hadn't thought of that – that the police would be investigating this, even though she had seen them arrive, had seen the dust that their wheels had kicked up on the gravel in the winter sunshine.

The idea of the police poking around the academy – interviewing Noella, the parents, Mr Alexandrov and his esteemed panel – nauseated her, made the whole thing feel darker, less hopeful.

'Children don't fall through ceilings every day, Steffie,' Greg said. 'The police will be all over this. Who knows – the academy might even be to blame.'

She stared at the television. She had forgotten it was on, had zoned out the quiet drone of voices in the background. A sports programme was on: a women's cycling race. One of the cyclists had something sparkly on her wrist.

It reminded Steffie of something. She looked back at Greg. 'Why was Jemima wearing Daisy Kirkpatrick's hat?'

'I don't know,' he said, shaking his head.

She put her head in her hands again. 'If only we could ask her,' she said.

'And we will,' he said, pushing his tea mug away. 'We'll find out exactly what happened – who or what did this to her.' He glanced at his watch. 'Not long till teatime, until we get the results . . . We'll have a much better picture then.'

She thought of her mother again – of how she would be pacing up and down. Steffie had told her she would ring after the performance. Her mother would be insane with worry by now.

'I should call Mum,' she said.

'Yes,' he said, 'but not yet. Wait till we've got something solid to tell her.'

Solid, Steffie thought. The ceiling at the Phoenix was supposed to be solid, reliable. Yet Jemima had fallen right through it.

Her eye was drawn again to the television. She watched the cyclists racing along the road, wheels glinting, helmets down, legs circling – hailing from a parallel universe alongside this one, where life wouldn't be beginning or ending at teatime tonight.

'I don't know,' Noella said.

They were sitting in Mikhail Alexandrov's soon-to-be office – had been there for twenty minutes going backwards and forwards over the same questions.

'Miss . . .' The detective sergeant sat forward to consult his notes. '. . . Chamoulaud,' he said. 'Forgive my pronunciation . . . No one's on trial. We're just trying to establish the facts.'

Noella gazed at the mahogany panelling on the door. They were positioned as though she were the one in charge, behind the desk. The two policemen were where visitors to Mikhail's office would sit.

She glanced around the room. It was half-complete. There were unopened boxes and files on the floor, pictures on one half of the wall and not the other. She couldn't see who the photographs were of. They were hazy, black and white. She would have relished a closer inspection, without the policemen's insatiable eyes on her.

'Mr Alexandrov's keen to ensure there's no hint of wrongdoing on the academy's part or on his.'

'I'm sure he is,' Noella said, immediately regretting her words.

The sergeant sat upright, interested. 'You have some personal feelings towards Mr Alexandrov?' he asked.

'Not at all,' she replied.

'Shared history?'

'No history.'

'And yet according to him, you were both in school together in Paris.' The sergeant sat back in his chair.

Noella stared at him coldly. She was tiring of this – was exhausted, thirsty, cold. She wanted to get to the hospital, to see Jemima, to explain to Steffie and Greg what had happened.

What if Jemima died? What if that had already happened?

She bit her lip, felt tears stinging her eyes. She hadn't cried yet, would not do so in front of these men.

'Look,' the sergeant said, 'it would help if you could stick to the truth. That way, we can all get out of here quicker.'

'So there's nothing you'd like to add?' the other policeman said.

'Nothing,' she said. 'I've told you everything. I was in the studio with Jemima. She left to go to the toilet just minutes before her audition. She was gone a long time. I couldn't find her. And then I found her lying in studio three. And you know the rest.'

'And there's absolutely nothing you can add? Nothing strange or unexpected that you recall?'

Noella thought of the kerfuffle in the café earlier – of

returning from the shop to find Jemima crying, and Steffie and Greg looking out of sorts. She hadn't enquired as to what was going on. She hadn't wanted to unsettle Jemima any more than she already was, had been intent only on getting her in the flow.

She thought of the hip flask lying secure within the lining of her bag, snuggled at her feet.

'No,' she replied.

'Then we needn't take up any more of your time,' the sergeant said, standing.

Teatime wasn't an accurate prediction. It was gone eight o'clock when Dr Mills came to find them. They had waited in the family room the entire time, sharing a packet of Mini Cheddars, flicking through books entitled *Understanding Childhood Illness* and *Effective Parenting*; watching cycling, golf and sumo wrestling on TV.

Steffie wouldn't have known the doctor's name, might not even have recognised him. It just went to show how impossible it was to spot criminals in a line-up, she thought, if even the man charged with saving your child's life was faceless. The doctor reminded her of his name, had evidently dealt with shocked parents so often that he knew to expect little in the way of social niceties, of the details that meant that someone was listening and cared. They cared. Just not about him. He was a white coat giving them news of terrifying importance.

'We have all the results back,' Dr Mills said, joining them at the table. He pulled a chair up and turned it round, his legs astride, his arms resting on its back. 'Jemima has a number of fractures: her ankle joint, her distal radius, her—'

'Distal radius?' Greg asked.

'Sorry. Her wrist,' Dr Mills said. 'She's also fractured her heel bone. And her elbow.'

Steffie gave a little cry and Greg reached for her hand. They linked fingers – a fragile connection that was of some comfort nonetheless.

'I know this doesn't sound great. But believe me, she's a lucky girl. I'm amazed there are no lumbar, thoracic or pelvic injuries.'

'So that's good?' said Steffie, reaching to the floor for her tissue supply, before recalling that she didn't have her bag with her.

'It's very good,' the doctor said. 'According to our tests, there are no neurological complications either. There's no brain swelling or tissue damage . . . currently.'

He coughed, curling his hand before his mouth whilst doing so. He was a polite man with tightly curled hair and a mole above his mouth that made him looked oddly coquettish. 'I say "currently" because the situation could change. Sometimes pressure builds as a result of the swelling of injured tissues, or an accumulation of blood . . . However, all this can be monitored.'

'But what do you think?' Greg asked. 'Can you give us a clearer picture – an idea of what you think Jemima's outlook is?'

'Well,' the doctor said, shuffling his feet. He appeared uncomfortable giving predictions, perhaps for fear that they would hold him to them. 'What I can tell you is that Jemima has a linear fracture in her skull.'

Once again, Steffie gave a little cry and Greg strengthened his grip on her, took her whole hand now and held it.

'The fracture's straight, thin and there's no bone displacement, depression or splintering.'

'So that's positive?' asked Greg.

'Yes,' the doctor said. 'However, I'd like to run some further tests in the morning.'

'And that's for . . . ?' Greg said.

The doctor dropped his hands from the chair back, clasped his thighs.

'I'm afraid that Jemima's current cerebral cortex activity would indicate that she's in a coma.'

'A coma?' Steffie said, pulling away from Greg and pressing her hands to her face. She could feel her cheeks burning, her head melting.

A coma.

'Please don't panic,' the doctor said, giving a little smile that pulled on the corners of his eyes. The smile then cleared and his expression grew serious once more. 'We have an arousal system in our brain – a collection of nerve cells called the brainstem.'

'The brainstem,' Greg repeated ardently, like a schoolboy revising for biology.

'When you go to sleep,' the doctor said, 'this arousal system shuts down and the cerebral cortex waves slow down. If you disrupt this system – with the kind of trauma to the head that Jemima suffered, for instance – then the result is unconsciousness. When unconscious, the activity waves are slow, just like they are when you're asleep – except that the patient can't be woken ... And this is what we call a coma.'

'And why shouldn't we panic?' said Steffie, fishing for something encouraging to go away with.

'Because from what I've observed so far,' the doctor said, 'I'm expecting Jemima's brainstem to start reorganising itself fairly quickly.'

'Which means?' Greg asked.

'That she'll begin to show signs of cognitive recovery: faster EEG waves, opening her eyes, squeezing your hand, watching you move about the room.'

Such small things – tiny movements that anyone could do.

And now they were to watch and hope and wait for their daughter to do them.

Steffie placed her hand flat against her mouth, trying to stop herself from crying.

The doctor was looking at her sympathetically. 'There's much cause for hope, Mrs Lee,' he said. 'More hope than anything else.' He tapped the top of his chair and then stood up. 'The good far outweighs the bad.'

The good outweighs the bad. Only a medic would say that. A mother could never see it that way. It was far too early to do so.

She couldn't bear to look at him, felt too ashamed to look him in the eye, for he would know then that she was unable to adopt his optimism – was only able to see pain. She put her head down on the table, not caring that there were tea stains and food debris there, and cradled her head in her arms. Her body felt weightless, unattached. The only way to look was down, at her feet, at the grey carpet.

How could this end well? How could they be positive, when Jemima was in a coma, might not wake?

Greg and the doctor were talking over Steffie's head.

'Will you be here for the duration?' Greg was asking him.

Steffie lifted her head then to look at the doctor, hoping to hear an affirmative reply.

Please be here to help us.

Please don't go anywhere.

'Yes,' the doctor said.

Steffie put her head back down on the table.

'Jemima will remain under my care until I'm satisfied that I've done all I can for her.' The men were shaking hands.

Steffie knew that she had to stand up, couldn't cower from this man and this situation.

She pulled herself to her feet, straightened her jumper, extending her hand to the doctor. 'Where is she now?' she asked.

'Back in her room. You can see her when you're ready.'

In her room.

That was *her* room now: the intensive-care room with the gingerbread curtains; not her little bedroom back in Wimborne.

Steffie welled up, withdrew her hand from him.

'Try to get some rest,' the doctor said. 'It'll be a long day tomorrow.' And then he left.

'We have to believe what he's saying,' Greg said. 'That she's going to pull through and start to show signs of recovery.'

Steffie nodded. Her head felt heavy.

They were just leaving the room when someone entered it. Steffie automatically looked away, didn't want to behold someone else's misery, or have them witness hers.

But then Greg said, 'Noella.'

Steffie stopped still on seeing her – the figure in black in the doorway – and tried to assess quickly how she felt. It was difficult to determine. There was little room currently within her for anything other than fear. And fear didn't like to share – was selfish, obsessive, liked to stretch out.

'Steffie . . .' Noella began nervously.

'Thank you for bringing our stuff,' Greg said.

Steffie realised then that Noella was holding their coats and bags. 'It was the least I could do,' Noella said, dropping her cargo and beginning to cry, face crumpled with grief.

Steffie remained motionless, unable to make a move because that would prove how she felt. A hug would suggest sympathy, when Steffie felt no such thing – felt nothing.

'What happened?' she said.

Noella fumbled in her coat pocket, produced a crumpled tissue, dabbed her nose. 'I don't know, Steffie,' she said. 'Jemima went to the toilet before the audition. I couldn't find her. And then I discovered her—' She broke off.

'Oh,' was all Steffie said.

She tried to remember the last time she had seen Jemima and

Noella together. It had been outside the studio. Jemima, in her leotard and tights; Noella, hovering in the doorway, eager to get started.

She thought of sitting on the sofa with Jemima, eating cereal on the night they had heard about the *étoiles* – just over a week ago; of the almond fragrance of Jemima's shampoo; of how she had wanted to freeze those morsels of alone time with her daughter – of how she wished now that she somehow had managed to.

'It's chaos at the academy,' Noella was telling Greg. 'Parents shouting, children crying. And the police . . . They have interviewed everyone under the sun. Have they been here?'

'Not yet,' Greg said, pushing his hands into his jean pockets.

'Then they're on their way . . .' She turned to Steffie. 'How is she?'

Steffie sniffed. 'She's in a coma.'

'A coma?' Noella said, her voice full of fear.

'We'll know more tomorrow.'

Noella blew her nose. 'I cannot understand it,' she said. 'She was in the attic, you know.'

'The attic?' Steffie said, looking at Greg.

'What was she doing up there?' he said.

'I've no idea,' said Noella. 'Perhaps the police will tell you more.'

Steffie nodded, then turned away, signalling an end to the conversation. She wanted to see her daughter, to no longer be in this dismal room talking to Noella.

'We were just going to see Jemima . . .' she said.

'Of course,' Noella said, withdrawing. 'I'll wait for news.'

'Where will you go?' Steffie asked.

Noella shrugged. 'Probably a local B & B. In case you need me.'

Steffie nodded. She wouldn't need Noella. At least, she didn't think so. But Jemima might, if she woke.

The thought of Jemima waking made Steffie want to be nicer to Noella.

'Thank you for bringing our things,' she called after Noella.

'Goodnight and God bless,' Noella replied hurriedly as she left, as though removing herself from view before breaking down.

As they made their way back down the corridor, through the children's ward, clutching their coats and bags, Steffie glanced up at Greg – at the man by her side.

He looked forlorn, shattered.

She could remember a time, long ago, when she had wanted to freeze her moments with him too – precious moments on honeymoon; on their first wedding anniversary; whilst pregnant with Jemima.

She had always been a hoarder – not of possessions, but of emotions. She had always fancied creating something like a dream catcher to hang near her, about her being – a key ring or necklace, perhaps – something to trap all the good feelings.

He had loved her so much.

And now . . .

She just didn't know; didn't know anything.

They arrived at Jemima's room. Jemima was lying in bed, the machines beeping, the sheets smooth on her bumpy form. The lights had been dimmed. There was a lamp above the bed – a strobe light built into the wall unit that gave her face an unearthly glow.

Steffie dropped her coat and bag down, and went to Jemima's side, reached for her hand then recalled that she could not hold it – that her left hand was in a cast, the right bearing a catheter.

She sat despondently in the nearby chair, oblivious to everything else, eyes only on Jemima, watching for signs of recovery, such as the doctor had described.

Brainwaves, transmissions, signals, perception, emotions – all things the eye couldn't see and that were deemed less substantial as a result. Until something tragic happened to teach you otherwise.

And by then it was too late.

AUDITION CANDIDATE NO.3

I didn't go into the rec room, but Jemima's mum told me the others had gone in there. I think it was when I was going to the toilet before my audition. I lost my sparkly beanie in the toilets, I think. I didn't see it again, until I saw Jemima Lee wearing it. I don't want it any more now.

My mum says that if I don't become an *étoile* after all the money she has spent on my lessons she will disown me.

I don't know what that means exactly, but I know that to diss something isn't very nice.

Daisy Kirkpatrick
Phoenix Academy of Performing Arts
Surrey Police interview transcript
20 February 2016

SEVENTEEN

Helena had been waiting by the landline all evening. All day, she had checked her mobile for an update from Steffie. She had kept looking at her watch, was barely able to concentrate on serving customers.

Lunchtime came and went with no word. Then teatime. She had shut up the shop with an uncomfortable sensation, pulling down the shutters, checking the lock twice, as though caring for an old friend whom she might not see for some time.

She knew there had to be something wrong. Even if Steffie had lost her phone or her signal had failed, she would have told Greg to phone, or would have found a payphone. She wouldn't have cut off all communications like this, not on such an important day.

By bedtime, she was nibbling her nails, traipsing up and down the lounge carpet. She couldn't go to bed, not until she had heard.

And then the phone rang. She plucked it up, heart racing.

What Steffie told her was beyond comprehension. Sat here with her damask curtains, her floral throws, her velveteen upholstered chairs, she couldn't for the life of her take in what Steffie was saying about a fall through the ceiling, a fractured skull, brain signals, signs of awakening.

Jemima was in a critical state, in a coma. They would update her again in the morning when they knew more.

Helena hung up, stunned. She stood in the lounge for some time without moving, unaware how dark it had grown around her.

Somehow Jemima had suffered a terrible accident.

What if she didn't make it? It would destroy Steffie. This was Helena's first thought.

After a camomile tea, she thought some more. Whose fault was this? That was her second thought.

Raised as part of a post-war generation that was fond of conspiracy theories, of being small fry in an unfeeling world that operated at a level beyond your control, Helena felt the desperate need to pin this on someone. It was also because she was too far away to do anything but cogitate.

She paced the carpet again.

Eventually, worn out, head thumping, she went to bed. But in the night, she tossed and turned so fitfully she lost half her bedding and woke stiff with cold, her jaw throbbing from having ground it so hard.

She hadn't found anyone to blame – didn't have enough facts to hand, was too much out of the loop. So she chose someone closer to home.

As she walked through to the bathroom and flicked on the light, she gazed at herself in the mirror. *Good morning, Madame,* she normally said aloud. But today she said nothing.

As she waited for the kettle to boil, she knew there was something bothering her – more than the notion of Jemima being in intensive care.

Worse was the thought that she had somehow helped put her there.

She should have told Steffie her doubts, should have voiced how she was feeling.

She thought back to their conversations in the shop. She had tried to air a few objections, but Steffie had told her off for being pessimistic, unsupportive.

The kettle clicked off, but Helena didn't move, remained transfixed, her eyes on the garden outside.

It was useless trying to pin this on something or someone. It was an accident – a terrible accident . . . but one that could have been prevented.

She fixed her eye on a cloud that was passing by. It looked like a headless body running by, legs splayed out.

Jemima had to live. She had to wake up.

Helena turned away from the window, went to the bathroom to clean her teeth.

'She'll be all right,' she told herself in the mirror. And then she went back to the kitchen to make a cup of tea and to sit by the phone.

It was impossible to sleep upright in a hard chair when you were six foot three, at the foot of your child's bed in intensive care, watching the monitors, listening to the beeps. The staff had turned the volume down on the equipment and had dimmed the lights, but the door was wide open and the corridor outside was brightly lit and noisy, with voices calling, doors slamming and staff scurrying around in Crocs – the footwear of choice here, it seemed.

The night staff had arrived – two nurses who didn't lower their voices or subdue their movements purely because it was evening. For them, the clock was unchanging – medical needs being what they were, regardless of the hour. Greg wasn't here to sleep. It wasn't a hotel. They stepped past his feet neatly enough, but scraped plugs into sockets by his head, talking over him as though he were invisible.

He understood that they were doing their job, that they were seeing to the priority here: the patient. Yet he still felt the basic human need for comfort, the minor disappointment of being disregarded; even though he felt for his daughter so deeply that it might as well have been him lying there.

He gazed at Jemima – at the drip, sensors, wires. There was a thin translucent tube leading from her nose to her stomach, feeding her so surreptitiously it was almost sinister. The equipment made the situation seem ugly, terrifying. Erase it from the scene and she was just a little girl asleep.

He smiled to himself, remembering when she used to climb in bed with them. He had loved that – waking of a morning, reaching out for Steffie, smoothing her crazy curly hair flat and then the door crashing open and in would run Jemima with her arms spread like a plane, aiming for their bed. She would wedge herself between them, smelling of milk and almond, and would rub noses with him, Eskimo-style.

Eskimo kiss, he would tell her.

Then they would rub foreheads: *buffalo kiss*.

Then he would flutter his eyelash on her cheek: *butterfly*.

His eyes stung with sorrow. He glanced at Steffie. She had finally fallen asleep on the pull-out bed, after hours of restless shifting about.

Poor Steffie. This would be killing her.

He gave a start as the doorway suddenly darkened, cutting off the pool of light from the corridor. Two men were entering the room, after a quick rap on the door.

Greg sat up straight; as did Steffie, who put her hand to her hair, fixing her rumpled clothes.

'Sorry to disturb you so late,' said one of the men. 'We were meant to be here hours ago. It's been a bit hectic. But we wanted to see you before the day was out.' He extended his hand in greeting. 'Detective Sergeant Lamb.'

Greg stood up stiffly, rubbing his face to rouse himself. 'Hello,' he said.

'This is my colleague, Detective Constable Whyte.'

'Pleased to meet you,' Steffie said, shaking hands with both men.

'Are you OK to talk for a minute?' the detective sergeant asked, looking about him. 'Perhaps somewhere we can speak more freely?'

'There's a family room ...' Greg said.

The sergeant didn't reply, was looking at Jemima. 'So how is she?' he asked, approaching her bed.

'She's stable,' Greg said. 'But she's in a coma. We'll know more in the morning.'

'I see,' the sergeant replied, looking now at Steffie. 'This must be very tough for you.'

'Yes,' Steffie said. She was watching the sergeant warily, the whites of her eyes more apparent than usual.

'Well, let's find this room, then,' the sergeant said.

The family room was more nocturnal than one might have expected. Half a dozen couples were sitting at intervals from each other, watching television, eating microwave meals, talking in hushed tones.

Greg led the detectives to a table. 'Would you like tea?' he asked, but they both declined the offer.

The four of them sat down.

Greg gazed at the sergeant, doing a quick audit of him. He was mid-fifties, Greg guessed, with sandy hair that was receding and chubby cheeks that suggested gluttony. His skin was shiny, oily, as though he tanned well, but didn't often get the chance to sunbathe. There was a speck of food on his shirt, which was untucked on one side. When he spoke, he did so out of the corner of his mouth, lips barely moving.

'So we've launched an investigation to find out why Jemima fell and injured herself so badly ... There are obvious things to establish, like was it the academy's fault in any way. And then there's the not-so-obvious stuff, like what is she like, what is her home life like – things that we're hoping you can tell us.'

The sergeant stopped speaking, clasped his hands together and rested them on the table.

'I uh ...' Greg began.

'Perhaps you could start by telling us about your daughter, Mrs Lee?' the sergeant said, turning to Steffie.

Steffie shrugged. 'She's a normal child. You know ... Does normal things ...'

Greg took the opportunity to assess Detective Constable Whyte, the quieter of the two men. He was maybe five years younger than his superior, was shaved bald and evidently worked out. He sat with his legs spread apart and his muscular arms taut. Yet there was something soft about him – his large eyes and big lips lent him a weakness that maybe he was at pains to disguise.

'And yet she's here auditioning to be one of these special *étoiles*, so she's not that normal,' said the sergeant. 'Tell me about that.'

'Well ...' Steffie said. 'She's always wanted to be a ballet dancer. And she's very determined and ambitious. Coming here was a dream come true for her.' Her voice wavered.

'It's OK,' the sergeant said. 'I appreciate how hard this is. Take your time.'

Steffie looked about her for a tissue and found none. Greg went to the kitchen where there was a dispenser with metal teeth. He returned to the table, handing her a blue tissue that was long and twisted, like a discoloured cheese straw.

'How did she feel about the competition at the academy?' the constable asked. 'Sounds pretty intense, by all accounts.'

'She didn't seem to mind,' Steffie replied. 'At least, she wasn't any more nervous than normal. She always gets nervous before performing.'

'How nervous?' the sergeant said.

'The usual sort of thing,' Steffie said. 'Nothing she couldn't handle. We've always encouraged her to control it, to keep herself calm . . . The show must go on.'

'Except that she didn't go on,' the sergeant said.

She looked unsure how to reply.

Greg interjected. 'Could you tell us how she fell?' he asked.

The sergeant turned to look at him. 'She landed on unsafe flooring that gave way. We're fairly sure she was swinging on a bar in the attic at the time.'

'A bar?' Greg said. 'What kind of bar?'

'The sort you'd find in an old-school gym. There's some gymnasium equipment in the attic, left over from its predecessors. The whole lot was due to be cleared out during the renovation work.'

Greg glanced at Steffie, thought of Jemima swinging, like a toddler on monkey bars and not a ten-year-old about to perform for the audition of her life. Steffie seemed to be picturing this too – was looking aghast.

'Was she on her own?' Greg asked.

He was trying not to imagine the fall, the moment when she slipped. There would have been a second – several seconds, perhaps – when she would have known for certain that she was done for.

'Yes,' the sergeant replied. 'We're fairly sure of that.'

'Oh,' said Greg.

She had been all alone, falling. And then the impact.

He closed his eyes briefly, folded his arms, clenched his hands into fists.

'We've had experts examine the site,' Detective Constable Whyte said. 'And it's hard to pin any of this on the academy or the construction team. It was made pretty clear that the area was off-limits. Plus all the parents signed to say they were responsible for their kids whilst on the property.' He held his hands up. 'What else could the Phoenix do?'

Greg shook his head. 'Nothing,' he said. 'We just don't understand what she was doing up there . . . How it happened.'

'Nor do we,' said Detective Sergeant Lamb, 'which is why we need to dig a bit deeper . . . So tell us about you – your marriage, Jemima's personality. All we have so far is that she's a normal kid who likes to dance.'

'Again, perhaps you'd like to go first, Mrs Lee?' the constable said.

Steffie sat back in her chair, still holding the string of tissue in her hand, like an unwanted hors d'oeuvre. 'When I say normal, I mean normal all round,' she said. 'There's nothing much to say. She's happy, has plenty of friends, loves One Direction, and everything cherry.'

'And what about her home life? Your marriage?' Detective Sergeant Lamb said.

Steffie blushed. 'We're separated,' she said. 'But it's amicable, as you can see.' She glanced at Greg. 'Jemima sees her dad all the time. Doesn't she, Greg?'

'That's nice,' said the sergeant. 'So why aren't you still together?'

Steffie looked again at Greg.

'Things didn't work out,' he said. 'Like they don't for a lot of people. But like Steffie says, we keep things friendly, and Jemima has a good life. Thousands of kids live like her and they don't end up in a coma.'

'Point taken,' said the sergeant. 'No offence meant. Just trying to establish the facts.'

'Which are?' Greg said. 'Because all we know is that our daughter fell from an attic when she was supposed to be on stage dancing. Is there anything else you can tell us?'

He didn't mean to sound aggressive, probably didn't, but

still he attempted to look placid in case they took him the wrong way. It was hard to decipher and control tone in the circumstances.

'Well, for starters – we know that Jemima was wearing Daisy Kirkpatrick's hat at the time of the accident,' the sergeant said, 'despite the fact that they weren't especially friendly. Is that right?'

'Yes,' Greg said. 'They weren't friends – hadn't had anything to do with each other that we know of.'

Detective Sergeant Lamb reached into his breast pocket for a notebook, which he flicked through. 'Yet you told Daisy Kirkpatrick to go into the rec room – into an off-limits area.'

Steffie's mouth dropped open. 'What? That's not quite—'

The sergeant was moving quickly on. 'We also know that Noella Chamoulaud was the last person to see Jemima before the accident.'

'How much do you trust her?' Detective Constable Whyte said, turning to Steffie.

'Noella?' she said. 'Implicitly.'

'And yet she lies,' Detective Sergeant Lamb said.

Greg looked at the sergeant in surprise. 'About what?' he said.

The sergeant shrugged, tucked his notebook back into his pocket. 'God knows. I just know she's hiding something.'

There was a silence.

'So why did Jemima go into the rec room earlier this morning?' the sergeant asked.

Steffie paused before replying; as did Greg.

'We . . . we're not sure,' he said finally. 'We didn't really get a chance to ask her.'

'Was it out of character?' the sergeant asked.

'Completely,' Steffie said. 'But then she didn't know any of the other children and might have been trying to save face . . .

211

After all, it was Zach's idea for them to go in. She was just tagging along.'

'Zach?' said the sergeant in surprise. 'Well, that's interesting.' He was looking at his colleague, smiling.

'According to the other kids,' said Detective Constable Whyte, 'Jemima was the only one who went into the restricted area. No one else broke with protocol.'

'What?' said Greg. 'That's a total lie! We saw them coming out! I was furious with them ... And that other woman was there – what's her name ... Mrs ...'

'Kirkpatrick,' said Steffie. 'Her daughter Daisy went into the room. And so did Freddie and Zach.'

The sergeant got his notebook back out and a stubby pencil. 'So let me get this straight,' he said. 'Four of them went into the rec room just before ten o'clock?'

'That's right,' said Greg. 'On Zach's instigation.'

Detective Sergeant Lamb chuckled. 'They were lying to save their asses. Scared stiff they'd get booted out of the academy.'

'Well, that says it all,' said Greg. 'If they're willing to lie about this, what else are they capable of?' He glanced at Steffie, but she was looking away – didn't want him to pursue this ropey line of conversation.

The sergeant was reading his notebook, his bottom lip stuck out in contemplation.

Greg thought of something. 'How did she get up there?' he asked. 'How did she gain access, or even know the attic was there?'

Detective Sergeant Lamb lowered his book. 'She got in via the rec room. There's a ladder in the corner of the room, leading up to the unknown. The kids would have spotted it earlier that morning. Pretty tempting, I'd imagine.'

'Not for Jemima,' Greg said. 'She would have looked at it and run a mile. Especially before the audition.'

'So either someone carried her kicking and screaming and made her hang on to that bar . . .'

'Are you serious?' Greg said.

'No,' said the sergeant. 'But that only leaves one other explanation.'

'Which is?'

'That she went up there of her own free will.'

Greg groaned, feeling suddenly drained.

'Mrs Lee,' Detective Sergeant Lamb said, turning to Steffie, 'your daughter sounds like a sensible kid. Why do you suppose she went into that dangerous area – twice?'

Steffie shook her head slowly. 'I really don't know.'

'Think,' the sergeant said. 'Is there anything else you can tell us?'

She sniffed, unwound the tissue, pressed it to her nose. 'No,' she said. 'I'm sorry.'

'OK,' the sergeant said. 'We should call it a day.' He pushed back his seat and stood, hitching his trousers up. 'I appreciate you taking the time to talk to us.'

'I'm not sure that we've been that much help,' Steffie said.

'Oh, I wouldn't say that,' the sergeant replied.

Something about the way he said this made Greg look sharply at him. But the words and their meaning had gone and the sergeant was shaking hands amicably with them both.

'We'll be in touch,' Detective Sergeant Lamb said. 'And in the meantime, we'll keep our fingers crossed for Jemima.'

They made their way to the door. The room was empty of parents now, everyone having left the hospital or returned to sit vigil by their child's bed. The place was even sadder without anyone there – just abandoned coffee cups and saggy cushions.

'By the way,' said the sergeant, stopping by the door, 'sorry if I come across as abrupt. It's my manner of speaking. But I do

213

care about your daughter, about all my cases. And I'm good at what I do.'

'Thank you,' Steffie said, unsure whether he was looking for gratitude exactly.

The sergeant gazed at them both. 'I always get hold of the truth,' he said, 'no matter how slippery it is.'

'Well, that's reassuring,' Greg said.

And then the two men left, hands in pockets, heads bent in thought.

PARENT OF CANDIDATE
ISOBEL QUINN

First thing on Monday we're taking Issie for psychological assessment after all the trauma. You can't be too careful about these things. Luckily, my husband's in the profession so it's easy for us to get a referral and a first-rate one at that.

This whole thing is awful for Mikhail ... That's Mr Alexandrov ... He's a close friend of ours. We're so worried about him. I know it's terrible for the poor girl and her family. I feel for them. But when all's said and done, the child went into a restricted area. It's outrageously irresponsible of both the child and her parents. Where were they? How on earth did they let this happen? It amazes me how negligent some people are – how careless they are with their own children. At an audition, of all things!

And what about Mikhail? He's done absolutely nothing to deserve this. If the girl dies, it'll be the end of his career.

Mrs E. Quinn
Phoenix Academy of Performing Arts
Surrey Police interview transcript
20 February 2016

EIGHTEEN

Noella woke to the sound of her phone ringing. For a moment, she didn't know where she was – didn't recognise the faded lilac wallpaper, the bouncy mattress beneath her. And then she recalled that she was in a guest house just a few streets away from the Royal Hospital.

Her head throbbed with the recollection of everything from the day before – of Jemima's accident, of the quiet looks of accusation on the Lees' faces last night.

She looked about for her bag and saw that she had left it on the pillow beside her, like an inert husband whose face was creased and leathery. She hadn't wanted to let the bag out of her sight since the accident, even though she had dropped the hip flask in a bin in Guildford outside a kebab shop.

She pulled her phone from her bag with trembling hands and took the call.

It was Mikhail. He wanted to meet her at the academy. She didn't have transport, she told him – was reliant on the Lees.

He would come to her then, he said. They could go for coffee in Guildford instead.

Noella rose and went through to the bathroom. As she cleaned her teeth, she stared out of the window that overlooked a gravel forecourt. There were flutters of snow in the air, delicate and pale like tulle. She thought of Jemima falling; light, like snow.

She tapped her toothbrush and packed it away.

She would not stay here another night. She would visit the Lees later today to offer her services in some meagre way. And then if they didn't mind, she would go home by train.

Better to be there than here, which felt like nowhere.

Poor Jemima, she thought. She hoped and prayed she would pull through. She had to, for all their sakes.

'*Ma petite chérie*,' she said, tears brimming her eyes.

An hour later, she left the guest house, her feet crunching on gravel, her breath outrunning her. She was meeting Alexandrov at a café several streets away.

As she hurried, she wondered what he wanted with her.

He would be worried about the impact of the accident on his career – was going to ingratiate himself with her and Lees.

Well, she would be having none of it. He hadn't wanted to know her before now – had been blunt, dismissive. She certainly wasn't going to suck up to him now that there was absolutely nothing to gain from doing so.

He was waiting for her outside the café, leaning back on a fancy car. She didn't know cars very well, but maybe it was a Porsche. He was wearing a blue blazer and his collar was turned up against the snowfall, his arms folded high on his chest.

On seeing her, he jumped up and reached out his hand. 'Noella,' he said, smiling.

She couldn't help but be a little frosty in response. She nodded hello.

'Shall we?' he said, gesturing to the café door.

They both ordered espressos. It was part habit – a quick

knock-back drink with a morning cigarette in Paris – and part an indication of the amount of time they were intending to expend on each other.

'Have you seen Jemima?' Mikhail asked, the moment they were seated. The café was busy. It was arty, she supposed. Perhaps he had chosen it because of that. The walls were purple and gold, the photography minimalist: a black-and-white tree, a stark flower.

She shook her head. 'No.'

'Oh. I was hoping you might have news for me.'

'No news,' she said.

'Oh,' he said again. He sipped his espresso. 'This is a very sorry business indeed.'

'Indeed,' she said.

Without looking down, Noella edged her bag closer towards her so that it lay between her feet. The hip flask was no longer there, but it might as well have still been hidden in the lining. It was haunting her – the suspicion that she had been responsible for the fall.

How much had Jemima drunk exactly? She tried to think back – had barely thought of anything else – but could not say for sure.

'I would like to do something for the parents,' Mikhail was saying. 'I would like to visit them, to pay my respects, but don't wish to barge in at such a private time.' He gazed at her. 'I was hoping you might go with me – to smooth my way.'

So it was exactly as she had thought: he wanted to use her.

'I see,' she said.

She wanted to tell him no, that she wouldn't be doing any smoothing – not for him, or anyone. But he was looking so earnest.

'Please, Noella,' he said. 'I know we didn't know each other intimately in Paris . . .'

Not intimate? How much more intimate could one be? They had had sex, many times!

Ah, she thought. He was talking about love, indirectly.

He had not loved her.

Even though she had already known this, she still felt stung. She drank her espresso with a shudder. It was bitter.

'. . . but I always knew you to be kind – to do the right thing,' he was saying.

She looked at him in surprise, wanting to laugh out loud – a guttural, guilty laugh. For she was good at many things – sometimes was even capable of kindness – but a tendency to do the right thing wasn't something that she counted in her skill set. 'So perhaps you could just do this one thing, for old times' sake.'

For your career's sake, she thought.

'Please,' he added.

He set his eyes on her then, and she found herself drawn in to them, unable to look away. She had never noticed before that his eyes were not fully brown, but contained flecks of bronze and gold, reminiscent of Van Gogh's sunflowers, and of the cornfields of her childhood.

She suddenly felt immeasurably sad, alone.

'You were always good to Delphine,' he said. 'She was so fragile, and you . . . were so . . . robust.'

His mention of Delphine broke the spell. She blinked in apprehension, picked up her coffee cup by way of distraction, but did not drink for fear of melting. Her heart was racing, her forehead tingling with perspiration.

'Do you ever hear from her?' he asked. 'You were such close friends.'

She stared at him.

How could he possibly have been so ignorant to the situation, to the truth: to her love for him at the time, to her sense of guilt?

Because – like most of them – he had been too preoccupied with his career.

Just like now. They were both here for their careers. He was trying to preserve his reputation. And she was trying to assuage her mounting sense of culpability regarding Jemima's accident. For if she hadn't forced the hip flask on Jemima, hadn't pushed her to audition in the first place, none of this would have taken place.

'No,' she said, finally answering his question. 'We lost touch ... After what happened.'

'Ah,' he said. 'That is understandable.'

She wondered bleakly where Delphine was now.

In a mental institution; homeless; selling Bibles door to door?

Wherever it was, it would be a sharp downturn from life in the Parisian ballet school.

They didn't speak again in the café, finished their drinks. Somehow it was agreed without words that she would accompany him to the hospital.

Outside, the snow was falling more rapidly, swarming. 'I can leave my car here for three hours,' he told her.

She nodded in response, thinking that she couldn't have cared less.

And they walked to the hospital in silence, heads bent against the tumbling snow.

It was some time that morning before Steffie looked out of the window and noticed the snow. They were in the family room, waiting for Jemima to get back from the latest series of tests.

'Look,' she said, pointing.

Greg joined her at the window. 'Snow,' he said flatly.

'Jemima loves snow,' she said.

She knew he was thinking it too: wondering whether Jemima would regain consciousness in time to see it.

They watched the snow. It was coming down harder, pitching on the paving stones and potted plants of the atrium below.

There was a noise behind them and Steffie turned, expecting it to be a member of staff coming to find them. But it was Noella and Mr Alexandrov.

Steffie pulled her jumper straight, pushed her hair from her eyes. She felt self-conscious all of a sudden. She hadn't slept, hadn't combed her hair or even looked in a mirror.

Mr Alexandrov was the first to speak. 'I'm sorry to intrude,' he said, shaking her hand and then Greg's. 'But I just wanted to enquire after Jemima.'

'Thank you,' Steffie said, lowering her shoulders. She had been holding herself taut. 'We don't know very much at the moment. But she's stable for now.'

'Well, that's good,' Mr Alexandrov said, nodding, glancing around him, taking in the shabbiness of the room.

It was slightly awkward, this meeting, for all sorts of reasons – none of which Steffie could identify. She was too tired, too preoccupied.

Noella looked even thinner than usual, and chronically tired too. She was clasping her bag with white knuckles, mouth knitted, frown lines pronounced. Had she always looked so old, so fierce?

Nothing could be judged correctly now – not until they were home, settled, out of trouble. Only then would anything look right. Until then, it was like looking at life through the side of a fish tank – trying to gauge space and depth and form through the distorting effects of moving water.

'Perhaps I could buy Jemima some books?' Mr Alexandrov said.

'Books?' said Steffie.

'Isn't reading aloud supposed to help?'

'Oh,' said Steffie. 'Yes. Perhaps. It's hard to . . .' She was going to say that it was hard to know what to do for the best, or for anything at all. Everything was so uncertain.

'Does she have a favourite?' Mr Alexandrov asked.

'A favourite?' Steffie said.

'Book,' he said.

'*Ballet Shoes*,' Greg said quietly.

'Ah,' said Mr Alexandrov, 'of course. Then allow me to get you a copy.'

'Please don't go to any trouble,' Steffie said.

'It's no trouble.'

Mr Alexandrov looked tall in here, in this room, with the low ceilings and slouchy sofas. He wasn't as tall as Greg, however, who loomed over him – made him look slight. Still, there was something majestic about the man, Steffie thought. Perhaps merely because he had held in his hand the very thing that Jemima had wanted more than anything else: a place as an *étoile*.

She turned away to the window to watch the snow again.

'Steffie . . .' Noella had joined her but stood at a distance. There was a barrier between them that had not existed before. Maybe it was the awkwardness of not knowing what to say to someone whose child was in a coma, and of Steffie having little to say in response. 'I think I'm going home this afternoon, if that's all right with you.'

Steffie didn't reply.

'Steffie . . .' Noella touched Steffie's arm.

'That's fine,' Steffie said. 'Go home, where it's comfortable.'

Noella was staring at her in dismay.

Had that sounded rude?

Steffie hadn't meant to sound dismissive, yet in order to explain that – to apologise, soften her tone, appease – she would have to speak more. And that meant burning more energy – energy that she was eking out slowly, like a frugal car owner monitoring petrol. A test result, a police visit, a sudden change

222

in Jemima's vitals would swallow energy in a greedy guzzle, leaving her on empty.

So she shrugged internally and didn't look at Noella.

'And what about some music?' Mr Alexandrov was saying.

Steffie wanted to tell him that she didn't care about music or books. She just wanted Jemima back again, whole, well.

But instead she nodded politely, vaguely.

'She likes Tchaikovsky, Prokofiev . . .' Noella offered.

'Then I'll purchase you some CDs and bring them here tomorrow, if I may,' Mr Alexandrov said.

'Thank you,' Greg said.

'Well, we'll leave you in peace,' said Mr Alexandrov.

'Goodbye,' Noella said hesitantly.

What was she waiting for? Steffie had nothing to say to her. Nor did Greg, by the look of things. He was approaching Steffie, turning away from their guests.

It wasn't ill-mannered. It was intensive-care behaviour.

So Steffie didn't wave goodbye to them, or see them out; she hadn't taken their coats, or made them tea, or offered them a seat; she hadn't thanked them profusely for their visit, enquired as to the traffic, the weather or their parking arrangements.

She turned back to the window, to the snow, to Greg who was gazing outside, looking as disorientated and lost as she was.

AUDITION CANDIDATE NO.2

My mum's taking me to see a therapist on Monday. I've seen one before about my chronic shyness. My parents say it doesn't pay to be shy in today's society so I have to do assignments and exercises to help me break out of my shell.

I don't want to break my shell. I like it. I also like tortoises and snails.

And I liked Jemima Lee. I liked her polka-dot leggings. They had holes in the knees. She said she draws on her knees sometimes. I'd have liked to have seen one of the drawings. I wonder if she can do spiders. I can do great spiders.

I'm writing her a poem so that if she wakes up and my parents let me speak to her then I can read it to her. It's all about how we can be friends if she goes to the Phoenix in September, and I can show her how to do spiders.

Isobel Quinn
Phoenix Academy of Performing Arts
Surrey Police interview transcript
20 February 2016

NINETEEN

'So I need to do a series of EEGs in order to monitor Jemima's electrical signals,' Dr Mills said.

'And what will that tell us again?' Steffie asked. Everything that she said was laced with the word 'again', in case she had already asked the same question, had just been given the answer, was failing to hear or respond appropriately.

'Well. . .' the doctor began.

Steffie reached for her tissues.

'. . . as I said last night, I'm hoping that things will start picking up. All the blood tests and X-rays have been reassuring . . . Aside from the fractures, it's a case of Jemima waking. But I'll be able to tell you more about that when I've seen the first set of EEG results.'

'OK,' Steffie said, 'sounds good.' Good was the wrong word. It was so hard not only to think but also to talk. Sometimes she just nodded, as she was doing now.

'When will she be going?' Greg said.

'In about ten minutes,' Dr Mills said.

Steffie and Greg sat down on their twin green chairs. They were still wearing yesterday's clothes – had nothing else to change into. At some point, they might do something about that, but not yet. It had taken quite a lot of effort to buy toothpaste and brushes at the hospital shop as it was.

'What shall we do while she's gone?' Greg asked Steffie, as though there were a multitude of possibilities.

She shrugged. 'A walk maybe?'

'OK,' he said, standing slowly, knees clicking.

They were both exhausted, hungry. But it wasn't an urgent feeling; just a vague, unpleasant sensation that there was something amiss.

When they got outside, they were surprised to see how deep the snow was. Steffie looked dubiously at her boots. 'I don't fancy wet feet,' she said.

'Maybe a walk round inside then,' he said. 'To the shop? I could do with some deodorant.'

She could have made a witty retort, but didn't. Wit felt outdated – something that other people did; before.

They made their way along the green-walled corridors, occasionally bumping into each other with fatigue, stepping out of the way for staff, or patients on trolleys.

'I've been racking my brains,' Steffie said, 'but I can't think of any reason at all why Jemima would have been in that attic. Can you?'

'No,' Greg said.

'I know kids do random things,' she said. 'We can't say what she would do in any given situation. But it just doesn't feel right. It doesn't feel like her.'

'I know,' he said.

'She wanted this, didn't she? She wanted this more than anything.'

He stopped, scratched his bristly chin. 'Yep. She did.'

They had stopped outside a café. It took them a while to acknowledge it, to realise what it was, even though there was a large sign saying, *Friends of the Royal Hospital Café*.

'Shall we go in there?' Steffie said.

Greg turned to look. 'OK,' he said.

Inside there were rose-coloured tablecloths, flower arrangements on the tables, old ladies sitting at tables around the edges of the room selling knitted things for charity. It was the sort of place that would have felt welcoming, but today it was wasted on them. They barely surveyed the menu board – opted for tea because it was first on the list.

'I thought the police were going to tell us more – to shed some light,' Steffie said as they sat down.

'Me too,' Greg said.

'I can't understand any of it,' she said. 'Are we missing something? Was someone up there with her?' She sat forward in her seat, pressed her hand on the table. 'Was Zachary with her?'

'No,' he said. 'He was on stage. Remember? We saw him.'

'Oh,' she said. 'Yes ... Of course.' She sat back in her chair, deflated.

'The other kids were in the auditorium too,' Greg said. 'I remember seeing them.'

'But they could have sneaked out,' she said. 'There was an exit at the back.'

'To what purpose?' he said.

The tea arrived on a tray. A white-haired lady with shaky hands distributed the cups with a smile.

Steffie lowered her voice. 'What about the Kirkpatricks?'

The old lady moved away. 'What about them?' Greg said.

'The mother was very uptight. Maybe they had something to do with it.'

'Doubt it,' he said.

'Why not?'

'Because being uptight doesn't make you a criminal. And besides,' he said, 'it's just a dance school, like you said last night.'

Steffie sipped her tea, unsatisfied. 'Then what?'

He gazed at her. 'You expect me to know?' he said. 'Because I've got nothing. None of this makes any sense to me.'

'But I have to know,' she said, putting her cup down.

'Then think about how she was,' he said.

'How she was?'

'Yes,' he said. 'How she seemed the night before, the day before, the week before … You're the only one who knows that – the only one who lives with her.'

She stared at him. Was there an edge to that comment?

Probably.

Or not.

She tried to think back. Everything was fuzzy. She was having trouble recalling the colour of the curtains in her bedroom at home, the contents of her wardrobe.

'Oh, I don't know,' she said.

Greg finished his drink, scraped back his chair and stood up.

'Come on.' He sounded jaded. 'Let's go to the shop.'

They returned along the corridor, Steffie barely registering where they were going, picking through her mind instead for fragments of information that would help get inside Jemima's head; a head that had always been so readily available, yet was firmly shut off to her now.

'Maybe we should have told the police what you were saying about the children playing games – about how they might—'

'No, Steff,' Greg said.

'Why not?' she said, stopping.

'Because it sounds ridiculous – as though we're paranoid.'

They were outside a lung department. A lady was being rushed inside wearing a ventilating machine. Steffie's stomach did a flip at the sight, at the omen of imminent death.

Greg was gazing about him, head swivelling. 'Where are we going?' he said.

'To the shop,' she said.

228

'Then this is the wrong way,' he said, steering her by the elbow to turn around.

They bumped into each other, their fingers briefly touching.

'Steffie . . .' he said, looking down at her. His eyes were red. His mouth looked dry. She wished, illogically, foolishly, that she could reach up on tiptoe and kiss his lips. It was the sleep deprivation, the distress, the worry. It all took a toll and weakened her, made her want to buckle into his arms and hide. 'I'm sorry.'

He meant everything, she realised: his affair, their separation, Jemima's accident.

'So am I,' she said.

When they got back to the children's ward, the two detectives were in reception. On seeing them, the men tossed their newspapers and magazines on to the coffee table and stood, shaking the creases from their trousers.

'Morning,' Detective Sergeant Lamb said, extending his hand to them both. 'Manage to get any sleep?'

'Not much,' Greg said.

'So how's the patient?' Detective Constable Whyte asked.

'They're doing some tests on her at the moment,' Steffie said.

'Well, we hope everything's going to be all right,' the sergeant said. 'And in the meantime—' Whatever he was going to say, he didn't finish for he was interrupted by the arrival of Dr Mills, who was looking flummoxed.

'Excuse me,' Dr Mills said to Steffie, 'but could I grab you for a moment? Perhaps in Jemima's room?' The doctor glanced at the detectives as he spoke, before turning back to Steffie and Greg.

'Of course,' Steffie said.

They walked down the corridor in silence and turned into Jemima's room. The space felt barren without her.

'It's concerning one of Jemima's blood test results,' Dr Mills said.

'Oh?' Steffie said, wrapping her arms around her, her heart skipping a beat. Greg was stood beside her, swaying slightly. She had noticed that the more tired they got, the less still they were.

'I'm sorry to have to tell you this,' Dr Mills began, avoiding eye contact, shifting his feet, 'but she had drugs in her bloodstream.'

Steffie and Greg both talked at once. 'What? I don't believe it!'

'That's not possible!' Greg said. 'Absolutely no way!'

'Again,' Dr Mills said, 'I'm sorry. But there's no arguing with the results. It's pretty conclusive.'

There was a noise behind them. 'Knock knock,' said Detective Sergeant Lamb, hovering in the doorway. 'Mind if we join you?'

Steffie didn't know what to say. The doctor was looking at her and Greg for guidance.

'That's fine,' Greg said, folding his arms, standing with his legs astride. 'Come on in. We're not bothered.'

Steffie felt bothered – immensely; Greg looked it too.

'Can you tell us what the medication was?' Greg asked.

Dr Mills paused, glanced at the sergeant, then turned to Steffie. 'Are you OK with this being discussed in front—'

'Yes,' she said firmly. 'Go ahead.'

She was taking her cue from Greg: that they had nothing to hide; even though her insides begged to differ.

'It was diazepam,' Dr Mills said at last. 'A standard dosage for an adult – a lot for a child.'

Steffie felt herself jolt in alarm. She gripped her jumper sleeves, her arms still wrapped about her waist. She was cold. It was cold in here.

'What the heck's diazepam?' said Greg.

'It's an anti-anxiety medication,' Dr Mills said, his voice respectfully subdued. 'It's a fairly standard prescription for anxiety and depression.'

'Huh,' said Detective Sergeant Lamb.

That was all he said, but the word hung heavily between them all.

'Well, I need to dash,' said Dr Mills. 'But I'll be back later if time permits.' And he left the room, causing Steffie to feel suddenly under-represented, exposed.

No one spoke for a while.

And then Detective Sergeant Lamb broke the silence. 'So Jemima had diazepam in her bloodstream when she fell?' he said, in his strange non-lip-moving manner of speaking. He had shaved this morning – had a nick on his chin that he had blotted with a piece of tissue paper that he'd evidently forgotten to remove. Steffie stared at that tiny fragment of white – at the dot of blood in its centre, like a bull's-eye.

'So it would seem,' Greg said.

The sergeant stepped away from the window ledge where he had been resting his elbows and stood up straight, his hands in his pockets. 'We don't wish to be intrusive. We know this is a delicate situation. But would you mind if we asked you a few questions – had a little chat about this?'

Steffie nodded.

'If at any point you wish to—' the sergeant began.

'It's fine,' Greg interjected, but his voice sounded strained.

'You see . . . I think this explains why Jemima fell.'

'It does?' Greg said.

'Yes,' the sergeant said. 'The bar that she fell from is in perfect working order. Even if she somehow lost her grip, she could have landed safely on to the beams. It was no worse than jumping from a tree. Sort of thing any kid could do . . . But Jemima went straight through the floorboards.'

Steffie winced, inhaled sharply. She kept her eye on the scrap of tissue on his chin, watching it as he talked, wondering why it hadn't come unfixed yet.

231

'But now it makes more sense,' he said. 'I can see how an athletic girl like Jemima managed to fall.'

He took off his watch with a flash of gold; rubbed the mark it had left on his wrist. Then he clipped it back on, shook his hand, looked at them both in turn.

'I don't suppose,' he said, 'either of you have ever had cause to use diazepam, or would know how Jemima came to have something like that in her possession?'

'No,' Greg said. 'Absolutely not.' He was looking at Steffie for affirmation. And then his face changed. She saw it – the flicker of something there: recollection, realisation, fear.

'No,' she said. 'Me neither.'

Greg's eyes widened slightly and then he looked down, away.

'You neither what?' said Detective Sergeant Lamb. 'You haven't ever taken diazepam, or you don't know how she had it in her possession?'

'Both,' she said.

'Then how did she manage to take it, would you say?'

'No idea,' Greg said. 'Jemima's just not like that. There's no way that she would have willingly taken a drug.'

The sergeant shrugged one shoulder. 'Maybe. Maybe not. Or maybe you don't know your daughter as well as you thought you did.'

And there was the abruptness that he had warned them about last night.

Detective Constable Whyte stepped away from the wall he had been leaning against. 'I'm a parent too,' he said congenially. 'Got two teenage daughters. God knows what they get up to.'

Steffie appreciated the commiseration, but she wanted to tell him otherwise, could feel herself growing warm with indignation. Maybe he didn't know where his daughters were, but she and Jemima were very close. They spent a lot of time together and there was nothing that she didn't know about her.

But then she thought: What if the sergeant were right?

He didn't appear to be testing or provoking them, but speaking frankly as though he said this sort of thing all the time to parents, which he probably did – delivering the disturbing news that all along you thought your child was one thing and all along they were something else.

Was that what was happening here – the piece in the picture that Steffie couldn't fathom?

She gazed at the space where Jemima's bed normally stood and felt its emptiness fill her too, as she realised that the girl in polka-dot leggings and the ice-skater sweater, with arrow eyebrows and French attitude and leaping legs and love of all things cherry, was an illusion of sorts; as colourless and transparent as the liquid in her drip sustaining her.

Steffie couldn't see the minutiae any more, the precious, delicious, evocative details that she had longed to freeze. That child was gone.

And in her place was a silent, lifeless child whose secrets slept with her.

Steffie felt the weight of disappointment inside her, felt her body sagging with despair.

The sergeant turned to Greg. 'This could be a serious crime, Mr Lee,' he said. 'If this is grievous bodily harm with intent, then someone could be looking at nine to sixteen years in custody.'

'Bloody hell,' Greg said, exhaling heavily.

'Bloody hell indeed,' the sergeant agreed. 'And as I said last night, I intend to find out exactly what happened to your daughter. If someone's behind this, then I'll get them. Mark my words.'

Steffie could hear the men still talking, shaking hands, but she wasn't really listening. She was letting herself catch up with what was going on. She was thinking. Minuscule calculations and chemical shifts were taking place within her, as her internal workings deduced that things were becoming a little too much to bear. She felt her heart beat pick up, her mouth go dry.

And as she did, one tiny speck of dust floated into her line of vision, falling softly, utterly undetected by anyone else.

AUDITION CANDIDATE NO.4

No. I didn't go into the rec room, or anywhere near it. I don't even know what it is. What is it?

I was in the café the whole time with my mum and dad. My sister Savannah needed the toilet so I took her. But that's the only time I left.

Can I go now? I'm starving.

Freddie Rawlings
Phoenix Academy of Performing Arts
Surrey Police interview transcript
20 February 2016

TWENTY

'Jemima's arousal system has been damaged. So the brainstem and forebrain are reorganising their activity. Unfortunately there are no changes yet, but I'm hoping to see faster EEG waves as Jemima begins to recover her wake–sleep cycles.'

'But should we be worried that nothing's happening?' Greg asked. 'Does that mean there's a chance that she might stay in a coma?'

'There's always a chance of that, I'm afraid, which is why I told you yesterday to prepare yourselves for anything. Some coma patients take years to wake up. Others have been known to suddenly sit up and get back on with their lives as if nothing's happened. We now think that perhaps this is because the brain was processing information even during an unresponsive period . . .'

Steffie was watching the space behind the doctor's head, the fiercely white sky through the window beyond. It had stopped snowing. The sun was out – a late afternoon sunshine that tinged the snow and clouds with a line of berry-red on the horizon, as though it were the crisp topping of a crème brûlée that she could crack with a spoon.

She was hungry. And dejected. And so tired.

She realised that both men were looking at her.

'Sorry?' she said.

'Questions,' Dr Mills said. 'Do you have any?'

'No, thank you,' Steffie said.

'Well, that's it for today. I'll see you in the morning. Try to get some rest. I know it's tempting to sit up with Jemima, but there's no knowing how long this could go on for. There's an onsite hotel if—'

'We're fine here,' said Greg, holding up his hand.

As the doctor left the room, Steffie looked at Greg. He was almost bearded now. She had never seen him with an almost beard.

'Maybe you should spend tonight at the hotel,' she said. 'We could take it in turns, if that makes you feel any better.'

'Maybe,' he said. 'But not yet.'

She understood. Sleeping elsewhere would feel like a betrayal, like abandoning Jemima. But soon they would be forced by necessity to leave in search of sleep.

'Maybe we should get some fresh air, stretch our legs,' Greg said, joining her at the window. 'If our feet get wet, we can always put them on the radiators.' He tapped the radiator nearest them.

'OK,' she said.

They got their coats, their movements typically clumsy, slow; and were leaving the room when Steffie said, 'Wait.'

She went to Jemima's side, stood looking over her. She and the nurses had just bathed her using warm damp towels. It wasn't a great success because of the wires and casts, but it was something and Jemima seemed more rested for it – or maybe it was just Steffie that felt better.

She felt it again then: that aching feeling of something being wrong, not only because of Jemima's condition, but because of their relationship, which felt impaired too.

She felt something fizzing in a dark corner of her body – a

truth that, were she more able-minded at that point, she would have acknowledged and identified.

But as it was, she clapped her gloved hands dully together, and said, 'Let's go.'

The main entrance of the Royal Hospital was like a modern version of a drawbridge: a white grid above the door suspended on poles. The whole thing looked as though it could snap down at any minute, barring entry.

The light was bright after being indoors all day. Steffie squinted as she looked about, hand above her eyes. There were a few cars and minibuses scattered around the forecourt, their tops laden with snow. The road opposite was grumbling with traffic. Immediately before them was a lawn that was cultivating baby trees that were feeble with winter, huddling together in bunches, like scrawny children.

'This way?' Greg said, pointing to the path that ran alongside the hospital. She nodded and they set off, snow creaking underfoot.

They got to the end of the path and came to a glass building. 'Here?' he said.

Again, she nodded and they traversed the length of the mirrored building, their reflections walking beside them. What would they look like, she wondered? A dishevelled woman with wild hair; an unshaven man in a tramp's coat.

'We've not really had a chance to speak since the police,' Greg said. It was true. They had been surrounded by staff since then, had been waiting in Jemima's room for the EEG test results. 'What are your thoughts?'

'I don't know,' she said.

'But you're shocked about the drug, about the ...?' He stalled, unable to recall its name.

'Diazepam,' she said.

He did a double take at her. 'Wasn't that . . . ?' he began.

'What?' she said.

'I thought perhaps—'

'No,' she said, cutting him and the subject off.

He knew her tone of voice – could read her well. And he said no more.

They arrived at a map on stilts, buried in snow. Greg wiped the map with his glove. 'You are here' appeared.

Steffie stamped her feet, watched her breath appearing and then disappearing before her.

'According to this, there's a place down here where we could try to get something to eat, if you fancy it?' Greg said.

'All right,' she said. 'Although I'm not very hungry.'

'Me neither,' he said. 'But if we don't eat something solid, we won't last.'

They turned the corner of the glass building and faced a stone building with pillars and a courtyard. A lady was walking across the courtyard towards them, her head bent, not looking around her. She knew where she was heading, Steffie supposed; or else she didn't care.

They made their way through an archway to the door beyond. The grandiose entryway reminded Steffie of Danube House, of the fact that it was only yesterday that they had arrived there with Jemima for her audition, and the thought pushed her further into melancholia, further into her coat.

As they entered the building, they were greeted by a blast of warm beefy air. They were near a restaurant. Signposts on chains dangled above their heads, wobbling.

'This way, I think,' Greg said.

They walked halfway down the corridor, Steffie glancing at the artwork on the walls: enlarged photographs of people smiling, mouths stretched, eyes laughing.

'Here we are,' Greg said, pointing to a closed door with glass panels in. Beyond, Steffie could see people carrying trays, could hear muted conversations.

She ran a hand through her hair, felt her hair tingling and rising with static.

Greg was looking at her oddly, hesitantly. 'Steffie ...' he began. He paused, unbuttoned his coat. 'Did you tell the police the truth?'

She stared up at him. 'The truth?' she said. 'About what?'

'About that drug.'

'Of course,' she said.

'Oh,' he said. 'It's just that I thought—'

'You thought what?'

He gazed at her and then shook his head. 'Nothing,' he said.

Greg was determined to sleep. He had asked one of the nurses for a pillow and a blanket, and was lying in the chair, his legs stretched out, arms folded. It was uncomfortable, but he was starting to realise that they could be here for the long haul and if he didn't sleep soon he would be incapable of making any decisions if required.

It took several hours for him to become drowsy. But in the early hours of the morning, the ward finally fell silent and the beeps on Jemima's monitor were more subdued. He didn't know whether this was his own body shutting down or if the nurses had turned the volume down on the equipment and on their own voices. But his last thought was: Ah, bliss.

And then he sat up so quickly that his pillow toppled and his head spun with dizziness.

Steffie was screaming.

'Get away! *Get away from her!*'

His head flooded with panic. He looked about him for a

weapon – saw the desk lamp that the nurse had given him earlier. He grabbed it as he stood up, the plug ripping from the wall socket. And then he threw it to where Steffie was pointing. It smashed against the wall and fell with a clatter.

There was the sound of running footsteps and the room was swamped in light. He put his hands to his face and stared about him in confusion, at the smashed lamp and splintered glass on the floor; at Steffie crouching on her pull-out bed; at the two nurses who were looking about in alarm; at Jemima lying on her back, her fractured limb in casts, her eyes closed, her oxygen mask in place, her drip secure.

'What the hell d'you think you're doing?' shouted one of the nurses. 'There's glass everywhere. Did you throw that lamp? You could have hit the patient!'

'I'll get a dustpan,' said the other nurse, hurrying from the room.

Greg was staring about him, stunned.

'Are you all right?' the nurse was saying, rubbing Steffie's back.

Steffie was opening and closing her mouth like a fish, just as silent as one.

'Can you speak?'

Greg leant back against the radiator, his legs heavy. The nurse was right: he could have hit Jemima, could have injured her on top of everything else. The lamp was an old industrial-looking one – a bulky thing.

'There was someone there,' Steffie was saying.

'Where?' the nurse said, looking in the direction where Steffie was pointing.

'By Jemima,' she said. 'They were going to hurt her.'

'Who?' the nurse said.

Her colleague had returned, was crouched down, sweeping the floor and picking up the large shards of glass by hand.

241

'Here,' Greg said, 'let me do that.' He took the dustpan and brush from her. 'I'm really sorry.'

The nurse tutted and moved away. Their primary concern was their patient. Men throwing heavy lamps were not acceptable or welcome on the children's ward. In that moment, he felt as though he were paying for every serial killer, rapist and abuser of his gender.

And then the nurse shouted as Steffie gulped for breath and fell forward on to the floor.

Greg dropped the dustpan, glass tinkling behind him as he dashed forward. 'She's passed out,' the nurse said, cradling Steffie in her lap on the floor. 'Get Nathan,' she said. The other nurse hurried from the room.

Greg knelt down. Steffie had opened her eyes. The nurse was stroking her forehead. 'It's all right,' the nurse was saying. 'It's all right.'

'Greg,' she said, looking petrified.

'It's OK, Steffie,' he said.

The other nurse returned with the night doctor, who sat Steffie up, held a finger before her, listened to her heart, looked in her ears and eyes, asked her her name, age, what day of the week it was.

Steffie had gone white. She was shivering, straining to draw breath, her eyes large and staring.

The doctor didn't seem concerned. He was talking in a low voice to one of the nurses.

Greg indicated that he would like a word in the corridor. 'What happened?' Greg asked him, when they were out of earshot of Steffie.

'Panic attack,' the doctor replied matter-of-factly. 'No doubt due to the stressful circumstances. The system becomes overloaded so it blacks out, like flicking a switch. Sort of a time-out, if you like.'

'A time-out,' Greg said pensively.

'Does she suffer from anxiety?' the doctor asked, licking his lips. He looked tired, thirsty. He frowned, waiting for Greg's response.

'You what?' Greg said.

'Anxiety,' the doctor repeated. 'Does she suffer from any form of it?'

'Yes,' Greg said. 'And no.'

'Oh? So which is it?'

'Well, she. . . ' Greg glanced over his shoulder, lowered his voice. '. . .She suffered from a phobia in the past. But I was led to believe that it was all better, that she was better.'

'I see,' the doctor said. 'Well ... emergency over. She's probably just exhausted. Make sure she gets some rest.' And he walked away, his Crocs squelching as though wet.

Greg watched the blue of the doctor's medical tunic until it had disappeared around the corner of the ward.

Then he thought about what to say and do next.

The nurses were busying themselves with Jemima now – checking her vitals, changing her drip.

Steffie was sitting on the pull-out bed. She was still shivering. He reached for her coat, draped it over her shoulders.

'Would you like me to make you a nice cup of tea, Mum?' the nurse asked Steffie. They had finished with Jemima.

Steffie made no response.

The nurse frowned in concern at Greg.

'Don't worry,' he said. 'We'll go along to the family room in a minute.'

'Right you are, then,' the nurse said. 'Give us a shout if you need us.' And they left the room.

Steffie turned to him. 'I thought I was dying,' she said. 'I couldn't breathe. My chest was so tight. And I couldn't hear. All I could hear was this hissing noise and . . .'

'It's OK,' he said, holding her hand. 'The doctor said it was understandable . . . Look what we're going through. You'd have to have nerves of steel not to be affected.'

'But what if it's come back? What if it's like before? What if. . .?'

He gripped her hand more forcibly than he had intended. 'Nothing bad's going to happen,' he said. 'This isn't like before. It's all going to be OK.' He loosened his grip.

She didn't look convinced. She was trying to smile. The sight of it made his heart wobble.

'I think you should sleep in the hotel tomorrow night,' he said. 'You need some rest.'

She nodded slowly with an expression that said, *We'll see.*

They said no more. He moved his chair to be next to her, to remain by her side for reassurance. As the silence fell again, he felt his eyes grow heavy with fatigue, and doubt.

He knew Steffie – knew when she was lying, when she was frightened, when she was hiding something.

If he had noticed the look of alarm on her face when the sergeant named the drug in Jemima's bloodstream, then surely the detectives would have done too.

They remained sitting like that – upright, without tea, without distraction or conversation – until dawn crept forward, across the snowy fields, ravaging the lawn of Danube House, creeping across the sleeping houses of Guildford to the Royal Hospital, where it tapped on the glass, crackled against the concrete, snapped their bones into standing and stretching; for a new day had arrived.

PARENT OF CANDIDATE
ZACHARY WILLIAMS

Zach's idea to go into the rec room? Are you kidding? I mean, Zach's my main man and all that. But the lad's never had an idea in his life!

Sorry . . . That's my phone . . . Just need to get this.

Mr T. Williams
Phoenix Academy of Performing Arts
Surrey Police telephone interview transcript
21 February 2016

TWENTY-ONE

Helena spent Monday morning unwrapping a delivery of greetings cards and putting them on the revolving rack. It was a slow day, snowing lumps of sleet, which was keeping people indoors by fires, and she was glad. She was too distracted to serve customers enthusiastically, could just about hold her hand out, take the money and that was it.

She kept her phone in her cardigan pocket, hoping that Steffie would ring with an update. She hadn't been able to sleep last night. So tired, she had taken the bus this morning instead of driving since she didn't feel safe behind the wheel. Far easier to let someone else take responsibility.

She gazed at the Easter card in her hand. Easter was early this year, just over four weeks away. She wondered whether Jemima would be home for it, would be well enough to do Greg's annual egg hunt at the lodge – foraging through wet rubbery plants, reaching into Jurassic undergrowth; *epic!*; pastel eggs mounting in the basket.

She moaned mournfully, continued putting the cards on the rack.

But what else had she just been thinking? About the driver of the bus taking responsibility. Helena had always been a bit like that – not lazy, but happy to relinquish control. She had never wanted to be a leader, not even of her own family; had always preferred to be led, within reason.

Her easy-going nature had suited the parenting style of the seventies, during a time when most mums had spent their days ironing, listening to the radio, preparing supper for husbands who expected a meal On The Dot. There were exceptions – plenty of them; it was just that Helena hadn't known of any in Wimborne. Parenting had been a bit vague, ethereal almost. The days were long, seat belts weren't law, cars smelt of petrol inside, washing machines broke down, the television needed time to warm up.

Motherhood back then had been rather like sitting on the bus, as opposed to driving it. There had been no point trying to take control because there had been little to take control of. There were no SATs, risk assessments, anti-bullying policies, key stages. It was a case of seeing your child off to school and then getting on with shelling peas or organising the airing cupboard.

Parenting had been practical then, in the main, focusing on manual skills: baking, sewing, gardening, painting, mending.

But modern mums had evolved into something infinitely more powerful. They weren't the rats on the wheels, but the ones turning them. They were drivers, not passengers. Practical was passé, to a certain extent; and in its wake had come knowledge.

Today's mums were astonishingly knowledgeable, Helena felt. They knew everything about everything – nutrition, healthcare, education – and how to apply that knowledge to everyday life. They went to the playground, meetings, doctors, coffee mornings, internet forums, armed with information that they used defensively, aggressively, helpfully, compassionately, as required.

To know all that – to have all that knocking around one's mind – would be exhausting. Yet modern life virtually demanded it. For if you didn't know how to do things, to do them well, on time, to maximum effect, then you would be caught short, found lacking.

Caught by whom precisely? Probably by one's self. Because from what Helena had observed in Steffie, sometimes the taskmaster driving her on each day was none other than herself. She didn't want to fail, to let anyone down.

Helena realised that her phone was ringing. A customer had entered the shop at the same time. She hesitated then reversed rapidly behind the counter, where she took the call.

It was Greg. He was speaking softly, saying something that she didn't catch.

'I beg your pardon?' she said. 'Can you speak up a bit?'

'Would you be able to come to Guildford?' he said.

'Uh ...' She thought for a moment. The answer was obvious, needed little contemplation, yet she was at an age where few responses were immediate or spontaneous. She was thinking stupidly of watering her plants, how much milk there was in the fridge, whether the ham would go off. 'Yes. Of course.'

'Good,' he said. 'There's a train station here. There'll be cabs outside, I'd imagine ... Ask for the Royal Hospital. And I'll settle up with you later.'

'Nonsense,' she said. 'I won't hear of it.'

'Well, we can argue about that when you're here,' he said.

She watched the customer who was flicking through a book on sheds – one of those amusing books that made gifts for men when desperate. 'What shall I do about the shop?' Helena said.

'Just put a note on the door saying closed for a few days.'

'OK,' she said. 'If that's all right with Steffie ... Does she know you're phoning me?' And then she suddenly realised what he was saying. 'What's happening, Greg?' She put her hand on the counter to steady herself. 'Is it Jemima?'

248

She had raised her voice. The customer was looking at her inquisitively.

Helena bent her head, gazed at the floor.

'It's not Jemima,' he said. 'There's no change there.'

'Then what?' she asked.

But she knew the answer.

She was a mother. And practical or not, bus driver or passenger, collector of Jasperware Wedgwood or Facebook Likes, she knew her child.

'It's Steffie, isn't it?' she said, feeling her face drain of colour.

'Yes,' he said. 'Just get here when you can.'

It was busy on the ward that afternoon. A new patient had arrived in the room opposite just after lunch and there had been a terrible kerfuffle – the mother crying hysterically, nurses running, alarms sounding. The child – a toddler, by the sounds of it – was evidently in a lot of pain, kept shouting, *Mummy, Mummy, Mummy!* Steffie had listened to the ordeal from inside their room, with her hand gripping Jemima's bed rail and her body tense. She had wanted to offer help, to do something, but as usual here felt an awful sense of redundancy – of being unable to change the situation.

Finally, when the child was sedated or the pain had subsided, Steffie could hear only the mother's sobs and a lower rumbling voice comforting her – the father, perhaps.

Steffie wondered what was wrong with the child – sensed that whatever it was the parents would eventually leave here changed in some way. They wouldn't know the change right away, but it would be there. Because no matter how much people told you that the past didn't count, that it was the present that was important, everyone knew that certain experiences – war, poverty, disease, death – never left the soul.

And now all was still. Steffie was sitting on her own beside her sleeping daughter – Greg had gone for a walk and the staff were preoccupied with other patients. Steffie could hear voices at the end of the corridor, footsteps hurrying; but as far as their little corner of the ward was concerned – the space occupied by Steffie and the faceless mother opposite – their children slept.

She gazed at Jemima, placed her hand on a small part of skin on Jemima's arm that wasn't covered by medical paraphernalia or a blanket. That was all she was allowed, that inch of her daughter.

She sighed, yawned. She was exhausted, yet sleep wouldn't come, especially not at night in a ward where darkness never fell and activity never ceased.

She was feeling rather sheepish about the fuss she had made during the night. It had been a long time since she had had a phobia attack. She hadn't expected to ever have one again.

There was a time before when dust had ruled her life, had brought her out in a chilling sweat, had driven her to bed. Yet she hadn't gone for therapy, hadn't discussed the problem with anyone but Greg – had even hidden it from her mother.

And she thought she had beaten it. But life thought differently. And the irony of anxiety was that it came to a head exactly when you needed it to disappear.

Greg had been extra careful around her this morning. He had a right to be concerned, but still... she found it vexing. It was the same patronising manner with which medical staff had treated her after childbirth, she recalled – taking any mention of tiredness or worry as a sign of neurosis or post-natal depression, scoring her responses out of ten on their mental health charts. She had found herself cracking jokes constantly back then, setting her face at Smile in the doctor's waiting room.

Perhaps it was then that she had begun to use humour as a mask, like her counsellor, Yvonne, had said.

Anxiety and motherhood often went hand in hand, yet were not allowed to.

She had hidden her phobia not only because she was ashamed of it, but also for fear of being accused of being a bad mother, of having her baby taken away. Because that was what sometimes happened to parents who failed to meet the grade.

Everything was graded now, from children to parents. No one escaped unassessed.

And now her mother was on her way; proof that Greg thought that she was unable to handle this without support.

She would be pleased to see her mum, who would arrive with smiles and open arms, disguising all the worry and concern. *Is Steffie coping?*

She yawned again, rubbed her eyes.

A sudden, quiet rap on the door made her look up. She hadn't heard anyone coming, wasn't expecting anyone.

To her surprise, it was Mr Alexandrov, clutching a paper bag. '*Ballet Shoes*,' he said, smiling. 'And music.'

'You didn't have to do that,' she said, smiling frailly in welcome. Today, one day deeper into hospital life, she wasn't self-conscious before this man, no longer cared about whether she looked ghastly, which she no doubt did.

She glanced at her toffee-coloured nails that had felt so exotic only days before, applied so carefully in order to impress at the auditions – in order also, if she were frank, to pretty herself in light of Olivia's glamorous appearance – and which now appeared utterly irrelevant, banal.

Mr Alexandrov stepped forward warily, halting a metre from the foot of Jemima's bed. Just the sight of him made Steffie feel woeful, for he represented all that was past: Jemima's health, her gift for dance, her future.

'How is she today?' he asked.

'There's no change, I'm afraid,' she said. 'They did some

more tests this morning, but the doctor said there was no improvement.'

'That's disappointing,' he said, putting the bag down on Greg's chair.

That was already Greg's chair, and this one hers, she thought. Funny how quickly humans claimed things as their own, set up routines, owned spaces, in even the most paltry conditions and settings.

'Is there anything else I can get you, or do for you?' Mr Alexandrov said.

She had temporarily forgotten he was there. He was standing so still, he blended into the backdrop.

'No,' she said. 'But thank you for the book ... I'll read it to Jemima.'

'Good,' he said, bowing his head slightly. 'Well, I'll leave you in peace.'

She nodded goodbye, and he left.

Really, there was nothing more they could say, nothing more he could do.

She wondered briefly whether they would ever see him again.

She rose to collect the paper bag from the chair and sat back down with it. Inside, was a hardback edition of *Ballet Shoes*, and a CD called *An Evening at the Ballet*.

The sight of the beautiful book caught her breath. She opened the cover, which creaked softly, and held the book to her nose, smelling the scent of unread pages.

There was a flutter as something fell from the book to the floor. She bent to pick it up. It was a compliments slip from the Phoenix Academy. There was something written on it in blue ink.

Never give up, Jemima.
Mikhail Alexandrov x

She gazed at the curly handwriting, at the kind sentiments. This was something that she would have cried at before. But her emotions had entered a vacuum until further notice.

So she tucked the slip inside the book, opened it to chapter one, and began to read.

As she read, the sun came out with sudden ferocity. Dust danced in the warm rays above Jemima's bed, a veritable swarm of particles.

Steffie was suddenly aware of footsteps approaching rapidly down the corridor, raised voices. She lowered the book and the floor wobbled beneath her, as though it were a treadmill just starting. She stared in concern, but the floor was still again.

And then the detectives entered the room.

'Mrs Lee,' the sergeant said. 'Here on your own?'

Greg had gone to stretch his legs – a quick walk around the corridors to brush off his fatigue. He wasn't just weary because of trying to sleep in a chair on a ward, but because sitting endlessly beside Jemima was disquietingly tiring. It was like sitting on a coach for a very long time without air conditioning or distraction; except that they weren't going anywhere.

Jemima's lack of movement dulled the senses, reminding him that intimacy was all about exchange. It made him realise that love was all about the impression that it made on the recipient. Loving someone was all about watching the other person's reaction – their mutual confessions, or kisses, or rebuttals. It wasn't about feeling it and not channelling it. To love was to pass it on.

And here was Jemima, unable to pass it on. All their love was flowing towards her and it was resting there, blocked, static. If it were a force field, she would have a yellow glow all around her; for love was not pink or red, as one might be led to believe by the Valentine's Day industry, but yellow, Greg sensed, like the sun. It was nurturing, warming, healthy; apart from when it was blocked. And then it was yellow for old, stale, unreplenished.

What would happen if it didn't get replenished? he thought. What would happen if she didn't pull through, if she didn't wake up?

He shook his head, tried to think of something else. But it was hard to. All he could see was yellow, and sadness, and exhaustion.

He didn't get very far with his walk, realised that perhaps he would be better off going back, getting Steffie and going outside now that the sun was out, rather than stumbling around the corridors. He always ended up getting lost, unable to get his bearings, having to rely on some doctor to point him back the right way.

When he got back to their ward, he was just about to clap his hands and force his voice into cheerful, when he saw the detectives in their room, their suits seeming big against the barren décor.

'Oh,' Greg said in surprise. There was always a possibility that the men would return, would be here at any given point. Yet he hadn't expected them somehow, hadn't wanted them here. It felt intrusive. He was beginning to care less about the case, cared more about Jemima waking up. The detectives took away from that, detracted from the most important thing.

He rested his hands on Jemima's bed rail, trying not to betray his thoughts with anything but a pleasant expression. Steffie was sitting in her usual spot at Jemima's side, holding a new book on her lap. He noticed the paper bag on the other chair. Evidently Alexandrov had been and gone.

'Hello, Mr Lee,' said Detective Sergeant Lamb.

The sergeant looked more dishevelled than usual – his hair sticking up, a handkerchief hanging from his trouser pocket. Greg glanced at Detective Constable Whyte, who was chewing slowly, looking slightly bored – an affectation, Greg suspected, intended to catch them off guard. The atmosphere didn't feel hostile, exactly; more cagey, he felt.

'We were just updating your wife on progress,' the sergeant said, 'concerning the medication in Jemima's bloodstream.'

'Oh right?' said Greg.

'We found a bottle of diazepam in a bin in the ladies' toilets near the studios in the academy,' Detective Constable Whyte said. 'It was prescribed by a GP in Bracknell. Do you know anyone in Bracknell, sir?'

'Bracknell,' said Greg. 'I don't . . .' He glanced at Steffie, who was gazing at the floor, her cheeks red in patches as though pinched.

'As you can imagine, we were very interested to find out whose bottle it was,' Detective Sergeant Lamb said. 'The name of the patient didn't match anyone on our records – no one associated with the academy. But then lots of professional women go by their maiden names.'

'They do,' Greg agreed. He folded his arms high on his chest, could feel his heart beating against his thumb.

'So it took us a while to trace its rightful owner, but when we did it was very enlightening.'

Greg looked at the two men. It was growing dark in the room, as the afternoon light dwindled. Their mouths were shadows, their noses black beaks.

'And?' he said.

The sergeant smiled. 'It belonged to Daisy Kirkpatrick's mother.'

There was a thud as Steffie dropped her book. 'I knew it!' she said.

The detectives turned to look at her. 'You did?'

Steffie blushed, bent to pick up her book. 'Well, not really. I don't mean that I knew, as such. Just that . . .'

'What?' said Detective Sergeant Lamb.

She shrugged. 'I thought the mother was a bit aggressive, that was all.'

'Aggressive?' said the sergeant.

'Yes. But then I just put it down to the stress of the auditions.'

'And what about you, Mr Lee?' the sergeant said. 'Did you think Mrs Kirkpatrick was hostile?'

'Not hostile,' said Steffie. 'I didn't say hostile. I said agg—'

'Sir?' said the sergeant.

'Well, to be frank, they were all like that,' Greg said. 'I didn't think she was any different. She was just more honest, perhaps – wearing her ambition more honestly.'

'I see. So your main reaction on hearing this news is that Mrs Kirkpatrick is honest?'

Greg opened his mouth and closed it again.

He didn't like this at all. Beyond the men lay his daughter, his only child. He wanted to tell them to get the hell out, to leave them alone, in peace.

'What do the Kirkpatricks say about it?' he said. 'Shouldn't you be there, grilling them, and not us?'

'All in good time,' replied the sergeant.

There was a pause. Then the sergeant spoke softly. 'Mrs Lee ...' Steffie gazed up at him anxiously, clutching the book against her, recoiling from the sergeant as though he were formidable, even though he had food on his tie, and inky hands. 'Is there anything else you can tell us, anything you can add, that might help us find out who did this to your daughter?'

Greg found himself holding his breath, waiting for Steffie's response. Even the constable had dropped his boredom act and was staring at her with his deep-set eyes.

'There's nothing,' she said.

Greg exhaled. The sergeant tutted as though disappointed;

only a tiny sound yet it unsettled Greg. What had the man been expecting?

Steffie stood now, shook hands with the sergeant. 'Thank you for updating us,' she said. And the two men left, saying good afternoon, wishing them a good night's sleep ahead.

Greg waited for Steffie to sit back down, to pick up her book and open it again, before he pursued the detectives.

'One minute,' he called after them.

Out in the corridor, the sergeant turned expectantly. Greg led them down to the reception before speaking.

His heart was racing. He wasn't sure what he was going to say. He spoke slowly, cautiously, concerned it would come out wrong. 'Please don't keep probing Steffie,' he said.

One of the nurses on reception glanced up. Greg lowered his voice. The nurse looked back down at her paperwork.

'She's in no fit state. This is hitting her badly, as you can imagine.'

'Yes,' said Detective Sergeant Lamb, 'we realise that, Mr Lee. But we have a job to do and we have to do it thoroughly ... You want a result, don't you?'

'Yes,' said Greg. 'Of course.'

'Then what is it that you're saying?' said Detective Constable Whyte, hands in pockets, legs astride. Away from the niceties of conversations by Jemima's bed or in the family room, this man was belligerent, Greg thought.

'That I'd like you to go easy on her,' Greg said.

'Go easy?' asked the sergeant, playing dumb.

'Yes,' said Greg, tiring of the sport. 'Whatever it is that you're looking for, it's nothing to do with her, with us.' He hesitated, then pressed ahead. 'You won't achieve anything by pushing her. You're just upsetting her.'

'So what would you propose that we do?' said Detective Sergeant Lamb.

'Just involve her less,' Greg said. 'If you need anything, come to me. But try to leave Steffie out of it. She's got enough on her plate.'

The sergeant was narrowing his eyes at Greg, his mouth open. After a few moments of speculation, he said, 'Fine,' and nodded. He slapped Greg's arm in farewell. And then they left, their footsteps clicking down the corridor, until they were no more.

TUTOR OF JEMIMA LEE

Medication? That is abominable! Completely inadvisable before an audition. Anyone who would think of administering drugs to a child to improve performance is utterly reprehensible, immoral in the extreme. They are just children, for goodness' sake. *Enfants*!

Oh. Well, I just assumed that it was to *improve* the performance . . .

Oh. Am I wrong?

Well, it was just an assumption.

No, it wasn't based on anything.

Ms N. Chamoulaud
Phoenix Academy of Performing Arts
Surrey Police telephone interview transcript
21 February 2016

TWENTY-TWO

Back home, in Wimborne, at the studio, in normal life, Noella could not settle. The day's sessions had gone past in a blur: a toddlers' dance class called Grasshoppers; a seniors' ballroom dance and coffee session, where she normally encouraged the pensioners to linger and socialise over Fondant Fancies. Today she could barely tolerate her pupils, had ushered them out with a tight smile and had closed the door promptly, leaning back against it in relief.

The police had phoned several times and she had successfully avoided them, but eventually she would have to answer.

What did they want with her?

No one had mentioned the trace of alcohol in Jemima's bloodstream yet. Maybe the matter had been clouded by something else, or the alcohol hadn't been detected, or wasn't of importance. If it did come up, she would flatly deny all knowledge.

Whatever the case, she sensed that no one would ever know about her minor indiscretion; unless Jemima told.

Career-wise, Jemima telling would be a small disaster for Noella. She hadn't broken any laws, but no one would entrust their children to her care thereafter.

Perhaps, in the event of that happening, she would move away – return to Paris even.

That was a possibility. But to run a dance school in Paris would be well beyond her means. She would be forced to the provinces, to the sidelines there, as well as here.

She gazed around her empty studio. She had hated it here, and yet now to have to give this up too? It felt insufferable.

She was truly repentant for what she had done. The entire thing had manifested because she had wanted to be recognised at last for her talent. And yet it had brought her nothing.

She sank down on to the floor and began to cry. She had always loathed crying – felt it to be weak, defeatist, and no more so than now.

And then she thought of something, of someone: Delphine.

And for the first time, the thought of her old room-mate didn't cause her to writhe with guilt but to leap up with something that felt rather like hope.

She ran to the cupboard behind the piano and flicked the light on within. Down from the shelf she pulled the shoebox once more and rested it on top of the grand piano, snatching off the lid impatiently.

She couldn't see what she wanted immediately, so tipped the box upside down, not caring about the mess, about whether anything perished. When she had found what she wanted, she would dispose of the rest anyway.

There it was.

She sat on the piano stool, holding a postcard. It was a note she had written to Delphine shortly after the accident.

She gazed at her childish handwriting – so big and gauche; loopy lettering, the dots in bold circles, exclamation marks running amok.

Guilt, fear, self-preservation had stopped her from sending the postcard. She had kept it all these years, a memento of a time when she broke a friendship, ceased communication, kept her head down – had been doing so ever since.

She turned the card over to look at the front. It was a complimentary postcard from Bartok, the sort of thing you picked up on the bar, trying to find one that wasn't beer-soaked or charred by cigarette ends.

She looked at the other side again, at the address that she had written.

Delphine had been well-connected, from money. She had spoken of a grand chateau in the Loire Valley, and a family residence in Saint Tropez, as well as an artist's studio in Montmartre, Paris, where she sometimes fled when things were too much at school.

The address Delphine had given her, that this postcard was addressed to, was the one in the Loire Valley. And it was this that Noella tapped into her phone now.

Sure enough there was a listing in an online directory for the family still at that address. But how to contact them more immediately?

She drummed her fingers on the piano, thought some more. Then she looked at the pile of junk she had emptied out of the box and rifled through it with her hands. She was sure it was here somewhere ...

Yes. There it was.

She opened a small address book. Again, it was childish: a picture on the front of a teddy bear holding roses; silly embellished handwriting inside. She ran her finger down the index, flicking the book open at the relevant page.

There Delphine was, complete with phone number.

Noella stood and leant back against the wall, gazing up at the high windows, at the snow amassed there in a fat wobbly line, like a grey moustache. The light was beginning to dip, one day ending in order to begin another indistinct, insufferable one.

The problem with being well-regarded, trusted, she thought,

was that when you did something wrong you often got away with it. It took a lot of digging to incriminate the good. And most people, unless driven by revenge or other personal motivation, didn't bother to dig.

Noella had lived for over twenty years with the concealed suspicion of having done something wrong, but not knowing quite what her part had been or how much she was to blame.

And now she found herself in the same position with the Lees.

The idea of living with more of a burden, of doubling the amount of guilt that she had to contend with was too much.

The answer lay in the past, with Delphine.

She would do what she should have done a long time ago: she would ring Delphine and ask how she was.

She would finally do the right thing.

And yet she did not call that afternoon, nor that evening. But sat instead with the book on her lap, the phone in her hand and her eyes on the growing darkness, revisiting a place in the past that she had not visited for a very long while, unable to tear herself away from its compelling secrets.

Helena arrived on the ward after teatime. The trays had been taken away but the smell of chicken curry and raspberry jelly lingered, and the habitual pre-night silence had fallen.

Hospitals were rhythmical, Greg had noticed – were places of routine that you grew accustomed to very quickly, acclimatising to the sounds and scents almost with fondness. He could recognise staff by the pace and weight of their approaching footsteps, could anticipate meals arriving on trolleys in the corridor, knew when the cleaners would come in to empty the bins, humming and whistling tunes.

Sometimes he nodded off, merely to be woken by a nurse checking Jemima's blood pressure – the crack of Velcro rousing him from sleep, although it was only just after lunch or early evening.

For somewhere so routine, time was irrelevant, eternal. And it was that that gave one the comfort – the sensation of security that came with places that were permanently open, always available. They existed whether you were there or not. When he and Steffie and Jemima left here, eventually, it would continue without them. And yet they wouldn't think of it again, only in the vaguest of terms. The routines would be forgotten, the vivid details would be no more.

So he was thinking when he heard the distinctive sound of a newcomer's footsteps, followed by a voice in the corridor. It was Helena, asking for directions; and on hearing her voice he felt a peculiar mix of happiness and sorrow.

Helena appeared hesitantly in the doorway, and then hurried forward and clasped her hand in his. They were a yard from Jemima's bed. Helena's eyes kept flitting past him to Jemima, her bottom lip trembling.

'Oh, Greg,' she said. And then she sniffed, gathering herself. She glanced around the room. 'Where's Steffie?'

'She's taking a break in the family room.'

'Oh,' said Helena. 'Well, maybe I should go and—'

'Come with me first, if you don't mind?' he said. 'Just for a quick cup of tea. I'd like to have a chat.'

'Oh,' Helena said again, pursing her lips. Then she gazed at Jemima. 'May I . . . ?'

Greg nodded, watched as his mother-in-law edged towards Jemima, holding her handbag before her. She didn't gasp or cry, but merely stood there at a suitable distance, gazing at the patient, the apparatus, the casts.

Then she gave a little nod and turned away. 'OK,' she said.

They went to the café, which was thankfully still open. Most hospitals would shut down their facilities as miserable night fell, but the Friends' café stayed open until late. Greg was sure that he wasn't the only person to be grateful for this kindness.

He ordered the drinks and returned with the tea to Helena, who was looking about her with attempted cheer. 'Well, this is nice,' she said.

'Yes,' he said, sitting down opposite her.

'So . . . what did you want to talk to me about?' she said.

She was still wearing her coat. Her hair was strangely flat; Greg didn't know much about hair but thought that it might be something to do with a recently worn hat. Some of her eye make-up was smudged. Her lipstick ran into crevices around her mouth. She was a good woman, and had not slept much lately. All of which he thought in a single glance.

'It's Steffie,' he said. 'She needs some rest. But it's impossible to sleep in that room.'

'Is there somewhere else she can go?' Helena asked.

'Yes, but she won't leave Jemima. Which is where you come in,' he said. 'I've booked a twin room for you both. The hotel's on the hospital grounds, but she'll still fight it. So I need you to persuade her to stay with you for a couple of nights until she's rested. And then we can swap round, because I'll need to sleep at some point.'

Helena nodded. 'Well, that all sounds sensible, Greg,' she said, picking up her teacup. 'I'm sure she'll see reason. It's natural for her to want to stay. But she needs to be strong for when Jemima wakes up . . .' She gazed at him, lips pursed. 'Thank you for asking me to come.'

'Thank *you*,' said Greg.

She hesitated. 'It's not been very nice being cut off at home – not knowing what's going on. I'd rather be here where I can be of use and where I can see with my own eyes what's happening, and how Steffie is.'

'Course,' said Greg. 'Hopefully it won't be too much for you.

265

It's quite gruelling, seeing Jemima ...' He trailed off, sipped his tea.

Helena sighed. 'Oh, this is a rotten business, isn't it?' she said. 'You must be exhausted too. If you like, I could stay in the room and you could sleep in the hotel?'

'That's kind of you to offer,' he said. 'But I think Steffie would be happier if I were here with Jemima. I don't mean that you're not a good substitute ...'

'It's all right,' she said. 'I understand perfectly what you meant.'

He added a lump of sugar to his tea, stirred it thoughtfully.

'Steffie had a panic attack last night,' he said. 'A phobia attack ... It seemed like before – like the old problem.'

'Oh dear,' said Helena. 'That's because of all the stress. Should she see someone? Take something? She's in the right place for medical advice.'

'No.' He shook his head. 'She won't want anyone to know. She'd kill me if she knew I was telling you.'

'I know,' Helena said. 'She always has to be seen to be coping. But I'm her mother. I know everything.' She smiled, without mirth.

'The police keep probing her, asking all sorts of questions,' he added.

Their eyes met.

There was a clattering behind them, a jangling of metal as cutlery fell to the floor. 'Good grief!' said Helena, putting her hand to her chest. 'That scared the heebie-jeebies out of me!'

The customer picked up the cutlery, the room settled; conversations resumed.

'And what about you?' Helena asked. 'How are you doing?'

'I'm OK,' he said wearily. 'The worst thing is feeling useless. There's nothing I can do for Jemima. I can't build her anything ... Can't even give her a hug.'

'You're doing something just by being here, by sitting with her day in and day out,' Helena said. She smiled consolingly. 'Somehow she knows that you're here.' She tapped his hand, before reaching again for her tea.

Greg swallowed hard, blinking back a sudden rush of hopelessness.

'What if she doesn't wake up?' he asked.

She didn't reply immediately. She held her teacup mid-air, her eyes rising upwards as she thought.

She seemed about to say something else, but changed her mind. Instead, she said, 'She will,' and left it at that.

When they returned to the room, Steffie was there. She tried to smile warmly at her mother. The two women embraced and then held hands, facing each other, talking in low voices.

Helena was telling Steffie that she needed sleep. Steffie was contesting it quietly, and then the matter was settled.

Helena's motherly dominance had won. Her opinion on what was best for Steffie superseded all others.

It had been cheap perhaps to call in the big guns, Greg thought, but Steffie was already more pink-cheeked due to her mother's presence. The two of them being together would do both women good.

Darkness had come. The world beyond was gone, the windows bluntly reflecting back their own room to them. There was no getting away tonight, no escaping the fact that Jemima was still lying there, unconscious.

Greg was moving more lethargically now, stumbling about, getting ready for a night on the fold-out bed. He said goodnight to Steffie and Helena, and then set off down the corridor to clean his teeth, wondering what fresh or stale news the morning would bring.

AUDITION CANDIDATE NO.5

I go to auditions all the time. They're boring. My parents make me dance because everyone they know has talents and they want me to have one too so that I'm not at home when they're trying to chillax. My dad pretends he's my best buddy but if he liked me that much he wouldn't always be on his phone. I don't even think he knows how to speak Japanese.

Jemima Lee seemed all right. I s'pose she won't be here in September, now that she's practically dead.

Zachary Williams
Phoenix Academy of Performing Arts
Surrey Police interview transcript
20 February 2016

TWENTY-THREE

Noella was sitting alone in her kitchen, her phone and the old teddy bear address book from Paris on the counter beside her. She was eating yesterday's risotto cold, with a glass of dry white wine. The risotto was not wonderful, but it would do. She had never been fussy about food, had never practised the level of mindfulness that meant that she paid attention to what she was eating. Rather, she ate on the run, or whilst tending to paperwork.

It had evolved from the fact that her family's mealtimes had been a physical activity, as opposed to sedentary. Food had been laid out on the long wooden table and her brothers came in and out, flicking flies away, stuffing home-made *pain au chocolat* into their mouths, cupping chicken drumsticks in their hands before rushing off again.

Her mother hadn't seemed to mind about this – hadn't striven for any sense of cohesion at mealtimes, nor any recognition. She had appeared happy, or at least prepared to accept her role as domestic servant. There were no thanks that Noella could recall. She couldn't even remember her mother ever sitting down and talking to them – sharing a joke, telling a story. She had been a shadowy form, endlessly rolling pastry, sugar shaking, carrying dripping laundry to the line, pegs stuck in mouth like monster teeth.

It was this early image of motherhood that had put Noella off for life. On the occasions when she had become close to a man in Paris – had considered, whilst languidly running a finger along a taut hairy chest, whether or not she might ever succumb to marriage or babies – her fantasies had been curdled by the thought of a life of slavery, exhaustion, over-eating.

How accurate a forecast that had been, she couldn't say.

All she knew was that she was here eating risotto, very slim, very alone.

She hadn't been the only one. Many of her ballet friends had sacrificed having babies in favour of careers. You couldn't perform whilst pregnant. And afterwards, the return to form would be long and arduous, if even attempted.

There were those who had their cake and ate it – albeit in tiny portions. A slim tall ballerina in Paris had carried her baby like a ping-pong ball underneath her sweater, taking the briefest of interludes before returning as though nothing had happened.

It wasn't for Noella, though. She had decided long ago not to become a mother – not to give up so much, for so few guarantees in return. Perhaps if she had had more support around her – a large flock of family who might have helped raise the child. But she had always been on her own, looking out for herself. Had she met the right man, he might have helped her. Yet she would have been too reliant on him.

It wasn't to be. For not only did one's own family determine the genetic make-up of future offspring, they also dictated the path in far more damning ways than mere biology.

Sometimes – mostly on Friday nights, alone in the studio, or on Sundays when families took over the parks, cafés and pavements as though on victory parade – she wondered whether she might be a mother yet.

But the moment soon passed and she told herself that the little ruddy infants whom she taught, with their grunts and flushed cheeks and wobbly limbs, were her children – that she was happy to settle for that. There were women the world over just like her – aunties, stepmothers, tutors, academics, teachers, nurses, midwives – women who surrounded themselves with babies without bearing them.

She gazed at the address book, paused to take a long drink of wine. As she did, a text appeared on her phone. She read it, chewing mechanically.

Thanks for calling. Sorry couldn't speak. No change today. Steffie x

Noella pushed her plate away, suddenly having lost her appetite.

She sipped her wine, thought of the first time she had met Jemima.

She could remember it clearly, although the occasion in itself had not been remarkable. She could not have known that the four-year-old girl twisting shyly around her mother's leg was going to light up Noella's world and her measly studio. And yet the child had caught her eye amongst all the others that spring morning at the beginners' enrolment class. There was a flap and flutter of raincoats and whispers and umbrellas folding and infants twitching, hanging on to mothers' skirts, as Noella tried to prise the children away, to get them to come forward and stand with her at the barre.

One child began to howl; another little boy simply stood still, picking his nose, his mother prodding his back. Twin girls were holding hands, shaking their heads vigorously.

Jemima was no better. She was still hiding behind her mother. But when Noella held out her hand, singled her out, called her '*ma chérie*', Jemima suddenly broke away and skipped forward. And as she approached, there was a look on her face that dried Noella's breath.

The child was wearing a very unreal shade of blue – a bright blue that one wouldn't find in the natural world, a blue that reminded Noella of saccharine cupcake frosting. The colour was stunning in the drab studio, but it was the expression on the child's face that had struck Noella most of all. For at that moment, when they had first touched hands, she had caught on Jemima's face the flash of something from the past, of someone. She had looked just like Delphine: enigmatic, easy to misjudge, to underestimate.

Noella turned her wine glass around on the kitchen counter, watching the wine shift and rock, as though afflicted by a miniature storm.

And then she picked up the address book and her phone.

'*Bonsoir*,' Noella said, when a lady answered the call. 'Is that Delphine's mother, by any chance?' She waited, still turning the glass, her heart racing.

'*Mais oui*,' said the woman. 'Who is calling, please?'

Noella hesitated. 'An old friend.'

'Your name, please?'

'Noella Chamoulaud.'

The woman paused. 'Noella . . . ' she said, as though to herself. 'No, that doesn't ring a bell.'

Of course it wouldn't. No one knew Noella Chamoulaud of Wimborne fame. 'How do you know Delphine?'

'We were at ballet school together,' Noella said, her voice wavering. She cleared her throat. 'In Paris.'

'I see.' The woman paused again. 'So how can I help you?'

This felt like a screening process. Delphine must have been in a worse way than she had imagined. Noella considered hanging up; if only she hadn't already given her name.

She cleared her throat again. 'I . . . just wanted to say hello, to find out how Delphine is doing . . . Is she . . . well?'

The woman laughed at that – a tinkly irritating laugh. 'Well? Ah, *bien sûr*!'

Noella was confused, slightly thrown. 'Oh,' she said, trying to think what to say next. Is there … is there a phone number that I could take for her, please?'

'*Oui*,' the woman said. 'Do you have a pen and paper?'

'*Oui*,' Noella said.

After the call, she gazed at the scrap of paper on which Delphine's number was written. In the quiet of the kitchen, lit only by the strip light above the oven, rain softly tapping on the windows, the numbers appeared to climb off the page, to dance around before her, teasing her to use them.

Delphine had been a tease, she recalled. She had teased Mikhail Alexandrov to near combustion, wearing risqué outfits to supper. It wouldn't be too long before the Dean noticed, or one of the kitchen staff who would jump her after lights-out. Noella had tried to warn her pretty friend – sweet Delphine who scratched her arms in the night.

'Do you know when you're doing that?' Noella had asked her once, trying to peer underneath the arm-warmers that Delphine always wore.

'*Pas du tout*,' Delphine had replied casually.

Not at all.

She had always been so light, so vivacious – Noella so creaky and stiff, by comparison. And she had been all set to bag the man whom Noella privately, distantly, adored.

They were all going to meet at Bartok that night. There had been a sudden downpour of summer rain, and the moisture on the pavements smelt hot and dusty through the open windows.

Delphine had been drinking since lunchtime. It was a hot evening and there was little ventilation in their room.

'Should you be drinking that?' Noella had said, trying to prise the vodka bottle from her room-mate. But Delphine had tittered with laughter, waving Noella away.

There were nine of them going to the bar – the Six Swallows and three men from Alexandrov's dorm, but it was obvious to all that it was really a date between Delphine and Alexandrov, who had been eyeing his prey with increasingly heavy-lidded, lusty eyes.

Noella couldn't think of the encounter, of the night ahead, of the idea of Delphine and Mikhail together in bed, without feeling sick with jealousy. She was trying to come up with a reason not to go to the bar – trying to think of a way not to have to spend the night here afterwards, listening to her room-mate fumbling in the dark, moaning underneath the sheets.

'Come on,' Delphine said, twirling around on her bed in a lavender chiffon gown. 'Let's party! Don't be such an old stiff!'

But Noella, who had spent the afternoon curled on her bed reading, nursing a headache, didn't want to party – wanted the world to go to hell and take Delphine with it.

And this was what she was thinking when she suddenly realised that Delphine was standing on the window ledge with her hands in the air, gown flapping. 'I can fly,' she was shouting. 'Look at me! Woo hoo!'

Noella screamed in alarm. '*Delphine*!' she said, jumping up and dashing towards her. 'Get down!'

But the sudden sound startled Delphine.

And the last thing Noella saw of her friend was the chiffon gown rippling like liquid, her hair spread around like seaweed, as Delphine fell.

Steffie had managed to read seven chapters of *Ballet Shoes* and was starting the eighth when she felt her mother's hand on her shoulder.

'Steffie, sweetheart,' she said, 'give yourself a break. Let's go and get a nice cup of coffee, hey?'

Steffie lowered the book, looked about her, glanced at her

watch. It was nine thirty in the morning. Her mother, neat in suede boots and navy dress, was standing expectantly, hand on bag. She could stand like that all day, her expression said. She had always been patient. And just as well, for Jemima was equally settled in this morning, lying fixed in her bed, unchanging.

Steffie sighed, stood up, paused as she passed Greg. He was asleep in his chair, shoulders hunched, face drawn with exhaustion. Escaping from his mouth was a faint trail of saliva.

The sight made Steffie feel terribly sorry for him. She reached for a tissue from her pocket and bent to dab his mouth. He closed his mouth with a little groan, but didn't wake.

Her mother had moved close to her side. 'That was kind,' her mother said.

And Steffie wanted to cry then – to dive into her mother's arms and feel the warmth of her body and smell the nostalgic scent of her perfume and feel the sweet soft wrinkles of her skin. But she couldn't do that – couldn't give in to self-pity, to sorrow.

Perhaps she would get Greg a chocolate bar or a newspaper from the shop to jolly things up, she thought.

They were at the stage where they were beginning to see things as long term, were trying to make things more bearable, liveable, were looking about the room and saying things like, *Maybe if we pulled the curtains a little more . . . or wheeled the bedside cabinet over there . . . or pulled your chair there?*

'Come on,' said her mother. 'Let's go.' She took Steffie's elbow, led her to the door.

'Wait,' Steffie said. 'Maybe we should put the music on?' She looked about her for the CD player. She had left it there somewhere, near the bed.

'No music. No reading,' said her mother. 'She's fine.'

Steffie nodded. There was no use arguing.

'My bag,' Steffie said. 'I'm not sure where it is . . .'

'There, look,' her mother said, pointing. 'Underneath the cabinet.'

'Thank you.' Steffie turned away and yawned deeply. She couldn't bring herself to tell her mother or Greg that she hadn't slept any better in the hotel bed than on the pull-out one here; that it wouldn't matter where she was, she would still be here, with Jemima.

But her mother would already know that; she looked shattered too.

Steffie had slept fitfully and woken at dawn in pain – not crushing, but enough to stir her. Had she not experienced this before, she would have feared she was having a heart attack. But as it was, she knew that the stabbing sensation in her chest was largely to be ignored.

Still, it had been unpleasant, hard to disregard, seizing attention as it did.

She had wheezed for breath in the hotel bed, trying to work out where she was in the dim light and foreign surroundings – her eyes scratchy, sore, the dark air swirling with dust that she was trying not to breathe in.

She had thought then that perhaps she might choke to death somehow. Yet on what? How?

She could feel perspiration on her hairline and back. She had cupped her hands either side of her nose and breathed in and out, shielding herself from the dust.

But it was no use. She had to stand up – couldn't get enough breath sitting down.

She had slipped quietly from bed, past her sleeping mother, and into the bathroom.

She hadn't put the light on because it was the sort that set off a fan and would have woken her mother. She had rested her hands on the sink, bent her head, breathing in shallow bursts.

She could sense the dust in the air around her. She had put the tap on. Her left hand was tingling. She had pressed it, held it under water, tried to wake it up but it still felt as though it had been stung by nettles.

Her mother had woken shortly afterwards and they had struggled through breakfast in a quiet hotel room, before hurrying along the length of the hospital in the snow to the children's ward to see Jemima, where they discovered Greg sitting up, eating toast.

They had greeted each other with sad humour, all telling each other how well they had slept, noting the bags under each other's eyes.

It was snowing again now, fat fluffy flakes landing on the window.

'Steffie?' said her mother, by her side.

'Huh?' said Steffie.

Where had she just been? She gazed about her absent-mindedly.

'Let's go,' her mother said, tugging her by the elbow.

'OK', Steffie said, but remained where she was.

'What is it?' her mother said.

Steffie didn't know. She just wanted to stay a moment longer, to watch Jemima.

Jemima's chest was shifting smoothly, her monitors the same as usual, the drip in need of replenishment. The nurses would be in soon to check her vitals, to cotton bud her eyes and ears.

'What, Steffie?' her mother asked again, sounding worried.

Steffie turned to her mother then, smiled quickly to reassure her. 'It's nothing, Mum,' she said. 'Let's go.'

And she went to leave the room, but then suddenly turned back round.

If she hadn't, she would have missed it.

She grabbed her mother's arm. 'Did you see that?' she said.

Her mother looked confused, startled. 'See what?'

Steffie hurried to Jemima's side, bent over her.

There it went again.

Her eyelashes were fluttering.

'Get a nurse, Mum! Quick!' Steffie said. And then she shouted, 'Greg! Wake up!'

But he was already standing, rushing forward.

Her mother had dropped her bag and was dashing from the room. 'Nurse!' she was shouting. 'Come quickly! Help! Nurse!'

'What's happening?' Greg said, joining Steffie.

'She moved,' Steffie said. 'I'm sure she did. Look ... Wait.'

They both stood still, watching Jemima.

The movement was more assured now, more rapid. Her eyelashes were flickering, as though she were ridding something from her eyes.

'Oh God,' said Greg. 'Is she ...?'

'I think so,' she said.

The nurses hurried into the room, followed by Dr Mills and two other doctors whom they hadn't seen before.

Steffie and Greg stood back. The monitor was beeping more rapidly. The white coats were flocking the bed. There were lots of voices talking at once – shouting instructions, medical stats.

But Steffie was gripped by the urge to draw close again, to find a tight but unoccupied spot on the opposite side of the bed next to the wall. And without thinking, she pulled Greg with her.

And so they were squashed against the wall, holding hands, holding their breath, when their daughter opened her eyes, frowned, then moved her head about to find them and saw them standing there, held captive, by her side.

PARENT OF CANDIDATE
FREDDIE RAWLINGS

If people can't hack the competition at these things then
they shouldn't come. Savannah wet the bed last night and
won't eat a thing. She'll be skin and bone by the end of
the week and it's all because of the Lees. Makes me so
cross.

Mrs L. Rawlings
Phoenix Academy of Performing Arts
Surrey Police telephone interview transcript
21 February 2016

TWENTY-FOUR

'Can you squeeze my hand? ... That's it. Good girl ... Can you close your eyes and open them again? ... Excellent.'

Dr Mills was bent over Jemima. There were four other doctors in attendance now, several nurses and a flock of medical students hovering near the door, keen to witness a patient emerging from a coma; they were writing notes, standing on tiptoes, clipboards sparring.

Steffie and Greg had stepped out of the way again, had rounded the bed and were waiting near the window. Steffie had her arms wrapped around her. Greg was standing close to her and was rubbing his stubbly chin, making a faint *tskh tskh tskh* sound. Helena was sitting in Greg's chair, handbag on lap, stiff-backed, staring at the staff, awaiting news.

'Now, can you tell me your name?' Dr Mills said.

The room fell silent.

Jemima frowned. Steffie nibbled a fingernail.

'Jemima Lee,' Jemima said croakily.

The medical students began to murmur and whisper.

'That's right,' said Dr Mills. 'And who's that there?'

Everyone, including Jemima, turned to look at Steffie.

Again, the silence.

'Mummy,' Jemima said.

At this, Steffie felt her face contort as she fought tears. She clenched her hands, smiled encouragingly at Jemima, tried to look as though this were a routine sort of a day, a general check-up.

Greg edged closer to Steffie, placed his hand lightly on her shoulder and then squeezed. Despite everything that had occurred between them, the hand was an anchor and she felt it steady her, felt it telling her that she could do this – could stand there and not cry.

They watched as Dr Mills checked Jemima's vitals and charts, as he consulted with colleagues.

'OK . . .' he said, approaching them, his voice low. 'Jemima's currently in a confusional state.'

'Oh,' Steffie said. 'Is that normal?'

'Yes,' he said. 'It's what I was hoping for.' He folded his arms, rose up and down briefly on his heels. 'She's by-passed the vegetative and minimally conscious states, which would have indicated damage to multiple brain areas. And now hopefully she'll make a full recovery. But it's impossible to say how long that will take, and whether she'll be left with any long-term health problems.'

'Long-term . . .' Steffie said. Greg's hand was still on her shoulder, squeezing. She nodded, trying to accept the doctor's words. 'OK.'

She hadn't thought of that – that there could be long-term problems, lingering after-effects. Maybe in days to come, she would look back and realise that there were holes and flaws all over her time here – big gaps, where logic and reality had poured through, as though in a giant colander. What else had she missed?

'Are you anticipating any problems?' Greg asked.

'It's impossible to say,' the doctor said. 'I don't want to give you false hope. That said, there's a lot to be thankful for this morning.' He smiled. 'I'd like to run some tests, and Orthopaedics will want to see Jemima about her fractures.'

Steffie nodded. She had forgotten about the fractures; faced with the big issue of the coma, the broken bones had flown straight through the colander.

'She's still got a long way to go,' Dr Mills said, 'but this is excellent progress.'

'Excellent,' Steffie said, knowing that she sounded fake.

'Well done,' Greg said quietly in her ear, removing his hand from her shoulder and stepping away. She had done it; she hadn't broken down. The staff were filtering from the room in a draught of noise and white jackets. One of the nurses was tending to Jemima's nose tube, removing it delicately. There was a faint sense of dismantlement. Everyone was moving – even her mother, rummaging through her handbag for something and standing up. Only Steffie stood still, wondering, absurdly, whether she would be the one left behind – that Greg wouldn't be here any more, would return to Olivia now, his job here done; Jemima would heal, walk, run, dance; only Steffie wouldn't change, wouldn't move on.

And then she snapped out of her reverie because the nurse was talking to her. 'So that's it for now, Mum ... Dr Mills will be taking her for tests about eleven. All right?'

'Fine,' said Steffie, nodding.

And then the nurse left the room, closing the door behind her.

That was new, Steffie thought. They hadn't closed the door before, had kept it permanently open in order to be able to access Jemima urgently.

Things weren't urgent now, were calmer. As a family, they were being afforded privacy, separation, as though somehow, subtly, with her awakening their daughter was being handed back to them.

Her mother was talking quietly to Greg. Steffie stole the opportunity to speak with Jemima alone.

She approached her daughter, feeling strangely shy, timid. Jemima had her eyes closed again, looking exactly the same as she had when unconscious. Steffie glanced over her shoulder at the door, wondering momentarily whether it were possible for Jemima to regress, to slip back into a coma. But that was stupid. They wouldn't have shut the door. They were safe now.

'I'm not sure . . .' she began. She was going to say that she wasn't sure how much Jemima knew about what had happened, but then changed her mind. It was best not to speak about it yet.

The staff could have helped them with that, she thought – could have told them what to say, how to behave.

But then that was stupid too. This was her child. She knew how to talk to her.

She reached forward to Jemima, touched her forehead, tucked her hair behind her ear.

'My dear sweet Mims,' she said. 'I love you so much.'

At the sound of Steffie's voice, Jemima opened her eyes and turned her head stiffly to look at her. A flicker of a smile touched her lips.

And then she opened her mouth and gave a shrill scream, her tongue curled, her eyes petrified.

Steffie stood back in shock.

Greg was wrestling with the door handle, calling for help.

The nurses came rushing in, darting looks of faint accusation, Steffie felt. Or maybe it was her imagination.

They were sitting with Jemima now, stroking her limbs, pressing a cloth to her head, calming her. 'It's OK, my lovely,' one of the nurses was saying. 'It's all right.'

Perhaps they could have warned us about that, Steffie thought, accusing them silently in return.

'Steffie, love,' said her mother, leading her by the elbow to her chair. 'Come and sit down. You look pale.'

Steffie sat down, held her hands to her head. Her mother was telling her that everything was going to be fine. But she couldn't really hear her – couldn't think. Her ears were still ringing with the sound of Jemima's scream.

She gazed at her daughter who was serene again, asleep, as though nothing had happened.

The nurses made a few notes and then left the room, leaving the door open this time.

Jemima had a liquid meal for tea which she managed to drink through a straw, her head propped up on pillows. She was sluggish, groggy, had slept most of the day. Her emotional outburst was down to her confused state, her inability to separate dreams from reality, and the trauma she had endured. More of such outbursts were to be expected and were entirely normal in the circumstances, Dr Mills had assured them.

The Orthopaedics had confirmed that no surgery was required for Jemima's fractures. As far as dancing went, they saw no reason why she wouldn't be able to participate at the same standard in future, but it would take some commitment on her part and great determination.

Looking at the wispy child lying in bed now, it seemed an unlikely outcome, even for an optimist. The hope that Steffie had sensed in the room during the short period when the door had been closed had been ushered out by Jemima's scream.

And now teatime had ended, the trays had been taken away, darkness had fallen, and the detectives had just arrived.

They were hovering by the door, where Greg was waylaying them. He was trying to tell them not to come in yet, to return tomorrow, but they were insisting on asking Jemima a few questions. Steffie could hear them countering Greg's objections, until sure enough, he stepped aside. And the detectives approached Jemima, heavy-footed, sombre in black trench coats, like undertakers.

Jemima was staring up at the ceiling blankly, a dab of liquid food on her lip. Steffie leant forward protectively, wiped Jemima's mouth with a tissue. She had drawn the chair beside the bed to be close to Jemima.

'Hello, Jemima,' the sergeant said. 'We haven't met before, but I'm Detective Sergeant Lamb. And this here is my friend, Detective Constable Whyte. We're very pleased to meet you. And we'd like to ask you a couple questions, if we may. Is that all right?'

Jemima didn't reply, made no sign of even seeing him.

The sergeant pushed his hands in his pockets, jangled his change. 'So how much do you remember about the accident, Jemima?'

Steffie glared at him in consternation.

'Do you remember falling, Jemima?'

Greg stepped forward. 'I really don't think you should—'

The sergeant held up his hand to Greg to stop him approaching or speaking. It wasn't rude, as such; more, assertive, dogged. He had come here for something and he was going to get it. 'Do you remember entering the rec room, Jemima? Either the first time or the second?'

Again, no reply, no sign of hearing or listening.

Maybe Jemima really couldn't hear the man, Steffie thought – was somehow blocking it, unable to remember or communicate yet.

'Is it that you don't remember? Or that you don't want to tell me?'

Nothing.

The sergeant exhaled, his lips puffing, cheeks wobbling. 'Well, young lady . . . it's our belief that someone has committed a serious crime against you. And we need to find that person. But we can't do it without your help.'

There was a patter of footsteps behind them. 'I'm sorry,' one of the nurses said, 'but we need to give Jemima her bath now.'

The nurse shot Steffie a quick smile when the sergeant's back was turned. It was a smile that said that no one else would be troubling the patient tonight.

The sergeant was nodding, but making no show of leaving. He gazed solemnly at Steffie. 'We'll be back tomorrow,' he said.

'OK,' said Steffie, trying to sound pleasant, nonplussed.

But in truth, they were the last people she wanted to see, for so many reasons – most of which had escaped her through the hospital colander.

Helena sat in a green chair by the window and watched Jemima sleep. She glanced at her watch. It was eight o'clock. Steffie and Greg had gone to get something to eat. When they returned, she and Steffie would head off to the hotel, and Greg would pull out the ward bed. It was a pattern that could go on for some time.

She had rung Wimborne Primary yesterday to report the news to the Head, knowing that Steffie wouldn't have thought of it in all the turmoil. Jemima had missed two days of school already. So much had happened since Saturday. Yet now there was hope.

She could remember feeling exactly the same as Steffie – petrified, witless – albeit on a lesser scale, when Steffie had gone to hospital aged seven to have her appendix out. Steffie had insisted on bringing her Sindy doll in nurse's outfit into the operating theatre with her. As they had wheeled Steffie and Sindy off, Helena had thought her heart would crack neatly, almost satisfyingly, in two, like a chocolate Easter egg.

And then it was over. Steffie had come to; and then was up and running again.

But the toll that the anguish took on a mother's heart was never forgotten, was always embedded there – could be retrieved just by the smell of a certain disinfectant or an emotive hospital drama on TV. Helena would never forget Steffie and Sindy being wheeled into surgery; Steffie would never forget Jemima's accident.

Creases in the heart – that was how Helena thought of a mother's painful experiences: tiny lines that no one could touch or smooth away. There wasn't a power iron in the world that could obliterate them – not a housewife's tip, a grandmother's trick or celestial intervention grand enough to have any effect.

And yet perhaps someone would think of a way to do that soon – a pill, a procedure that would remove anything painful or unpleasant from the heart, from life as a whole.

Certainly, Helena thought, looking around her at the weary décor – at the industrial bins, the equipment, the stark metal and chipped woodwork – no one liked hospitals. They were a reminder of mortality, of the fragility of life. A short stay here – even just a daytime admission for something minor – would serve its message loud and clear, with recovered patients returning home brimming with gratitude and thankfulness. And then life continued and the gratitude dissolved and everyone went back to cursing the traffic or the rain.

But those little lines on the heart? They couldn't dissolve, were permanent.

They were the privilege of motherhood – a badge of honour, that you were there, that you served, that you cared, that you loved.

Helena heard a little noise that caught her attention. Jemima was trying to sit up, for the first time in Helena's knowledge.

She was struggling, wincing with pain, her left side helpless in casts.

'Wait . . .' Helena said, standing up and hurrying to her grand-daughter. 'Lie still, poppet. Don't wriggle. You'll hurt yourself.'

As Helena approached, she glanced at the open door furtively. She wasn't sure why exactly. It was just that the situation felt clandestine. She didn't think Jemima ought to be jiggling about. She was still wearing the wrist catheter and sensor pads on her chest.

And yet Helena wanted to encourage this progress. She plumped the cushions behind Jemima's head, helped her raise her head slightly without disrupting the wires.

Then she sat in Steffie's seat. 'There,' she said.

'Grandma,' was all Jemima said.

Helena nodded receptively, but felt intrigue prickling her skin in goosebumps.

Beyond the room, the corridor sounded very quiet. The little child from the room opposite – the one that cried a lot – had left earlier and hadn't been replaced. Maybe sometimes everyone left at once and the beds were all empty. She wondered if that ever happened.

She looked at her granddaughter, placed her old sun-spotted hand on Jemima's casted hand. 'Talk to me,' she said.

Jemima was staring at the ceiling, frowning. 'Who were those men?'

Her voice sounded different, Helena thought. It sounded as though it had been at the bottom of a river for a long time. It was thin, reedy.

'Policemen,' Helena said. 'They're investigating why you fell.' She said this tentatively, not sure how much she should say, how much Jemima could recall.

'Where's Noella?' Jemima asked.

'Noella?' said Helena. 'Well, she's back at her studio, I think.

She was here for a little while and I expect she went home because there was nothing more she could do.'

'Oh,' said Jemima.

'Do you need her for something?' Helena asked.

Jemima shook her head. 'No.'

She said this rather adamantly, Helena noted. Was there something in that?

She gazed at the door, aware that at any moment one of the nurses could enter and tell her off for interfering with the patient. Or Steffie. Steffie would be cross with her. They hadn't tried to talk to Jemima yet about anything other than whether she needed a drink of water or a change of position.

'Am I in trouble?' Jemima said.

She looked so different, Helena thought: so much older than before, so ashen, so perturbed.

'No, poppet,' Helena said, tapping her hand, 'absolutely not.'

'So why were they asking me about the rec room?' Jemima said, looking away from the ceiling and at her bed sheets. Her breathing was laboured now. Helena was beginning to feel uncomfortable, as though speaking to her granddaughter was a very bad idea.

Yet she couldn't stop herself. 'Why do you ask?' she said. 'Do you remember going in there?'

Jemima didn't reply.

Once more, Helena glanced at the door. She stroked Jemima's hand. 'Tell me.'

Jemima rolled her head to look at her. 'I remember it all,' she said. Two tears trickled from her eyes. Helena reached forward, wiped them away. Somehow they seemed like evidence. 'But you mustn't tell anyone.' Suddenly, she grabbed Helena's hand. 'Grandma, you *mustn't*.'

Helena gazed at Jemima's bloodshot eyes. 'Jemima,' she began, 'I'm—'

'Everything OK?'

It was Steffie. Helena immediately sat back in the chair. Jemima had closed her eyes, was feigning sleep.

'Any change, Mum?'

Helena, who didn't want her granddaughter to hear that she was lying for her – hadn't, in fact, made up her mind yet whether to do so – replied wordlessly with a shake of her head.

Steffie sighed, straightened the bed covers, smoothed Jemima's hair. Greg was unfolding the bed from the wall. Their little evening routine had begun.

Helena watched her granddaughter lying there innocently, mutely, as Steffie tidied the room, gathered her things.

She felt guilty, and sorry for Steffie – her tired, hard-working, loyal daughter – for whatever betrayal this was. For it was most definitely one of some sort, even if just a whisper behind a back that had stood watch so faithfully, for so long.

And Helena knew in that moment that she was going to have to carry out her own betrayal too. She would tell her daughter what had just occurred. Because that was the other thing about being a mother, no matter from which decade they were sprung, no matter how smooth or lined their heart: their own child came first.

Diazepam? Yes, I take it occasionally. Who doesn't?

Do you seriously expect me to cope with my children, with all this – with the clubs and lessons and homework and assessments and exams and awards and performances – unmedicated? Have you any idea what my average day looks like?

Mrs U. Kirkpatrick
Phoenix Academy of Performing Arts
Surrey Police telephone interview transcript
21 February 2016

TWENTY-FIVE

Lavender chiffon; it was lying on the forecourt like spilled paint.

And then everyone had started screaming.

Noella had stood at the window, her hands clenched before her, the smell of summer rain in the air, the fading sunshine lighting the puddles.

Some of the staff were tending to Delphine – first-aiders whom Noella recognised from backstage during productions, when they always needed physiotherapists or medics to administer drugs or massages or even splints.

The bottle of vodka had fallen with Delphine, was lying in smithereens on the concrete below.

Noella couldn't look at the head, at the neck, at the hair, at the body. The chiffon was far easier on the eye.

Eventually, she didn't look at all – turned and sat down on the bed, shaking violently. Until a knock on the door startled her and in came Mikhail Alexandrov.

He did not know the news – had somehow missed it on his journey here, his head and groin filled with the promise of pleasure. He was wearing a fitted white shirt. His black hair hung either side of his face in a sexy fringe. His nose – broken from a dance injury – was still perfect, above a mouth that was equally well-drawn.

Noella had smiled at him in greeting, straightened her blouse, edged the leg of her trousers down with a raised bare foot. But he was looking about the room for Delphine. The curtains were billowing and there suddenly came the sound of crying and shouting below. And Noella realised, with shame and horror, that she had forgotten about what had just happened – had been too arrested by Alexandrov.

He too forgot something – waylaid it in all the upset and shock, and never found it again. He forgot that she had looked pleased to see him, had somehow been smiling, even with her friend lying there on the forecourt.

He was looking out of the window, yelling, holding his head in his hands.

It was some months before Noella made her move. But Alexandrov was eventually hers; at least, for a dozen nights.

She picked up the phone and the scrap of paper bearing the phone number. She had already got rid of all the contents of the shoebox – had taken it outside to the bin in her courtyard garden. The scrap of paper was the only thing left – the only thing linked to the past; that and the swallow tattoo on her neck.

She touched the tattoo now, waiting for the phone to be answered.

'Hello?'

Noella took a quick breath in. She recognised the voice at once: breezy, nonchalant. 'Delphine,' Noella said.

'*Oui?*'

Noella sat down on her bed with a thump, wondering what to say next.

It was the last part of the problem – the thickest part of the knot. And yet a kind word from Delphine – an assurance that she was fine and bore no grudge – would ease the knot free.

All that would remain would be a faint kink in the timeline of Noella's life that no one would ever notice or care about.

Even the Lee situation seemed to be improving. She had rung Steffie earlier and was thrilled to learn that Jemima had woken, and might even dance again. The news had felt wonderfully liberating, until she had panicked about Jemima speaking up about the hip flask.

She was bound to do so. She was a little girl. Little girls couldn't keep secrets. And Noella's school would be no more.

And then Delphine spoke, her voice crackling down the line.

'Noella?' she said. 'It's you, isn't it?'

Noella's heart lurched. 'Yes,' she said. 'How did—'

'My mother told me that you rang yesterday.' There was a sharp inhaling sound, followed by an exhalation. Delphine was smoking. 'What took you so long?'

Noella wasn't sure what she meant precisely. Did she mean the twenty-four-hour delay before calling, or the twenty-year lapse?

'What do you want?' Delphine asked sharply.

This was unexpected: the anger. Noella immediately stiffened in defence. And yet perhaps Delphine had every right to be cross. Noella hadn't once enquired after her health in all these years.

'I just wanted to know how you are,' she said.

'Me?' Delphine said. 'I'm perfect!' Noella thought of the scratched arms, the shards of the vodka bottle on the forecourt, and doubted that.

'Where are you living?' Noella asked.

She had long pictured Delphine in an institution of some sort – one that gave out complimentary arm-warmers on the door.

'Paris,' said Delphine, dragging on her cigarette again.

'Doing?' said Noella.

Delphine laughed. 'Working for Chanel, of course.'

'Chanel?' said Noella, her heart picking up pace.

'*Mais oui. Bien sûr*! I'm Head of Marketing and Communications, *ma chérie*.'

Noella stared at the bedroom wall in shock.

Delphine was laughing again. 'But what about you, Noella? Are you still in your little studio in uh . . . what's its name?'

'My studio?' Noella said. 'How do you know—'

'Misha,' she said.

Noella sat up straight, nearly pulling the cord from the phone. It was a traditional phone with a rotary dial that had seemed elegantly retro, but now felt unfashionably old and ungainly. 'Mikhail Alexandrov?'

'Of course!' Delphine said. 'Who else?'

Noella knelt up on the bed, her eyes burning. 'How do you know him still? How are you in touch with him? He didn't mention he had spoken to you.'

'Ah,' said Delphine softly. 'So you are in contact with Misha too. I might have guessed . . . Poor Noella and her little crush.'

Noella felt light-headed. She held her hand to her forehead.

Hearing Delphine's voice, it was as though they were back there again in their room, hiding their Swallow tattoos, smoking, sneaking alcohol into the dorm, pretending to be friends, hating each other.

That had been the worst part of it all, Noella thought: the hating.

All the academies were like that at this level: their old school in Paris, the Phoenix in Usherwood. Everyone felt it – every pupil, without exception. They all succumbed to that crushing pressure. It was the same in any field – any field at the top.

Her heart was beating so rapidly, it was starting to ache. She could remember that aching feeling being prevalent back then, too – the rapid heart beating whenever competition met the air, which was most days. It had felt as though every day were a day of reckoning, a final judgement that would declare Noella once and for all Not Good Enough. And each day, she had somehow eluded it, had escaped certain death.

'We all knew about your pathetic crush,' Delphine was saying. 'Everyone except Misha. But then he was so wrapped up in his dance ... So how long did you wait before jumping into the sack with him? A couple days, I hope?' She laughed, then dragged on her cigarette.

Noella's head was spinning. Her mouth felt dry. She looked about for a drink. There was none here. She couldn't hang up or move – she was tied to the phone cord.

'Misha's father and my father are old friends, Noella. We see each other from time to time, for supper whenever he's in town.'

Town meant Paris. Not Wimborne.

If there was a day of reckoning, it was now. Twenty years on, but now nonetheless.

Noella was no one – had always been no one. She had no connections, no money, no one to fight her corner, no one to fluff up a committee, no one to visit her on parents' day, no one to influence the board, no one to subsidise her enterprises or misdemeanours.

In the game of dance, of competition, of elitism, where the most eloquent or wealthy parents won, Noella of Galgon – with her kitchen-sink mother, and father with gappy teeth and field-worn hands – had never stood a chance.

'I'm not to blame for what happened to you,' Noella found herself saying.

Delphine gave an affected little gasp. 'But of course not! You tried to warn me – to help me not to fall, correct?'

'Correct,' Noella said.

'And then you slept with Misha. Correct?'

Noella didn't reply.

'Which is why it has taken you this long to contact me … And so I repeat my initial question: what do you want?'

Noella closed her eyes. The answer was obvious.

'Peace,' she said.

Delphine laughed. She was going to swear or hang up, Noella sensed.

'Don't,' Noella urged her. 'Please, Delphine. Just say goodbye and good luck. And mean it.'

Delphine was quiet for a moment. Noella could picture her frowning, sitting cross-legged as she was prone to do, her scratched arms hugging her chest.

'Goodbye,' Delphine said at last. 'And good luck.'

'Goodbye,' Noella replied. Her voice was breaking. She had to say it quickly. 'Good luck.'

She dropped the phone on to the blanket, exhausted, and leant forward to unplug the socket from the wall.

And then she sat with her head bent, her hands pressed to her eyes, wondering where on earth to go now, whether there existed a corner small enough for her to fit in.

Greg was in the family room when he saw Mikhail Alexandrov walk past the doorway.

It was Wednesday morning. Steffie was bathing Jemima, who had just managed to walk to the bathroom on a frame with a nurse either side. It was quite an achievement. She wasn't able to support herself, with her left arm out of action, and her ankle and heel bone unable to bear weight, so had eased forward timidly, looking determined, her mouth creased in pain, Steffie hovering beside her, murmuring encouragement.

They had somehow made it to the bathroom door – a little

gathering of staff, parents and patient, all holding their breath and bones tightly — at which point Greg had wiped his head clear of sweat and bailed out in favour of getting a coffee in the family room.

He had thought it might be easier to sleep, with Jemima being awake and out of danger, yet he had spent the night lying tensely on the fold-out bed, watching her fitful movements, listening to the twang of her bedsprings and the crackling of her water-repellent mattress as she tossed about.

Sometimes she called for a drink, sometimes said that her casts were itching or that she had pins and needles, or that her wrist catheter was stinging. And sometimes she said things in her sleep — strange, incoherent mumblings that he strained to hear.

Even when she was quiet, he found himself unable to nod off, began picking back over her behaviour since waking yesterday.

She had not acted the way he had expected her to, even in these strange circumstances. It wasn't just the screaming episode, which he could partly understand, but the way she had behaved in front of the detectives.

He might have put it all down to mental confusion, if it weren't for the fact that she had been *compos mentis* enough to watch television earlier on her bedside screen. She had even laughed a couple of times — tight asthmatic laughs.

He had been pleased to see this at the time — a glimpse of the old Jemima — and had dared to believe that it was a sign she was making progress.

So it had come as a surprise to see her shut down in front of the policemen — not to help out as she normally did, not to offer help towards finding who had done this to her.

And yet, it could be explained; Dr Mills would have an explanation for it, if consulted. Jemima was coming out of a coma. It was an extreme situation. There were no rules, no standard patterns of behaviour. She might not ever even be the same child again. Dr Mills had told them this yesterday, Steffie turning away in abhorrence of the suggestion.

Still, Greg didn't like it, knew there was something wrong.

Sometimes he felt like that with work, knew when something was off, even though there was no way of telling what. He always respected the feeling and did something about it – went back over calculations, paperwork, handiwork. And sure enough there it always was: a flaw, an oversight.

So he was thinking, when he saw Mr Alexandrov pass the family room.

Greg jumped up, hurried after him, calling his name.

Mr Alexandrov turned and waited as Greg approached. 'Good morning, Mr Lee,' he said.

The two men shook hands.

'I was just on my way to speak with you,' Alexandrov said, glancing over Greg's shoulder back to the family room. 'Were you in there? Shall we . . . ?'

Greg nodded. 'Yes. I just made a coffee, if you're interested.'

'No, thank you,' said Alexandrov, tapping his stomach.

'Probably a wise decision,' said Greg.

They went into the room and Greg retrieved his mug. He didn't want to sit down, was tired of sitting, so he led Alexandrov to the window where they leant on the sill.

'So how is Jemima this morning?'

'She's well, thank you,' said Greg. 'In fact, she just walked on a frame.'

'Fantastic. You must be very pleased.'

'Yes,' Greg said. 'Although, not as much as you might think.'

Alexandrov gazed at him thoughtfully. 'I can imagine.'

Greg blew on his coffee mug. 'So how can I help you?' he asked.

It was nice of the bloke to come, but he wasn't sure that this was the place for him; not any more.

'Well, I actually came to tell you something,' Alexandrov said, putting his hands in his pockets and leaning back against the window.

'Oh?' said Greg.

'I don't know if this information is of importance to you. But I do know that part of being a great dancer is constant striving – a fierce desire to succeed.'

'Oh, right,' said Greg.

He knew that he sounded passive, weary. But he couldn't get pumped up about this conversation; not with Jemima struggling to walk.

He turned to look out of the window at the empty courtyard, the neglected plant pots and benches. No one would be out there today. The television – permanently on in the family room, whether anyone heeded it or not – was talking softly beside him about weather warnings: snow showers, then rain and gale-force winds.

The windows were already rattling, the wind howling plaintively.

'Mr Lee, your daughter is one of the most promising young dancers I've ever seen – far superior to her contemporaries.'

'Really?' said Greg, turning on his heel to look at Alexandrov. 'Blimey, that's . . .'

'News to you?'

'Yes,' said Greg, smiling.

Alexandrov shrugged his mouth downwards. 'But you knew she was good. Why not the best?'

Greg thought about that for a moment: Jemima, his daughter, the best.

But then he thought of her in casts and crutches, and shook his head.

'I'm not saying now. I'm not saying next week. I'm not even talking about this year perhaps,' said Alexandrov quietly. 'But some day, some time, your daughter could be truly remarkable, my friend.'

A silence fell between them, broken only by the murmuring of the television.

'It's good of you to come,' Greg said, at last. 'I appreciate it. But I don't know whether Jemima will want to dance again.'

'Ah,' said Alexandrov with a humourless laugh. 'She will dance, trust me.' He slapped Greg's arm firmly but gently. 'And when she does? Send her back to me.'

Greg was surprised. 'You would still take her?'

'Always.'

The conversation felt poignant, moving. Greg nodded. 'OK,' he said. 'Thank you.'

'Please pass on my best wishes to Jemima,' Alexandrov said, moving towards the door.

Greg watched the man walking away. 'I don't think she'll want to come now,' he called after him.

Alexandrov stopped, turned. 'How so?'

Greg shrugged. 'Not after what happened.'

Alexandrov rubbed his chin pensively. 'So what about her tutor?' he said.

'Noella?' said Greg. 'What's she got to do with it?'

'How close are the two of them?'

'Very,' said Greg. 'Why?'

Alexandrov smiled. 'Perhaps if the tutor came, the child would follow.'

'I don't get it,' said Greg. 'Why?'

'I would offer the tutor a job at the Phoenix. She's an accomplished dancer and tutor. Jemima is evidence of that, yes?'

'Yes,' said Greg. And then he folded his arms. 'But why would you hire Noella? Why are you even here today?'

Alexandrov inhaled heavily, took a step towards Greg. 'Because, Mr Lee, I care about talent. I care about not letting it go to waste. And I care about my career.'

Greg stared at him. 'But you're not to blame,' he said.

'Really?' Alexandrov laughed. 'Some of the parents are saying that the school is unsafe, that I'm unsafe. All this could ruin me.'

'And Jemima attending would fix it?'

'Perhaps ... But ...' He held up his hand. 'That is not the purpose of this visit. I would not be so distasteful. I'm merely telling you that you must not underestimate your daughter's talent. And that if she wants to come to my school, the door's open.'

Greg assessed the man's expression. He seemed sincere enough.

'OK,' Greg said, reaching to shake Alexandrov's hand. 'Thank you for your honesty ... We'll see how this plays out. But it's not really under my control.'

'Of course,' said Alexandrov. 'And good luck.'

And they parted company, Greg sipping his coffee, which had grown cold.

After bathing Jemima, Steffie went with Greg to the Friends café, leaving Jemima in bed with a bag of Maltesers, a TV screen and her grandmother for company.

The café was busy this morning – the busiest they had seen it. Greg was telling Steffie about Mr Alexandrov's visit, his voice raised over the clutter of noise around them, and Steffie was trying not to gloat about the knowledge that Jemima was the best of all the *étoile* candidates.

But the news was bitter-sweet. She wasn't sure whether Jemima would want to have anything to do with the Phoenix now. Jemima hadn't even mentioned Noella. And that – not quoting Noella, or talking about her, or radiating Noella-ness – had been unheard of prior to the accident.

'Maybe if we told her what Alexandrov said,' Greg said, 'it might help her recover … Because maybe it's just me, but she doesn't seem in a hurry to get her life back.'

Steffie put down her teacup. 'What do you mean?'

'Oh, come on, Steffie. Don't you think she's acting odd?'

'Odd?' said Steffie. 'She's just woken up from a coma!'

'Exactly,' said Greg. 'And no one's talking about that. No one's talking about how she fell. And I think it's wrong. We should be encouraging her to remember.'

Steffie opened her mouth to speak and then looked quickly around her, before turning back to him.

'She does remember,' she said.

'What?' said Greg, startled. 'How do you know?'

'I'm sorry,' Steffie said. 'I wasn't keeping it from you. I just didn't want a scene in front of Jemima and this has been our first chance to speak on our own …' She leant towards him appealingly. 'Mum told me first thing this morning that Jemima remembers the accident, but doesn't want us to know.'

'Eh?' he said. 'Why?'

'I don't know,' she said. 'But I don't think we should push her. There's obviously something wrong. It could be trauma – something that she can't deal with yet.'

'So maybe we should talk to Dr Mills about it?'

'But he keeps saying that we need to tread lightly – not to provoke her.'

'So what about asking for a therapist to speak to her or something?'

'Yes,' Steffie said. 'Maybe.'

'Maybe?' he said.

She stared at him. 'Why are you being so hard about this?' she asked. 'Why can't we just take baby steps?'

'We can,' he said gruffly. 'It's just . . .' He put his head in his hands, rubbed his face. 'I'm getting to the stage where I want answers . . . Aren't you?'

She paused. 'Yes,' she said. 'But I want the right ones. When Jemima's ready.'

'Fine,' he said.

She looked at her watch. 'We should get going,' she said, standing up. And they made their way back to the ward, where they found Jemima playing rummy with Helena.

The detectives returned just after lunch, when a sleepy lull had descended on the ward during the handover of staff. Jemima had just eaten tangerine jelly and a forkful of fish pie, before sitting back listlessly, with her back and head propped against her pillow.

Detective Sergeant Lamb hesitated at the door. 'Is this a good time?' he asked.

'Yes,' Steffie said. 'Come on in.'

Steffie wasn't pleased to see them exactly, but on some level she knew that Jemima's reluctance to open up to them would force the issue home to Greg: that they were to give their daughter more time.

The sergeant approached, hands in pockets. Detective Constable Whyte, following behind, nodded hello to them, his grey suit appearing shimmery under the harsh hospital lighting.

'Hello, Jemima,' Detective Sergeant Lamb said, halting. 'Mind if I . . . ?' he asked Steffie, pointing to the green chair next to the bed.

'Go ahead,' said Steffie. She would relinquish her chair, would squish up against the wall on the other side of the bed to give the men space.

'Ta.' The sergeant hitched his trousers at the knees and sat down. Detective Constable Whyte assumed his usual stance, elbows on window sill, leg propped against the wall.

Greg went to join Steffie on the other side of Jemima's bed and Helena sat down in Greg's chair, handbag on lap, as though waiting for a dentist's appointment. They were all shuffling about, getting in place, and then it fell quiet. The only one who had not moved the entire time, who had remained entirely motionless, was Jemima.

'How are you feeling?' Detective Sergeant Lamb asked her.

She didn't reply, made no sign of having heard him, her eyes fixed on an imaginary object amongst her bed covers.

'Answer him, Jemima,' Greg said.

Steffie flashed Greg a look.

Don't interfere. Don't push her.

'Jemima,' the sergeant said, 'I need your help. I'm trying to solve a case. It's my job. And I have to find out what happened to you. So ... do you think you can tell me? Can you tell me why you fell?'

Steffie gazed at Jemima, waiting. She sensed that it wasn't going to be that easy – that Jemima wasn't just going to crack and tell. She would need coaxing and careful handling. The last person she would open up to was this strange man with his stuck-up hair and dishevelled appearance.

But then Jemima did move – began to struggle, turning towards Steffie, trying to reach for her hand. But the catheter was caught in the holes of the waffle blanket.

'Mummy ...' Jemima said, her voice panicky as she tried to wrench her wrist free.

'Wait,' Steffie said. 'Sit still.' She unhooked the catheter from the blanket, noting the strong smell of the transparent medical tape that kept it in place; such a peculiar smell, one that she would never forget.

She held Jemima's hand firmly, looked into her eyes with an expression that said that everything was absolutely fine, that there was nothing to be frightened of – that Mummy was here, always.

But it wasn't working. Because Jemima looked terrified, was beginning to cry, her frail shoulders shaking.

'I don't think she's ready for this yet,' Greg said. 'Perhaps we could leave it a few days?'

But the sergeant wasn't heeding him, was gazing resolutely at Jemima.

'I think I know what's happening here ...' Detective Sergeant Lamb said. 'But it would be a lot easier if I heard it from you, Jemima.'

Steffie continued to grip her daughter's hand, who gripped her hand back.

The power between them at that moment – the energy, the warmth – was huge. Steffie felt it ripple over her body, leaving goosebumps in its wake. Her skin felt tight, stretched with love and potential.

So when Jemima spoke, it was such a shock to Steffie that she dropped her daughter's hand and the connection was broken.

She could almost smell burnt metal in the air as the wires were cut.

'I wanted to fall,' Jemima said.

AUDITION CANDIDATE NO.3

My mum's obsessed with winning. There's only first place. She won't even wear silver jewellery, only gold.

I thought that if Jemima Lee was better than me, my mum wouldn't love me any more.

Daisy Kirkpatrick
Phoenix Academy of Performing Arts
Surrey Police interview transcript
23 February 2016

TWENTY-SIX

Greg felt the blood sink from his head in a horrible rush. Steffie had stepped backwards, forgetting she was pressed against a wall, her head banging against it.

Helena was the first to try to say something coherent. She stood at the edge of the bed, looking dazed. 'Why?' she said.

Jemima began to cry – high-pitched wails. She was holding her broken hand in front of her face, masking herself. Her other hand, having been dropped by Steffie, was still stretched in that direction – seeking her mother's protection and guidance, as she so often had before. Yet Steffie looked fossilised with disbelief; an imprint of what she had once been, only moments before.

'Tell us what happened,' Detective Sergeant Lamb said. He was perched on the edge of his seat.

Jemima opened her mouth, then closed it promptly.

'It's OK,' the sergeant said gently. 'You're not in any trouble. You have my word.'

This kindness seemed to stir Steffie. She moved away from the wall and stood upright, swaying unsteadily.

'I went into the rec room . . .' Jemima said.

Detective Constable Whyte flicked a notepad open and began to write. 'What time?' he asked, chewing.

Jemima sniffed. 'In the morning. I don't know when.'

'And you were with . . . ?' the constable said.

The sergeant glanced over his shoulder at his colleague and held up his hand in restraint. 'We can get to specifics later,' he said.

The constable gave a grunt and put the pad away.

Jemima, evidently sensing that she had lost her mother's favour, stopped reaching for her, and began to fidget instead with the blanket, poking her finger through the holes.

'So you went in there because Zachary said it would be fun?' Detective Sergeant Lamb said.

Jemima nodded. 'It wasn't, though. Everything was covered in cloths.'

'I see. So what then?'

'We came out, and Mum and Dad found us and Dad was really cross.'

The sergeant glanced at Greg, who nodded.

Then the sergeant turned back to Jemima. 'But something else happened before then, didn't it, Jemima?' he said.

There was a silence and then the rain lashed harder at the windows, rattling the panes.

Jemima dropped the blanket, began to cry again, gazed at her mother for help. But Steffie was unmoved, her thoughts and sympathies unknown. Greg watched with some mild alarm. He had never known Steffie not to respond to Jemima. It was unnerving to witness.

'We went up the ladder to the attic,' Jemima said.

'Why?' asked Detective Constable Whyte.

'Just 'cos,' she said.

'Because Zachary thought it'd be a laugh?' said the constable.

Jemima nodded.

'And what happened up there, Jemima?' the sergeant asked.

'Zach swung on a bar,' she said, wrinkling her nose as a tear fell. 'He told us to try it too, but no one wanted to. Freddie kept saying we needed to leave.'

'And what else?' said the constable.

'Nothing,' she said. 'We came back down.'

'OK.' The sergeant stood up, bent his legs briskly, stretching. 'So let's fast forward to just before the audition. Tell us what happened.'

The wind howled. Greg thought of all the rain lashing down, melting the snow, causing flooding. Everything felt unstable, even the ground under his feet.

He looked at his shoes. They seemed real enough and yet he imagined that they weren't his, that this wasn't his daughter, his problem, his life.

He thought of his work, of something to ground him. But all he could picture was wood floating away on floods of water like rafts.

Jemima shook her head vehemently. 'I don't remember.'

'But that's just it, Jemima,' said the sergeant. 'I think that you do.'

Noella was teaching a class – preschool ballet. It was a sweet collection of sticky, sucky, milky limbs – little babies who tried their hardest to shine despite the fact that they hadn't yet mastered riding a bike without stabilisers. Somehow their parents felt that they would excel here, at the barre. And some of them did. It was just that many of them didn't.

'And that's it ... And one and two and three ... don't bend ... Heels! And one and two ...'

Still, Noella was not in a position to judge – had proved that thoroughly.

She stopped in front of the wall of mirrors, surveyed her lonely figure. She had never been one to feel sorry for herself, but at that moment she felt that there was not a more pathetic soul alive.

'And one and two and three and four . . . and . . .'

She looked away from her reflection, tried not to be emotional. It was difficult, on the verge of forty years old. One began to fight all sorts of hormonal battles – feelings arriving en masse like minuscule enemies, attacking one's eyes and nervous system.

Her phone was ringing in her pocket. Ordinarily, she didn't answer it whilst teaching. But it didn't seem to matter now that she was on her way out of business.

It was Mikhail Alexandrov. 'What do you want?' she said, turning her back to the children to take the call, one hand pressed against her ear. 'I'm in the middle of class.'

'You speak on your phone in class?' he said. 'I'll have to make a note of that.'

'A note?' she said, frowning. 'Why would you—'

'Would you consider working here for me?' he asked. 'As a tutor?'

'And one and two and three and four . . .' she called out to the infants, waving to the pianist to continue. Thankfully, there were no parents observing class today. She turned back to the phone. 'Why would I work for you?' she asked.

'Because you are ruthlessly ambitious?'

'So what's in it for you?' she said, ignoring his comment.

He laughed. 'Tut tut, Noella, must you be so cynical?'

She didn't know.

Must she?

She glanced at the children. 'That's it, *mes enfants*. Keep going!'

'So?' he said.

'I don't understand,' she said.

'It's on the condition that Jemima Lee attends here too.'

'Ah,' she said. 'Now I understand.'

There was a pause.

And then something occurred to her. 'Mikhail,' she said. 'Tell me. The day of Delphine's accident . . . when you came to our room . . . Did you notice. . . ?'

She hesitated. She wanted to ask whether he had noticed her smile – that she had been pleased to see him, had temporarily forgotten her friend's ghastly plight.

'Notice what?' he said. The tone of his voice implied that he had already moved on, wasn't even thinking of the scene that she was conjuring.

He hadn't noticed anything. He had been focused on himself; just like every other dancer at the top of their field.

And that, she saw now, was what she had been guilty of all along: self-preoccupation. That single untimely smile might have revealed the contents of her soul, had anyone witnessed it. She had been focused purely on her own interests, on the man who had seized hold of her heart; and recently on getting Jemima to the top, no matter what it took.

She could no longer punish herself for that – had to come to terms with the fact that it was simply the way she was wired. It was what had made her a great dancer once.

'So will you work for me?' he asked.

'I'll think about it and will let you know,' she said. And she hung up.

It should have been good news. It was what she had wanted – a chance to claim an equal stance amongst the elite.

Yet she had messed everything up. He didn't know what Jemima Lee knew – the little piece of information that she would eventually tell her parents and the police.

And so Noella turned back to her class despondently. How ironic. She had finally won her prize. And she couldn't receive it.

*

312

'I went to the toilet,' Jemima said. 'Just before the audition.'

'Go on . . .' said the sergeant.

Steffie was standing with her arms folded, heart thumping like an angry fist on a door. She kept thinking about what her mother had said first thing this morning – that Jemima had betrayed them by keeping secrets.

Steffie had thought it too strong a word to use, especially about Jemima.

Yet that was the word that came to mind now as she watched her pale daughter who was fidgeting with her casts, her eyes flitting nervously at the grown-ups gathered around her bed.

What else was it but a betrayal?

Perhaps this was what parents felt when their child self-harmed, or worse . . . A gut-wrenching sense of disloyalty and rejection in the extreme; an embarrassment, almost, at having one's gift returned. For no one gave a child life, only for it to be belittled. Even in the event of mental problems or terrible complications, one's child hurting themselves, sabotaging their own life, was the ultimate kick in the parental teeth.

'Who did you meet in there?' Detective Sergeant Lamb asked.

Everyone stared at Jemima. The wind howled, the rain lashed against the window panes.

'I . . . can't . . .'

'Yes, you can,' said the sergeant. 'Who did you meet?'

Jemima shook her head, her hair falling into her face, and she kept it there, like a veil. Then Greg reached forward and tucked her hair behind her ears.

Jemima looked up at him imploringly and Steffie bristled with emotion – with the sudden urge to comfort her child – but clamped her jaw shut, her feet to the floor.

She wouldn't stop this. Jemima had to tell the truth.

Jemima hung her head, picked at the holes in the waffle blanket. 'Daisy Kirkpatrick.'

'And what happened?' said the sergeant.

'She gave me a pill,' said Jemima.

Steffie's mother gasped. 'A pill? Why on earth—'

But the sergeant was holding up his hand with a warning look, eyebrows low. He didn't want reaction. He wanted things to trickle slowly forward.

He was bending towards Jemima so keenly now, he could have slipped off his chair. He looked like a man watching a chick hatch from a rare egg: tentative, excitable, avaricious.

'Why did she give you the pill?' he asked.

Jemima shrugged.

'Why, Jemima?'

'She said all the others—'

'Could you speak up a little, please?'

Jemima cleared her throat. 'She said all the others were taking the pills – that they were relaxing and would help me dance better.'

'That's what Daisy told me too,' said the sergeant.

At this, Jemima looked up fearfully.

'But why did you want to take it? Why did you want to dance so well?'

Jemima shrugged again. 'Because I really wanted to be an *étoile*,' she said.

Steffie was watching Jemima closely. She was doing something that she sometimes did when lying – something that perhaps only a mother might spot: she was sucking in her cheeks, staring into space.

Greg suddenly spoke, a loud voice at Steffie's side. 'Why would Daisy Kirkpatrick have given Jemima a thing like that?' he asked.

The sergeant looked up at Greg. 'The diazepam belonged to her mother,' he said. 'Daisy knew that Jemima was the best performer, and that made her a threat. She couldn't have known exactly what the drug would do, but it was worth a shot.'

'Bloody hell,' said Greg.

Detective Sergeant Lamb sat back in his seat. 'That's what you get your when your parents are hell-bent on winning – when it's all they care about.'

'It's a wonder something like this hasn't happened before,' said the constable. 'It probably does, all the time, mind you, but goes untraced.' He kicked away from the wall, folded his arms, the suit jacket tight on his inflated forceps. 'Schools like this, at this level, are bound to attract a certain type.'

'That's as may be,' said Steffie, looking at Jemima, 'but why would you even think about doing such a thing without coming to us, or Noella?'

At the mention of Noella's name, Jemima flinched, looked away. Perhaps it was because she couldn't bear to have let her mentor down.

Everyone was looking at Steffie now. It was the first time she had spoken. The sergeant was considering her as though she were an interesting piece of evidence, his head cocked, mouth open.

'It's not like we haven't supported you,' Steffie said, feeling she should say something else, now that she had started. 'It's not like we haven't been there for you every step of the way.' She was becoming warm as her indignation mounted. 'You heard the constable. Some of the parents at the academy are monsters. But we weren't like that. We—'

'But that's the whole point!' Jemima suddenly shouted.

Everyone stopped, stared.

'What?' said Steffie, astonished.

'I didn't want to do the audition!'

'Hey?' Greg said. 'Why?'

'When I saw Zach swinging on the bar,' Jemima said, 'it gave me the idea.'

'The idea?' Greg said. 'What idea?'

Jemima shed a tear and then lifted her casted hand to her face, touched her lip. It was an odd, plaintive gesture that made Steffie feel horribly sorry for her.

She was thirsty, Steffie intuited, reaching to the bedside table for the jug of water and stack of plastic cups.

'What idea, Jemima?' the sergeant said, echoing Greg's words but more coaxingly.

'To . . .' Jemima began. She was faltering, as though trying to find the right words. 'To . . . swing on the bar like Zach. And drop on to the beams like he did. He was really good at it – said it was easy as pie. So I thought I could . . . I could do it differently and fall on the beam with a twist.'

'A twist?' said the sergeant.

Jemima lowered her voice, talked to her bed sheets. 'I knew I could twist my ankle easily.'

'Twisting your ankle?' said Greg. 'Why the hell would you have wanted to do that?' He stepped forward. 'Jemima . . . ?'

Steffie was handing the cup to Jemima, who was reaching up for it with a shaky hand.

Their eyes met with painful timing, perfectly aligned for when the words hit the air.

'Because then I could go home,' Jemima said. 'Because that's what Mummy really wanted.'

There was a ghastly silence. Even the wind stopped moaning, the rain ceased.

Steffie could feel her mother's eyes on her, enlarged by fear.

'I took the pill to make me brave,' Jemima said. 'I was scared. I didn't want to twist my ankle. I knew it would hurt and I really wanted to dance for Mr Alexandrov and be one of his stars. But I knew . . . I knew that would break Mummy's heart. So . . . So I made it impossible for me to dance.'

Jemima was biting the side of the plastic cup, eyes staring blankly ahead.

Greg spoke then. 'Excuse me, Sergeant,' he said, 'but this all seems a bit—'

'But there was a problem, wasn't there, Jemima?' the sergeant said, ignoring Greg. 'The pill wasn't what you thought it was, what Daisy said it was, was it? ... Tell us about that. Tell us what happened.'

Jemima lowered the plastic cup, spoke quietly, slowly. 'It didn't make me stronger. It wasn't a performance enhancer, as she called it.' Another tear fell. It was such a neat fat tear, she almost could have caught it in her cup. 'It made me funny ... I couldn't hang on to the bar. I fell and it wasn't as I had planned. I didn't land on the beams like Zach did. But I went into something else – something with a smack and then ...' She trailed off.

Helena was crying, her face buried in her hands. It was a long time since Steffie had heard her mother cry. The sight filled her with guilt, with the sense that she had inflicted this on them, was ultimately responsible for everything.

'Is this true?' Steffie asked, prising the cup from Jemima's hand and placing it on the cabinet. 'Is what you're saying totally true?'

Jemima wouldn't look at her.

'Because I don't see how it can be,' Steffie said. 'Didn't I encourage you to come here? Wasn't it me over the years that took you to all the rehearsals, that made your costumes and—'

Jemima murmured something that Steffie didn't catch.

'I'm sorry ... ?' said Steffie.

The sergeant was sitting back in his chair, hands clasped smartly on his lap, his demeanour peaceful though attentive, as though attending an organ recital. He had done his bit. And was watching them now.

'I heard you cry,' Jemima said, clearly now.

Steffie stared at her. 'What?'

'The night before the audition.' Jemima's bottom lip wobbled and she began to cry wretchedly. Normally this was the point where Steffie's resolve cracked, no matter how embroiled or heated their dispute, and she would try to comfort Jemima. But currently she was too preoccupied – was back-pedalling through her mind, trying to locate this particular detail: the night before the audition.

What did Jemima mean?

Where had they been the night before the audition?

She couldn't think.

'You called me . . . your dear sweet Mims . . .' Jemima said. She was trying to wipe her face with her cast. 'You said that you didn't . . . that you didn't . . . know what you would do without me . . . if I went to the ac-academy.' Jemima stopped talking, hid her face.

Steffie felt the floor wobble underneath her. Greg and her mother were both staring at her in confusion.

'Steffie . . . did—' Greg began.

'No,' she said, turning to him. 'I didn't. I mean, I didn't mean it like that. I thought Jemima was asleep. I was tired and emotional. It was taken out of context.'

'By a ten-year-old girl who just wants to please her mum,' said the sergeant.

'Just like Daisy Kirkpatrick,' added Detective Constable Whyte.

That felt like a dig too far. Steffie felt her limbs stiffen. 'Jemima's *nothing* like Daisy Kirkpatrick,' she said.

'Oh?' said Detective Constable Whyte. 'Not competitive, self-disciplined, ambitious, a perfectionist? None of that sounds familiar? Because that tends to be the prototype of young gifted children, so we've found.'

Once again, the silence fell. But it was quickly quelled by a lashing of hail on the windows that made Steffie jump.

'OK,' Greg said, nodding slowly. 'Even if this is what I think you're saying it is ... How exactly have you managed to get to this point?'

'Meaning?' asked Detective Sergeant Lamb.

'How you knew?' Greg said.

The sergeant looked uncharacteristically abashed. He gazed at the floor, thumbs circling his clasped hands. 'I ... uncovered a piece of personal information,' he said.

'What personal information?' Greg asked.

Steffie was staring at Greg imploringly, horror rising in her veins, having guessed what the sergeant was going to say before he said it.

Yet it was too late. The sergeant was speaking, his thin lips moving in that barely mobile way of his, his tone regretful, his eyes solemn.

It felt like an actual person when it finally came forward, when it emerged into daylight on that rainy February afternoon in the Royal Hospital and stood there before them, squinting, dusting itself down and shyly introducing itself.

It was the truth. Everyone recognised it at once.

'I know about the other Jemima,' he said.

No one ever asked me why I danced. Everyone was supportive and wanted me to be the best I could be. That's my school motto. But no one asked me what it was for. They just thought it was what I wanted to do – even Mummy. But if they'd have asked, I would have told them.

It was because it was the only time that I saw my mum and dad together. They always came to watch me dance and sat together and cheered. It was the only time that I saw them like that any more.

And there was the crying. Mummy didn't know I knew . . . But I could hear it through the walls. We have a small flat and there's a small partition between us and sometimes I could hear her crying at night. I never asked what it was, just like she never asked me about dancing. But I knew it was something bad and that it had always been there, even when I was small.

The only time it went away was when I danced.

Jemima Lee
Phoenix Academy of Performing Arts
Surrey Police interview transcript
24 February 2016

TWENTY-SEVEN

Not all concealments were bad. Some were instinctive, natural – the soft body of the tortoise hidden by the shell, the defence of a long deep burrow for a rabbit. Nature was full of devices designed to protect creatures from harm. And so it was with secrets.

Steffie's secret had been born of a will to survive, to protect herself.

She hadn't tried to fool anyone – hadn't even considered that she was doing so. She had just come up with a way of coping that worked for her. Greg and her mother were accomplices, the only ones who had become closer as an outcome of the concealment, bonding over their mutual reluctance yet desire to make her happy.

It was pretty basic in design. It was a lie by omission, a rearrangement of facts, as though Tipp-Exing over a calendar of life and rewriting the details.

Jemima Lee was born on 1 July 2005.

That was the new fact, the lie that wasn't a lie. It was there on Jemima's birth certificate. It was an actual fact.

And on this truth the construct of the lie was based.

Scrape the Tipp-Ex off, hold the calendar to the light and there was something else there entirely.

Jemima Lee was born on 3 June 2004.

*

3 June 2004 was a warm day with a breeze that went unde-tected by those inside the maternity ward of Oxford City Hospital. Jemima Lee was, like all babies, utterly adorable, and Steffie and Greg were besotted – tickled pink with love and pride for this product of their love.

They hadn't been back that long from their honeymoon in the Dolomites. Their marriage was still basking in the glow of the mountains at sundown – in Alpenglow – and it felt as though their daughter were part of that too, that her limbs and hair and blue eyes were tinged with gold.

At eight weeks old, Jemima was thriving – smiling, cooing, beginning to take note of the world around her and to reach out for it in a way that thrilled Steffie.

One morning, during the last week of July, Jemima woke at her regular time with a temperature. Steffie felt it the moment she picked her up – the heat radiating from Jemima's tiny body. Steffie knew that these things were par for the course, especially in the summer, but she took Jemima to the doctor just in case, who said she had a nasty cold and that Steffie was to keep her well hydrated.

By teatime, Steffie was struggling to keep Jemima awake. Normally at this hour Jemima would be fitful, fractious, but wide awake. It was difficult to judge, but Steffie felt that some-thing wasn't right. Yet the doctor had insisted that everything was fine. Still, she ended up sitting up all night in the rocking chair next to Jemima's cot, watching her feverish sleep.

In the morning, Steffie was relieved to see that the symptoms had subsided. She pulled back the nursery curtains with a happy sigh and eased open the window. Then she took Jemima down-stairs and strapped her into her bouncy chair in the kitchen, whilst she did the laundry in the adjacent utility room.

But when she checked on Jemima, she was alarmed to see that she had been sick and that her body was jerking, rocking the bouncy chair.

She rang Greg and told him to come home immediately. They drove Jemima back to the hospital that she had been born in, only five minutes' drive from their house.

On arrival at hospital, it was established that Jemima was very ill. Steffie felt a stab of guilt when the nurses said that her baby's temperature was unacceptable. She reached for Greg, who held her hand and didn't let go.

Jemima was raced to intensive care, where she was hooked up to a ventilator.

As night fell, they were told that Jemima had a rare viral infection causing inflammation of the brain. The cause would probably never be established. If she lived, she would most likely be brain damaged.

They waited, watched, for four days. Little information was passed their way, but they both knew what was going to happen and tried to prepare themselves.

But there was no preparation for it.

At the end of the fourth day, the staff unhooked the ventilator, dressed Jemima in a Babygro with a bunny rabbit appliqué on the chest, and placed her in Steffie's arms.

By dawn, on 1 August 2004, Jemima had passed away.

What Steffie recalled the most of those days in August – of that August that stretched ahead endlessly, like a record going round and round – was the silence.

Sometimes silence could be so loud that it made you scream.

She sat for days in the bay window of their lounge, knees drawn to her chest. She watched gulls circling the air, their wings brilliant white in the sky; watched bin men scooping up the recycling; watched the postman sweating along the street in his shorts. There was plenty going on out there that August, but it was happening with the sound on mute.

It was the same inside the house too. When Greg spoke, she

watched his lips moving, with little regard for the information being passed her way.

It was the funeral tomorrow, he was telling her. She had to get dressed. There was still time to get something from the doctor as the health visitor had suggested – something to help get her through the day.

Greg took her lack of response as consent, made her a doctor's appointment. And sure enough there was a pill on her bedside table that night, neat and polite on a small saucer.

Diazepam.

It was certainly hypnotic, appealing. She only took it for a couple of days, was frightened that it would prove addictive, like the doctor warned. But those few days in its company were warm and soft, with an overpowering sense of relaxation that she would remember for a very long time.

She had got through the funeral with Greg on one arm, her mother on the other and diazepam in her veins.

Her father had been dead for fifteen years. Her mother hadn't expected to endure another tragedy, and the shock showed on her face. Yet Steffie barely heeded it, was concentrating only on the miniature coffin adorned with lilies that was elevated on the rostrum behind the woman who was saying that Jemima had lived only for a short while but had brought her parents so much joy in that time.

Then the officiators pressed a button and there was a whirring noise, a small door opened, and Jemima was slowly moved on a conveyor belt beyond view.

They chose a brass plaque near the fish pond in the grounds of the crematorium. The other choice was the rose garden. They felt that Jemima was the sort of baby who would have liked fish more.

They scattered her ashes by the pond.

Ash. Dust.

These things were strong in Steffie's mind that day – the notion of things diminishing to ash; burning; gone.

She resumed life without diazepam, life by the window on mute, knees drawn to chest, watching not the world outside now but the dust swarming by the window in the sunbeams – dust that was death, ash, coffins, plaques by fish ponds.

Greg tried to entice her away with phone calls from friends, offers from her mother to stay, talk of a holiday in the Dolomites, a change of job perhaps or even of city. How about moving back to her childhood home in Dorset to be near her mum?

But Steffie wasn't listening, was watching the dust.

By the end of August the dust was so thick in the air of her home she could barely breathe.

She went to bed where she hid under the sheets – where Greg watched her with alarm, asking her what it was that she was so frightened of, what she was cowering from. He called a doctor who said she should rest.

So she did. She stayed in bed, or by the window, listening to the silence, watching the dust.

Until one day, at the end of September, as summer dwindled, as the leaves became insecure on trees, she heard a sound that stopped her heart.

It was a baby crying.

She knelt up on the window sill, peering out of the window.

A mother was passing by, pushing a pram, bending forward slightly to appease her crying infant.

And at that moment, Steffie could hear again – could see details, hear voices, could see a future.

She didn't trick Greg, nor mislead him, nor was she forth-coming with information. It wasn't difficult to get a man to make love, especially not your husband and a grieving one at that. So they just did so, night after night, until she got what she wanted.

And on 1 July 2005, Jemima was born.

'I didn't deliberately mislead anyone,' Steffie said, crying. Greg was rubbing her back. Her mother was holding her hand.

'I know,' the sergeant said. He was standing now, hands in pockets, head bowed. 'These things have a habit of evolving in a way that you don't always foresee.'

'I thought that if we had another baby—'

Steffie began to cry too bitterly to speak. Her mother took the helm. 'It would mean that the other one hadn't existed,' she said.

Jemima was sitting upright, staring at her family – at the three adults she most relied on – with a look of complete displacement.

Steffie felt her insides smite with shame and grief. She looked at the floor, leant into her mother.

'It's called a replacement child,' her mother said, stroking Steffie's hair tenderly.

The sergeant nodded. 'I've encountered it before,' he replied.

'Then you'll know that it's more common than you'd expect.'

'Quite,' he said.

'I didn't plan it like that,' Steffie said, wiping her face with her sleeve. 'Aside from our very close friends, most people – work colleagues, old friends – assumed that Jemima was the same Jemima. And then when we moved away to Wimborne, no one knew anything about it. I could just get on with life, as though nothing had happened.'

'Except,' said Sergeant Lamb, 'that you couldn't.'

'No,' Steffie said. 'It was always there – the past, our little lie . . .'

The dust, she added mentally.

One day, when she was settled into the new house, with Jemima as a toddler at her feet, Steffie had looked up the replacement child phenomenon online.

What she read had filled her with dread.

Psychiatric.

Pathognomonic.

Unresolved parental grief.

Restrictive, overprotective parenting.

More often than not, the replacement child developed psychiatric problems – anxiety and confidence problems. They would also be likely to experience difficulty dealing with separation, the website had said.

This was bad information indeed – information that she couldn't share, but which anyone – including Greg – could have accessed at any point for themselves. It was there for them to see: the potential damage that she could be inflicting on their child.

Her choice was to either carry on as they were or resurrect the pain they had left behind in Oxford.

It seemed like no choice at all. She had felt tense with indecision, and the amathophobia that had begun in the aftermath of Jemima's death – the fear of dust – returned now, exacerbated, intensified.

It seemed an innocent, harmless sort of phobia. Dust itself could be easily dealt with – could be swept under the metaphorical carpet simply enough. It felt like a very private, rather stupid fear. The best way to deal with it, she had felt, was to forget all about it, try to deal with it herself as best she could until it went away.

Yet it was neither innocent nor harmless. And before it went, it destroyed their marriage.

Greg had been surrounded habitually by dust, by wood chippings and sawdust. It was all around him, all over his clothes and hair, in his very skin, in the air hanging inside the lodge, in the air above it.

She began to turn away from him, too often. He was grieving also, she knew, but she just couldn't love him the way he wanted. But Olivia could, and had.

Moving to the apartment with Jemima had helped – her phobia, at least. Her anxiety abated, the dust settled.

And in Oxford a little brass plaque near a fish pond grew cloudy and dull, for no one went to polish it.

The sergeant was reaching for their hands in farewell. 'I'm sorry for everything you've been through,' he said.

Steffie forced herself to stand up straight, to shake the sergeant's hand.

'I hope things get better from here,' he said. And then he and the constable left, closing the door behind them.

Steffie turned to Jemima, who was crying softly into her broken hand.

She approached her cautiously, perched on the edge of the bed, reached out to tuck Jemima's hair behind her ear. She was petrified that Jemima might reject her, recoil.

But she didn't. She looked up at Steffie. 'I didn't want you to be sad any more, Mummy,' Jemima said.

Dr Mills came to see them off when Jemima was discharged a month later. He shook hands with Greg, before turning to Steffie with a smile. 'I'm so pleased how this has turned out,' he said, not knowing the half of it, seeing only the medical outcome. 'The best of luck.'

Steffie was surprised by how short he was. 'Thank you so much for everything you've done for us,' she said.

She could have sworn he had been a lot taller when they had first met him. When she mentioned it to her mother on the way home in the car, Helena told her that this was a recognised phenomenon: when you met someone whilst in a state of shock and perceived them to be your rescuer, they appeared larger than in real life. She had read it in *Reader's Digest* only the other week, she said.

Steffie smiled, went to reach behind her to hold Jemima's hand and then thought better of it. She turned forward again, kept her eyes on the road ahead. Jemima didn't want to be prodded about, or even touched at the moment. She was coy with them, reticent, processing things. But the promising thing was that she was listening to her headphones again – was getting back into ballet, although walking on crutches and her left arm still heavily casted. And they had just stopped off to buy purple gobstoppers.

As Jemima slurped on a gobstopper, kicking her good leg against the car seat in time to the music, wearing her grey skater sweater and polka-dot leggings, Steffie glimpsed more than a flash of the old Jemima; and beyond her … the old, old Jemima – a ghost whom she couldn't dispense with lightly, who didn't deserve that, and yet whose memory made Steffie's heart twist with pain.

As a mother, there was no delete button; there was no way of sidestepping the truth. She had to admit that her first baby had died. And that her second baby was sitting here with them now, real enough, brimming with talent and life.

She reached for the radio and turned it on, listening to the soothing murmur of low voices.

She sighed, glanced at Greg beside her and her mother behind her.

The police inquiry was closed. They weren't pressing charges against the Kirkpatricks. They wanted the matter over with, to get back to some form of normality.

They were going home, much changed from when they had left – how, exactly, time would tell.

*

One week later, they were in their apartment after school, when Jemima hobbled forward and stood looking at Steffie. 'I'd like to go to Noella's,' she said.

'Oh,' said Steffie, who was just taking off her coat, dropping her work bag on to the sofa. 'Yes. Of course.'

Jemima remained still, leaning on her crutch.

'Now?' Steffie said.

Jemima nodded.

'Oh, OK.' Steffie picked her bag back up and reached for her coat. 'Do you need to bring anything?'

'No,' said Jemima. 'Let's go.'

'Oh,' Steffie said again. She glanced around the apartment, tapping her coat pockets to check for her keys.

Outside in the street, it was quiet. Rain was falling lightly. The occasional car passed, tyres shrill on wet tarmac. It was the last day of March. Trees were beginning to bud; daffodils in pots by front doors nodded their heads in greeting.

Steffie and Jemima walked slowly, Jemima hobbling but refusing help. The determination that the physiotherapists had spoken of was beginning to prove itself. The idea of Jemima dancing again didn't seem ludicrous, but inevitable.

Evening was approaching, but it wasn't yet rush hour. It was a peculiar time of day when a lull fell as a changeover approached, reminiscent of life on the hospital ward, Steffie thought.

Jemima still hadn't spoken much about the accident, nor about the events leading to it – about the past. It would all come eventually. But for now everything was fine, was healing. Except for one missing thing, or person: Noella.

Jemima hadn't mentioned Noella at all, had resisted being drawn into conversation about her. It was most odd, but Steffie hadn't pushed it. Something had evidently occurred between the two of them that Jemima wasn't ready to discuss. Or perhaps it was simply that Jemima associated Noella with an old world that she no longer wished to haunt.

Either way, Steffie thought it was progress that they were on their way to the studio at last. It seemed a shame that two people who had spent so much time together were now estranged, for an inexplicable and probably trivial reason.

So she was thinking as they rounded the corner of Peach Street and Noella's studio came into sight. The top windows were open and Steffie felt a little pang of nostalgia and regret when she saw the yellow light spilling out and heard the tinkling of the piano and, as they drew closer, the hypnotic chanting of Noella's instructions.

And one and two and three and four . . .

They stopped at the door. Steffie turned to smile sentimentally at Jemima, but Jemima was standing still, foraging through her coat pocket for something.

It was an envelope, one of Steffie's brown business envelopes. Jemima held up the letter, motioning towards the letterbox.

'Wait,' Steffie said. 'We're not going in?'

'No.' Jemima hobbled forward, pushing the envelope through the letterbox. And then she took off slowly again, her crutch making a plaintive creaking sound that Steffie hadn't noticed before now.

'Jemima!' Steffie said. She stood gazing up at Noella's for a moment. The music had stopped. She couldn't hear Noella's voice. It felt as though everything were stopping as Jemima walked away.

And then Steffie hurried after her. 'What's going on?' she asked. 'Why won't you see Noella? What happened between the two of you?'

Jemima was crying noiselessly.

'Mims,' Steffie said. 'You have to tell me.'

They stood looking at each other, Jemima squinting up at the rain and the streetlight that they had stopped underneath.

'It's nothing, Mum,' she said.

'It doesn't look like nothing,' Steffie said.

Jemima wiped her eyes. 'Please,' she said ardently. 'Let's just go home.'

Steffie hesitated and then took Jemima's arm.

'OK,' she said, helping her along.

Jemima didn't resist the help now, was weakened somehow. And Steffie was glad to help – decided finally to leave the Noella issue, to focus all her energies on helping her daughter walk; and to dance again, if that was what she wanted to do.

Noella bent to pick up the envelope on the mat. She didn't recognise the handwriting.

When she saw the name of the writer, it caught her breath.

Dear Noella

i hope you are well and enjoying classis!

i am sorry i havent been to see you but i dont know what to say. i am not sure why you gave me the drink at my etivals audition but i dont think you meant to hurt me and im not going tell any one in case it gets you into trobble.

i dont think you should come to the pheenix in septembur because it wont feel like a fresh start. i think you should stay at Noellas and help ordenairy people be great dancers. You may even find anothur star like the epic Jemima Lee! ☺

if you care about me, you wont come.

Thank you for teeching me ballet. i wont forget you.

Love from Jemima Lee x

Noella sat down on the bottom step of the stairs leading to the studio.

She read the note again. And then folded it back up and put the envelope in her skirt pocket.

She sat for a long while in the darkness. Her pupils had gone home. It was just her in the studio tonight, and every night.

She gazed at the closed door, a creak of light lining the side where the streetlight seeped through. Otherwise it was blank, dark.

So ... she thought, she was to stay here with the *ordenairy* people.

She thought she might cry or scream. But instead she felt calm. It wasn't a calm of resignation, nor of numbness, but of something else.

It was the calm of possibility.

Was it possible that Noella was back where she had started ... looking for gems in the dirt of her childhood back yard – digging for scraps of china or plastic beads that she might rub clean on her dress and hold up to the light and admire?

Was it so very bad that she had ended up where she had begun, where she was supposed to be all along?

An ordinary life, amongst the ordinary. Not elite, not competitive, not high-profile or esteemed.

Entirely ordinary.

She tapped the envelope in her pocket, stood up.

'Very well, *ma petite chérie*,' she said. 'So it must be.'

And she climbed the stairs to the apartment that lay at the back of Noella's School of Dance, Wimborne, knowing as she climbed that she was going to have to start looking for some merit in that title, starting now.

That summer, when Jemima could walk without a crutch but still with a labouring limp, just two weeks before her induction at the Phoenix Academy, they took a trip to Oxford.

They were never going to be one of those families who talked about their grief, aired it alongside photographs and shrines. They had chosen another route and it was too late now to change course. And that was all right, Steffie sensed; at least, it would have to be. And yet there was something that they could do to honour the child they had lost – something they could do now and in the future.

The crematorium was on the outskirts of town. It was an attractive place with a long gravel driveway and sweeping views of the surrounding countryside.

They gathered at Jemima's plaque by the duck pond, Greg and Steffie side by side, heads bowed, their living daughter between them.

There was no evading the pain. The pain was dust, death. No one could remove them.

And yet that day there was no dust there. The air was clear, the sun was warm. The afternoon smelt of roses. The pond was wobbling slightly as fish moved about, rippling the water, life moving on.

Steffie knelt down, began to polish the plaque with a yellow duster until it shone, until she could see her face reflected in the brass.

She stood back up, tucked the duster into her coat pocket.

'I'm glad we chose the fish pond,' was all she said.

'Me too,' said Greg, his voice unrecognisably low.

Jemima was fiddling with something – the clasp on her satchel. And then she stepped forward and gently looped something over the edge of the plaque.

Steffie stared at the object. It was the tiny ballet shoes that Jemima cherished – the little charm that she had fallen asleep holding the night before the audition.

Jemima was gazing up at Steffie, seeking her mother's approval.

'Thank you,' Steffie said, overwhelmed. And then she reached for her daughter's hand. 'Come on,' she said, forcing a smile. 'Let's go.'

TWENTY-EIGHT

Helena was in the Silver Tree when Steffie said she needed to go out to run an errand. Helena murmured a goodbye. It was very busy in the shop that morning. It was a warm September day and the shoppers were out like greedy wasps, up and down the high street in search of treats.

Jemima had been gone a week. Her fractures were almost healed. She had worked hard at her physiotherapy with a grit and fortitude that hadn't surprised her family, but may have surprised the healthcare practitioners.

And there were other surprises. Several of the children from the academy had visited Jemima at the apartment during August. One was Daisy Kirkpatrick, and the other was Isobel Quinn.

Daisy Kirkpatrick – whose mother was nowhere to be seen but who came to visit with her father en route to business in Poole, and who stood looking around the little flat with a blatantly wrinkled nose – came to apologise and to present Jemima with her own sparkly beanie.

Everyone had forgotten about the hat. When asked later, Jemima said she had found the hat in the toilet just before the accident – that she had put it on in order to become the sort of person who would do what she was about to do.

But the morning after Daisy's visit, when Steffie emptied the bins, she found the new sparkly hat there, still in its gift wrapping.

The visit from Isobel Quinn had gone rather better. The child, on her way to their holiday home in Cornwall, only came in briefly, leaving her large family out in the car with the motor running.

She had brought Jemima a get-well card and a poem. The poem was all about Jemima's polka-dot leggings and her purple gobstoppers. Evidently the child was proposing friendship and loyalty at the Phoenix.

Not an offer to be sniffed at in the circumstances. And, unlike the beanie, the card and poem made their way to Jemima's bedside table.

The final visit had been from Mr Alexandrov himself. He had come expressly to see her, he said, and to run through a few details with staff-to-be Noella.

His visit had the biggest impact of all. It had become apparent then that Jemima had not been deterred from her course – wanted to be an *étoile* now more than ever. It had not all been for nothing, the accident.

'Remember, Jemima: the scariest boxer is the hungriest one,' Mr Alexandrov had said as he left.

Helena had been there in the apartment with them that day. Jemima had turned to her. 'What does that mean, Grandma?'

'It means,' Helena had told her, 'that the most precious things are those that can be taken away.'

It was absolutely true.

Life, and one's children, were deeply precious.

But sometimes the fear of losing them could be more crippling than the loss itself.

Jemima had gone to the Phoenix, and Steffie had survived, was surviving.

And now she was off to run an errand on this fine September day and Helena had smiled wisely in response for she knew that it wasn't Pilates, nor counselling, but something far more moving, and overdue.

It wasn't quite autumn, but there was that smell in the air that hinted something was set to change.

September had always been Greg's favourite month. It was a new term, a fresh start. He normally took on a big project in September and this year was no exception: an art deco mansion on the edge of town that he had admired in passing for years. His clients were renovating the building in order to turn it into an exclusive hotel, and Greg had secured the contract to fit the kitchen area.

The property reminded him architecturally of Danube House. It felt apt to be working on a project that brought to mind his daughter and her new life in Usherwood. Each time he arrived at the mansion, he thought of Jemima – of the work that she had to do, of the fight ahead of her, of the strength of character she had displayed that summer. He couldn't predict the future, whether she would thrive in the pressure of the Phoenix, but he did know now that she was tough and that she wouldn't give up easily. And it was that thought – the look on her face when she had first tried to walk again, the sweat on her back when she tried to do up a shoelace – that he focused on during pensive moments.

That morning, he was working in the outhouse at The Fishing Lodge, sawing in time to Fleetwood Mac on the radio, when he heard the crunch of tyres on gravel.

He put down his saw, wiped his brow by pulling up his T-shirt.

Who would that be? He wasn't expecting any workmates today.

Not Olivia, surely?

He groaned. He had been really clear with her, but she had taken to leaving messages again on his phone over the past couple of weeks. He hadn't listened to the voicemails, had pressed delete.

If it was her . . .

He stood squinting in the bright sunshine, hand held above his eyes.

It wasn't Olivia.

The day Jemima left, Steffie had thought of two very distinct things.

She had thought of the helium balloon that she had first imagined in Noella's studio the day she had told them about the Phoenix – her daughter as a beautiful balloon struggling to be released.

And she had thought of the mirror that she used to think of whilst watching Jemima dance: the mirror that reflected back the child to its mother.

The mirror, she knew now, wasn't something toxic, like in *Snow White*. It wasn't to be avoided, broken or covered. It was just part of being a mother.

So she had dropped Jemima off at the Phoenix that September morning and driven away. She had told her mother and Greg that it was something that she wanted to do alone, and she had managed it . . . just.

Thankfully, the lovely Issie Quinn had arrived at the same time as Jemima. The two girls had held hands as they walked down their corridor to their new rooms.

There had been a moment when Steffie had hesitated, full of doubt. Jemima was walking away, chatting, and Steffie wasn't sure whether she was supposed to follow or to wait or leave. The girls were already settled in their rooms – Jemima's gear was unpacked – and they were going off to a welcome meeting in five minutes.

Steffie lingered, waiting for Jemima to look back over her shoulder or wave or grin. But there was nothing.

She turned and walked away, down the corridor alone. And then she heard something: the pattering of uneven feet – Jemima trying to run.

Steffie smiled ecstatically, holding out her arms. 'Don't run, Mims!' she called out. 'You'll—'

But Jemima had arrived and was hugging Steffie so hard she thought her ribs would bend.

'I love you, Mummy,' Jemima said.

Steffie stroked Jemima's hair, kissed her on each cheek. 'I love you too,' she said.

And then she walked away.

Don't cry, she told herself.

Don't cry.

She cried all the way home, but something had shifted.

It was too early to say what.

And now, one week later, she had just rushed out of the Silver Tree leaving her mother in charge, and was driving along through the warm September morning, sunshine rippling on the ceiling of the car, trees flashing above her in a rush of vibrant green.

She felt giddy, feverish, alive.

She gripped the wheel and told herself to stay calm.

She was on the outskirts of Chelton now, deep in country-side. The hedgerows were thick and overgrown. Telegraph poles poked surreptitiously out from ivy and brambles. An old phone box had been besieged by nettles.

She took a left turn and went along the dirt track to the lodge, the tyres kicking up dust in clouds. Just before coming to the driveway, she stopped the car.

The engine creaked as it cooled; the dust clouds were dissipating.

She took a deep breath, pulled her phone from her bag, keyed in the number for the Silver Tree and waited.

Her mother took a while to answer.

'Mum,' Steffie said. 'I just wanted you to know that I suffer – not always, just sometimes – from a phobia. It's a dust phobia. It's called 'amathophobia'. I don't really want to talk about it. I just wanted you to know.'

She paused. She could hear her mother's breath – quick, light inhalations.

Then her mother gave a little laugh. 'OK, Steffie, love,' she said.

'OK then,' Steffie said, laughing herself, rather awkwardly. 'Well, I'll see you shortly. Gotta dash.'

She hung up and then dialled another number.

'Steffie! How lovely to hear from you!'

'Hello, Yvonne,' Steffie said. 'I know it's been a while . . . and that I left things a bit . . . you know . . . But I was wondering whether . . .'

'You can come in and see me?' Yvonne said.

'Yes.'

'Of course you can.' There was a flap of paperwork, the turning of pages. 'I'm free at your old time next week if that's any good?'

'That's perfect,' she said.

She ended the call and then eased the car forward into the driveway, turned off the engine and sat gazing at the house before her.

It was so quiet. A blackbird was hopping about in yesterday's puddles. A squirrel was sitting on the front doorstep, paws raised, head twitching, assessing danger – which it deemed high when Greg came out of his workshop.

He approached, flapping his shirt, ruffling his hair, sweeping his arms free of sawdust. 'Shouldn't you be at work?' he said.

She got out of the car, walked towards him. They met near the front door.

'Yes,' she said. 'But I was passing by and thought I'd stop to see how you are.'

'How I am?' he said, squinting.

'Yes,' she said. 'What with Jemima being gone.'

'Oh,' he said, taking a handkerchief from his back pocket and flapping it out of its folds. He wiped his forehead and the back of his neck. 'Well, I'm fine, thanks for asking.'

'Good,' she said. She looked at her feet. The squirrel was nowhere to be seen, but the blackbird was still about, pecking amongst the gravel for crumbs.

'And you?' he asked, tucking the handkerchief into his pocket again.

'I'm good too.'

'Excellent,' he said. 'Have you spoken to Jemima today?' He was wearing a T-shirt that was ripped on the shoulder, fitted to his chest. The hospital beard had long since gone and he looked healthy, tanned. Just beyond him, hanging in its habitual place on the hook outside the work shed, was his black donkey jacket. She liked seeing it there, as though it were a steadfast pet.

'She texted first thing,' she replied. 'She said it was tofu stir-fry for lunch.'

He smiled. 'Well, I'm glad she's all right,' he said.

She coughed, kicked the gravel. 'I've been thinking . . .' she said.

'Yes?' And then he stared in surprise over her shoulder. 'Why's your car full of stuff?'

'Oh,' she said, pushing her hands into her pockets. 'That.'

'Steff?' he said. 'Are you moving out?'

'Not out,' she said. 'In.'

'In?'

She prodded him in the tummy. 'Don't be slow,' she said.

He looked at her blankly.

She would help him.

'I'm moving back in,' she said. 'I want to start again. It's what Jemima wants. And it's what I want. And I think it's what you want. At least, I thought it was, but you're not saying anything . . .'

'Of course it's what I want,' he said. 'But I can't believe it. Why now?'

She looked up at him shyly. 'It's not because I'm desperate or lonely – it's not because Jemima's gone.'

'It's not?'

'Well, it sort of is . . . But not for the reasons you think. It's because it's given me some space. And even with just a week gone by I can see that I belong here . . . Or at least, I need to see if I do . . .' She trailed off.

For an awful moment, she thought he was going to say no – that she had left it too late, or worse: that he was back with Olivia.

Too many times she had rejected him. Too many times, she had—

And then he bent down and kissed her.

He tasted of salty sweat, of sugary tea, of sawdust, of love.

'Come on,' he said, putting his arm around her. And they went to the car to get her belongings, the blackbird watching them inquisitively.

Somewhere, not so far away, Helena was serving customers, Noella was counting aloud to her Grasshoppers class, Jemima was holding the barre in studio four . . . and Steffie had just crossed the threshold at the lodge.

The sight of her old possessions – her beloved Venetian mirror and the oil painting of Big Ben – hanging exactly where they belonged suddenly filled her with remorse, with painful regret.

She turned to Greg. 'I'm sorry that I didn't handle things better, that I neglected you, that I didn't get help for my ... my phobia ... and that I...'

'Stef,' he said. 'It's all gone, in the past.'

'But I don't think it has all gone,' she said.

His face clouded.

'I think we need to deal with it,' she said. 'So I just told Mum about, you know ...'

He smiled. 'You did?'

'Yes. And I've booked to see Yvonne.'

'Yvonne?'

'My counsellor.'

He smiled again and stooped to kiss her. 'Well, that's great,' he said.

They broke away and stood looking at their home.

'So...' he said. 'Is everything all right? It should be exactly as you left it.'

'It is,' she said looking about with satisfaction.

And then she reached for his hand and stood breathing in the old air, willing the dust to show itself, knowing that she would fight it when it did.

Because her secret had finally come to light.

And now she no longer feared it.

ACKNOWLEDGMENTS

During the writing of this book, there was a lot of media attention on the issue of testing in primary schools and the pressure that this places on children. I'm thankful to my lovely, anarchistic friend Ali Carter who featured in the local press for striking against the SATs. She drew my attention (and everyone else's) to how heartfelt this issue is. I'm grateful also to all the parents whose conversations in the playground – their criticisms and praise of our education system – enabled me to create the parenting climate featured in this story.

Thank you to my talented editor, Emma Beswetherick, for her enthusiasm and spot-on guidance. Thanks also to Dom Wakeford for his help with the manuscript; and to all the team at Piatkus Fiction who helped give this book life.

Special thanks to Sally Pasche, Bec Vaughan, Brenda Corbett, Anita Rowden, Lisa Parker and Catherine Adams, and to my beautiful big sister, Lisa Gannaway. Having kind friends who encourage me is something that I don't take lightly.

Finally, you can't write about family without being part of one: thank you to my dad for building a giant plastic roller-coaster with my boys during the holidays so that I could write; thank you to my mum for the lovingly-made bakewell tarts for sustenance; and thank you to Nick, Wilfie and Alex for being the icing on the cake.

Mothers

Reading Guide

READING GROUP QUESTIONS

1) What do you think are the main themes in *Mothers?*

2) Do you think Steffie is a good mother? If so, why?

3) What are the biggest challenges that Steffie faces as a mother? Are they realistically handled?

4) Does Steffie make the right decision in allowing Jemima to pursue her dreams and leave home at such a young age?

5) Do you think Steffie and Greg made the right decision to part? Should they get back together?

6) Can you talk about the grandmother's role in the story? Why do you think the author included her?

7) Do you think too much pressure is put on children in today's society?

8) What do you take away from the secret that Steffie has kept for so many years? Was she right to keep the past hidden, in the circumstances?

9) Should Steffie have been more understanding about Greg's infidelity? Should we forgive one-off indiscretions?

10) Do you like the way in which the story is punctuated with police interviews? What effect did they have on you as reader?

AUTHOR Q&A

1) Can you tell us a little about what inspired you to write Mothers?

When I write a book, I like to pick a subject that I don't quite understand so that I can explore it and make sense of it. In doing so, I hope that my readers come to understand the subject a little more too. I know that I'm not the only one who finds modern parenting stressful. I wanted to look at the pressure that mothers are under. And when it came to writing about it, I found inspiration all around me.

2) Can you see any of yourself in Steffie, or in any of the other mothers in the story?

I see myself in Steffie because she's a fairly average person with no strong views on parenting, so it's easy to identify with her. There's a line in the book about how she stands in the middle – not pushing at the front, nor lagging at the back. As such I created an open-minded character, who gets swept along by the forces around her, which is how I think many parents feel these days. However, unlike me, she is sometimes unaware of what is going on around her – of how competitive the ballet academy is, for example. I would have sensed the pressure the moment I walked in, and would have been more guarded.

I also see myself in Helena because I often find myself identifying with older mothers, given that I'm not completely in tune with some elements of modern parenting and have a hankering after the carefree style of my Seventies childhood. I was raised in the countryside and thought I was Huckleberry Finn. Helena's more relaxed parenting style is attractive to me, if only because I'd love to be that way myself.

3) Competitive parenting has become a huge issue of late. How do you see it affecting children today?

I think that our children are growing up too quickly and that's it our duty as parents to try to prevent this from happening. We know about the harmful effects to children's health if they're not allowed to grow at their own pace. Yet still we march on. It's like a wave that we keep riding because no one knows how to stop it, or where it came from. Worst still – we don't know where it's going.

4) Single parenting is also explored in depth in this story. Do you think Jemima suffers because of her parents' living arrangement?

Of course it would be better if Jemima were at home with both her parents. But her parents separated because of an undisclosed tragedy and unfortunately, Jemima is affected by that. She lives in a cramped flat with her mother, on a temporary basis. Given that children don't cope well with unpredictability, it's the impermanence and uncertainty in her life that is the most harmful, I feel – and not the fact that she is being single parented or living away from her dad.

5) What is the message that you would like your readers to take away from this story?

That we have to try to trust our children to live their lives without our constant interference. There are times to be pushy, and times when we need to fall to the background. Often in the story, Steffie is watching Jemima. I think that's a sensible stance: alert, interested, but not right on top, suffocating. If we mould our children too much, how will we ever know who they were supposed to be?

6) Can you tell us any more about the tragic concept of 'replacement children'?

I came across it by accident whilst doing research and knew that I had to use it in a story which is about how we can negatively affect our children, often unconsciously and whilst meaning well. However, I also realise that it's a sensitive term for some because it almost implies wrong doing on the parents' behalf, which is not the case. The term was first used in the 1960s by psychologists following research carried out with children who were rescued from the Holocaust. It stems from a time when infant mortality was high and parents were advised to have another child as soon as possible after losing one. It's quite a vague term, since it's immeasurable and not exact. Just because you have lost a child and have had another, it doesn't automatically make the new child a replacement child. But in Steffie's case, she tries to deny that the first child lived, even calling Jemima by the same name. So the term does apply to Steffie and she cannot thrive until this is fully realised and addressed.

7) Who is your favourite character and why?

Noella! I enjoyed my time with her. I'm a bit of a Francophile. I lived in Paris, and I am still in touch with the French pen pal that I was given at school. Her surname is Chamoulaud, Noella's name in the story. But it's not just Noella's Frenchness that I liked. I enjoyed writing her story – her frustrations and struggles. I felt for her and I hope that she finds what she is looking for in life: self-worth and a little applause.

8) Were there any challenges that you faced when researching or writing the book?

My biggest challenge was how to write about pushy parents without being critical. It's easy to slip into judgemental mode and point the finger. But really this book was about looking at ourselves, not at others. And I wanted to do so compassionately. I think humour always helps. When I felt like I was about to criticise someone in *Mothers*, I softened it by poking fun.

9) How does it feel to see your second book in print?

Fantastic! Nothing really compares to it – not for me anyway, as it's what I've worked my whole life towards. I like how my books complement each other too. *Mothers* leads on nicely from *Blind*, my debut. My hope is to create a whole host of stories that sit side by side, offering my readers both comfort and escapism.

10) Are you working on anything else at the moment?

I have just finished writing my third book, *The Wife's Shadow*. After *Blind* and *Mothers*, I felt as though I had explored the aspects of parenting that I wanted to look at and could move on. The main character in *The Wife's Shadow* is a parent, but this is secondary to the story. Central is her fierce desire for control. I think control is a huge issue in modern society and I wanted to take a long look at it. In *The Wife's Shadow*, the main protagonist loses control of her life and is desperate to win it back, at all costs. Darker than the first two books, it was quite intense to write and is packed with secrets. I'm very excited about it.

WHY I WROTE *MOTHERS*;
THE INSPIRATION BEHIND THE STORY

When I sat down to write a book about competitive parenting, I didn't know how I was going to go about it, but I did know that I wasn't going to be mean. Anyone who currently has a child in school will know about the pressures that parents face. We can all offer up anecdotes about overbearing parents around us. However, I think that behind every pushy parent is someone who means well. No one aims to make their child break down through stress. Yet that's where many of our children are headed. Statistics claim that 10% of children in the UK aged between five and sixteen have a clinically diagnosable mental health problem.

So I wanted to write about the pressure that our children are under: pressure to do well, to be better than the child next to them. Surely this is exhausting, especially for primary school children. Anyone who has had a competitive friend or family member will know that it can be the most draining relationship out there. Yet we are raising our children from a young age to be competitive in almost every aspect of their lives, with pressure being treated like the norm. Primary schools are running anxiety workshops and in doing so we are saying that mental health problems are part of the framework of modern education.

When I wrote *Mothers*, I was concentrating more on the gifted and the elite. Yet increasingly these high standards seem to be creeping into our living rooms and 'average' is becoming a word that we loathe hearing applied to our children, even though it means precisely that: the majority of children. The other night I came across *The Voice Kids* on TV, a talent show for children aged 7 to 14. I was transfixed by the children's vocal talents. Yet when one young boy – the same age as my son – came on stage looking vulnerable, I began to feel uncomfortable. When the judges rejected him and he began to sob, I was so upset for him I had to turn the show off.

We know that pushing children can be toxic. Yet still we do it. We have made competition and pressure such an integral part of our children's lives that it's our Saturday night entertainment.

Yet all is not lost. It's never too late to step back, dial things down, relax our schedules and expectations. I try to make sure that my children smile more than they frown. It takes a little effort, but it's easy enough because kids want to laugh; they want to have fun. And we shouldn't stand in their way.

I wish you well and I wish you happy parenting. It's not easy, but we'll get there – not one step ahead of each other, with no winners or losers; but together.

Cath x

FURTHER READING

The following books were helpful to me when I was gathering information about competitive parenting, not with a view to writing this book but to raising my own children. There are lots of alternatives out there if you are interested in further reading, particularly on the subject of children growing up too quickly, or the power of play. However, I was especially interested in education – in how to ensure that my children fulfilled their potential whilst still having fun and not feeling pressured.

The following are the books that helped me find my way. They are on my bookshelf and I often reach for them, especially *Simplicity Parenting*. Whilst most of them were written a decade or more ago, they still remain relevant and wise. All are available at Amazon.

Reclaiming Childhood by William Crain; Holt Paperbacks.

The Over-Scheduled Child: Avoiding the Hyper-parenting Trap by Alvin Rosenfeld and Nicole Wise; St. Martin's Griffin.

The Hurried Child by David Elkind; Da Capo Press.

How Children Learn by John Holt; Penguin.

Simplicity Parenting by Kim John Payne & Lisa Ross; Ballantine Books Inc.

MY TOP FIVE TIPS FOR ASPIRING WRITERS

1) *Try not to read fiction whilst writing*

I was given this piece of advice years ago and it was one of best that I've received. It's helpful not to read fiction when writing your own, especially in the early years when you're developing your voice, since other authors' voices can be highly infectious. I tend to stockpile books and read them when I have stopped writing. When I'm writing, I turn to non-fiction. Every writer is different and some people can read and write without mimicking. But if you are a sponge, like me, then stick to non-fiction so that you can easily find and hear your own voice.

2) *Write what you know . . . with extras*

This is age-old advice and it's excellent, to a point. Not everyone can write what they know if they wish to produce a wealth of books, since our experiences are limited. Once you've written what you know, in those early largely autobiographical works, you have to look outside of yourself. So I advise you to practise curiosity and to listen. If you want to write a narrative from the viewpoint of a sixty-year-old male then find one and listen to him. Find out what he thinks, how he feels, and the words that he uses. This doesn't have to be in depth. It's amazing what you can learn by watching the world around you, in cafes, park benches, on train journeys. People are giving you material all the time, for free! So absorb it all and use it.

3) Enter competitions, however small

Writing competitions are – to the aspiring writer – heaven sent. If you want to find out if you are any good, enter competitions and if you start winning them then you will have your answer. Don't just go for the big ones, but the little ones too – especially local ones. There are so many short story competitions in the UK, particularly attached to literary festivals. I entered my local one twice and came second twice, and when my short story was selected to be produced for BBC Radio Somerset, I was blown away. Hearing my work produced by professionals made me really believe that I had a shot at a career in writing. Do not delay – enter now!

4) Don't be afraid to let your work go

And not just to your mum and best friend. Close friends and family do not make the best critics. Don't trust them when they say you are a literary genius; or at least, look further than their opinion. Make your work as good as possible and then let it go. It's rather like parenting. I know how hard it is to show your work. I have floor-paced for hours whilst awaiting feedback. But the only way to progress is to show your work to others. So submit it to literary agents and if you are lucky enough to receive professional feedback, not only is this an achievement in itself but use every morsel of advice that you are given. Because once the initial sting of criticism fades and time sets in, you will undoubtedly see that they were right.

5) Never give up

I tried for twenty years to get published. No one knows more than me how hard and soul-destroying the process can be. I had no contacts, nothing to nudge me up the ladder. I didn't have a unique viewpoint or angle. I had nothing except my passion for writing. My mum told me that it was all I wanted to do as a child. So surely some day it would happen for me? I just kept trying, kept writing. And if you feel the same way, then so must you.